REAPER

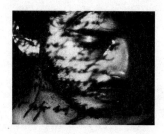

DEATH AND DECEIT IN A WORLD WHERE FRIENDS ARE AS **DANGEROUS** AS ENEMIES

THE FIRST BOOK IN THE ADAM CAINE SERIES

Captain Doug Beattie MC

FireStep
Press

FireStep Publishing
Gemini House
136–140 Old Shoreham Road
Brighton
BN3 7BD

www.firesteppublishing.com

First published by Firestep Press, an imprint
of Firestep Publishing in 2016
A Unicorn Publishing Group company
www.unicornpress.org

ISBN 978-1-908487-04-9

Cover by Ryan Gearing
Typeset by Vivian@Bookscribe

Printed and bound in Great Britain by
Marston Book Services Ltd, Oxfordshire

Contents

We are the Pilgrims, master;

We shall go Always a little further:

it may be Beyond the last blue mountain barred with snow,

Across that angry or that glimmering sea.

Prologue
FAROUK BASHIR – NORTHWEST FRONTIER

George Gethin ran through his pre-flight checks.

Diligently, he followed a long list but didn't really need to. He knew the routine off by heart.

Everything was in order. It always was; the ground crew made sure of that. They were thorough and took pride in their work. None wanted to be the guy who forgot to tighten the bolt that held the prop that propelled the aircraft that crashed because someone had not done their job correctly. Nobody on the team wanted either the loss of $10 million worth of equipment on their conscience or the inevitable harm to their career that would follow, as certain as night follows day and a bollocking follows a fuck-up.

For the final time George checked the weather. The latest meteorological report, the one he held in his hand, had been issued just seventeen minutes earlier and had not changed significantly from that he had seen a couple of hours before at the pre-flight briefing.

Further north, deeper into the mountains, deeper into enemy territory, thunderstorms were forecast for later on, great masses of electrically charged cumulonimbus cloud rising more than ten miles into the atmosphere creating sheets of lightening and ferocious vortices of boiling air able to break a plane in an instant. For all his training and experience, for all the firepower and technology at his fingertips, George was well aware that man and machine do best to avoid battles with these particular elements. Anyway, he already had enough on his hands with the Taliban without making an enemy of nature, which is why he had allowed both extra fuel and extra time in his flight plan to skirt the edge of any storm that might block the return path.

Absentmindedly George fingered the winged badge delicately sewn onto his left-breast pocket. Though he had been flying for almost a decade, the feel of it inspired confidence, reminding him he was one of the elite. Over the course of the ten years George had completed 189 operational missions not to mention thousands of hours on training and test flights. Each and every foray skywards was dutifully recorded in his logbook. It read like a travel guide of the world's least welcoming places: Iraq, Somalia, the Yemen, Pakistan, Afghanistan. There had been many hairy moments along the way but he was a veteran aviator and there were very few, if any, more accomplished pilots in the US Air Force; even if he said so himself. But familiarity with the job had neither dimmed his sense of excitement, nor dulled his senses. He loved what he did and recognised every operation was slightly different. Ask any pilot; there is no such thing as a routine flight.

Through his headset George could hear the radio traffic from the tower as controllers gave instructions to other pilots. Then they were talking to him.

"SAT73 taxi into position and hold."

"Taxi into position and hold," George confirmed the instruction.

Gently he allowed the aircraft to inch forward, over the threshold and onto runway 23. Very precisely he turned the plane so the nose sat directly over the broken centre line stretching, south-westerly, two miles into the distance, a heat haze shimmering above it. Thirty seconds later and the tower was talking to him again.

"SAT73 cleared for takeoff."

George depressed the blue transmit button and repeated the direction he had been given.

Smoothly but firmly, without undue delay, he pushed the throttle all the way to the stops, holding the aircraft on the brakes as the power built. Finally he released the anchors and the plane surged forward, easily, rapidly gathering pace. Less than 400 metres down the tarmac it reached

V1; the speed at which George could commit to the takeoff. Reassured by a last check of the instruments – oil pressure good, engine temperature spot on – he eased back on the stick and the craft was airborne. George felt a small flutter in his stomach as it rose, rolling slightly to the left as a breeze caught the starboard wing. A nudge of the controls and the smallest amount of rudder brought things back into shape.

Already the plane was two hundred feet high, the pilot adjusting the trim tabs to aid the climb so he wasn't fighting a heavy stick.

500 feet came and went.

It was going to be a long day but George was used to that.

1000 feet.

He was already desperate for a piss though. It was all that Coke he had been slugging. Would he never learn?

2000 feet.

George Gethin could no longer contain himself. Engaging the autopilot, he slid back his chair, pushed himself stiffly to his feet, arched his shoulders, rubbed his eyes and headed for the toilet.

8,000 miles away the unmanned, remotely-controlled, MQ-9 Reaper drone continued to claw its way towards the heavens, leaving Kandahar far below and behind, ready to receive its next set of instructions from the control centre at Creech Air Force Base, Nevada, the HQ of 432nd Wing.

———•———

If you take the N55 highway out of Peshawar in the Northwest Frontier province of Pakistan and head south, first through the town of Kohat and then beyond, you come – after some fifty miles of driving – to a right hand turn. If the junction were in possession of a signpost, one of the pointers would direct travellers towards Kachkai, a small settlement in a deep cleft valley in the heart of the semi-autonomous tribal regions over which the politicians and functionaries in Islamabad had long since given up any pretence of governing. The journey – even by vehicle – from junction to destination is interminable, thanks to the myriad potholes, ruts and ridges that scar the route, jarring the bones and sapping the energy from even the hardiest voyager.

But for the inhabitants of communities like Kachkai, there are few alternatives other than to endure the trip if they want to sell the meagre produce they grow and livestock they raise. In fact there are no alternatives: for who would come to them?

As a matter of routine Farouk made the journey to market in Peshawar alone, the battered pick-up he borrowed from his neighbour – or rather leased, for little comes for nothing in this part of the world. Normally the pick-up would be stuffed high and wide with goats for the slaughter, plus a few boxes of succulent pomegranates and melons, but this particular trip had been different. Of the ten animals he had ready for the table, he had saved three for his own, for there was soon to be reason to celebrate. Farouk glanced in the rear view mirror and caught a glimpse of his daughter Sameena; fifteen years old and to him a beauty to behold. Her dark brown hair framed a delicate face in which were set the pair of exquisite, brilliant emeralds she called eyes. The ravages of life had not yet exacted a measurable toll on her complexion, nor had the hardships and privations managed to beat out of her the sense of fun and wonderment so obviously present from the day she was first able to express herself.

But in a month's time she was due to be taken – in marriage – from Farouk by another man, to live with her suitor and his family in a neighbouring valley. In return Farouk would receive a small amount of money, paid as a dowry by the parents of Sameena's husband-to-be. In exchange for this inadequate sum this man would be able to take Farouk's most precious belonging, yet Farouk knew no quantity of riches could compensate him for his loss, whether double, quadruple, one hundred times the agreed sum.

But at that moment she was still his, still there in the mirror, gripping tightly to the sides of the truck, trying to avoid being flung out at every rotation of the wheels. And despite it all she was smiling. Out of sight, at his daughter's feet, lay the material they had just bought in Kohat to make her wedding dress. It was not silk from the famed trade routes that run through the Khyber Pass further to the north, nor Kashmiri, but it was the best the family could afford. Not that Farouk had had any idea what to purchase. No, that had been a matter for the third person in the pick-up; his wife Salma. She sat alongside him, staring ahead, grimly clutching the grubby handle fastened to the passenger door. Unlike her daughter, the cumulative privations of time were clearly marked in her complexion, a network of lines mapping the different parts of a harsh life spent on the edge of one sort of calamity or another; famine, fever, drought, war. Farouk peeked across at the woman he had married 35 years earlier and smiled. Despite the creases in her skin, despite the grimaced expression, he could still see traces of the beauty which had attracted him to her and which she had passed on to Sameena.

The softness of her features had also been strikingly evident in Khalid, their son, though Farouk had no way of knowing whether the gentleness, the warmth, the attractiveness were still there, because he had been absent for three years, ever since he walked out of the house and out of their valley to make his own way in the world.

A blaring of horns brought Farouk sharply back to the present.

He swerved hard to the right, just able to squeeze between the oncoming lorry headed straight for him and the side of the road that dropped steeply away to a wooded area twenty metres below. His palms were sweaty even though such moments were common in an environment where survival is constantly balanced on a knife-edge. He took comfort from knowing the village was now no more than twenty minutes away.

"Want a drink?" Mike O'Donnell teased his pilot.

"Yeah, funny. Why don't you just pour it straight down the john and cut out the middleman?" George Gethin snorted to the sensor operator sitting to his right.

For George it had been a slow couple of hours. In the first sixty minutes after take-off, other than taking a leak, there had been little to do other than enjoy the view generated by the Reaper's camera. For all his familiarity with the technology, for all the murderous undertones to the flight, he still had a grudging awe for both the capabilities of his craft and the otherworldly nature of the terrain he was flying over. Looking down at the desolate Afghan landscape, he found it hard to believe it supported a supposed population of 26 million, so desolate did it appear.

The second hour of the flight offered less time for making holiday plans. The moment was nearing when the Reaper – a hunter-killer unmanned aerial vehicle – would earn its keep by going to work, going to war. Some 45 minutes earlier the UAV had left Afghanistan behind and crossed into Pakistani territory. There was no call to air traffic controllers at the Lahore Area Control Centre South to inform them of the change of jurisdictions and at an altitude of 25,000 feet the Reaper's progress would have gone unnoticed. If by chance someone had been watching, and if by chance they had bionic vision they would have been rewarded with a view of the drone's underbelly. Under the bulbous nose was the ball turret containing the camera with daylight, thermal, and infrared imaging sensors. At the other end of the fuselage were three stabilising fins, the two larger ones above the horizontal, forming a flattened 'V'. Driving the UAV forward, impossible to identify at the speed it was spinning, was the Honeywell-powered turbo-prop. The 950 horsepower engine was more than enough to ensure a steady flow of air over the Reaper's wings – combined span, 66 feet – and hence keep it airborne. An observer would also have seen the six stores pylons clamped to the underside of the drone. Sometimes used for external long-range fuel tanks, their more common purpose was to carry the weapons which gave legitimacy to the UAV's popular name – in today's case, a pair of Hellfire II AGM-114Ks, laser-guided, air-to-ground missiles, each one 50 kilos of bad-arse weaponry, tipped with a 20 lb high explosive warhead. Developed and honed over 35 years they were quite capable of destroying heavily armoured tanks.

The UAV had now been overhead the target area for the best part of fifteen minutes. Repeating standard rate turns to port – passing through three degrees each second – the unflinching eye of the camera capturing every movement, every shadow, every fold of land several miles below.

On his main screen George could make out two plumes of dust, tight together, almost as one, making fast progress along the twists and turns of the highway. For a moment he lost sight of them as they took a sharp bend and the UAV was left blind by an overhanging rock face. But it was only a temporary blip. As quickly as they had disappeared they re-emerged, barrelling along a straight piece of road towards another sharp curve again bordered by a rising sheer face of rock to one side and what looked like a large drop to the other.

Without taking his eyes away from the bank of screens in front of him, George spoke to the man who had been sitting quietly behind them since take-off.

"Sir, can you confirm the orders once more please."

"Just the same as they were earlier George," soothed Justin Cathcart, the mission commander. "No ambiguity here. Take out both the vehicles you see and those in them."

And that was it, no more information, no details of who the cars contained, just the bald instruction.

The small convoy was perhaps half a mile from the end of the straight.

"Your show now then, Mike," George said to his sensor operator.

"Ok, I am going to hit them as they slow for that next corner," Mike replied matter-of-factly.

It was not as if Mike would miss if he fired when the vehicles were travelling at full pelt, but what was the point in making things difficult if you could make them easy?

Mike followed their progress, lazily making ballpark calculations. The missiles had a speed of mach 1.3 – some 450 yards per second. The target was a bit over four miles away – call it 7000 yards, close to the missile's maximum range – giving a travel time of about 14 seconds. To hit the trucks just before they turned the corner would mean firing… now.

Mike pressed the button to unleash the first venomous tube and the UAV shuddered slightly as the solid fuel rocket of the portside missile burst into life. As the $68,000 weapon dropped from its cradle, it surged forward, a thin con trail left in its wake, homing in on the reflected laser beam aimed from the Reaper.

———◆———

Farouk eased back on the accelerator and transferred his foot to the brake, slowing for the right hand bend, aware that just round it he would catch his first glimpse of home. For all the privations and hardships the family had to endure there was something majestic, mystic almost, about his small bit of the globe. Farouk was well aware that to many outsiders this corner of the earth was regarded with distrust, seen as a breeding ground for extremists and villains. Yet the war on terror had never come to his door though often it did pass close by.

As Farouk negotiated the bend, he saw a vehicle approaching him, a second tucked in behind it. Enclosed 4 x 4s, with blacked out windows, these were not typical farmers' transport; bigger, newer, more expensive than anything he was used to, they were affordable by only three types of people: the meddling, do-gooding foreigners who worked for the aid agencies, who rarely ventured this far from the safety of their compounds; drugs lords; or those fighting the foreigners – Taliban or Al Qaeda.

Because his attention was on the road and not the sky he was oblivious to the thin white streak of vapour being scored onto the blue canvas above him, approaching at an angle of about 40 degrees to the horizontal.

The missile struck the roof of the lead Toyota, punching a gaping hole in it and entering the cabin. The nose of the projectile narrowly missed the headrest of the driver's seat but did hit the driver, smashing through the flesh and bone of his right shoulder. Barely deviated from its course it demolished the car radio, corkscrewed through the bulkhead and struck the engine block. At which point it exploded.

If George hadn't blinked at the wrong moment he would have witnessed a brilliant flash erupt from the lead car. Mike saw it however. "Boom" he said to himself with animated mouth movements.

It was a familiar picture, one he had witnessed many times before; it was a mark of success, proof their handiwork had been spot on; that the predator had once again lived up to its name and its billing. Even as Mike allowed himself a small smile of satisfaction, he leaned forward in anticipation, waiting for the second missile to strike.

Farouk was almost level with the lead 4x4 when it disintegrated before his eyes; what had taken hours, days, weeks to put together on some car production line was instantly and violently disassembled. Amongst the devastation there was also blood, bone, flesh, hair; organs and parts of organs; limbs and parts of limbs; great chunks of muscle and tissue, and barely noticeable slivers and slices of human meat, for the vehicle wasn't the only thing ripped to shreds – so were its occupants, the resistance they offered the destructive power of the warhead significantly less than that of their transport.

Instinctively Farouk wrenched the steering wheel to the left as the catastrophe unfolded just yards in front of him. The pick-up slewed across the road, an avalanche of debris wrapped up in a blanket of heat, light and pressure enveloping it. Momentarily the Toyota stood up to the onslaught, channelling the initial surge up, down and around its body. But the laws of physics and chemistry were against it and inevitably it was overwhelmed. Pressed-steel panels were punctured, glass smashed, tyres slashed. Pretty much the same happened to Farouk's wife, the red-hot maelstrom scything through her. She died there and then. But Farouk did not. Because Salma's final act on earth was to shield the man she loved from the worst of the explosion.

And then the second Hellfire struck.

As Farouk's car left the road, toppling and then tumbling down the steep bank towards a thick crop of trees at the bottom of the gulley, he caught a fleeting glimpse, of something in the mirror. It was the face of his daughter, but not as he had ever seen it before. There was a gaping hole in her right cheek, while from her left eye a metallic lance protruded. And then there was her smile, or at least a macabre, twisted version of the one he loved so much, the edges of the mouth pulled back at the sides, the lips apart, almost as if she was cackling with demonic pleasure, though he knew – but could not hear – her cries were of terror. It was the last image Farouk ever had of the girl he lived for.

For George, the elation of a job well done was tempered by the fact, that while Mike could now relax, he still needed to get the Predator home and with the thunderstorm having pushed further south than predicted, the detour required on the way back to Kandahar would be greater than he had hoped. Even once the aircraft was down safely and in the hands of the ground team, George and Mike would have their paperwork to do and a debrief to attend. He understood why a post-flight analysis was necessary, he just wished it did not have to be him who did it. Flying was his passion; targets hit and bad guys killed his measures of success. And by those yardsticks he would sleep easily in his bed that night. The proof was there on the video. Mike had been spot on, taken out the two vehicles as ordered. A nagging doubt lingered in George's mind however, that a third vehicle had emerged out of nowhere just as the first missile struck, but the hot spot caused by the sequence of detonations had obscured his view – blinking hadn't helped – and by the time the picture cleared there was no sign of it. Just before turning the Reaper for home, he had zoomed out slightly to view a wider area but there was no other indication of life, or violent death, in the vicinity, just a silvery stream, part-shaded by a heavy canopy of overhanging trees, rare splashes of colour in the barren environment.

———•———

At the joint surveillance, targeting and acquisition cell situated in Khost in eastern Afghanistan, it had been a busy morning which had begun early with a dawn raid on an insurgent stronghold deep in the south of Helmand Province, well beyond, or so the enemy had thought, the reach of the coalition forces. Since then there had been a number of other attacks of an important and specialised enough nature to warrant the team's attention. The destruction of Mule – the codeword allocated to the twin targets – wrought by the Reaper was just the latest action they were keeping tabs on. Its progress had been monitored throughout, courtesy of the aircraft's own camera and satellite imaging, which came, literally, from another dimension. It took four minutes and 17 seconds for the success of the strike to be fully assessed and confirmed.

The duty watch-keeper punched the single call key of the secure phone.

No more than ten seconds after the receiving mobile had started to ring, a bleary voice answered it with a curtness borne of tiredness.

"Yes?"

"Sir, it's the STAP Cell," the watch-keeper said hesitantly.

"Go on," said the voice, a fraction more alert than before.

"We have bingo on Mule, Sir."

"Good, thank you, give my congratulations to the crew." The man now sounded almost happy.

Four time zones away Cyrus Vincent slumped back on his pillow, hanging up on the watch-keeper before he had time to offer a goodbye, the digital clock on his bedside table winked repeatedly at him, letting him know it was 3.30 in the morning, DC being eight and half hours behind Afghan. The news of the successful strike on the 4x4s in Pakistan was a slight distraction given the size of the problem he was dealing with in this part of the world.

Vincent saw things in primary colours. There was no shading in his life. His job was simple. Track down the bad guys and wipe them out. It was simple profit and loss. As long as they died quicker and in greater numbers than the good guys then things looked rosy and his career would remain on track.

Chapter 1

ADAM CAINE – OBJECTIVE SILAB

Stiffly, one at a time; Adam Caine stretched his legs. The cramp had set in soon after his stint in the covert observation post had started. Now, two days later, it had become a never-ending battle just to keep the circulation going; a distraction he could have done without.

There were four of them packed into the forward position that had been crafted into a corner of the demolished compound 550 metres from the target complex. Three hundred metres to the rear in a separate location was the five-man Bravo team, providing rear protection, an aviation link and immediate support if things went to shit. For those at the back, things might be mildly uncomfortable but at least they could move. For Adam, wedged into the OP with the rest of Alpha Team, uncomfortable didn't come close to describing of how he was feeling.

"Control, this is Alpha-11," whispered Mo, the radio-operator.

Despite the thickness of his Clyde-side accent, the Glaswegian's words were crystal clear and carried a tone of authority that demanded he be listened to.

"We have two Tangos south, moving towards Lima X-ray Two Five."

The 117 tactical satellite radio gave Mo a direct link with the operations room back in Sangin where men in t-shirts and shorts – cooled by the air conditioning – were logging all the comms traffic and marking and remarking the 1:25,000 gridded aerial photography map pinned to the wall, plotting the scope and progress of proceedings.

Next to Mo lay a second SAS trooper. Like Mo, he had a C8 Carbine beside him. But where his colleague had the radio set, the other man had a pair of x12 high intensity laser range finders pressed hard to his eyes through which he scanned the target area. Where Mo was lanky and wiry, Nick was short and stocky, the toned shape of his body clear even beneath his loose fitting UK military uniform which carried the markings of the standard disruptive pattern. Against this statement of military conformity, his 1970s style tennis shoes and the shamagh wrapped around his head and shoulders looked totally out of place.

Neither man wore a helmet.

Adam studied the pair at point blank range. He could understand how Nick might have passed selection: he just looked the part. But Mo? How had such a weedy looking man secured a place in the world's most elite fighting unit? Then again, over the last few months Adam had seen plenty of men who looked as if they'd be better suited to working in a library than fighting in such a bloody conflict.

The routine in the observation post was simple enough. There were four positions covering the cardinal points of the compass.

Armed with the range finders with thermal imaging capabilities, the observer kept his glues on the target, a group of compounds, dominated by a large two-story complex made, like the others, of the rock-hard mud which on this bit of the planet doubled as bricks and mortar. A flat roof topped the building off. It had been designated LX25.

Along with the observer, the radio operator was responsible for all communications plus logging and reporting the daily pattern of life, as well as movements in the target area.

The third position – and Adam's current role – was security, watching for any hostile or passive movements towards the team's covert position.

At any one time only the fourth person would be getting any rest.

During the down time not only did you have to get some kip, it was also the only chance for attending to other basic human needs. Food was cold, extracted from multi-climate rations packs, the rubbish placed away in the Bergans to be carried out on collapse. Having a piss or a dump meant squatting down in the small space in front of the other team members, depositing your waste in a wag bag, the chemicals in the bottom capturing and dealing with the results. This too was sealed and placed in the pack for removal from the site; no sign to be left behind showing British forces had ever been in the area at any stage.

Dave was the fourth and final component of the team, and its commander. He'd done his business first thing and was now tucked up in the single sleeping bag that had been brought into the position. He too was a member of the regiment, a sergeant and a veteran of Iraq, Northern Ireland and Columbia where he'd helped US Special Forces in their fight against the drug lords. He sported a short dark beard that he took pride in – spends more time in front of the mirror than a bloody girl, Mo had said – which complemented the intense, sinister look created by his sunken green eyes. Altogether he portrayed the grizzly appearance of someone who had been there, done that and enjoyed it all far too much.

Struggling to sit up straight, a dark Afghan cloak wrapped around his shoulders, Adam gently shook the lump to his right.

"Dave, time to rotate," he whispered. "Dave…."

"Roger, heard you the first time," came the muffled, slightly irritated, reply.

The two days so far had been a torture. What kept him focused was that this was the endgame to a plan he had set in motion. It was his mission.

The SAS troopers were there because of him. The differences between them were stark and not lost on Adam. They were seasoned NCOs, who'd been nurtured on the training hardships imposed by places like the Brecon Beacons, and further nourished on operations they could not and would not talk about with Adam. He, originally a regular commissioned officer, processed like so many others at Sandhurst, was now a human intelligence expert, a product of the classroom, one of the few to successfully pass through the five-month-long Op Achilles programme.

For the last three months Captain Adam Caine had been cultivating a HUMINT source from the northeast of Helmand Province called Assadullah Hakim. Hakim was the Taliban second in command in the Upper Sangin Valley but dabbled with entrepreneurship. Fighting the Russians with the Mujahedeen in the 1980s Hakim had been responsible for the movement of ammunition and weapons through the mountain paths of northern Afghanistan using the old silk routes. He'd learned them inside out. Later, once the Russians had gone, Hakim put this knowledge to lucrative advantage, using the same paths to move his poppy and opium crop, happy to work with the local militias and warlords, as well as the ruling Taliban. Although the Taliban rulers were anti drugs they permitted Hakim to continue his business in order to help finance their regime. For a while the business did well. After 2001 in did better still.

The US led invasion of Afghanistan and the ousting of the Taliban meant Hakim no longer had to use any of his income to support the government. Law and order collapsed and the warlords filled the vacuum. Over the years Hakim had used some of his increasing wealth to form a militia of his own, and backed by loyalty bought with money rather than presumed through blood, he became one of the strongest players in the in the area. Meanwhile the price of Heroin had rocketed and Hakim had started to make more cash than he ever dreamed possible.

Hakim had made his home in Now Zad where he lived with his three wives and four children, two of whom had entered the family business.

In 2006 his fortune changed once more when NATO forces expanded their mission into southern Afghanistan to try and tackle a resurgent Taliban. Hakim was faced with hard choices. He calculated that his best interests would be served by again coming to an accommodation with the Taliban. His reputation and connections meant he quickly became the Taliban's deputy commander in the Upper Sangin Valley. But it was under sufferance.

And it was this weakness that Adam had identified and was sure could be exploited.

"The choices are simple, Hakim," Adam had said through his interpreter. "Either you work with us or I will ensure the Taliban know about your enterprises. On top of that I will also unleash the NDS onto your little operation. You'll be getting crap from both sides and you know as well as I do that your sons and daughters won't survive a month in Bost prison. Your money won't buy them protection. There are too many people who will be happy to exact revenge for some aspect of your past."

"My children have nothing to do with this," Hakim had protested but Adam called his bluff.

"It doesn't matter Hakim, the NDS will believe whatever we tell them, and actually I won't have to make much of it up. Most of it will be the truth. You will lose everything and you know it."

Adam let the words hang in the air as Hakim ran through the alternatives.

"What do you want me to do?" Hakim asked, dropping his head low. If nothing else he was a pragmatist and he knew he had nowhere to go.

"I want you to tell me what is happening in the Sangin valley:

Taliban operations, smuggling, local tribal elder meetings with top Taliban officials." Adam reeled off a long list. "I want to know if any Al Qaeda come into the area, any foreign fighters, I want to know what you are doing before you do it."

"How am I supposed to do this?" Hakim had replied, a touch of the bravado returning. "The commander won't allow me to know everything, and if anything he does share ends up being used against him then he'll know I have passed it on to the infidels."

"Hakim, I don't think you understand. *You* will be the commander."

"How? I mean, what? ..." Hakim struggled to comprehend.

"Because we are going to get rid of Mullah Karimi and you are going to be the natural successor," Adam said as if this was something he had arranged a million times before. "All I want from you is information as to when he will be in his village next and the location of his safe house."

A smile came over Hakim's face. It was his turn to lay down some rules.

"Because you are asking me this you will know exactly how Mullah Karimi operates. You will know he is based in Pakistan in Quetta and controls everything from there, not just through me but with the help of his family and his advisers. If you want me to be effective then it's not just Karimi you need to kill but also his lieutenants."

Adam suppressed a grin. Even with his back to the wall Hakim was working an angle.

———◆———

"Stand-by, stand-by," Mo said steadily staring through the binos. "I have two vehicles, each with four up and a number of armed Tangos moving towards Lima X-ray Two Five."

Nick repeated the observation into the mic of the 117 TacSat.

"Ok, I can see four unknown males getting out of the lead vehicle and walking towards the target. Three of the four are armed." Now Mo was speaking for the benefit of those jammed in beside him.

Also viewing the scene, Adam hadn't thought making the decision to act would be so hard. His role sounded simple: to identify Objective Silab, give the codeword, then the rest would just happen. There was no mistaking Karimi, even at more than half a kilometre. He was accompanied by a handful of others whom Adam was in no doubt the world would be better off without. But there were others crowding around: at least half a dozen children curious to see who the illustrious visitor was. Some of them would surely become casualties. Standing in the door of the target compound was a pair of women, each with a baby in their arms.

"Well?" Dave urged. "Do we have a positive ID on Silab or not?"

Adam remained silent watching the scene in front of him. He knew what a Hellfire missile strike would do to those in the target area, innocent or not.

———

The plan Captain Caine had hatched and which had been agreed at Task Force level was simple. Once they had identified Silab a missile strike would be called in using a number of Reaper UAVs to destroy the target and the surrounding area. This would be followed by a couple of US Cobras flying in to mop up, making it look like a normal chance engagement and not a covert, intelligence-led strike. The last act would be a small team of tier-3 US Special Forces – US Rangers in this case – flying in to conduct a Battle Damage Assessment to ensure the objective and the mission parameters had been achieved. The observation team would remain in place beyond the strike to monitor ground traffic before they extracted after daylight. Simple. But giving the codeword for the strike to eliminate Mullah Karimi and propel Assadullah Hakim to the top job was far harder than Adam had envisaged.

"For fuck's sake Adam do we have a positive ID or not?" Dave pushed again.

The pause between Dave asking and Adam responding seemed to go on for a lifetime.

"Mo, get onto CHOSIN and ensure the Cobras are turning and burning," Dave said, then turning to Adam. "You need to make a call on this. Forget about what you are looking at. You've got one job to do. Tell me if you have a positive ID on our objective."

"Georgetown," Adam responded letting his own binos slip from his eyes. "Georgetown."

In an instant the codeword was being repeated over the airwaves and the final phase of the operation was underway. Simultaneously, Nick and Dave began packing kit. If everything went to plan with the strike they wouldn't be leaving immediately. But if it didn't, and they were compromised, then they would have to bug out sharpish, probably under fire.

There was similar hurried activity amongst Bravo team. Only Dan remained unmoving, hunched over his radio set. In his lap a map was spread open, the target set clearly marked in blue non-permanent marker.

A US Marines Anglico, Dan was expert in calling in naval gunfire and other indirect fire. He was also a political pawn, there as a sop to the fact that the Upper Sangin Valley sat in American controlled territory. As sops go at least he had a use. As well as managing firepower he was also qualified to direct air assets; in this case two Cobras, a Blackhawk and the extraction chopper.

"MUD 51 this is CHOSIN 49. How copy?" Dan spoke rapidly into the mic establishing comms with the Cobras back on the pad at Camp Leatherneck.

"CHOSIN 49 we have good copy send your traffic," the pilot of the lead Cobra responded.

"Roger MUD 51 we have 'Georgetown'. Request you move your

packet to holding area Foxtrot and wait for call forward."

"We are lifting with 2 MUD call signs, 51 and 52 as well as TF 81 Blackhawk."

"What the fuck is that?" Nick said. Adam turned to look in the same direction as the other members of the team.

"What you got mate?" Dave asked.

"I can hear helicopters coming in from the north."

"Fucking Yanks," Mo chipped in. "Can't keep their helicopters back long enough for the strike to go in. They're going to blow the fucking op."

"Nick, get onto CHOSIN and tell him to hold the Cobras back. If we can hear them it means the target can bloody well hear them too."

"Roger, already on it."

"This is going to a bag of fuck Adam, we should have kept those fuckers out of the planning and done it ourselves," Dave said, looking beyond Adam to the north. "Too many moving parts. This should be a simple op and we've made it complicated."

"Boss we got a problem," Nick said agitatedly. "CHOSIN says he has no comms with those fuckers. His airframes are still to the southeast en route to holding area Foxtrot. He has no idea who these boys are."

"Could it just be some random US pilot not reading his map right and straying through the out of bounds box?" Adam asked.

"No way," replied Dave. "Too much of a coincidence, there's been no over flight for 48 hours and yet suddenly we get this. I don't like it. Nick, get onto higher I want to know what is going on."

"Roger Boss."

"Keep packing," ordered Dave. "Mo, see if you can get eyes on those aircraft."

"Yeah, got them now mate, three US Marine Chinooks coming in from the north. Two are dropping around the 611. The third looks to be going down south of the compounds."

"Shit, that's a cordon going in," Dave said.

"I think you've nailed it Dave. I now have a pair of Blackhawks coming in with little birds in over-watch. Looks like Delta," Mo said.

"That makes no sense," Adam tried to compute what he was being told. "We're about to level that area and they're sending people in?"

"Boss," Nick interrupted brusquely. "We have a call from higher to begin extraction. They've given us a movement corridor southeast into the Dashte."

"Ok, that's good enough for me. Lads, lets get the fuck out of her," Dave whispered. "Nick, tell Bravo they have five mikes and we want to be out of here. Meet them at the ERV."

"What's going on Dave? Extract in daylight? I thought you said we would have a twelve-hour window after the strike to bug out in darkness?" Adam asked, stuffing the sleeping bag back into his Bergen. "And why have the skies suddenly become busier than Heathrow? What the fuck is happening Dave?" He stopped to look the SAS sergeant in the eyes.

"You're right Adam this is fucked up," Dave replied. "But we're playing a different game now. Can't you see that? The cordon, the Blackhawks. I bet my bottom dollar this isn't a kill mission anymore. The Yanks are going for a snatch and once they've got their guy the enemy are going to be tearing it up looking for us. We need to be somewhere else and fast."

"What do you mean a snatch, that was never the plan?"

"Maybe not, but that's what my money is on now. Seems like you aren't being kept up to date with all the operational changes mate," Dave said with a sarcastic smile. "So, are you fucking coming or what?"

————◆————

By now the Chinooks had straddled the village and deposited their human cargo to fan out and create an impenetrable perimeter: nobody out. The Blackhawks made a single pass overhead before they too set down, less than 100 metres off the target compound. Under the cover of a barrage supplied courtesy of the fire support helicopters, the occupants spilled out. Some darted straight for the compound; others dealt with the pockets of fire coming from local Taliban fighters.

For the first time in two days, Adam stood up. Fighting the cramp, he braced himself against a crumbling wall pillar to get a better view of what was going on. He watched the Delta teams stream towards their goal, cutting down anything that moved. Three old men, who had been hurriedly crossing the road to get to the safety of the bazaar didn't make it, felled in a hail of bullets.

Small firefights were springing up everywhere. The struggle for control of the target was intense, confused and murderous, aerial gunfire ripped up the ground, laying a carpet of fire for the specialists to move over. Then came the sound of flash-bangs going off; the stun grenades easily distinguishable from their HE counterparts by their high pitch detonations and blaze of light. The use of the non-lethal weapons signified only one thing: they had reached Silab.

———•———

Adam's response was instinctive and one he knew he'd probably come to regret, but he did nothing to check it. Grabbing hold of his C8 carbine and shrugging off the Bergen hanging from his shoulder, he darted from the OP and headed towards the target compound.

"Adam, what the fuck?" Dave yelled after him. But Adam ignored the shouting.

"Well fuck you, you're on your own." Dave was furious, spitting the words out. "Fucking amateur Ruperts."

With his uniform concealed beneath the long Afghan cloak he wore, Adam was under no illusions over what would happen if the Americans saw him: they would shoot first and ask questions later, if they bothered doing so at all. After a couple of hundred metres of hard running across the open ground, he ducked left and collapsed into a bone dry irrigation ditch. He wriggled to get out of the cape, his eyes stinging from the sweat dripping into them. As he struggled to undress, company arrived; two armed Afghans hurrying down the same arid watercourse but in the other direction, towards him, keen to put some distance between themselves and the mayhem unfolding behind them. Confronted with Adam, they stumbled to a halt, unsure of what they were seeing, looks of bewilderment spreading over their faces. The moment's pause was all Adam needed. Finally managing to free his rifle he half raised the weapon and fired two rounds at the man in front. The first bullet struck him in the throat, clipping an artery and sending a spray of blood shooting from the wound. The second round embedded itself in his groin. Adam didn't hesitate, letting go another burst as the man crumpled to the ground, putting the Afghan's fate beyond doubt.

Reacting to the plight of his comrade the second man started yelling, bringing his battered AK47 to bear on Adam and wildly firing a volley of shots, but not so wildly that he missed completely, a single round glancing off Adam's shoulder, knocking him sideways. Losing his balance saved his life. As he dropped to his knee, another brace of bullets flew past inches over his head. Adam took aim and fired before the Afghan could get set up for another attempt. The round hit the second Afghan square in the chest and he collapsed too. Wary that others might be following in the wake of the pair he had just felled, Adam turned to inspect the furrow on his right shoulder. A voice shouted in his ear.

"Adam, this is Dave, check."

"Dave roger, got you," Adam replied.

"You need to get yourself back here, we're bugging out now."

"Listen Dave, I have spent too much time on this thing to watch it disintegrate just because someone thinks they want to change the operational parameters," said Adam, taking deep breaths, steadying himself for the next dash forward. "I want to get to Delta and find out when the orders were changed and by whom."

"Come on mate, they won't know," said Dave trying to sound reasonable. "Raise it higher when we get back to base."

But Adam was no longer listening. He had pulled his earpiece out, stepped over the corpses at his feet and was charging along the ditch. The deep channel took him almost to the compound's edge. There was no sign of the fighting letting up. Whether or not the Americans had got Silab, it was clear his comrades were not going to be a pushover. Adam kicked his way up the steep mud bank and flung himself against a wall, cursing loudly as the movement jarred his injured arm. Sucking air into his lungs he was acutely aware that he was wounded, alone and without anything that could adequately be described as a plan. Peering round a corner Adam found himself looking at the inside angle of an L-shaped building. At its apex was a door, slightly ajar.

He made a run for it but as he closed in on the aperture, he was showered with dust as the wall above him was torn apart by a Talib's bullets. Darting through the doorway he crashed headlong into another Talib who like him had decided the room would make a good place to take cover.

Entwined in a mass of rifles and limbs the two fell to the floor. As his weapon fell out of reach, Adam grasped the barrel of the Talib's AK and forced it away from him, trying to shut his mind to the scorching pain of the red-hot metal burning into his skin. With his other hand he groped for the Sig pistol holstered on his thigh. A crescendo of noise filled the tiny space as Adam's opponent pulled the trigger of his weapon sending a spray of 7.62mm short thumping into the ceiling.

With a short waist-high jab Adam rammed his pistol into the enemy fighter's solar plexus with all the energy he could muster. He was rewarded with the sound of ribs cracking. Without pausing he squeezed the Sig's trigger repeatedly and four 9mm rounds punched into the Talib who buckled under the fatal onslaught. For good measure Adam pumped another couple of rounds into the figure now sprawled at his feet. Only then did he release his opponent's rifle, the shape of the barrel branded on his left palm.

Trying to calm himself he switched the magazines of both his weapons, wincing at the scald on his hand and the sting of his bullet-creased shoulder. He holstered the pistol and raised his rifle, preparing for the next move.

'Ok Adam, these fuckers can't shoot for shit' he persuaded himself, 'just move fast, stay low and don't stop'. He was off again, spinning out of the doorway.

Dashing out, the fire was back on him in an instant, rounds churning up the sun baked earth at his feet. He made it as far as the animal pen, its occupants, a handful of sheep, lay there dead, their mangy fleeces sodden with blood. He scuttled over to an earthen shelter into which the livestock must have been herded at night or in bad weather. But now he was in trouble: pinned down by a handful of the enemy, his protection being systematically eaten away by bullets fired by men who clearly could shoot and who were ensconced in what looked like a barn only fifty metres away.

Grimly he kept his head down, trying to make himself as small as possible, figuring a way out of the nightmare. He couldn't simply back up. That would put him out in open territory again and no match for the enemy who had found their range. Pushing on didn't look like a good long-term proposition either. His best hope was that the Yanks would finish their business in the larger compound and come and see what all the noise was about. He had to admit this didn't seem like a banker either. As if to highlight his predicament his C8 shuddered violently. He was not reassured when he saw the metal framed stock had been buckled by the force of an enemy round.

A terrific explosion drowned out the sound of the small arms fire. Daring to raise his head just slightly Adam saw a trio of men he recognised crouched in the lee of the barn, stacking up ready for an assault. On the silent count of three Dave and Nick posted grenades underneath the bulging set of wooden double doors. After three seconds more they detonated, blowing the doors open and sending a billowing cloud of dust and debris out into the open. Mo led the way in, bursts of silenced automatic gunfire heralding their arrival to the structure's disorientated and wounded occupants. It took less than half a minute for Dave to reappear, this time at a window. He looked directly at Adam and gave him two signals. A thumbs up, and the five-minute sign. The message was clear. He'd been given a second chance to do whatever he felt necessary, but take longer than the allotted time and there would be no one coming to his rescue.

Adam replied with his own thumbs up before remembering the earpiece he'd wrenched out whilst in the ditch. It still dangled from his neck. He shoved it back in.

"You listen in Adam. We'll cover for the next few minutes then you need to get yourself out of there. Bravo team is to the west watching our flank and preparing to cover our extraction. There's no leeway here mate, get on with it, get it done and let's go."

Dave's words were delivered as rapidly as the rate of fire from his C8.

"Cheers Dave," Adam said. "You don't…" but Dave cut him short.

"Yeah, yeah, whatever, just fucking hurry up."

Adam didn't need further prompting. He was gone, heading towards LX25, nervous that the absence of shooting indicated that the Delta unit had got their man and were heading for exit. Adam knew he was in a race, a fact confirmed by a knot of American troops slipping into sight, making for the spot where the Blackhawks had deposited them minutes previously.

Carried along in the middle of the group, smaller than the burly US soldiers, but just visible between them was the man Adam had come to kill. Hooded and with his hands bound by plasticuffs, the slightly overweight Afghan was bundled towards the waiting aircraft, falling every few feet and having to be hauled up by his minders. Adam ploughed on.

"British soldier! British soldier!" he yelled, raising his rifle above his head to show he was no threat.

One of the Delta team turned and covered him as he got to within a few yards. The man regarded Adam with a degree of suspicion, but mainly bemusement. Behind him his colleagues were about in position to board the first of the two choppers that had now landed.

"Who the hell is in charge here?" Adam demanded, pulling up short because of the American rifle pointing directly at his heart.

"Stay back, Sir," the Delta operator replied in a mild, almost apologetic voice completely at odds with the violent disorder going on all around. Adam chanced another step forward. Now the response was more aggressive: "Stay fucking back, Sir."

"Listen I need to speak to the man in charge here," Adam shouted, trying to make himself heard over the whining of the helicopter. "You're fucking up a long term operation." His protests were ignored, the soldier, rifle still levelled, now retreating slowly towards the choppers and the rest of his team.

Adam looked on impotently as Silab, the man he had spent three months targeting, was shoved inside an aircraft. But it wasn't one-way traffic. Flanked by a pair of bodyguards, a portly figure clambered out of the same Blackhawk and strode towards him.

The man was several years older than the rest of the Delta Force members, not in prime physical shape and instead of being dressed in US style MTP with a Kevlar helmet, ops vest and an array of gadgets, antennas and radios hanging from the kit, he wore previous era US military fatigues. There were no badges of rank, no helmet and his pistol sat snug in a beaten-up old holster.

He walked on confidently until he stood in front of Adam.

"Captain Caine it's nice to meet you. My name is Cyrus Vincent and I work for US intelligence. I would just like to take this opportunity to thank you for your work in targeting our man. I would understand if you had a few questions..."

"A few questions?" Adam shouted. "Are you fucking kidding me? I have more than a few questions. Who gave authority for the mission parameters to change?"

"Well I think that's a little obvious Captain don't you?" Cyrus replied without changing the calm tone of his voice. "Mullah Karimi, or Silab as you like to call him, is far too valuable to merely kill. Our government needs sources like him and so, I would have thought, does yours. I should say thank you for doing the hard work for us. We'd had trouble tracking him down. Without your assistance we could have been looking for him for who knows how much longer."

"You played me and my men. Why didn't you just tell me what you wanted and we could have come up with a joint plan. We're on the same side aren't we?"

"Don't be naïve, Captain," Cyrus shot back, a degree of impatience finding its way into his voice. "You and your European partners turned your backs on this country and are walking away. Not for the first time it will be up to good ol' Uncle Sam to sort the mess out. This is bigger than Afghanistan, this is regional, and the whole stability of the area depends on us defeating Al Qaeda, the Taliban and whoever else gets in the way."

Cyrus was on rapid fire now, not affording Adam a word in edgeways.

"The killing of Bin Laden looked good on paper and was great for the US administration but our real target, the man who we need to remove to end the coherency of any insurgency is Mullah Omar. If we deliver him up, if we can reduce or erase the Taliban footprint, then the people of the US will have the appetite to retain a presence in Afghanistan for longer and give us the opportunity to control this whole region. People like Karimi are part of that process. Look, we're the ones here indefinitely and I'm not ashamed to say we're looking out for ourselves. If that causes our esteemed allies a few problems along the way then hell, that's a price I'm happy to pay."

Cyrus turned to leave, but Adam seized his arm.

"We could have controlled the whole of the Sangin valley, saved countless lives, made it better for the Afghans. Doesn't that count for something in your mission statement?" Even as he spoke Adam knew he sounded like some bleeding heart aid worker.

"Look Captain," Cyrus tried to keep his composure. "To be frank I don't care if we lose a few hundred soldiers in this shit hole or if the locals hate us for having a dung filled life. My aim is to find out what is going on between Afghanistan and Pakistan and make sure the ground is set for a long-term intervention in this region by the US. The Kabul government has already forgotten what the likes of you and I have been doing for them since 2001 and even now are speaking to the Russians. Meanwhile the Chinese continue to buy up land and fund projects all over the country. The United States is not in the business of being undermined by a bunch of chancers and opportunists. We will dominate this part of the world and Karimi's information will help us do it. If you can't see the bigger picture Captain then I think you should be looking for another line of work."

"But what about the people you have killed here today?" Adam said desperately still gripping Cyrus's arm.

"No more than you would have killed if you had called in that missile strike," the American replied acidly. "Now. Let. Go. Of. My. Fucking. Shirt. Is that clear enough for you?"

"You arrogant bastard" Adam shouted. He lunged for Cyrus but was way too slow. The American's two minders held him back as their boss pulled himself free. Unhurriedly he returned to his transport.

Chapter 2
MAN DOWN – SANGIN VALLEY

Another round ricocheted off the doorframe.

"Dave this isn't funny," yelled Nick, crouched behind the crumbling woodwork. "It's getting a bit tasty here mate and I'm not sure we are going to be able to get out if we don't get some support in shortly or begin our extraction."

The situation for the three SAS troopers, left huddled in the small compound as Adam argued his piece, was getting dire. With the Yanks heading for the exit, the enemy's confidence was growing and the odds were rapidly stacking in their favour again.

Dave didn't answer straight away. Instead he kept staring across the ground toward the HLS north of LX25, as if a parent debating whether they should go after an errant child. He could see Delta Force making for their rides home, weighed down by enough kit and weaponry to start a big war in a small African nation. Dropping to one knee, he sighed:

"Alright you two, I had better go and get him."

He pressed the release catch on the left side of his carbine and ejected the half-empty magazine, replacing it with the full one he had retrieved from his ops vest.

"Covering fire now," Dave yelled, breaking into the open and running north towards Adam.

Two hundred metres and several hundred gasped breaths later he arrived in time to see the retro-dressed American striding towards his helicopter, his guards in tow, edging away from Adam, careful not to turn their backs on him completely.

"You got your fucking answers now lets get the fuck out of here,"

Dave insisted, grabbing Adam by the shoulders and spinning him around. As if to emphasise the dangers a large explosion ripped through the sky and both men ducked. "The enemy are all over the fucking place, I don't have permission to call in IDF or heli support until this lot are long gone and we need to get to the ERV. Sharpish."

"Ok," Adam replied dejectedly. "Let's go."

As he spoke they were engulfed in a blanket of Afghan dust as, in turn, the two Blackhawks carrying Vincent and the Delta teams, lifted and turned, accelerating rapidly, low across the landscape, before the pilots pulled back on their sticks to gain height and safety. Their paths crossed those of a trio of lumbering Chinooks inbound to retrieve the marines.

"We are going to be left here with our bollocks hanging out all because you needed to throw a sodding tantrum," Dave shouted as the two men ran, chased on their way by a growing number of Taliban bullets.

Both men crashed into the redoubt to find Nick and Mo preoccupied, furiously engaging enemy fighters who were closing in.

"Right, Nick," Dave shouted. "Get onto Bravo team and have them provide covering fire for our extraction, we will go out the same route we came in."

"Roger," replied Nick, wrestling with his small personal transmitter to relay the message.

"Also give CHOSIN a call. See if we can finally get those Cobras in to give us backup."

Dave twisted round to look at Mo.

"On my shout I want you to head to the track junction about 150 metres south. Secure it as a rally point and wait for us to reach you. Got it?"

"Got it mate, on your call for move and secure," Mo repeated.

Everything was happening at once. With Dave frantically trying to orchestrate the battle, the numerous and increasingly emboldened Talibs converged on the British contingent. Several paid the price for their overconfidence, but even as they fell to SAS bullets, others appeared behind them. Dave understood it was a numbers game. No matter how skilled he and the others were; the sheer weight of the opposition would see them quickly overwhelmed. The stink of cordite from the weapons being fired testified to the intensity of the engagement. Empty magazines and cartridge cases littered the floor, each man going through a practised routine of acquiring a target through the holographic sight on top of their C8s, shooting and moving on to the next, using their carbines not in full automatic mode firing bursts, but on repeat, to give better accuracy and conserve ammo. Still, to Adam, the rate of fire seemed incredible.

As for the incoming, most of it was Kalashnikov 7.62, but not all.

Another RPG warhead snaked towards them. It was mesmeric. Unlike the bullets snapping past at supersonic speeds, the RPGs seemed to defy gravity, so slowly did they wend their way across the battlefield, almost as if they had been lobbed by hand, their approach heralded by the sound of the large back-blast as the weapon was fired. Almost too late, Adam tore his eyes away from the projectile and dropped behind the window as it slammed against the wall and detonated; slivers of shrapnel flew through the opening inches above his head.

"Dave," came the shout from Nick. "Bravo team are in a secure area and can cover our extraction from the compound, they are engaging enemy now."

"Alright, let's get some fire down, begin taking out those targets. Mo… Go. Go. Go."

In a second Mo was barging out of the door, rifle in one hand, his grab bag dragged along in the other, day-sack over his shoulder. Out of the corner of his eye Adam glimpsed him leave. An instant later the whole room was filled with heat, noise and scything metal. There was a yell of pain as fragmentation from the explosion of another RPG sliced through Nick's forearm. Disorientated by the violence Adam shook his head in an attempt to reorder his thoughts. His ears were ringing and his eyes stuffed with grit. He fought to clear his vision. Mo had been blown back into the room as the round struck the door. He wasn't moving.

"Man down! Man down! Dave, Mo is down."

"Treat him and get him ready to move," Dave said, blasting at the enemy. "How's it going with the air support Nick, spoke to CHOSIN? Now would be a good time to have it."

"Roger mate, got good comms, they are going to give us suppressive fire. Airframes will be inbound in two mikes. CHOSIN will use the Cobras to get us back to the ERV and then give them their original target package."

"OK, keep giving fire, I'm going to check on Mo and get our kit ready."

Dave dodged over to Adam who was kneeling beside Mo, a hand on his throat, feeling for a non-existent pulse.

"He's dead," Adam said, almost in a whisper.

"What did you fucking say?"

"I said Mo is dead."

"What? He can't be fucking dead." Dave shoved Adam aside and put his own fingers on his friend's neck searching for signs of life.

"Took the full force of the RPG, didn't stand a chance," Adam explained.

"I hate to bother you two," shouted Nick, oblivious to the conversation behind him. "But there are Talibs all over the fucking place and I could use a hand."

"Nick, get onto CHOSIN again. Tell them we have... tell them we have a T4. Mo's gone."

Nick hesitated and looked over at the huddle, two soldiers bent over the prostrate body of a third.

"CHOSIN 49 this is Alpha-11 we have one T4 and need immediate extraction."

Dave looked up. Adam could see hatred in his eyes, could feel the accusations being silently hurled at him: here was a man, an outsider who they had accepted into their team only for him to rip apart their tight group through his injudicious, selfish actions. Adam couldn't hold the gaze any longer.

"You get him on your shoulder," Dave ordered Adam, his voice as cold as ice. "You killed him, you carry him. I will sort out the kit for blowing."

For Adam, time went haywire. There was so much on his mind that when the Cobras arrived on station he couldn't tell whether they had been ten seconds or ten minutes in the coming. The helicopters pirouetted around the wafting red smoke released by Nick to mark friendly force positions, using their 20mm Gatling cannons to scribe an arc of destruction through the enemy positions.

As the three men left the compound, it was rocked by another blast. But this was the Brits own doing. Dave had made the improvised device by connecting a handful of plastic explosive to a couple of phosphorous grenades and placed it amongst the pile of equipment he'd bundled together and taped up. When the bomb went off it showered everything with burning lumps of phos. The clothing was the first thing to ignite, but soon everything was ablaze.

Dave had taken up point with Nick at the rear covering the enemy who were now scattering beneath the Cobras as they made another pass. Adam, Mo's body over his shoulder, was sandwiched between them, the burden of carrying the dead weight only slightly eased by the adrenaline coursing through his veins. As they approached the track junction they could hear Bravo team shouting instructions and firing at the enemy in the distance. CHOSIN, his American accent easily discernable over the sound of battle, was talking continuously on the radio to both the Cobras and the Medical Emergency Response Team helicopter inbound to recover the casualty's body and probably extract them too.

———•———

"Bravo this is Alpha we're going to head straight to the HLS, secure the area and wait for you to close in," Dave said, his small transmitter now in range of Bravo team.

"Roger Alpha," a disembodied voice replied. "We will continue to cover with SAF, CHOSIN is going to keep the Cobras on task until extraction."

———•———

Alpha team reached the track junction.

"Right," Dave said sucking in air, "stop for two, catch your breath."

Automatically, Nick adopted the prone position covering north. Adam collapsed with Mo's body.

"How far Dave?" Adam asked.

"It was in the fucking orders Adam. What's the problem? Mo giving you difficulties is he? Here's a thing, maybe if you had stuck to the fucking orders from me, he would still be alive."

"Listen mate nobody is more sorry than me, but who is to blame here?" Adam tried to reason with Dave. "This is a US fuck up and when we get back…"

Dave interrupted.

"I'll tell you who'll be more sorry than you. Mo's wife. And his two young kids. They're the ones who'll be really sorry. Sorry that an arsehole amateur like you cost them their dad. Now stop whining and let's move."

Adam heaved the body back over his shoulder with help from Dave and Nick. The enemy fire had died down noticeably thanks to the intervention of the Cobras.

Another ten minutes of progress, then Dave shouted back to the rest of the team.

"About 80 metres till we hit the ERV and Emergency HLS." Dave stopped and looked back at Adam and Nick. "Once we get there, Nick I want you to cover north and call in Bravo. Adam you watch west."

Orders given, Dave turned and took a pace forward. There wouldn't be another.

The blast from the IED buried beneath the track ripped up through the surface following the course of least resistance. It took the team leader with it, throwing him several feet into the field of corn bordering the path, his mutilated legs and groin a bloody mess, barely recognisable as body parts.

None of this registered with Adam as he too was engulfed in the chaos of the situation, pummelled by a hail of mud, sand and metal. Falling to the floor, he lost consciousness.

Chapter 3
KHALID BASHIR – US PRISONER HOLDING FACILITY BAGRAM

The fluid was as vivid as anything he had ever seen, luxuriant almost. So rich it oozed more than flowed, meandering slowly down Khalid's arm. Its purity seemed to draw him in. As the trickle of blood moved in one direction Khalid cast his eyes in the other, trying to trace the crimson smear back to its source. Going cross-eyed he lost sight of it.

The spring nestled amongst the mass of coarse black matted hair that hung around Khalid's face, sodden with sweat, with water and now with blood.

If Khalid had been able he would have reached up to stem the flow but both his wrists were bound to the heavy metal chair he sat slumped in. His legs were also fastened to the chair that was itself bolted to the ground.

Khalid shivered with the cold, his naked body struggling to maintain its core temperature. He felt as vulnerable and as helpless as a child, reliant on others to ensure its wellbeing. Only in this case there was no parental solace or comfort to be found, just the unrelenting noise, energy sapping fatigue and unpredictable torture.

Khalid attempted to focus. He thought it was about an hour since his tormentors had last paid a visit; they'd taken it in turns to beat him with lengths of plastic piping. The bouts of violence were short and sharp, intended to intimidate, to leave Khalid scared and isolated. The torturers never spoke, never gave any indication they wanted anything in particular. They simply went about their well-practiced task. It was crude, effective conditioning. Without hope of appealing to his captors'

47

compassion he had no way to get them to stop, the anonymous figures meting out the punishment devoid of emotion.

Khalid let his mind drift again to try and find some peace elsewhere. He took himself back to the start. To the place, high in the border region of Pakistan, that had been his childhood home. To the people who had shaped him; his father most of all.

———◆———

Standing above the tethered creature, its legs bound by coarse twine to two posts driven firmly into the ground behind the house, Farouk offers the rough wooden handle of the weapon to his eldest child and only son. The just-sharpened blade glints in the harsh midday light as Khalid reluctantly takes the knife.

"We shall do this together," Farouk says gently sensing the young boy's nervousness. Khalid feels his father grasp his wrist and lets him guide him towards the goat, ignoring its pleading bleats. The pair of them kneel down, the older man grabbing the head of the animal and pulling it back to fully expose the long line of the neck. Before Khalid realises what is happening, the person he admires more than any other has yanked his arm and plunged the dagger through the animal's skin with a force and speed that leaves him stunned, the honed metal slicing effortlessly through everything it comes into contact with. For a moment neither of them move. The first trickles of blood start to seep from the cut, the surge held back by the knife left stuck where it has been thrust. It is only when his father jerks the blade free that the full visceral nature of what they have done becomes shockingly obvious, red liquid pumping over the pair of them, splattering and staining their clothes, splashing their skin. Farouk ignores it.

"Never hesitate. Once you have decided to act, then act quickly."

Khalid listens to his father, feeling his warm breath on his ear.

"Killing is not to be enjoyed, but when it has to be done then always,

always, be strong and be certain. Next time," his father says wiping the blade on the end of a long cloth thrown over his shoulder, "you will do this on your own."

Transfixed by the corpse Khalid hardly notices as the older man gently releases his hold and steps silently away. The image of the limp, lifeless goat will remain with Khalid forever. So too the wisdom of the words.

The open palm slapped the side of Khalid's face, a heavy hand grabbing him by the hair and wrenching his head back. Khalid yelled out in surprise and pain, the picture of him and his father and the goat smashed. The image in front of him now is that of a tall muscular figure in a dark boiler suit with a black balaclava over his head. The eyes that peer through the slits betray nothing.

"Please," Khalid whispers in Pashtu, the language he has used since being taken. "What do you want? I can't help you if you don't tell me."

The guard doesn't bother responding. Instead he retrieves the blindfold lying on the floor beside Khalid and slips it over his eyes to plunge him into darkness again.

"Why are you doing this? Tell me why?"

Khalid shouts this time but still there's no answer. He is left to count the man's footsteps as he walks away. Eighteen of them. About fifteen metres. Then came the sound of a door being opened and closed. Behind the blindfold Khalid couldn't see anything but he'd already taken in his surroundings. The room was cold and damp – he didn't need any vision to know that – and the stone floor and walls were stained with dark green watermarks. A single bulb hung from a length of flex in the centre of the ceiling, inadequate to produce enough light to penetrate the shadows that obscured the furthest recesses of the space.

With the guard gone the noise restarted. Not rock music now but white noise; piercing and relentless. Khalid tried to escape back to his past. He remembered the day he told his family he'd be leaving Kachkai to join the border police. He remembered the time two years later when he had proudly returned to tell his family of his selection to go to England to be trained at the most famous military academy in the world. And then he remembered that his family were no longer with him; that a US missile had ripped them apart and the vengefulness welled within him. He imagined the torn up bodies of his mother and sister. And he shuddered at the thought of his crippled father.

The old man lays flat out on a filthy mattress in the grubby hospital, draped only in a ragged sheet soiled with the bodily fluids of previous temporary owners. The face – where the tangled beard does not hide it – carries the same hues as the cloth that covers him for Farouk is also stained: with the blemishes of age – liver spots and moles, deep pores and blotches – and with the marks of violence; cuts and bruises that refuse to heal, and a zigzagging wheal which runs from his cheek, past his temple and disappears into the hairline.

There is no way of telling what is happening in the soul because the windows are closed, the eye lids pulled down like shutters. But it is the shape of the head that offers the most obvious clue as to the harm suffered by the old man. The top left side of the skull is cratered, concave when it should be convex, the grey locks absent where an overworked, underpaid, ill-equipped doctor has tried to ease the pressure on the brain with little hope of properly reconstructing the now staved-in protection surrounding it.

Throughout the hospital people are rushing to and fro: harassed staff, worried families, indifferent policemen, they're all doing urgent things. Yet the old man remains oblivious to the goings-on. Just as everyone seems to ignore him, so he ignores them. For Farouk Bashir is in a state of suspension, and has been ever since the women of his family were wiped out by the American missile. Five months after the attack there is no indication that the life – if that is what it can be called – of Bashir senior will ever be anything more than one spent in a coma. Nothing in the motionless, emotionless, façade he presents suggests he is being tormented by what has happened to him. If that anguish exists, then it is locked far from prying eyes, those of his son included.

Khalid weeps as he squeezes the hand that had guided his own in the slaughter of the goat so long before. For more than an hour Khalid is there, first sitting on the edge of the bed, then lying on it, cradling the skeletal frame, all the while talking softly to the spirit of the man he once knew, not to the shrivelled physical form stretched out in front of him, not to the body that more closely resembles a corpse than a human being. Over and over he quietly repeats his vow.

"Father, how can this be? Every step of the way you protected me, taught and encouraged me, loved me. You tolerated my foolishness and endured my stupidity. You were calm and forgiving when I offered you nothing but pain and anxiety. For as long as I can remember you were there for me. Now it is my chance to repay you. I promise you this: I will avenge the deaths of my mother and my sister. That is my pledge to you."

Khalid stops talking and squeezes the hand in his fist even tighter, determined the old man should feel his presence and gain some comfort from it. Or is it he, Khalid, needing the contact? He remains stock-still as around him the perpetual motion continues. Above the neighbouring bed there is a small square aperture, at least eight feet off the ground. The window contains no glass. Instead it is covered by a screen of tightly weaved mesh that is supposed to keep out the flies and mosquitoes, the effectiveness of which is singularly undermined by a large tear. Through the hole, a shaft of light cuts across the room. During the time Khalid has been with his father it has made gradual progress towards him and his father, like a lighthouse beam slowed to a snail's pace. At last Khalid rises to his feet, turns and walks away. Harnessing all his willpower he resists the overwhelming desire to look back. He harbours a dreadful fear: that he has seen his father for the last time. He moves down the tiled corridor, between whitewashed walls, the noise from every step reflecting off the hard surfaces and adding to the hum of noise.

Ahead of him he sees the young doctor who offered him directions to his father when he first arrived. He pores over the top sheet of a pile of papers held in the crook of his arm. Khalid approaches him, noticing how grey the man's hair is for someone so junior. Perhaps he shouldn't be surprised. The ravages of life are quick to leave their mark in this part of the world and there is no reason to believe a man of medicine should suffer the effects any less than anyone else.

"Excuse me doctor."

The young man glances up from his files.

"I'm sorry doctor, but my father, what is the prognosis?" Khalid asks the question though he is afraid of the answer. The doctor appears confused.

"Farouk Bashir," Khalid persists. "The old man with the head injury caused by the missile attack, he's in a coma. Down there."

Khalid gestures in the direction he's just come. The prompt triggers in the medic some recognition and a degree of sympathy.

"Ah yes. I am sorry," the doctor replies. "Although he has made a strong recovery in physical terms, he would need a lot of rehabilitation and stimulation to stand any chance of regaining consciousness. His vital signs are good – heart, breathing, digestion – but there is nothing to indicate when or if he will again be aware of his surroundings or be able to communicate his feelings. It is very sad, but there is not much we can do here. With specialist help and a lot of time, neither of which we are able to offer, then there is the slightest chance he might regain some of his faculties. But it is very unlikely. We will try our best, however..."

The voice trails off, but there is no mistaking what has gone unsaid. In a place of so few resources and so many demands the plight of an elderly patient with little likelihood of recovery and no ability to fight his own corner will not feature particularly high on anyone's agenda.

The electricity shot through Khalid's body causing him to bite his tongue. It didn't stop, the ongoing blast of energy rattling his nerves. Through clenched teeth he let out a miserable groan, his eyes rolling in their sockets, nails splintering as he clawed at the metal of the chair. For six, seven seconds, a lifetime, the force field engulfed Khalid. Finally turned off, he unclenched his muscles, the sweat pouring from him. He barely had chance to recover before the process is repeated. There is not time to say anything and anyway there would be no point in doing so because no one would listen. The reason for the violence is not to get him to reveal anything but to grind him down, to keep him awake when he wants to sleep, to make every moment a misery.

Running through his treatment there was a simple theme to the abuse. Deprivation. Of rest, of company, of food, of water, of comfort, of quiet, of warmth. The whole time his guards, his torturers, say nothing and ask nothing.

It is only late on the second day, when he thought he could take no more, that he finally felt strong arms free his bindings and drag him from the chair. He is virtually carried to a small room hidden behind one of the two stone pillars that support the roof of the main chamber. Forcing him to crouch, Khalid's gaolers pushed him through a low opening into a tiny cell too small for him to stand in even if he had the energy to do so. There was barely any light, only that which seeped from the room he had just been taken from, but it was just enough to allow him to make out a ragged, stinking hessian mat piled in the corner. He crawled to it and pulled it over his shoulders, anxious to protect himself from the chill. The deep sleep came almost immediately.

The Mujahedeen fighters had been sat for many hours beneath the treeline, in the undergrowth, separated from the dusty track by a broad, irrigation gulley, waiting for the enemy soldiers to come by. They are being led by an elderly warrior. His seniority is a product of his age rather than any great tactical ability. The old man is aware of his failings, but that doesn't make him any more accepting of Khalid's presence amongst the group. Rather the opposite. He resents the idea of being shown up by this new arrival who is already being feted as a remarkable tactician. Certainly he will not show Khalid any favour or allow him any influence. The plan for the attack he is about to instigate has worked before, so why would it not work again?

The previous evening, under the leader's direction, the insurgents – Khalid amongst them – had dug a hole in the track into which a homemade mine had been laid, before the soil was scraped back into position over the top of it. The disturbed ground was drenched with water from the ditch and left to bake hard in the early sun of the following morning.

The mine will activate when it is trod on, the weight of a soldier compressing two electrical contacts and completing a circuit, allowing a current to flow to the detonator. As other troops move in to help the casualty the Afghans lying in wait will use a mobile phone to set off a second, radio-controlled, mine they've planted. In the following chaos the insurgents will open fire at close range with their assortment of AK-47s, PKMs and RPGs. Such is the plan.

Concealed amongst the foliage and the shadows Khalid and the others barely allow themselves a breath as the American troops finally come into view. They move ever so slowly, their progress deliberate and cautious, the patrol's lead man scans the ground in front and to the side of him with wide sweeps of the long wand he holds in his hands. Suddenly he halts, the wand left hovering over a patch of ground three feet away.

"Stop!" he warns. Khalid watches with a certain detachment, confident

of what the infidels next move will be. The remaining members of the US unit take up defensive positions, scanning the terrain in all directions. Closest to Khalid a thick-set marine has dropped to his stomach and is adjusting the M-240B general purpose machine gun he's been carrying and, despite the tension, no doubt feeling some relief at being able to put it down. From a distance of no more than twenty metres Khalid stares into the face of the gunner as his enemy strains to locate any threat in the foliage. For a moment they lock eyes but only one of them is aware of it. Khalid thanks Allah for the lush vegetation and the burning sun at his back that makes the job of peering into the gloom within which he is hiding all but impossible for the soldier. The man with the wand shouts out again.

"I've found an IED."

There is nothing Khalid can now do. The insurgents' advantage has evaporated and whatever happens next depends on the judgement and action of the veteran commander. Khalid prepares himself for things to unravel very quickly.

As the Americans' attention is diverted by a flurry of barked orders from the patrol leader the Mujahedeen commander, a few feet to Khalid's left, gestures wildly at a subordinate indicating he should explode the second charge. The man with the mobile presses the green button on the keypad having already tapped out the number. When nothing happens, he tries again, but still it does not work. For a moment the operator wonders whether he has input the wrong digits, substituted a four for a three; a seven for an eight; what else could it be? For a third time he tries, and fails, to set off the bomb. Beside him the old man is indignant. More than that he can sense twenty pairs of eyes boring into him, silently pleading that he do something.

The 57 year-old makes his fatal decision. Only too well aware of the growing doubt and uncertainty amongst his men, his fear of losing face easily outweighs any fear of being killed. He pushes aside the branches that conceal him and rises to his feet, yelling.

"Allah Akbar!"

And shooting.

The fusillade of 7.62mm short explodes from the barrel of the Kalashnikov he is firing from the hip. Cartridge cases spill on to the ground. If they had allowed themselves time the other fighters who follow the old man's lead and leap to their feet might have thought better of the idea. But most are simply grateful an example has been set and a course of action undertaken. No matter that it is the wrong one. A growing torrent of lead is flying across the ditch, but none with any accuracy. The response from the US Marines, already in good firing positions, is swift and murderous.

The US soldier adjacent to Khalid is also one of the closest to the Mujahedeen commander and, by a fraction, the first among his colleagues to react. He does not have to adjust his aim more than a few degrees to have the prize in his sight. Even as he squirms a couple of inches to his right and pulls the butt of the M-240B tighter into his shoulder he is firing. The first volley of shots streams straight over Khalid's lowered head. The second volley cuts his senior almost in half. Two of the half-dozen bullets that strike the aged warrior rip open his stomach and intestine, the third shatters his pelvis and slices through the femoral artery. The fourth bullet destroys a pair of his lumber vertebrae severing the spinal cord as it does so. The force of the impacts spin the victim on his heels and send him crashing to the floor. The trademark black turban he wears snags on a branch as he falls, dislodging it from his head. Even as he dies, blood spewing from his wounds, he cannot understand how things have gone quite so badly wrong.

But Khalid can.

As far back as the early 1970s British soldiers started carrying electronic counter measures equipment. The ECM kit was introduced exactly to thwart republican terrorists deploying radio-controlled bombs. The equipment would jam the trigger signal being sent either by telephone or the sort of radio controlled server used to fly model aircraft. The Americans were slower to take up ECM because before Afghanistan they were never in a conflict where they needed it. But they had it now; the three antenna protruding from the backpacks of a number of the US soldiers had confirmed as much to Khalid before the mayhem began.

In the second or two it has taken the gunner to fell the old Afghan, the other members of the US unit have assigned themselves targets and opened up, the deep-throated solo of the M-240B all but drowned out by the chorus of 5.56mm calibre M4s chattering away repeatedly and accurately.

The storm of bullets scythe through the foliage and at least three of the Afghan fighters who jumped to their feet alongside the old man. Nose pressed into the earth, Khalid can hear the screaming of his colleagues above the cacophony of gunfire. Any hope of winning the engagement has evaporated, so too the blind courage displayed by the dead and dying. Shocked by the onslaught, the rest of the group now have thoughts only of self-preservation. In a panic, the surviving members struggle to their feet, diving through the undergrowth and plunging into the field of man-high stalks of maize bordering their position.

The move does not go unnoticed. Still hidden from view, it is just a few seconds later that Khalid hears the first 105mm shell whistle overhead and detonate amongst the crops. It is followed in quick succession by three more rounds propelled by the big guns he knows are located at Forward Operating Base Jackson some five miles distant. He has already made his mind up to try and creep away at a tangent to his fleeing colleagues. The bombardment confirms the wisdom of that decision. The pummelling continues unabated as Khalid, brimming with disappointment and anger, slithers along the treeline; his frustrations directed not towards the enemy but the old man who has thrown away his life and those of the men. And what for? Absolutely nothing. Khalid swears he will never be involved in such a calamitous attack again. Uniquely amongst those that fight the infidel he truly understands the enemy: their strengths and their weaknesses.

The trio of men looked at Khalid through the peepholes bored into the prison's wall. Two of the three wore the dark boiler suits Khalid was familiar with. The third had no such uniform. Instead he was dressed in canvas trousers, hiking boots and a white cotton shirt. Content with what they had seen the men stepped away from the observation point.

"Has he spoken at all?" the man in the casuals asked.

"He keeps shouting out in Pashtu, asking us to stop," one of the guards replied.

"Have you spoken to him?"

"No Sir. As per your orders we have said nothing."

"I want to keep it that way, I need him isolated and vulnerable, do you understand? But write down anything he says. And that includes what he utters in his sleep. Got it?"

"Yes Sir, but…"

"What?"

"I cannot write," said the first guard.

"Fuck." The Westerner turned to the second guard. "And you?"

"I can write a little Sir, in Dari."

"Dari will have to do then. Just scribble down whatever you can and I will get it translated. I want it all."

The two guards exchanged a nervous glance.

"For fuck sake. Now what?"

"We do not have any paper or pencil, Sir," the second guard said sheepishly, avoiding the Westerner's gaze.

"Unfuckingbelievable!"

The Westerner delved into the pockets of his trousers and retrieved a pen and a small spiral bound notebook. He flicked through it and tore out a few pages that already had notes scrawled on them, before handing it, with the biro, to the guards. Without another word he walked out of the holding facility and up the long flight of steps that would take him back above ground. Squinting in the stark daylight Cyrus Vincent lit a cigarette and absorbed his surroundings, familiar though they were to him: the anonymous buildings, the wooden watchtowers, the double fence and razor wire. He fumbled for his mobile phone.

"Hello? This is Charlie Victor 2855. Can you put me through to the J2 collation cell duty watch keeper?"

"One moment please while we verify," the voice replied. "Thank you Mr Vincent, I'm putting you through now."

"J2."

"Hi this is Cyrus Vincent I'm calling to asset check 19 Sierra."

"We can confirm biometric profiling and data collection has identified 19 Sierra as Khalid Bashir a member of the Pakistan Border Force."

"I see. Anything else?" Cyrus asked, drawing heavily on his cigarette.

"There is a reference to him taking part in an overseas training program in England Sir, some Internet references, and UK intercepts are showing him as a person of interest."

"Is that it"?

"At the moment, yes."

"Well I want you to get some resources on this thing. I want to know what the UK link is and I want to know where and when the biometric readings were gathered. Are they UK archive or are they live readings. Do you understand?"

"Of course, Sir. I'll form a team right away and get on it," the voice replied.

"I will be moving the asset to Khost in the next 12 hours and I want full profiling by the time I get him there."

Cyrus hit the red button on the sat phone to end the conversation without allowing the voice at the other end to answer.

This was big; Cyrus could feel it. He just didn't know how big.

Chapter 4
COURT MARTIAL – NORTH OF ENGLAND

"Captain Caine you have been found guilty of disobeying a direct order resulting in the death of Lance Corporal Maurice James Quinn," the court judge read from a prepared script.

Adam had stood to hear his fate, fingering the two decorations pinned to his dress uniform: one acknowledging his general service in Afghanistan, the other – the Queen's Gallantry Medal – recognition of an action in the same country where he'd rescued a comrade trapped in an upturned vehicle in a canal. The award marked him out as a hero. But he wasn't being treated like one now.

"This court fully understands the extraordinary pressure and dangers faced by soldiers every day in Afghanistan. It also appreciates that each man and woman who place themselves in such a theatre of operation does so knowing they risk life and limb."

Adam couldn't help but touch his forehead, tracing the heavy scar from just above his left eye until it disappeared into his hairline.

"As an officer responsible for the wellbeing of his men it is incumbent on you to ensure their safety to the best of your ability. In disobeying a direct order you put the lives of your men in unnecessary danger resulting in the death of one and the serious injury to another. That the toll wasn't worse still is only due to the life saving skills of other members of the patrol."

Adam risked a look across the courtroom towards the shrivelled figure in the wheelchair. Minus both legs and a hand, a colostomy bag hanging from the side of his carriage, Dave also had a red-raw burn over much of one side of his face. There were very few ways in which the SAS sergeant resembled the man Adam had met six months previously in Helmand but the eyes were unmistakeable. Dave had concentrated on Adam throughout the three-day hearing ignoring the others present, focusing all his bitterness and loathing on the person in the dock. Beside Dave, sat a striking woman in her early thirties; tall and slender, a platinum band on her ring finger, she was immaculately turned out in a long black dress as if attending a funeral. Perhaps in a way she was, Adam thought. Perhaps, having to nurse Dave with his appalling injuries meant every day felt like a living hell where the prospect of death – as a way out – would not be such a bad thing. Where Dave projected an air of complete anger, she instead had a look of utter sadness, someone for whom the future held out not a sliver of hope. Adam caught her eye. He made to mouth the words 'I'm sorry', but she had already lowered her head.

"Captain Caine, this court takes into consideration the pressure you were under and the danger you faced. It also notes your previous exemplary service. Taking these factors into account you are to be dismissed from Her Majesty's service immediately. All pension rights will be paid as per Queen's regulations but you will no long be able to wear the uniform of Her Majesty's forces as either a regular or in reserve service. These findings will be annotated on your record."

There was more to come from the judge. He outlined Adam's right to challenge the verdict but the subject of his comments was neither listening nor interested. There was silence in the courtroom as Adam walked out, his lawyer just behind.

"You heard what he said, you can appeal," his counsel reiterated.

"What for? The judge was right, my actions did kill one man and as near as damn it killed another."

"Well if you change your mind you have fourteen days to let me know. You've got my details. Good luck."

"Sure. Thanks."

Adam halted as the other set of doors to the chamber opened

and Dave was wheeled into the corridor. Adam waited until he was safely out of sight, squared the peak cap on his head and exited the Court Martial Centre too. He started to cross the car park of Catterick Garrison making for his rusty old Lancia. As he groped for the keys a man he didn't recognise approached.

"Captain Caine?"

"If you're media you can fuck right off."

The man chuckled.

"I've been mistaken for many things in my time, but not for a gutter journalist. My name is Peter Ryder, can we talk?"

"About what?"

"Well, Afghanistan, Sandhurst, HUMINT, the CIA. Some or all of them. Take your pick. I have a proposition for you, if you're interested. Why don't we talk in the Central Café?"

Without waiting for a response he headed for the greasy spoon at the heart of the base. For want of anything better to do, Adam trailed behind.

Five minutes later Peter Ryder was tucking into an all-day fry-up with Adam sitting opposite him, sullenly nursing a cup of tea.

"You don't know what you're missing," mumbled Ryder through a mouthful of bacon and egg.

"Not hungry," Adam replied. "And to be honest I wouldn't be that comfortable eating with someone I don't know."

"Mmmm, I see. Well I know all about you," said Ryder. "Stop me if I get any of this wrong. You are the only son of a housewife mother who died from cancer when you were at primary school and an engineer father who you adored but was killed in a car crash while you were at Newcastle University. You are a formidable athlete who won the national cross-country championships in your teens. You enjoyed college and were popular with the men and the women alike and were all set for a career as a surveyor. But your dad's death changed everything for you. You re-evaluated your priorities and started to think of something more stimulating, something, dare I say it, more risky and adventurous to do with your life. Probably you wanted to make the most of life while you could, acutely aware that, as was the case with your parents, there is no guarantee that you can leave things today and do them tomorrow. And that's why you went for the Army. How am I doing?"

Adam said nothing.

"At Sandhurst you excelled at everything, probably because having coped with being orphaned everything else seemed, well, almost trivial. You went on to win the Sword of Honour, presented by the Heir to the throne to the best student of his or her intake, your only disappointment being that there was no one from your family there to witness it.

After Sandhurst you did your trade training as a 2nd Lieutenant troop commander in the Royal Engineers at Chatham. Your first operation was Afghanistan and this is where you received the QGM for your selfless bravery in helping a colleague. You loved Afghan and ops, but when you got home you were posted to the Army Foundation College in Harrogate to bring on under-18 recruits. It was during your time there that you applied to, and where accepted for, Operation Achilles and after three months you had gained your basic human intelligence qualification. The advance course soon followed."

"Then it was back into theatre in Afghanistan, a place you found thrilling and rewarding in almost equal measure. You devised a plan to replace the Taliban's commander in that region with his second in command who you had cultivated as a source. And that's where it all went spectacularly wrong. Your mission was compromised, an SAS man got killed and the Director Special Forces demanded your head, which your boss was more than happy to provide as he had very quickly come to regard you as somewhat of an embarrassment."

Peter stopped talking, picked up his last piece of toast and chased the final few baked beans round his plate.

"I think I'll take myself somewhere else," Adam replied, draining his mug and moving to leave.

"Just a minute Captain Caine. I believe I've shown I know more than most about you. I also know how bitter you are about the actions of the Americans that precipitated the situation you now find yourself in. I've got some sympathy with you on that. Let's just say your experience is not unique. The US might be one of our closest allies but they can be a scheming, conniving bunch of bastards."

"That's the polite way of putting it," said Adam, sinking back onto his chair.

"Look, I've studied your operation to capture Mullah Karimi. Operation Silab was well planned and had an intended outcome that would have been very welcome to British intelligence not to mention NATO and the Afghan government. But the shadow of Washington hangs over us all. Too often we play to their tune and if they apply pressure then we bend over backwards to accommodate. In some ways we seem to be more scared of them, our allies, than we do of our enemies."

"Ok, so you've won Mastermind and are my new best friend, but you still haven't told me who you are."

"Like you I am, or was, a HUMINT operator and surveillance specialist. Now I work for a Government organisation known as the Det."

Adam considered what he had been told.

"The Det. 14 Intelligence Company. Sure I know. Thought they had been wound up when the Ulster problem went away though?"

"They were, kind of. The end of The Troubles – or should I say a rather big lull for I'm not sure they'll ever completely disappear – meant we could vanish into the woodwork and regroup. Morph into something different, ready for the next challenges," Ryder spoke quietly now, despite the hubbub in the café. It was difficult for Adam, let alone anyone else, to hear what was being said. "It would be quite hard to determine our legal status. I suppose we're beyond the realms of the strictly legitimate, and even SIS are rather pissed off by our freedoms. But we fill a need, if you understand what I mean."

"Not completely. So what is this about? Karimi or Assadullah Hakim?"

"Neither. They're history I'm afraid. You're going to have to put that episode behind you. I've got a rather bigger problem to deal with and I hope you are going to be able to help me out. After all, what else are you going to be doing?"

Good question, Adam admitted to himself. What else am I going to do? As much as he was reluctant to get involved with anything else over which he didn't have full control, his options were rather limited. He was about to be booted out of the military – not dishonourably discharged as such, they didn't do that anymore – but to all intents and purposes disgraced. If nothing else maybe Ryder would offer up an opportunity for him to redeem himself.

"Alright, I'll give you another ten minutes," said Adam. "After that I'm out of here."

"Good man. Look I'll get you another brew. And while I do, perhaps you would consider what the name Khalid Bashir means to you. This photo might help jog your memory."

———◆———

Adam was still staring at the picture when Ryder returned with the teas. It had been taken on a cloudless day. There were hundreds of soldiers standing on parade in the background but the attention of the photographer was on three individuals in front of the masses. They were immaculately dressed in their Blues and standing to attention on a parade ground. The pale-stoned Old College building of the Royal Military Academy Sandhurst sat directly behind. The person in the middle of the three was Adam. A younger version, fresher faced, smiling, but him all the same, and he was holding the sword of honour. A young woman with her skirt just below her knee was to Adam's left. To the right was a man: smaller than Adam but not significantly so; his complexion much darker.

"I take it that's Khalid Bashir?"

"That's the chap," said Peter brightly.

"I remember him, but until you told me I wouldn't have recalled his name."

"Do you know anything else about him?"

"Not much really. He wasn't in my company. But he was talked about. Came from Pakistan if I remember correctly. Was with the Border Force."

"The Frontier Corps, that's right. But that's just the start. It might take rather more than what's left of my ten minutes to tell you though."

"I've stopped the clock. Go on."

"Khalid Bashir was born in the northern tribal areas of Pakistan, the son of a Pashtu family from a village called Kachkai. Khalid didn't have much contact with the outside world apart from the odd trip to market to help his father sell the livestock he raised and the vegetables he grew. Like most youths in that area Khalid grew up in circumstances of extreme hardship: cold winters, hot summers, very little food. Typical subsistence living. There wasn't any reason to think his horizons would ever extend much further than the valley he called home.

"But Khalid had one thing that set him apart. His father. It was the parent who ensured that he made the daily eight-mile round trip – on foot of course – to the local school. Even at a young age he had already gained a little knowledge of English thanks again to his father, who himself had been taught the rudiments of the language by his own father who had served in the Indian Army prior to partition. As well as English, the guiding principles of life in that part of the world were also drummed into him: honour, loyalty, trust. It was religion of a sort.

"Bashir's chance of escape came in his late teens when a patrol from the Pakistani Frontier Corps came wandering by. It probably was a once in a lifetime opportunity. They were searching for intelligence about a tribal leader who had power in the area. Of course Khalid knew nothing of the tribal leader and even if he had he wouldn't have said anything, but as the unit hung around for refreshments he got talking to some of the men. They said most of them had been very much like him: from humble backgrounds and with little hope of advancement in life. But the Frontier Corps had offered the opportunity for education, a decent salary and some excitement. Though he didn't march out of Kachkai there and then, Khalid did decide that his future lay with the Corps and a couple of months later he did join up. And if that was a good move for Khalid it was just as fortuitous for the authorities. Khalid was the star recruit. Strong, brave, clever, and quick and willing to learn, and it did him no harm that he already spoke some English. In fact, so good was he that he was identified by a US/UK mentoring team working in Pakistan as part of Op MONACLE. On their recommendation, his government put him forward to attend the overseas officer cadet training programme at Sandhurst."

"A floppy," Adam interjected.

"Yep, indeed, and one of the best." Peter stabbed the photo on the table with his finger. "As you see."

Adam was intrigued by the story. He wanted to know where it was going. Ryder filled him in.

"Having won the overseas officer cadets' award, after the commissioning parade Khalid returned to his village. He hadn't been in touch with his family since departing for England and he was desperate to get back and tell them of his achievements. He was sure they would be proud of what he had done. And I am sure they would have been. Except they never got chance to find out because the family was pretty much wiped off the face of the earth: mother and sister confirmed dead, father left a comatose vegetable. Collateral damage in a US UAV strike. You can see the bitter irony can't you Adam?"

"There's Bashir being trained up by us, happily sampling the joys and privileges of life in the English Home Counties while our coalition partners are bombing his family to fuck," Adam offered.

"Correctamundo. And what would you do if your nearest and dearest were casually taken out by some fat fingered yank?"

"Go looking for revenge?"

"Of course you would," confirmed Ryder calmly. "And that's exactly what Bashir has since done. He's switched sides and is wreaking his vengeance. In the most brutal fashion. The instances of low or no metal IEDs have increased dramatically. The issue is not the bombs themselves – there was always going to be a next step in bomb technology – no, the real problem is that thanks to Bashir's inside knowledge the Taliban know how we are going to react. He knows our TTPs, where we set our blocks, our route selections, our surveillance measures. He knows because we bloody well taught him and now he's passed all he's learned on to the Taliban so they can use it against us. Our best guess it that he is now involved in well over half the attacks against British troops. As for Americans, he's killing an even bigger proportion of them."

"We have no leads on where he is holding out?" Adam queried.

"That's the thing, he knows our targeting procedures, he moves daily, not just from area to area but from district to district, province to province. And the word is spreading."

"What do you mean?" Adam was confused.

"There's already a rumour doing the rounds that a foreign fighter, trained by Western forces is operating in Afghanistan. He is known as the Western Muslim in many villages and it is beginning to get noisy."

"So what's the plan?"

"To be frank we don't exactly have a plan at the moment. The bottom line is that if the US finds out that the man responsible for the majority of their soldiers' deaths was trained at Sandhurst it would – to put it mildly – be a diplomatic nightmare for the UK government. And it'd only get worse if the public here realised UK troops are being murdered by a Pakistani we'd trained to be a killer. I wouldn't want to be the PM answering questions about that in parliament."

"I can see where you are coming from on that one, but where do I fit in?" Adam persisted.

"I am putting a team together to track Bashir down and I want you on it," Ryder explained.

"Why me?"

"Maybe Khalid will recognise you, maybe you have something on him we can use, who knows. But right now you seem like a good option. And, to be blunt, you're available."

"But I'm not on the payroll anymore, didn't you hear? Discharged immediately."

"As I said, the Det are made up of all sorts, some soldiers, some not. You will be one of the nots. What do you reckon?"

Adam wasn't sure what to think. Ryder had done a good sales job, but he was uncertain whether he could bring anything to the party. The photo from Sandhurst clearly put them in the same place at the same time, but it didn't make them bosom buddies. Still, it was a chance to try and do something to rebuild his shattered reputation. And what was the alternative? The dole?

"Ok, you've convinced me. Why not? So what's next? Oh, and you still haven't told me who the fuck you really are."

"First things first. You'd don't just walk straight into the Det. We need to get you briefed and up to speed on the way we do things.

Maybe then you can find out more about me. But don't worry about my pedigree. Just you concentrate on Bashir."

Ryder scraped his chair back, away from the table, stood tall and offered his hand to Adam.

"I will be in touch in the next 48 hours. Until then, enjoy yourself."

Chapter 5
RENDITION – KHOST

The wet cloth clung limpet-like to Khalid's face, following every contour of his strong features: the square chin, the full lips, the prominent nose now swollen and blocked by congealed blood caused by the methodical beating he had already received from his captors.

Stretched out on the horizontal wooden board, roughly hewn and without give, his feet fastened at one end, and – with arms outstretched – his wrists tethered at the other, Khalid was full of panic.

With each drawn breath he took down more moisture, the burning lungs and sensation of drowning compounded by pain from ribs cracked by the fists and boots of those intent on causing him suffering. For the moment, deprived of his vision by the sodden rag, he could not see his gaolers but their form were seared on his brain. It wasn't as if there was much to remember for each was similar if not quite identical in appearance and manner. Dressed in brown sweatshirts and tan trousers they had short, though not shaven, hair and wore wraparound black sunglasses. There was nothing that indicated individuality: no tattoos, no watches, no rings, no jewellery, not a single visible thing that could be described as a distinguishing mark or feature which would set them apart in a line-up. Nor could Khalid distinguish any by their accent, because none of them had uttered a word.

They simply went about their business, taking it in turns to pour more water onto the cloth, oblivious to Khalid's muffled cries of agony.

The feeling of suffocation was intense; far worse than he could have imagined. In fact it was unimaginable, because there is no way to prepare for not being able to breath, no way to envisage the hurt. Burn yourself with a match and you can perhaps anticipate the misery of being engulfed by flame. Cut yourself with a knife and it is at least fathomable how being slashed with a sword might be hellish. But there is no similar experience that hints at the horror of not being able to absorb oxygen. As Khalid could testify, the experience was terrifyingly unique.

In Pashtu, he cried out.

"What do you want? I will tell you what you want. Just stop, please."

But his tormentors didn't stop. They stood and watched and then doused the cloth with yet more water.

"Please," he screamed again this time in Dari. The response from his tormentors was the same. More water. More pain. His captors didn't appear to want anything from him other than to see him in agony.

Khalid tried to move his head, to shake the covering from his face, but the pair of boards secured vice-like against the sides of his skull prevented him from dodging the discomfort.

As well as the water, the opaque cloth let through a degree of light, but this was fading rapidly as if someone was turning down a dimmer switch. Khalid knew he was about to pass out. He welcomed the escape. Two seconds later he slipped into unconsciousness.

———•———

Twenty yards away from the Khalid, on the other side of a brick wall, Cyrus Vincent looked down at the cell phone vibrating in his hand, the screen flashing. He noticed the power indicator was showing the battery was dangerously low on juice. He wasn't surprised. The device had been clamped to his ear for much of the past 24-hours and there had been little recent opportunity to recharge it, certainly not on the flight to the US base at Khost from their other piece of what was effectively sovereign territory at Bagram. Cyrus had not been the sole passenger aboard the Blackhawk. His prisoner had come with him and so too a pair of guards. Not that Khalid gave much trouble.

Heavily bound and gagged and smothered by a sensory deprivation hood that denied sight and sound, he was sealed off from the outside world. As soon as the airframe had touched down and taxied to a halt Cyrus had been the first to disembark, heading straight for the room he knew was set aside for VIP visitors, somewhere he could get some food and sleep. He hadn't bothered looking back to see the others leave the helicopter. Just as he had a designated place to stay, so too had the more unwelcome guests. As befitted their status it was rather less hospitable.

Extending the sat phone's antenna Cyrus hit the green accept button. "Hello?"

"Good day Sir. This is Mrs Elias. I am the case officer for asset 19 Sierra."

Sat in a cramped, windowless side room of the Joint Intelligence Centre in Washington, the woman gave no indication she knew Cyrus even though she had met him socially on at least two occasions. She would not have described him as charming exactly, but he could be disarmingly frank and that was a rare and delicious quality amongst the circle of lawyers, mid-ranking public servants and junior politicians she moved in thanks to the relentless networking of her foreign service husband.

"What have you got for me Mrs Elias?" said Cyrus with a slight impatience, conscious that his phone might cut out at any moment.

"Sir, you have the basic information on the prisoner you now hold. Intelligence indicates he is a member of the Pakistan Border Force who was selected for the UK overseas officer program run at their military academy," she précised data she knew Cyrus already had.

"Eighteen months or so ago he completed his training and returned to his unit. Prior to taking up new duties he was given leave to return to see his family who are from a mountain village close to Peshawar. But he never came back."

"So do we have any idea why?" Cyrus probed.

"To be honest, no. That's where there's a big gap in the profile," Mrs Elias replied. "But there are some clues. Within the last year we have seen a significant change in insurgent tactics. The use of non-metal content IEDs grew significantly. That in itself was no major surprise. What was a surprise was where the IEDs were being placed."

"Go on." Cyrus spoke softly to let the caller know he was still listening.

"Ground analysis and learning accounts of all the IED incidents show the enemy has changed its siting profile and is now increasingly placing the IEDs in known ICP locations, cordon positions, medical evacuation routes and follow-up positions."

"That could just be good guess work or basic intelligence gathering by the enemy studying the routines and reactions of our patrols?"

"Possibly, but information preparation of the battlefield has shown that an incident in say Musa Qala, creating a reaction in Kajaki, has been directly targeted. It's as if they know the way our forces operate from district to district. But it's not confined to just one province, the same pattern has been appearing in Kandahar, Urezgon, Kabul and Nimruz."

"So what has J2 come up with?"

"Well initially we thought, like you, it was just good enemy TTPs. Until recently, that was. During an incident in Paktia Province, a metal-free IED was exploited; forensics gave a positive match to a similar IED in Helmand. Cross checking the match with the NDS, UK intelligence and Pakistan ISS, we came up with a name. Khalid Bashir. Our British-trained Pakistani Border Force officer. Biometric profiling of the man you now hold confirms it is one and the same person."

"Are you sure? Khalid Bashir? He's the same man I have in custody here?" Cyrus asked, his heart racing.

"Yes Sir, you are holding a major IED facilitator with a direct link to numerous insurgent groupings throughout Afghanistan and Pakistan. He has been given the codename Tabasco."

Cyrus couldn't resist a smile. The phone lodged in the crook of his neck, he picked at his nails and mulled over his good fortune. The odds against Khalid Bashir falling into US hands made the chances of winning the lottery seem positively good. Yet it had happened. Best of all Bashir was alive. Funny how things turn out, mused Cyrus. But then he had never been one to discount luck. Big events can turn on the smallest of things. Sometimes things work in your favour, other times against you. The key thin was to mitigate the disasters and milk the successes. Gleefully, Cyrus was about to do the latter.

"Sir? Are you still there?"

Cyrus had forgotten all about his failing battery.

"Yes, sorry. Has this information been passed to the director?"

"No, Sir, routine asset handling is down to local operators. That information would come from your team."

"You're right. Thank you for your help," Cyrus answered, terminating the call before he was tempted to become engaged in trivial goodbyes.

Already an idea had begun to formulate in Cyrus's head but first he had to find out what had happened between Bashir leaving the UK military academy and turning up on the Jalalabad road.

———•———

When Khalid awoke it was to find that there was no relief from his nightmares. He remained tied down, the sodden rag still draped across his mouth and nose. Almost immediately more water was poured onto it, faster than before. He started to gag. The more he struggled to breath, the more oxygen he needed to do so and the deeper he tried to inhale. The result was predictable.

In his last brief moments of consciousness he yelled out. In English.

"For the love of Allah, please stop."

Then the darkness returned.

When he came to he found the cloth had been removed. His whole body convulsed as he retched. A cascade of watery bile and puke spewed up. Unable to swivel his head to the side, he could not prevent half of the stinking liquid sitting in his mouth. He swallowed some of it back down, only for this to bring on another bout of vomiting. At last he lay still, exhausted, motionless except for the heavy rise and fall of his chest, the relief of taking in full lungs of air overriding the extreme discomfort of doing with fractured ribs.

Khalid tried to look around. There was no sign of his identikit guards. But he wasn't alone. In the clones' place was someone as far removed from anonymous as it was possible to be. Cyrus Vincent loomed over his prize, his expansive stomach spilling out over the belt of his trousers, the buttons of his shirt struggling to contain the flesh. His face was a mass of deep pores. Upon his head sat tangled threads of light-brown hair. Strapped to his wrist was a chunky gold watch. On anyone else it would have looked huge and ostentatious but against Cyrus's bulk it seemed almost understated.

"So Mr Bashir, you do speak some English?" Cyrus observed, lighting a cigarette.

"Some," Khalid admitted, unable to keep up the fight.

"Some? Probably more than you are willing to admit, but that's ok, we have a starting point at least. Let's see how we get on."

"What is it you want?"

"Well let's start by me explaining to you that I didn't make your life unpleasant to force you to talk. Nor did I do it because it gave me a cheap thrill. I did it just to show you that I could." Cyrus remained calm, his voice offering no trace of emotion. He knew the next few minutes would decide if Khalid Bashir was of any further use to him.

"I can't tell you anything you don't already know."

"I think you can Mr Bashir. Do you mind if I call you Khalid?"

There was no reply. Cyrus took this as a positive assertion.

"Two days ago you were travelling in a truck with a group of men on a road leading out of Kabul. You were heading eastwards towards the Afghan/Pakistan border and the Khyber Pass. That's right isn't it Khalid?"

Khalid still didn't answer so Cyrus continued.

"Unluckily for you, your group was stopped at a checkpoint where the local police did their normal cursory check for drugs and guns before demanding a small fee to allow your lorry to pass. Your driver, who understands these things, dutifully paid. And that would have been that had the Afghan police not been working with a US Marines mentoring team. Well one thing led to another. They were inquisitive. One of your guys was nervous. Throw in some weapons and before you know it there's a firefight going on which, in all truth, the Americans were always going to win. Say what you like about our guys. They finish what they start. Anyway, you end up in captivity and after a bit of routine biometric checking it is discovered you are a person of interest. Hence you get to speak to me."

"I don't know why you think I am anyone special. I did nothing wrong, I was heading to see my family in Pakistan when I was stopped," Khalid said weakly. "I am a simple man, I was working in Kabul, working on the roads, working for ISAF. I'm your friend."

"Now Khalid if you're happy letting these other fellas look after you then I'll back off. But I don't think you really want that and to be truthful nor do I." For the first time there was menace in Cyrus's voice. "You showed up on the biometric system because you've left your mark on our databases. Before the Pakistani Border Force sent you to England for all that jolly officer training you had to go through a series of security checks, is that not right?"

Khalid didn't answer but lowered his eyes as if to mask his surprise.

"We know about your time at Sandhurst. We know what it was like for you. We know you were awarded the overseas cadet award. We can even tell you when you began your reign of terror in Afghanistan. Oh yes Khalid, we know plenty about you. So don't give me the friendship shit."

"What will you do with me?"

"Well that depends how open you are with me now."

"What do you want to know?" Khalid replied raising his head in what he hoped looked like defiance. He met and held Cyrus's gaze.

"Why don't you tell me more about what you have been up to? Fill in a bit more of the detail." Cyrus didn't take notes, he didn't need to; a pair of microphones – one in the ceiling and the other tucked discretely under the torture table – were picking up everything being said. All he had to do was focus totally on Khalid and keep him talking. "You have been successful Khalid, your IEDs, your mines, have accounted for a lot of NATO casualties. You must be pleased."

Khalid ignored the false praise.

"I understand the term IED," he said contemptuously.

"I know you do. Tell me about your training in England then."

"You know about my training in England, I spent one year in their military academy. I arrived, they trained me, I graduated and then I left," Khalid was starting to regain his composure.

"OK then tell me about how you were recruited into the Taliban," Cyrus probed.

"I went to a man named Amir Khan in Peshawar, he put me in touch with a Mullah in the local Madrassa and from there I was sent across the border to join a local Kalay unit".

Khalid found some reassurance in that what he was saying was not a betrayal of those to whom he was loyal. A false name, some general locations, a procedure that could be guessed at. None of it was going to cause harm to his colleagues.

Cyrus had been slowly circling Khalid as he talked. As he came level with his head he paused. So far the questions, and hence the answers, had been of little consequence, more of a way of striking up a conversation than revealing critical information, but it was time to get to the heart of the matter. In an almost head-masterly tone, but with the retained trace of threat, he said:

"Personally I believe there are two things that scare men more than anything else. One is fire. The other is water. Before they've been shown its full horror – gone through what you just have – many believe death by submersion to be a quick and painless way out." Cyrus stopped talking to drift around Khalid once more. "As I am sure you can testify this is no easy option. I heard the terror in your voice. I see it still in your eyes: it is terrifying and that's why it is used in these circumstances. Did you know that water boarding has been around since the Spanish Inquisition? I have been using it for a mere eighteen years and I swear there is no more effective method of inducing dread."

"I understand you will do whatever you need to do to get information from me – but I don't know anything that would be of any use to you"

Cyrus ignored Khalid and continued with his history lesson.

"A few years ago – as part of an experiment – some of my CIA colleagues voluntarily subjected themselves to water boarding, just to understand its effects. In the interests of science you could say. On average, they lasted for fourteen seconds before crying out for help. Fourteen seconds – that's it. Some argue this technique is a waste of time as confessions secured through its use are unreliable because people will say pretty much anything to get the misery to stop. I know I would. But the point is I won't stop until I have all the information I need."

Cyrus halted and snapped his fingers. Out of the shadows two of the practitioners of torture stepped into Khalid's view. Now the CIA man raised his voice.

"You can forget Amnesty International, the Red Cross, UN checks and balances," Cyrus snarled. "You are well and truly beyond the scrutiny and help of the sanctimonious, self-righteous liberals who enjoy freedom but criticise the practical ways in which it is secured. You will either tell me what I want to know or you will never leave this place alive. Now why, after being the Border Force star pupil, after excelling during training in England, did you turn against us? Surely not because they called you nasty names at Sandhurst and spat in your food? So what was it? What?"

Khalid said nothing but, as far as he could manage it, turned his head away from his interrogator.

"Do you never want to see your family again?" Cyrus asked, his voice back under control.

The mere mention of family lit a fuse within Khalid.

"My family, what do you know of my family?" Khalid responded with as much venom as he could muster. "To you lot, you Westerners, we are people to be treated with contempt. Hardly better than savages. Our lives are of no consequence to you. On the scales of justice we are inconsequential. Our history, our religion, our culture; they are all alien to you. You do not understand them and you do not want to. What would you care about my family? How they lived? How they all died?"

"Your family are all dead?" Cyrus asked, successfully hiding his surprise.

"Dead. Slaughtered. Gone because your war on terror is a war *of* terror. It has no regard for the innocent who will die so you can strike your target."

Khalid had opened up, driven on by a rage; his tongue loosened by recognition that whatever his fate, it was no more than his mother and sister and father had already suffered.

"I don't suppose you have ever heard of Kachkai. No reason why you would have. But it was my home. And that of my family. There is only one road in and out of the village. And it was on this road that your drones attacked two cars carrying your enemies. They were successful. The vehicles were destroyed. But so was a third; the one carrying my family back to their sanctuary. And as your aircraft returned to their bases and their pilots drove home to their loved ones, my mother and sister lay dead in the twisted remains of their truck. My father lay there too, as good as dead. I gave the West everything. I was persuaded to choose your ways and your values, and in return you took from me that which was most precious."

Cyrus smiled to himself. There was always a motive and now he had Khalid's. He had to play to it; use the vulnerability to present Khalid with a proposal that he would have no choice other than to accept. Cyrus's tone changed again. He soothed and sympathised.

"I am sorry to hear that Khalid. Really, I am. It has never been the intention to harm the innocent. We are striving to protect them. War is a terrible thing. Heaven knows, I have seen too much killing and bloodshed over the years. But we must endure in the hope of victory, for if we step away from the fight – and the years have shown me this too – then the monsters will fill the gap and wreak their misery. But you will know all this. Have been taught it at Sandhurst and learned the lessons from history. Tell me more about what happened. Perhaps there is something I can still do."

For the next 30 minutes Khalid was free with his words. He recounted it all, from the earliest hardships of his youth; the brutal but liberating experiences of serving in the Border Force; the sequence of events that led him to the outskirts of a small town in Surrey in England and the most famous military training centre in the world. Despite his anger he spoke with pride of graduating from Sandhurst and being awarded the Overseas Cadet Medal by the son of the nation's sovereign. He remembered how all he wanted to do was journey back to Kachkai and tell his father of his adventures and his achievements.

And then he told Cyrus of how his dream had been shattered by a Hellfire missile.

Through it all, the CIA officer remained motionless, giving Khalid his undivided attention. Only speaking to move the story on.

"So what became of your father? Is he still in the village?"

"Not in the village. After the drone strike, some other travellers came across the scene. They searched through the wreckage and discovered that my father was the only one still breathing. They hauled him up the slope, dumped him in the back of their pick-up and made for Peshawar. Several hours later, they laid him out on the reception floor of the city's hospital. He remains in the hospital today. I went to see him. He is barely clinging to life, tucked away in a filthy room with little attention and less hope. I sense the doctors are resentful of his presence. He gets no better and no worse, and because his condition does not change and there is nowhere else for him to go, he continues to take up a bed that someone else could use. I vowed to avenge him. I promised I would do whatever I could to slaughter the enemy and bring to their families the same misery I have endured."

He explained how everything he learned from the British – standard operating procedures, electronic counter measures, the tactics of bomb disposal teams – were now being used against the coalition. Then Khalid smiled.

"It has been surprisingly easy. Your allies trained me well. I have killed many NATO soldiers and it brings me satisfaction. If Allah wills it then I will kill many more."

At last Khalid was silent. The emotion spent. Exhausted, he shut his eyes. Quietly Cyrus backed away and exited the torture chamber.

———•———

The multi-media control centre next door was far removed from the bleak, Spartan cell that contained the prisoner. It was modern and well lit, with an air-conditioning panel embedded in the ceiling, its output set to keep cool both the human occupants and the array of equipment at their disposal. Another pair of identikit guards sat at a bank of screens and consoles, a handful of which displayed the closed circuit TV feed from the multiple cameras angled and focussed to capture Khalid's confessions and admissions, and every aspect of his discomfort. Four speakers brought Khalid's words into the room. There were also moving images acquired from much further afield; live satellite feeds beamed directly from the surveillance and target acquisition teams in Kabul and Washington.

"Did you get that?" asked Cyrus of one of the men sitting behind the electronics. His query was more out of politeness than concern.

"Yes Sir. I'm just plotting Kachkai now, the road to Peshawar, Peshawar hospital and the layout schematic."

"I also want a feed of what, historically, our UAVs have been doing in that area. What were the targets, what were the outcomes; was there any collateral damage; personnel or infrastructure?"

"Take me about an hour Sir," the man replied.

"Half an hour would be more helpful."

Cyrus turned to another pair of guards lounging on a sofa, one of them reading a copy of Sports Illustrated. It wasn't quite porn, but as good as you were going to get in the Afghan desert.

"Another session of water boarding will keep him focused, don't your think? But don't damage him, I want him lucid when I get back from the Joint Ops Centre."

Cyrus needed to send a report up the line to the CIA director's operations officer along with some suggested courses of action, though in his own mind it was increasingly clear how they should proceed. He wanted to put Khalid back into circulation then handle him as a high value target and asset. Cyrus was excited. He believed he could get this man to the very heart of the Afghan and Pakistan Taliban, possibly Al Qaeda. It was too good an opportunity to miss. Cyrus took a step towards the door, then stopped abruptly and turned to his team, waving his phone.

"Hey, I take it we have got a God-damn charger somewhere in this hi-tech set up? I have a feeling I'm going to be on the phone quite a lot in the near future."

Chapter 6
THE 'DET' – SOUTHEAST ENGLAND

The quartet of men – Adam and three others – sat silently in the drab lecture theatre sipping coffee from chipped mugs, glancing suspiciously at each other. There had been only the briefest of pleasantries as they'd each arrived; firm handshakes, half-hearted smiles and the standard, uninformative, introductions. 'Hello mate', 'Alright buddy?' 'How you doing pal?'

At first glance, thought Adam, they could just have been the latest recruits to enrol for the Op Achilles programme. But further inspection revealed these four weren't run of the mill HUMINT operators, SF gurus or local 'rent a soldier'. Behind each man's reticence lay a steely confidence. There was an air about them. If you had to put money on it you'd say these men had been there, done that.

Everyone turned when the double doors at the side of the auditorium swung open and Peter Ryder marched in, a large file under one arm and an obligatory cup of coffee in his hand. He strode towards the lectern ignoring the other occupants of the room. It wasn't until he had deposited the folder on the wooden stand and shuffled some papers that he raised his eyes and gave the select group a broad smile.

"Good to see you all. Great you could all make it."

Peter spoke with a soft Northern Irish accent, mellow and low enough to make the men in front of him strain to hear. It was a trick he had learned from his time teaching at the Defence Intelligence Centre. Confident he had everyone's full attention he spoke some more.

"I'm not going to take up too much of your time. You've already received individual briefings so you have the basic gist of what our mission and tasks are going to be. This is an opportunity for you to meet each other so it might be a good idea if each of you gave a quick intro so the others know a little about you. No need to go into personal stuff, just your working background. Who wants to start?"

Peter knew none of them did so he took the initiative.

"Ok, you all know me as Peter Ryder, I am an ex ranger. That's Irish Ranger not US. I spent eight years in green before I joined 14 Intelligence Company working mostly out of the province."

Peter spoke in an easy manner.

"I spent six years in 14 Int before it became the Special Reconnaissance Regiment and I became part of the permanent cadre. I left the SRR just over two years ago to work with the UK Intelligence services and in that time I have been responsible for setting up a network of teams – Dets – that work for the UK government on covert operations around the world. I'm in charge of Det 3 and about the only thing that is permanent about the team. The other members – like you lot – are brought in as required, your capabilities matched to those required for the task being undertaken. Right, so, is anyone else going to say a few words?"

The man to Peter's right reluctantly got to his feet.

"Hi fellas. My name is George Mallon. Rocky to my friends. I am ex-3 PARA and spent two years with the Pathfinders in 16 Brigade. I have completed three tours of Afghan and one each of Iraq and Kosovo. I'm a trained forward air controller and more recently I have worked for the Bancroft Group in Somalia."

"Cheers Rocky," Peter said as Rocky sat down. "Good to see you again, it's been a while."

"Thanks boss, glad to be here," said Rocky raising his coffee to his lips. Rocky's neighbour started talking.

"My name is Al. I'm a former 'scaley' who's been involved in the information war in Afghanistan and East Africa over the last few years. I've spent time with 264 Signals Squadron SAS and more recently I have been working for a freelance HUMINT Company in Afghanistan monitoring Afghan Government transmissions between various insurgent factions, warlords and drug lords. Oh yes fellas, I'm a bleep," Al said with a rye smile.

"Al will be our comms expert while we are in the sand. Good to have you on board," said Peter.

It was Adam's turn. He suddenly felt very self-conscious. In all likelihood he was the only officer in the room and would have the least experience and least to tell. He thought about embellishing his story.

"Chaps, my name is Adam Caine. I'm a Royal Engineer and as you have probably worked out I am a Sandhurst-trained Rupert." Adam smiled but nobody took up the invitation to smile back. He ploughed on. "I did one tour of Afghanistan before I joined the OP Achilles programme and deployed back to Helmand as a HUMINT operator." Adam took a deep breath. "On my return I was court marshalled and discharged from the military." He could almost see the members of his audience prick up their ears. That's got your bloody attention he thought. "In all I have spent four years in the army." Adam finished and went to sit down.

"What were you court marshalled for?" Rocky asked.

"I don't think it matters at this time lads," Peter said quickly.

"No problem Peter," Adam interrupted. "No point keeping secrets. It'll come out anyway. I was court marshalled for disobeying orders which resulted in one of my men being killed and a second being seriously wounded."

Peter jumped in before anyone could protest.

"Adam has vital knowledge of our target and will brief you en route to Pakistan with as much info as he has. For this operation he will be our HUMINT face."

The last man in the group introduced himself.

"I'm Simon. Not much to say really. I'm an ex RLC AT. I have worked in Afghanistan as part of the counter IED team. Did a bit of UK based AT work before leaving to join the peace support team in Kenya as a civilian contractor. You could say I like to blow shit up. Oh, and I've never been court marshalled."

Adam didn't bite back. Instead he looked at his companions. It was hard to say what physically distinguished them because they were all so similar in appearance, deliberately so. They'd all dyed their hair near black. The beards they'd grown were the same shade. Even the hairs on their arms had been coloured. Their eyes were dark too, though only Al's were a product of nature – the rest wore tinted contact lenses. Where they didn't have naturally acquired deep tans they had applied make-up. Adam stared at Simon. He thought he could just about distinguish some freckles beneath the slap but it was hard to tell.

"There is a sixth man in Det 3," Peter said. "He is our facilitator and will join us at a later stage. At the moment you don't need to worry about him. To keep you in the loop he's busy conducting a recce of the landing site in Pakistan and the route through the Khyber Pass into Afghanistan."

Peter Ryder sifted through his folder as he spoke. It gave the false impression that he was absent minded and disorganised.

"OK," said Peter. "Let me just recap who we have in the team. George, sorry Rocky, will be responsible for all air assets if and when needed. He will be the team second-in-command and will be our primary driver, though clearly you will all be taking your turn behind the wheel."

Peter stopped to copy some details from Rocky's file onto a single form: blood group, next of kin and team ID – Det 3 Bravo.

"As I said, Al is comms." Peter stopped to write some more. "Simon is weapons and explosives. You happy with that, Simon?" Peter stated rather than asked.

"Right down my street boss."

"Finally Adam's our HUMINT interface and interpreter coordinator. Adam will be the man who does the walking and talking. He is the guy who we as a team are trying to get into position to make contacts and find sources, including our target. To that end he is, by far, the most important man in the team. The crown jewels you might say."

Adam could feel three sets of sceptical eyes tunnelling into him. He shifted uncomfortably in his seat.

"Best make sure we keep and eye on you then," Al said in a friendlier manner than Adam had been expecting. "I'd be embarrassed being paid if we lost the treasure."

Al chuckled. After a second or two so did the others. When he was sure they were all laughing, Adam dared to join in. Peter took the opportunity to hand out a set of papers to each man.

"To finish off fellas, here's some light reading. You have until 2000 hours tonight to get through these, memorise their contents and hand them back to me personally. I'd like to remind you that prior to deployment you will be searched for any information or identification."

Peter knew they'd understand what he meant. They'd be sterile. Their kit would be sterile. There'd be no trace back to the UK government.

"After the homework we will meet up in the mess for a beer and a bit more of a get to know you session. Tomorrow morning there'll be time for a quick jog, a bit of GLF and then we'll hit the range for a final CQB practise. We depart at 2200 hours tomorrow evening. Happy studying."

———◆———

Adam woke the next morning with a hangover and cursed. He had promised himself he wouldn't drink too much but surrounded by his new colleagues at the bar he was damned if he was going to be the first one to cry off for an early night. As it was he'd been the last to leave alongside Rocky who with each passing drink had been increasingly happy to talk about his exploits in the Horn of Africa and the number of rags and skinnies he'd killed. Rocky had ribbed him about his QGM which, annoyingly, Peter had brought up.

"Have you sold it yet?" Rocky had asked. "No? Well what use is it to you mate? It's just a bit of cheap metal and to be honest whatever Al says I wouldn't put money on your likely return from this gig. Fancy giving it to me for safe keeping then?"

It was with a distinct lack of enthusiasm that Adam joined the others for the run. Each step flung his brain against the side of his head and was a reminder why it is never a good idea mixing beer and whisky, certainly not in the quantities he'd been necking it. There was worse to come in the gym. For 40 minutes they used punch bags to carry out hard impact drills, maintaining a steady rate of blows against the lumpy, leaden weights. Now and again the physical training instructor would mix things up. A blast on his whistle was the signal to go like fuck and each man would thump as hard and fast as they could, also using their elbows, knees and heads to batter the target. For sixty seconds they had to keep this going before a second blast of the whistle allowed them to catch their breath.

The men were tired but the adrenaline was high and nobody slacked. As a special treat the last go-like-fuck session went on for two minutes. Not long into it each man was gasping for air, trying to match their air intake to their exertion.

"Stop," the PTI finally shouted. "To the loading area now. Quickly!"

They moved to a long trestle table where matching Glock 9mm pistols sat alongside 5.56mm HK53s.

"Load and go to the start line," ordered the PTI. Adam and the others hurried up the corridor and stopped abreast of each other, Peter just behind.

"Move," Peter shouted and almost instantly a set of six targets appeared 30 metres ahead. Adam, Al, Simon and Rocky dropped to their knees and opened fire. Above the noise they heard the instruction to move repeated. This time only the outside pair advanced: three, four, five, paces, still shooting as they went. They knelt again and the inside pair, still firing too, stepped up to them to reform the line. Peter came with them. He was using his weapon too, firing over their shoulders, inches past their heads, even between their legs. As a unit they closed in on their quarry, their opponents defiantly standing their ground despite being shredded by the ferocity of the onslaught. The attackers got to within point blank range and put the final rounds through the paper and wood targets.

As the noise ceased and the echoes drained away so did the adrenaline. The men were exhausted. The test had served its purpose. Pumped up with aggression they had kept their discipline and maintained their trust in each other. But then it was only a drill.

Chapter 7
DANNY AKERS – HELMAND PROVINCE

Private Danny Akers couldn't stop shaking. He wasn't cold. How could he be in the middle of an Afghan summer where daytime temperatures routinely hit 40 degrees? No, Danny was shivering with terror. Small beads of sweat congregated on his brow and then – one by one – trickled down his face, some ending up in his eyes – mixing with the tears he'd desperately tried to hold back – causing them to sting. He blinked furiously, but it was a losing battle. Danny would have wiped his face on his sleeve to staunch the flow but it was impossible, the makeshift cuffs – plastic cable ties – pinning his hands tight behind his back ensured that; the same restraints that prevented him from wrapping his arms around his body to hug himself still.

The perspiration and trembling weren't the only physical manifestations of Danny's fear. As his fate had become increasingly and unalterably clear, he'd lost control of his bodily functions; his groin was soaked with piss and, kneeling down on the dusty floor, the back of his boots were pressing his own filth against his skin.

———•———

Sitting on faux leather chairs, around a non-descript conference table that could best be described as functional, there were eight men. All of them were nominally powerful, yet at that moment they found themselves trapped in a state of complete group impotence. Seven of them were watching Danny Akers on a giant plasma TV mounted on the wall furthest from the single door that allowed visitors to enter and exit Cabinet Office Briefing Room A, the abbreviation for which gave the special ad-hoc committee occupying it its name – COBRA.

As for the eighth man, he stared at a single sheet of paper held in his left hand. He too was shaking, not much, but enough to be noticeable should anyone care to look closely, the tremor caused by the onset of Parkinson's disease. Robert Adamson, Chief of the Defence Staff, was sixty-three years old and his best years – certainly in physical terms – were now far behind. The illness developing in his body irritated him constantly and he was realistic enough to accept things would only get worse. But that particular afternoon he didn't find his ailment quite as distracting as normal. For once it was easy to put his frailty into perspective.

The General broke the silence as he read from the prepared brief.

"The man you are looking at is Danny Akers, a private in 2 Platoon, A Company, 3rd Battalion, The Rifles. An only son, he comes from Middlesbrough, Tyne and Wear, and is eighteen years and two months old."

It was basic factual data extracted from the soldier's electronic personal military records.

"He arrived in Afghanistan just three weeks ago on his first operational tour. His unit is based in Lashkar Gah, the capital of Helmand Province. Four days ago Private Akers' platoon was on a routine foot patrol in the Babaji area northwest of the town supporting the local Afghan Police in that area. At about 1630 hours the patrol was making its way back to base when the enemy engaged it using a mixture of small arms and rocket propelled grenades. According to the report made by the patrol commander, he ordered his men to take cover. In the melee Private Akers became lost from view and was not seen again."

The general glanced up at the TV. Danny remained on his knees, centre screen.

"Until now that is."

Danny could not remember a time when he did not want to be a soldier. Growing up, he had a one track mind: as a four and five year-old running around in the back garden with sticks shooting his friends; as a youngster at primary school endlessly clambering over the climbing frame and swings he regarded as an assault course; as a youth, talking with his dad about his experiences in Northern Ireland and the Gulf; as a teenager devouring every book about the conflicts in Iraq and Afghanistan he could scavenge. Danny hadn't much cared about the whys and wherefores of Britain's invasion of Saddam Hussein's country, or indeed the events that precipitated involvement in Afghanistan. Geo-politics weren't his thing. All he wanted to read about was the action, the fighting, the blood and guts, the heroics. He was inspired by the camaraderie, the loyalty to one's mates. It all left him with an overwhelming thirst for adventure.

———•———

As the boss screamed into the radio for everyone to get down, Danny was already scrambling off the dusty road and about to slither down the bank into the stream. For the first time in his life he was being shot at and it gave him an adrenaline rush. His pulse was racing. He was a bag of nerves, but also as excited as hell. He had got what he wanted. The excitement. The danger.

The drop into the irrigation ditch was further than he expected and he found himself well below the level of the track, his legs sinking into the soft mud at the bottom of the ditch. Trying to pull his feet free of the quagmire he cursed Afghanistan. For a country with so much desert there seemed to be more than enough fucking water about. Bullets zipped high over his head and somewhere – was it to his left? he couldn't be sure – there was a small explosion as what he assumed to be an RPG detonated.

Struggling to move, Danny saw the irony in the situation. Having finally joined the British Army and got into his first firefight his immediate concern was not the enemy, but the hole in the ground he was stuck in. The teenager was about to allow himself a wry smile when his face twisted into a look of the utmost surprise. Legs buckling beneath him, he collapsed under the weight of the blow to the back of his neck. His first – last – thought was that he had been flattened by an express train. His shaken brain began trying to compute how this could be the case given that he was not on a railway line but in a gulley in Afghan. He never reached a conclusion because no more than a second after being struck, and before the sensation of surprise could mutate into any real feeling of pain, Danny's world went pitch black.

With his attention, like that of the others, now held by the TV, the General studied what was being portrayed. Behind Danny stood three men. The man to the left was wearing a brown, flowing shalwar kameeze, black turban bound tightly around his head, while the man on the right wore the uniform of the ALP, topped off with a blue peaked cap complete with the insignia of the Afghan Police. Both men had long matted beards sprouting from their chins. Across their chests they gripped Kalashnikovs, the barrels pointing towards the ground. The man in the middle was taller than the other two, and to the General he appeared to be younger, fitter, in a way more professional, if that was possible. His eyes gleamed. He too had a weapon, but because, like the General, he was clutching a piece of paper, the rifle had been slung over his shoulder making it impossible for the viewers to distinguish its make and model.

The backdrop to the whole scene was a banner that extended out to the edges of the screen, jet-black except for the two sentences of Arabic written in white, a translation of which had been thoughtfully included in the General's notes. It read: '*Allah is great. Death to the infidels.*'

For the first few hours after his capture by the Taliban the teenager hoped for the best. Surely the other guys would not leave him? But as time passed, and no rescue mission materialised, the optimism evaporated, drop by drop. Then the horror truly set in.

Danny worked out that he had regained consciousness pretty quickly because as he groggily came to, he could still hear the sounds of the battle raging nearby – a battle he should have been playing a part in. For a moment or two he wondered how, given the way he was feeling, he was able to walk through the maze field enveloping him on all sides? Then he understood. Others were putting in the effort for him; at each shoulder was an insurgent – for want of a better term – their arms hooked under his, propelling him through the dense vegetation, the stalks and leaves slapping him in the face before grudgingly parting to make way for him and his captors.

The echoes of warfare became steadily quieter. Understanding he was being lead further and further from the rest of his team, Danny attempted to yell out. But he couldn't. Something had been stuffed in his mouth. From its taste and feel, it was a filthy bit of rag. He shook his head violently, trying to spit out the gag. It was no use. The only thing he succeeded in doing was make his head feel as if the express train that had flattened him earlier, had reversed back down the track to finish the job off. The pain made him feel sick, the vomit rising from his stomach up his throat. If it hadn't been for the piece of cloth he would have heaved his guts out. As it was the bile nearly choked him.

Suddenly he and his minders emerged from the tangled crops. Fifty metres away sat a pair of pick-ups with more of the enemy standing beside them. Danny was forced towards them, a dig to the kidneys helping him on his way, ensuring he didn't have too much time to regain his composure. He saw one of the welcoming committee turn and release the tailgate of the nearest truck to reveal a scruffy green tarpaulin. Another stepped forward to meet him and with strong hands forged by hard work, tugged at his helmet, half-heartedly at first and then, when it resisted, with undisguised spite. As it gave way and slipped off Danny's head, the aggressors turned their attention to his backpack, body armour and webbing. The equipment was swiftly and greedily picked over, the man with the fat fingers passing the items around, the recipients inspecting them and hanging on to anything that particularly took their fancy – ammo, food, water, knife, first-aid kit, map, flares, bayonet, personal radio. In less than a minute, the scavengers had all but picked him clean. The only bit of his equipment Danny couldn't account for was his SA80(A2) rifle. But there was no opportunity to dwell on it because Danny was quickly bundled underneath the canvas, face down against the filthy floor of the pick-up, pinned by the feet of at least two gunmen, the muzzles of their rifles pressed hard against his body. He tried wriggling to get more comfortable but the response to the movement was a flurry of blows, one of which struck the left-hand side of his face. A tooth broke from his gum and a warm, coppery-tasting liquid began to seep around his mouth. Then the metal floor beneath him started to vibrate gently as the engine rumbled into life. With a lurch and scrabble of rubber on gravel the vehicle moved off.

The man with the piercing eyes started to speak, but not in a language understood by the Prime Minister. Robert Samuels looked and listened a little longer, but as the incomprehensible rhetoric continued, he swivelled his chair and faced the General.

"So do we know who these people are? Do we know where they are?"

The General declined to look directly at the PM, instead peering down at his piece of paper, even though he was painfully aware there was nothing on it to help him, nothing that might cast a better light on a dismal situation.

"No Sir, collectively we don't – although the man on the right in the Afghan Local Police Uniform is Asa Sher-Wali, a member of the Ali-Zai tribe and a relation through marriage of Abdul Rahman-Jan, the former Helmand Chief of Police. He joined the ALP around three months ago." The General read the facts without analysis. "The Islamic Freedom Movement has not previously appeared on our radar."

The PM stared at the General expectantly.

"I am also afraid there is nothing to place what we are watching to a particular village, town or province. Or indeed country. It could be Afghanistan, it could be Pakistan. It could be somewhere else entirely. At the moment we just don't know."

No one doubted the sophistication of *'the enemy'*, whoever they actually were. The Taliban, Al Qaeda, affiliated groups – all had previously proved their ingenuity and their ability to plan complicated missions with devastating results. Now the IFM had done so too.

"Where exactly did this video come from?" The PM tried another line of questioning.

This was something General Adamson did know the answer to.

"It was anonymously posted on a file sharing site favoured by those with, shall we say, extreme views of, and antipathy towards, the Western world, at 0700 hours GMT today. A link to the video was sent to an Arab press agency that put it out on its wire service two hours ago. The story is currently running on just about every newspaper website across the globe. It is leading radio and television bulletins in this country and beyond. The original site was closed down after we applied pressure on the government of Bahrain in whose country the hosting company is based, explaining that the arms deal we are negotiating with them has yet to be signed. However this only happened after the video had already been viewed 3.8 million times and begun to appear elsewhere.

We will continue to have a quiet word where we can. Unfortunately we're not involved in multi-billion pound weapons' contracts with that many countries."

————•————

Chained to a beam in the ceiling of a pitch-black room, the terror was suffocating. Danny had always had a vivid imagination. Now, in the cell, his thoughts were as dark as his surroundings. For as long as he had strength the young soldier tugged at the metal leash that held him, trying to pry it from the wood it was anchored in. It gave him a focus, a way of resisting the mental torture. But all too soon his physical strength evaporated just like the hope. He tried to sleep but with his mind working in overdrive it was impossible, the same thoughts of fear and loneliness bouncing around his head whether his eyes were open or shut. No one arrived with food or water to sustain him. The removal of the gag aside, not even the smallest gesture had been made to indicate anyone was interested in either his short-term wellbeing or long-term survival.

Which is why, when the door to his cell was flung back and light – daylight – ate into the murk, the soldier had no expectation that anything good would come of it.

Again Danny found himself being dragged along, first down the narrow corridor, then out of the house and across a large courtyard, the huge earthen walls of the compound – of the prison – hemming him in on every side, the sun intensely bright way above him. After twenty paces Danny and his escorts reached another building, very much like the other, and another room. Primitive. Forbidding. Heaved roughly back into the gloom, Danny wasn't allowed to stop. At the back of the room, there was a curtain, a thin man with bad skin standing next to it, holding an assault rifle. He yanked back the heavy drape and suddenly it was if Danny was back outside, the brightness making him squint.

But he wasn't outside. He was in a second chamber, the light coming from a pair of huge lamps. Between them was a silver video camera, mounted on a tripod, its legs buried in the dirt floor. Behind it, the operator was engrossed, fiddling with the buttons, tilting the image screen so he could get the best possible view of events as they would unfold in front of him, setting the exposure correctly, checking the focus, making sure the battery was charged. He sat wide-legged on a wooden stool, a battered AK47 carelessly dumped beside it. Before Danny could say or do anything, someone took another stab at his kidneys and kicked him in the back of the knee. He crumpled to the ground. Out of sight, a man started speaking in Arabic.

On the floor, gasping for breath, the soldier looked at the camera pointed straight at him, the unblinking lens capturing his humiliation, the illuminated tally light confirming the device was recording. Danny might not have been well educated, but he wasn't stupid. He had seen the news reports, watched footage on the net of hostages being killed, the miserable end of a human life taped for posterity in rooms very much like this one.

His shaking had become uncontrollable, and he'd wet himself and soiled his trousers. He didn't want to die, certainly not like this. He wondered how much it would hurt? He wondered what his parents would say? Wondered how they would react? He knew it would break his mother's heart. She never really wanted a soldier for a husband; definitely not one as a son.

Then something happened which, cruelly, gave Danny the briefest moment of optimism. He heard English being spoken.

———•———

The accent was neutral, the words well formed.

"You might not have heard of the Islamic Freedom Movement. But you will know those we are fighting for. The people of Afghanistan being terrorised by soldiers from Britain and America, and their stooges around the world." There was a pause as the man reading the statement looked up from the paper to stare directly at the camera.

"The Afghans did not create this conflict. The Taliban did not create it. You and your kind did that. You would not accept there are those who are different from you, who hold different values, do not aspire to be you, who do not fit into your way of thinking".

The man went on. He outlined the ideology of the Muslim fighters currently engaged in a struggle with the Western powers. He referred to the infidels, the crusaders and their attempt to marginalise the Muslim world and the true word of Mohammad – *'peace be upon him'*. At no stage did the statement ask for anything; it neither demanded anything nor offered solutions.

"We are fighting back – defending our homes, our traditions, our beliefs, our future. We do not respect you and we do not fear you. And we are not afraid to die. I am not afraid to die. If I am killed then dozens will take my place. My family will take pride in the fact I fought the infidel".

The prepared statement had been discarded and now the man stood staring straight at the camera, speaking from memory as if relaying his own personal circumstances.

"But you Prime Minister, how do you regard death? Are you happy to watch your soldiers killed? What price do you see as acceptable in your struggle against us? Do you remain the puppets of the United States? Do you accept their murderous actions without question? Do you apply their disregard for the life of innocent families destroyed during this war without a moment's loss of sleep? Ours is a fight for survival. We will oppose you at whatever cost. But how far will you go? Where do you draw the line? What is your resolve compared to ours?"

The eyes of everyone in the COBRA meeting room remained fixed on the television set. The PM knew all those present were desperate to turn and look at him, to see how he was reacting. Two things prevented them doing so. Their fear of him and their fear of missing anything on the screen, a morbid fascination keeping them glued to a hideous piece of reality TV.

The show's host folded up the piece of paper he was still holding and stuffed it into a pocket. Then he reached behind his back and took the rifle that had so far been out of view. He cocked the weapon and checked the safety catch was off before raising the barrel, pushing it against the soldier's head. He did not rush his actions, but nor did he hesitate; there was not a hint of nervousness or indecision but a confidence in how to handle the weapon and what he was about to do with it.

When Danny heard his mother tongue spoken his heart had initially leapt. For an instant he allowed himself to believe help had arrived. Three things very rapidly shattered the illusion. First was the voice itself. Calm, deliberate, it was the same one that had delivered the sentences of Arabic. Next was what was said. His earlier hunch had been right. His impending death was being proclaimed.

The third thing was the 5.56mm bullet which took off the top of his head and blew away much of his face, splattering blood, bone and tissue across the unflinching optics of the camera. What Danny didn't see and never knew was that the round that killed him was fired from his own weapon.

The noise of the shot made those in the briefing room jump. As Private 30621604 Akers slumped gently out of frame the sound of the detonation reverberated between the walls of the chamber of horrors.

The man who had executed him – the one with the impeccable English – looked down, towards a spot, out of view of the camera, apparently inspecting the consequences of his actions. In his hand was the British rifle he had used to murder its owner.

The screen went blank.

For several seconds there was little further reaction from the eight men sat around the briefing room table. The Secretary of State for Defence was as white as a sheet. A man supremely unsuited to the rigours of his job, he gripped the edge of the table to prevent himself passing out.

"Bunch of fucking animals," he said.

It was the head of the intelligence service that first recovered the power of coherent speech. Slowly he pushed himself out of his chair and arched his back, stretching his muscles.

"There is a little more intelligence the General hasn't given you, Prime Minister."

He spoke reluctantly as if he didn't want the PM to hear what he was about to tell him. "We have spoken to Pakistani ISS and they have identified the English speaking insurgent as one of their Border Force Officers – his name is Khalid Bashir."

"My God, he was one of theirs?" said the PM angrily. "How are we supposed to defeat these terrorists if our allies keep producing them?"

"I'm sorry prime Minister but it's not quite as simple as that"

"What do you mean?"

"Khalid Bashir is also a graduate of the Royal Military Academy. He recently attended the overseas officer cadet programme. We were made aware of his activities about a month ago as our casualty rate in Afghanistan spiked. It seems the US also noticed a spike in trade."

"So let me get this right," the PM said. "Our casualties in Afghanistan have increased and we believe it is down to a Pakistani officer who we trained at Sandhurst – is that right"

"Yes it is, Sir."

"Do we know why he is doing this? Does the US administration know its young men are being killed and maimed by someone taught by us?"

"No Sir," the intelligence chief answered.

"No to which part?"

"No, Washington is unaware of Bashir's background and no we don't know why he does what he does," the intelligence chief lied.

"So what are we doing about it, you say we learned of his activities about a month ago, so what have you done about it?" the PM asked accusingly.

The General stood and stepped towards the intelligence chief as if to show solidarity and support.

"As soon as we learned about the possible link between our casualty count and Khalid Bashir we set about collating information," the General began. "We have formed a team of human intelligence officers and special forces to go to Pakistan to track Bashir down."

The PM clasped his hands in front of his face and rested his forehead on the fist they created. Now in the second year of his second term as prime minister, nothing that had gone before had vaguely prepared him for what he had just been told. Heaven help him if the British public found out what was happening. His choice was stark. Give the team the go ahead in the hope it could quickly deal with the situation before more details got out or come clean with the Americans and ask for their help.

"General Adamson, what do you suggest?" the PM spoke without raising his head from his hands.

"Sir I believe if given the opportunity our team should be able to track him down within a few weeks, it's not as if he hasn't left a fair few footprints for us to follow."

"We already have satellite and digital audio surveillance looking for him," the intelligence chief added. "What we need now is boots on the ground."

The PM sighed.

"Alright. You lot are always moaning about how important it is to preserve spending on the military and I have done that haven't I? Well its time to show you've put that money to good use. You have clearance to send in your team, but I want regular sitreps on their progress, is that clear?" He looked icily at those around him. "And don't be in any doubt. Its not just my neck on the line."

———•———

Four thousand miles away, Cyrus Vincent's phone rang again. He ignored it again, knowing that if it was important they'd try him on the cell.

The landline went silent and a few seconds later his mobile began to burble and vibrate. Shaking steadily the Nokia crept towards the edge of the bedside table, Cyrus watching it go, wondering whether it would reach the precipice before the answer machine kicked in. The answer was yes, though just before it tumbled off on to the floor, Cyrus caught sight of the number of the incoming call. Withheld. That confirmed it then. Someone from work was trying to reach him.

He leant out of bed and foraged for the handset. Retrieving the source of the disturbance he speed dialled his office number. A voice he recognised answered.

"What is it Beth?"

"Sir, sorry to disturb you. We have news from Khost. The British soldier is dead, and its already making front-page news round the world. Just thought you would like to know."

"Thank you. What are we hearing from London?"

"Nothing much Sir. We don't believe they know Bashir is working for us but we do think they know about his past and are sending a unit to track him down."

"Alright, goodnight Beth."

Slumping back onto his pillow, Cyrus put the phone back onto the table and mulled over the latest developments. He liked a problem to work through. Almost as much as he liked his sleep. Within seconds he had drifted back into unconsciousness, snug in his own bed.

Chapter 8

KACHKAI – NORTHWEST FRONTIER PAKISTAN

None of those on board the Lear jet had clamoured for repeats of the in-flight movie but they got them just the same. Three times they were treated to the twelve-minute video of Danny Akers' death. The ending was always the same as much as they might have wished it otherwise: the terror of the soldier, the jolt of the gunshot, the splatter of blood on the camera lens. Peter Ryder urged his team to look past the murder and concentrate on the man committing it. Only Adam had had any real exposure to the killer. For the others, this was as close as they'd so far come to Khalid Bashir and understanding what he was like.

The film was put on almost as soon as they had taken off from Manston airport in Kent and banked through 180 degrees so they could coast out at Dover and begin in earnest the seven-hour flight to Pakistan. Ryder wanted the guys to get as much sleep as they could, but first they needed to see what they were dealing with. He hoped it wouldn't give them nightmares. If nothing else it illustrated the importance of their mission. For Adam there was a thin recollection of the man from Sandhurst. It wasn't the way Bashir looked which resonated most with him, but the way he spoke: quiet, polite, articulate, yet intensely determined. Adam shuddered. He wanted to believe it a product of tiredness and altitude. But he couldn't be completely sure. More likely, he admitted, it was apprehension at what lay ahead.

———•———

The landing strip they arrived at was unmetalled, dusty and bumpy. It lacked any obvious markings or lighting, and couldn't have been further removed from the gigantic tarmaced runway they'd taken off from back in the UK – so big, someone said, it had been a diversion destination for the space shuttle. Adam knew this airfield would not feature in any commercial aviation guide. When the plane had taxied to a standstill Adam thanked God it was daylight. That had at least meant the pilot had been able to see where he was supposed to be touching down. As he followed the others down the stowaway steps, Simon leading, a pair of 4x4 Nissan vehicles swept up beside the jet. Simon ignored the transport and ducked beneath the aircraft's underbelly. Impatiently he waited for the internal locking mechanism to click free so he could open the cargo hatch and begin offloading the kit. Adam went to help. Rocky, Al and Peter moved to the vehicles to check some of the equipment they were expecting to be collecting. They paid only cursory attention to the pair of Pakistani drivers who'd got out to greet them and were now standing around awkwardly, not sure what to say or do. Neither looked much beyond their teenage years.

"For Fuck's sake, Peter," Rocky shouted, popping his head back out of the first truck.

"What's up?"

"There's a Blue Force Tracker fitted to the vehicle – I can see the box in the glove compartment – but there's no monitor, what the fuck use is that?"

"Same in here," Peter shouted back from inside the second Nissan. "I guess our CIA friends aren't keen on us seeing their troop dispositions but want to keep tabs on us."

"That's fucked up," said Rocky.

"It might well be. But if we want to move through their area of responsibility we'll just have to suck it up."

It took 20 minutes to get everything square. Al was the last to finish. Methodically he checked the comms kit they'd been gifted and established a Sat-phone link with London. He also spoke to CIA ops in Khost via the TacSat using the preloaded frequency.

Det 3 broke down into two groups and finally boarded their transport: Al at the wheel of the first pick-up with Peter beside him: Adam and one of the Pakistanis in the rear. Rocky and Simon were in the second vehicle with the other Pakistani who, like his colleague, having handed over the ignition keys to the new arrivals, would act as an interpreter rather than a driver during the move northwest into the mountains.

———◆———

The journey was long and increasingly uncomfortable. Initially they managed to keep up a steady 60kph despite repeatedly jerking sharply left and right to avoid the road's potholes and crumbling edges. The traffic was light and nobody gave the vehicles or their occupants a second glance; the men inside all dressed in the local style. The weapons were stowed out of sight, though close to hand. Even the GPS was below the level of the dashboard. After two hours progress they prepared to leave the main road.

"At the next junction take a left," Peter said. "Our marker should be a building about 100 metres before the turn."

Al grunted confirmation.

A small compound loomed ahead and Peter acknowledged it as what he'd been expecting. The exit appeared and Al swung the lead vehicle off the pitted tarmac road and onto a rough dirt track less than a vehicle and a half wide. A cloud of brown dust engulfed the convoy and their speed dropped to no more than 40kph.

Two hundred metres further on they passed the confirmation marker, another turning, acutely angled back the way they had come. Peter slumped back in his seat. He wasn't anticipating another change of course for a couple more hours.

The track wound its way along the bottoms of valleys and along the steep sides of hills. Occasionally they lost height but the overall momentum was upwards. There were few signs of human life other than occasional, primitive villages that straddled the route. They looked as if they had not changed in appearance for hundreds of years. Once, rounding a blind bend, they were faced with a herd of goats blocking their path, forcing them to come to a shuddering halt. One of the interpreters leaped out, but despite screaming and shouting at the old herder it took several minutes for the animals to amble clear.

"You ok, Al?" Adam asked. "Do you want me to take over the driving for a while?"

"No thanks mate, I'm happy enough."

"Hardly worth it anyway," added Peter. "It should only be another 30 minutes drive to Kachkai. As we approach I want you to pull over short of the village by about 75 metres. I'll let you know when."

"Roger Boss."

"Adam once we stop you, me and Simon will head into the village. First thing we want to do is find an easy access route for the vehicles so we can call them forward. Once we've done that then it's time for you to earn your keep and find Khalid's family. You happy with that?"

Adam nodded.

"I want a soft approach. No weapons on display, side arms tucked out of sight. Grenades, phos and spare ammunition in a grab bag. I'll take the TacSat strapped to my chest."

The pair of Nissans pulled up in a passing place at the side of the track just ahead of the village's outlying huts and houses. As Al established comms with Khost Rocky made himself snug alongside the vehicles and viewed the scene through the Schmidt and Bender sight sitting on his L115A3 sniper rifle. Looking up the road and into a tightening group of buildings he watched as his three colleagues and one of the Pakistanis moved into the sight picture, striding towards the settlement.

———◆———

Peter and Adam walked in front, casually looking about, a nervous interpreter at their shoulders, Simon covering the rear. There was nothing out of the ordinary about the kalay, just the usual jumble of compounds and huts. To the right of the road the ground stretched out flat but after one hundred metres or so it gave way and fell sharply to the valley floor below. Two or three of the compounds were noticeably larger than the others with high surrounding walls. Each had a large cast-iron gate preventing anyone seeing inside. They were grouped around a narrow open space, a village square you'd call it back home thought Adam, though not much of one. At the centre of the square was a grove of spindly trees bordering a stone well that sat in disrepair, a battered hand crank connected by a tatty rope to, presumably, an unseen bucket down the shaft. To the left of the road the ground rose and a gaggle of homes stepped their way up the flank of the slope. Two small children ran towards them as they walked, startling a tethered knot of goats much to the annoyance of a wizened old man who sat cross-legged, tending them.

"Adam, you pop over and make friends with goatherd and I'll have a quick check and call up the vehicles"

"Sure," Adam said, beckoning the interpreter to come with him.

"Salaam alaikum."

Adam raised his right hand to cover his heart.

"Walaikum salam," the old man responded, struggling to get up.

Adam went through the extended pleasantries particular to this part of the world. He could read suspicion and confusion on the elder's face. Adam had the appearance of a man from the region, but he was betrayed when he opened his mouth. Through his interpreter he recognised the seniority of the man before him.

"Though I am not the elder of the village," the old man said.

"Do you know where I can find him?" Adam pressed.

On cue a small delegation trooped out of one of the compounds and paced towards Adam, preceded by a gaggle of laughing children. After more pleasantries Adam was ushered to the shade of a yew tree.

Following the Afghans' lead he sat down in the circle they'd formed. The conversation started without him.

"What are they saying?"

"They think you are an American soldier and are here to look for Taliban," answered the interpreter.

"Who is that doing all the talking?"

"I don't know. He may be the local Imam."

"Is he the village elder?" Adam asked.

"No, the man with the brown cloak is the elder. He is listening to what the others advise."

Adam was wary the hangers on might prove a bad influence on the elder but he knew there would be no chance of speaking to the senior figure on his own. He needed to put his case in front of them all. He waited for a moment to interrupt then, speaking louder than was polite, broke into the discussion.

"I am looking for a family called Bashir. The father's name is Farouk."

There was a long pause before the senior man spoke.

"We have not seen Farouk for a long time. He is sick. In a Peshawar hospital."

"Is he ill?" Adam asked. "Can I speak with his wife or his daughter?"

The man ignored Adam's questions.

"Why have you come to speak with the Bashir family?"

"I want to ask Farouk a few questions about his son, Khalid. Nothing important. I understand he is in the Border Force. We were hoping he could help us," Adam was speaking more softly now, with deference.

"Farouk's family – his wife, his daughter – are dead, killed by an American missile strike," the elder said coldly. "Farouk was very badly hurt. He will not recover."

"And his son?"

"Khalid came to visit soon after the attack, but we have not seen him since. He will not be back here."

"Do you know where has he gone?"

The old man shifted uncomfortably and turned to those around him. Even without a translation it was clear to Adam they were debating whether they should say anything more to the stranger; wondering whether they'd already said too much. Their deliberations were interrupted by the arrival of a boy heaving a large kettle. A second child carried a tray of glasses. Working as a team they poured tea for the adults. A glass was offered to Adam who accepted and took a sip.

"Shukran," he said, nodding.

"Have you got anything yet, Adam?" Peter whispered, sliding into a position just behind him.

"Not quite," Adam murmured.

The interpreter turned to face him.

"They are speculating about what you could be after. It is hard to make everything out."

Adam was worried the mood would turn against him if he gave them too long to think.

"I am sorry but it is very important that we speak to the son of Farouk Bashir. We mean him no harm and we are willing to pay you for some information."

Adam wanted to keep the conversation moving, rephrasing his questions to try and wheedle information out of the increasingly stony faced men. He repeated his offer to compensate them for their time and trouble. He tried $1,000. Then $2,000. But the villagers stubbornly kept their counsel.

Adam made a show of draining his glass and standing up. The others mirrored his actions. Adam bade farewell with as much politeness and ritual as he had used for the greetings and turned away towards the vehicles which Simon and Al had brought forward as the meeting progressed. Adam was conscious of a man standing aloof to the group he'd just been talking to. Throughout the discussions he had leaned against a tree, detached from the proceedings, listening to what was being said but contributing nothing. Now he was trying to catch Adam's eye. Adam let him do so. The pair stood in silence while the village elder led his party back to the compound they had emerged from.

"Ask him what he wants," Adam said to the interpreter. "Quietly."

"He says his name is Lal-Jan and he claims to know about Khalid Bashir."

"What does he know?"

"He says Bashir is fighting with a small Taliban group in southern Afghanistan. He makes mines and has already become a famous Jihadi."

"Does he know where he is now?"

"No. But he says he does know the Taliban leader he is fighting with. He claims he can help you."

"Ask him how he knows the leader and how he knows about the Taliban group," Adam instructed.

"Because he fought with him before being wounded in the leg."

The interpreter told Lal-Jan to lift the leg of his trouser blouse. He did so, revealing a ragged scar that stretched from his knee to his ankle.

"You were Taliban?"

"I fought with the Taliban because they paid me. When I was wounded and I could no longer fight the money stopped. So I came home," Lal-Jan explained.

"Do you think you could find this Taliban leader?"

"Possibly," he answered. "I can take you to his tribal area and home village, we might be able to trace him from there."

Adam studied the man stood in front of him. He understood the basis of the deal. This was purely about money; nothing to do with ideology. But that was ok. It was how things worked. And anyway, what other lead did he have?

"Which house belonged to the Bashirs?"

"I can show you if you like. But there's nothing there. I've looked."

"Well, I'd like a look too," Adam said pointedly. "Wait here a minute."

Adam strode over to Peter and Simon.

"What do you think, Adam? Can this guy be trusted?"

"I don't see why not. He could also act as a local guide, do a bit of running around. At the moment he seems like our best option."

Peter thought for a while.

"Ok let's go for it. In the meantime we have been given orders to head to Khost to speak with the CIA head before we start charging around Afghanistan."

Simon looked offended.

"Typical of the Yanks, sticking their noses into other people's private business."

"You can't blame them can you? It is their operational back yard. We'd be the same," Peter answered. "Right. Adam, Rocky, I want you to pop up and do a quick check of the Bashir compound. Simon, you and Al sort out the vehicle – I want to be on the road within thirty minutes and across the border before last light."

As it was, they were out of Kachkai in half that time, the search of the pathetically humble compound where Khalid Bashir had grown up revealing nothing of importance. Even everyday items were absent; there were clearly those in the village who thought Farouk Bashir would never have further use for his pots, pans and utensils.

The convoy retraced its route for about 15 kilometres before sweeping onto an obscure feeder road. Their journey would take them through Landi Kotal, close to the top of the Khyber Pass and the Afghan/Pakistan border. Rather than risk complications at the crossing between the two countries the plan was to jump the N5 and join up with one of the old silk routes that snaked through the mountains to hurdle the frontier. The risk came not from border guards, but a little local difficulty: the Afridi tribe were at war with the Pakistan Taliban, fighting each other for control of the critical smuggling routes.

"My map shows a large river south of the N5," Adam shouted from the back seat as they approached Landi. "Do you want me to ask Lal-Jan if he knows a way across it?"

"You can check, but I am happy with the route. My source has already conducted a check of the river and has plotted a 10 figure into the satnav. It should be ok, shallow enough for the vehicles to get through."

"Roger. But just so you are aware, he is indicating duchman are present in the area."

"Duchman?" Peter shouted back.

"Tribal fighters, they call them duchman," Adam explained, dragging his HK MR223 rifle up from the rear foot well of the vehicle and checking the magazine. Next he fished for the Glock pistol tucked into a side holster under the gray over-vest he was wearing; reassuring himself it too was fully loaded. Peter spoke to the other vehicle over the radio warning them they were about to hit the main highway. Once over the main Khyber road they were to adopt tactical vehicle movements and keep 60 metres separation.

Rocky was on the TacSat to get a link to both Khost and the air operations control centre at Kandahar where UK Special Forces maintained a constant liaison officer presence to assist all covert ops running in the region. Any call from 'Det 3' would get priority treatment. From Khost a US Reaper could be on task within ten minutes of any call for help.

Joining the Landi Kotal road the traffic was at a near standstill. There was a long snaking queue of vehicles waiting for their turn to cross into Afghanistan. Large jingly trucks, overflowing with goods, sat bumper to bumper while entrepreneurial traders hurried between them trying to sell the drivers anything from fruit to CDs.

The Nissans struggled to negotiate a passage through and the hawkers regarded the new arrivals as another sales opportunity. What they hadn't anticipated was Al's response. Raising the rifle from between his legs so it was now clearly visible, he mouthed the words *Fuck off*.

"For fuck sake Al," Adam said angrily. "What was the point in that?"

"I hate these fuckers. Had enough of rags trying to sell me shit in Iraq. They never take no for an answer."

"Yeah well, very subtle with your reaction."

"Who are you? Mother fucking Teresa?" Al shot back. "What's your problem?"

"Ok Al, that's enough," Peter jumped in. "Adam's right. It was a pretty stupid thing to do. If we're to be stuck here much longer I'd rather not draw attention to us. Just keep an eye out for a break in the traffic and cut directly across. We'll edge west until we hit the track past the hospital."

For the next few minutes they all sat in stony silence as Al wormed his way through the jam of lorries.

"Have you travelled this area much before?" Adam asked Lal-Jan as the tension eased and they regained some momentum.

"Often. We moved our weapons across the border using these tracks. After I was wounded it was through this pass I was carried out on a donkey train."

"Do you know the tribal elders? Can you talk to them?"

"No, no, they are Afridi Pashtu. All they want is money. If they stop you they will kill you to get it. They will take the vehicles, take your belonging and leave you to rot in the sun."

"Yet you and your Taliban train were able to pass?"

"We crossed at night, using the animals. They didn't see or hear us. It was risky though. That's why vehicles stay on the Khyber road and don't come down here."

"What's he saying, Adam?" asked Peter.

"He's telling us not to stop, and if we come across anyone we don't like the look of shoot first."

It was an hour of bone jarring driving later that the lead vehicle halted on a bend high above a valley set out in front of them. The second truck pulled over some distance back. Looking down they could see the river they had to ford before the final climb into Afghanistan. Peter, Al and Adam got out to take a look. It looked deep and fast flowing, though a pronounced track led down to the river's near-side edge and reappeared directly opposite on the far bank.

"What do you think Peter?" asked Al.

"The route is obvious enough and it matches the 10 figure grid on the satnav. I guess this is our crossing point."

"It would be all too easy for the local tribe to place an IED here or here abouts. Guaranteed to catch someone," said Adam.

"What does Lal-Jan reckon?" asked Peter. Adam walked back to the truck to find out. He was quickly back.

"Well he thinks that if they were intent on robbery, it wouldn't make sense if they destroyed the vehicles they were trying to steal."

"Ok, but would you back him on this one?"

Adam reacted with irritation.

"Not being fucking smart Peter, but he is ex-Taliban, has fought for money and is only with us for money. I have only just met him and I wouldn't be surprised if he happily sold us out to the highest bidder. How the fuck would I know if he can be trusted?"

"Fair one mate," Peter answered untroubled by Adam's outburst.

"One thing I am sure of though," Adam continued, his anger spent. "He has no comms on him and if he's is in the first vehicle and knows there are IEDs set he will tell us pretty quick. Whatever else he might be, I don't take him for a martyr, do you?"

"Now that's clever thinking. Let's go," Peter said decisively.

The first vehicle mounted up and moved off: Peter commanding, Al behind the wheel and Adam in the back seat with Lal-Jan squeezed between him and the interpreter. They left the second crew behind them. Rocky over watched with his rifle in hand and radio set close to. Simon had made himself comfy on the edge of the ravine in a stable firing position. He scanned the ground ready to take a shot.

Al took the truck down the zigzagging track and out onto the plain, inching towards the river. Stopping only briefly to judge the flow he nosed the vehicle confidently into the water, pushing a small bow wave ahead. For a second it felt as if they might drift off into the stream, but the truck settled, finding purchase on the stony bottom despite the rush of the water.

"Keep it steady Al," warned Peter. "We don't want to swamp the engine."

"Roger Boss, but I'm fighting the current here. It's pretty strong."

The torrent was at least sixty metres wide, but they were making progress. Then there was a shout from Rocky.

"Alpha, this is Bravo, standby."

"Roger, I got it mate," Peter said.

With the Nissan closing on the far bank, Rocky had spotted two clouds of dust appear on the skyline ahead. They started to tumble down the slope. As they rapidly gained ground Rocky saw that at their core there were a pair of flatbed Rangers, packed with armed men. Mounted on the back of one was what looked like a 12.7mm Duskha.

"Adam, keep your weapon down but be prepared to exit right," Peter spoke softly. "Al I need you to stay with the vehicle. If we lose it then we're fucked."

"Roger Boss. Are we going to bluff this as far as we can?" asked Al, trying hard to concentrate on his driving rather than the welcoming committee bearing down on them.

"Yeah, I reckon they will wait till we are out of the water and then stop us."

"They will come to my window first," Al said apprehensively.

"Adam. If that's what they do then I want you to take the first man through the side. Once he's down, you exit. Al, you spin the vehicle as close to the technical as you can before the fire gets too heavy."

"Got you, Boss," Al replied, relieved to have a plan.

"Roger Peter. This will kick off on my shot," Adam said lifting his weapon slightly so he'd be able to fire over Al's shoulder and through the window.

Three hundred metres back Rocky had been busy. He'd already received confirmation that a Reaper was airborne and patrolling to the north of Khost. It was theirs if they wanted it. Simon peered through the telescopic sight and tried to count how many of the enemy there were.

"Alpha this is Bravo. We have two vehicles and eight up, I reckon" Rocky relayed what Simon had told him.

"Ok. Don't engage yet because if they hit us in the river we'll never make it out. We are going to go through this like an IVCP drill. Once we take the road man out I want you to take the Duskha and then the drivers."

The approaching vehicles slowed and stopped, the first just short of the water, the second, with the Duskha, further back up the track, covering the territory in much the same way as Peter had laid out his own unit. It was a game of chess. From the lead vehicle, three men climbed out: two stood at the sides with their rifles raised, whilst the third walked round to the front and leaned against the bonnet.

"Ok fellas, let's just keep calm. No nervousness now. Let's get them close by," Peter said, nearly to himself.

Al slid the vehicle out of the water and drove towards the two roadmen with their AK47s.

"Fifteen metres to go, 10 metres, 5 metres. Standby, standby," Peter counted down softly.

The tribal fighter closest to the Nissan held up his hand, fingers splayed. Al drew up slightly short of the man forcing him to move towards them. As he neared, Al lifted his hands off the wheel to show he was of no threat. The man rapped sharply on the window. When nothing happened he moved to repeat the exercise, a scowl on his face. What he didn't see, because he didn't have time and wasn't looking, was Adam thrust his rifle forward until the muzzle was almost touching the driver's window and then pull the trigger. Out spewed a six-round burst of 5.56mm ammo, the spent cases ejecting and striking Al on the back of the head. Inside the confined space the noise was deafening.

The glass shattered, as did the fighter's face. Even before the body had slumped to the ground Peter was out of his door and advancing on the enemy closest to him, firing several rounds from his C8 carbine. The man's astonishment at the turn and speed of events had left him rooted to the spot. The bullets thumped into his chest and he spun to the floor. His body bucked as Peter followed him down, hitting him with even more ammo.

"Move!" yelled Al swinging his pistol out of the broken window and aiming at the last of the leading trio. Behind him Adam had exited the rear door and a moment later they were both firing at the same target. Their victim reeled as he was struck, first in the knee. Another bullet bore into his groin. He had the trigger of his AK depressed but the rounds were flying wild and high. Back across the river Simon heard the shots with only a fraction of a delay. He fired at the image he'd lined up in the centre of his scope. There was a solid kick to his shoulder as the bullet left the barrel of the heavy L115A2 and homed in on the Duskha operator, striking him just above the right ear and reducing his brain to mush. The energy of the impact toppled him backwards over the truck's tailgate. He was dead long before he landed in the dirt. Simon shuffled to one side to get a good aim on the driver of the second vehicle. He lined up his rifle and squeezed the trigger again. A hole appeared in the windscreen and the man behind the wheel slumped sideways out of view. With fire coming from Rocky and Simon on the high ground Adam moved in on the wounded roadman beside the first enemy vehicle. Firing repeatedly as he went he saw in his peripheral vision that Peter had pushed out to the right and taken up a position behind a giant, oddly shaped rock where he was engaged in a battle with two more fighters tucked in behind the first vehicle. He heard Peter yell out.

"RPG!"

The warhead struck the ground just a few feet away but bounced harmlessly past, the short distance it had been fired over meaning there had been no time for it to arm. Satisfied that the man in front of him was now well and truly out of action, Adam moved to outflank the pair of men Peter was entangled with.

"Go firm, Adam," shouted Peter.

"Roger, firm, move now."

Hearing Dam's shout Peter pushed away from the rock to get an angle on the fighters behind the vehicle. Instinctively the pair scrambled round the vehicle to take cover from Peter's changing position, but they ran straight into Adam's line of fire. It was almost too easy for him to cut both down with short bursts.

"Tangos down," said Adam breathlessly.

"Moving to the second vehicle. Put fire onto it. Can you get the tyres?"

"Nope, not easily."

Peter looked elsewhere for help.

"Bravo, can you shred the tyres?"

"No chance, they're protected by a line of boulders but we think we have taken the driver," Rocky replied. "There is still one Tango near the second vehicle. We're scanning for him now."

"Understood, we are going to climb up and see if we can find him. Cover us."

Rocky passed on some good news he'd just been sent by Khost ops. He was almost laughing.

"We will have a UAV on task in about three minutes, call sign Ghostbuster."

"Ghostbuster? Are you fucking kidding me?"

———•———

Moving one at a time, Adam and Peter edged steadily up the stony incline one covering the other. Nobody was shooting now. Reaching the lip of the ridge both men paused to catch their breath. Gingerly they raised their heads and scouted the land in front. Just ahead was the second enemy vehicle, a neat aperture in the screen and a twisted, wrecked body sprawled behind it.

"Adam, you move left."

"Moving now."

As he started his dash he heard Peter's shouted warning.

"Enemy right! Enemy right!"

So that's where he is thought Adam bitterly. The remaining enemy fighter had appeared from behind a bevel in the rock face, firing a burst in Adam's direction. Instinctively Adam dived for the front of the Ranger as Peter opened up. But it was Simon who did the damage, the force of the .338 round he fired exploding the enemy's head.

Relieved, Adam staggered to his feet, dusting himself off. It was shock then that the Ranger's engine suddenly revved madly and it shot forward, its twisted bumper clipping Adam's shin, sending him sprawling and making him squeal. The vehicle arced round as the driver, staying as low as he could, attempted a U turn to escape back the way he had come. The move caught everyone else as much by surprise as it had Adam, but they recovered quickly, bringing fire to bear on the retreating truck, hitting it repeatedly. It didn't stop, finding cover in the billowing plume of dust it was throwing up.

"Bravo this is Alpha, we can't let him get away."

"Yep I'm on it," replied Rocky. Then to the Reaper's forward air controller: "We have a single red flat bed vehicle moving west from our present position, how copy?"

"Good copy – my pilot is reporting a number of vehicles in the area can you mark your position and give time and space."

"Roger, marking with red smoke. Vehicle will be approximately three minutes from our location west at about one kilometre."

On the valley floor Peter flung a smoke grenade then backtracked with Adam to their truck.

"Det 3 Bravo, this is Ghostbuster. Confirm what you want done, over."

"We need this vehicle and its occupants eliminated."

Fifteen seconds later.

"We've got a good ID. Circling for attack run now."

"Det 3 Bravo, roger out," Rocky terminated the call. With Simon he started gathering up their kit and stowing it in the vehicle.

Running down the slope back to the river Adam and Peter saw Al standing over a jumble of clothes strewn in a hollow. They moved over for a closer look. The injured man was oozing blood from at three wounds, staining his ragged dress. His face was contorted with the pain conjured up by the bullets embedded deep within him. He still clung to his rifle, though without the energy to use it.

"Got a live one here Boss," Al shouted.

"Then sort it," said Peter curtly.

Al drew his pistol and took aim at the head of the crumpled figure at his feet. Without hesitation he shot the man once in the skull before double tapping into his body.

"Right that's it, lets get the fuck out of here," Peter said.

Chapter 9
CIA HQ – KHOST

Cyrus sat ponderously behind his flat-pack desk in the small glass-fronted office that took up one corner of the Joint Operating Centre. Its position gave him a good view of the planning map that filled a wall of the JOC and provided a focal point for the members of the various agencies, his of course included, that made up the Afghan CIA HQ in Khost.

Cyrus had arrived back in Khost three days previously. It was a regular stopping off point but he reckoned that nowadays he probably spent more time in Kabul and Islamabad and, when he was lucky – which seemed to have been quite often recently – Washington. As the man in charge of the Near East Desk his patch stretched for many thousand of miles, but the current situation dictated that Khost be the hub of his activities. A knock at the half-open door interrupted his train of thought.

"Yes?" Cyrus said looking up from his computer screen. A young man in flannel trousers and a white shirt hovered at the entrance.

"Sir, I have a Mr Ryder to see you."

"Ryder?"

"The British operator you were expecting."

"Ah yes. Of course. Is he alone?" Cyrus inquired.

"Alone."

"And the rest of his team?"

"We have put the others in the DFAC to get a bite to eat and some coffee."

"Perfect. Well please show Mr Ryder in," Cyrus answered, closing down the windows on his screen then turning it off.

Det 3 had reached Khost just before midnight. They'd been expected. The Blue Force Tracker had ensured that. Still, their credentials had been exhaustively inspected at the camp entrance before they were directed to the secure compound housing the CIA facility. Over grabbed refreshment, Peter had carried out a mercifully short debrief and then the party had split to go to their various accommodation: the interpreters and Lal-Jan traipsing off to a block set aside for locally hired civilians; the others to a prefab transit hut encased in concrete. It felt as if they had been in the country for days yet they had not even reached the 24-hour mark.

The shrill of the alarm at 0530 hours had come as a rude awakening but by 0600 hours they were checking their equipment and tidying up the battered trucks. The driver's window of the lead vehicle was cleaned of ragged glass though there was nothing to replace it with. Nor was there much to be done about the bullet holes to be found on most of the panels. Not that they were particularly worried about the state of the bodywork. What was important was the engine bay and running gear. These were thoroughly examined for any damage incurred during the firefight. Peter sent a situation report to London and Al checked the preset frequency for the TacSat to ensure continued communications with the CIA JOC. After all of which it was breakfast time. Adam was hobbling slightly; the bang on the shin he had taken the previous day still causing him grief. Peter had barely started his food when he was ushered away for his meeting with Cyrus. Swearing, he wolfed down a final mouthful of hash browns and beans and followed the messenger.

———•———

"Good morning, Sir. My name is Peter. I think you have been kept up to date with my details."

"Yes indeed Peter, good to see you," Cyrus said, emerging from behind his computer and shaking the hand being offered. Cyrus gestured to a couple of chairs in the corner, making sure Peter took the smaller, less comfortable of the two.

"Would you like a coffee?"

There was nothing he wanted more.

"No thank you, Sir."

Peter waited while Cyrus poured himself a cup, adding cream and sugar, and settled himself down.

"So how can I help you Peter?" Cyrus asked savouring his drink.

"Well I'm hoping we can help each other. I'm sure you are aware of the insurgent fighter who recently executed a British soldier."

"The one on the internet? Doesn't make for good viewing does it. Awful stuff. I take it you are here to hunt him down? What has that got to do with us though?"

"We have discovered a number of things about this man which you and your government need to know."

"Really, such as?"

Peter rattled off the Khalid Bashir story from beginning to end. Cyrus rubbed his chin.

"Thanks for sharing that, though to be honest much of it we are already on top of. "

"I thought you might be," Peter said mildly. "But I thought I would give you the rundown anyway. In the interests of transparency."

"Appreciated. So what now?"

"It's believed Bashir is working in the north of the country and has been ever since the execution of the British soldier."

Peter told Cyrus about their visit to Kachkai, the meeting with the village elder and the hiring of Lal-Jan.

"We are hoping you might be able to provide us with some HUMINT on insurgent activity in the area, give us the low down on tribal issues. Basically help us on our quest."

It was a strange conversation. Both men expected the other to be, at best, economical with the truth, and at worst to be lying. To Cyrus it didn't really matter. There was nothing the British could possibly know about Khalid that he didn't. Bashir was his agent for Christ's sake. What he did want to discover though, was whether Ryder and his team were getting anywhere close to catching his man. If they were then Cyrus would have to reconsider their relationship.

"So when you find Bashir what is your plan?" Cyrus inquired.

"I've been told to attempt to take him alive, believe it or not."

A quizzical look crossed Cyrus's face. He made sure it did not become one of concern.

"Alive? Surely it would be easier just to kill him. An awful lot less mess."

"I agree," Peter shrugged, shifting forward in his low chair. "But UK intelligence are keen to talk to him. Between you and me I think they are rather embarrassed about the whole thing and want to take him to task. Stop the same sort of thing happening again."

"And any information you gain through this 'debrief' you will pass onto US intelligence I'm sure."

"Of course. In exchange for your valuable help in tracking him down."

"What info do you think he will have? Seriously, he is pretty low key, despite his handiwork in front of the camera."

"As a Pakistani national and one time member of the Border Force we believe he's had assistance from the Pakistan ISI and Military Intelligence. We think they are trying to wage war in Afghanistan remotely, using individuals like Bashir," Peter lied.

"So what if you find him? What do you think you can do to make him come peacefully? In truth your team is pretty light and eventually you will have to call in the big guns and that will go noisy."

"That's true but we have a link with his past; the time he spent at the Royal Military Academy. One of my team trained with him. We are hoping that connection will give us an opportunity to bring him across. Worth a shot anyway."

"Seriously?" Now Cyrus did look surprised. "You dragged along someone who knew him at Sandhurst?"

"Not exactly dragged along, we have a HUMINT operator who knows Afghanistan and knows Khalid Bashir. His name is Adam Caine, a decent fella if a little green."

Peter paused, looking for any glimmer of recognition from Cyrus. There was something familiar about the name, but for the moment Cyrus couldn't place it. He'd been exposed to hundreds of people and names over the past 18 months and most he'd assessed and filtered out as unimportant. Very few had any lasting impact on him or his job.

"Interesting. Well let's go and meet your team so I can say hello and see how we can help. I've got a couple of ideas though."

"Such as?"

"Well, why don't you let me re-route one of our satellites to have a look in your target area. That should help pinpoint activity. At the same time I'll get my HUMINT assets to see what the word is on the street," Cyrus said standing up. "Might take a couple of days though."

"That's kind, but unfortunately I don't have a couple of days."

Cyrus looked aggrieved. "As I say, it might take a couple of days."

The pair moved to the door and stepped through. Cyrus halted.

"Just a moment, I had better make a quick call before we go."

"No problem," Peter said. He turned to look around the JOC. His attention was immediately drawn to the large planning map. He couldn't really miss it. He studied the location of the units under CIA control highlighted by the Blue Force Tracker.

Back at his desk Cyrus hit five on his phone. Impressively fast the duty watch keeper answered.

"Bryson, hello?"

"It's Cyrus. I want you to do some things for me. First I want a background check on a man called Adam Caine. This might be a false name but do a check of the UK Sandhurst commissioning course Bashir was on. You can do a face recognition check using images taken by the cameras when he entered the base last night."

"No problem, Sir."

"Also get some of the CivSec team down to the LEC compound. There's a Lal-Jan who has just arrived. I want him arrested. He's a former insurgent. Is that understood?"

Cyrus hung up and rejoined Peter.

"Sorry pal, let's go."

———◆———

"Hopefully we will be out of here soon," Adam said as they sat around after breakfast, surrounded by empty plates and mugs.

"This is alright by me. Could be worse," Simon replied. "We could be out in some crappy village drinking chai and having to shit in a ditch."

"True but I'm a little uncomfortable around these people."

"Americans?"

"Spies."

"I thought you would be happy in the company of spooks," Rocky chipped in. "Mind you, having seen you operate yesterday I have to say you have a skill set beyond what your average spook might possess."

"Maybe it's just a previous bad experience with US intelligence putting me on edge," Adam answered lowering his head.

"Like what?" asked Al. All eyes had turned expectantly towards Adam. He said nothing.

"Come on you prick tease. You can't give us a sniff of the pussy without revealing all the juicy detail."

"My last outing in Afghanistan," Adam began reluctantly. "Thanks to the CIA, things didn't go exactly according to plan."

Adam supposed there was no reason why the men he was fighting with shouldn't know his story, not now, not after the skirmish they'd been in. Adam figured he'd already made some amends for what had happened previously. He was just about to come clean when the door to the DFAC was flung open and Peter appeared, just ahead of someone who Adam recognised.

"For fuck's sake," he said. "I don't fucking believe this."

Chapter 10
THE INSURGENT – CENTRAL AFGHANISTAN

For several hours, Khalid's narrow view of the world had changed little. Sat deep amongst the tangled undergrowth beneath the tree line, concealed by the foliage and the long shifting shadows it cast, separated from the dusty track by a deep, wide, irrigation gulley, the scene before him had only sporadically been enlivened by people passing by, oblivious to his presence. At times the cramp threatened to become debilitating but Khalid understood patience was key to the success of what he did and discomfort had to be mastered; a price to be paid. He could teach the Jihadis many things but the virtue of endurance was an inner strength he knew not everyone possessed.

He judged that enemy patrols would be routinely operating in the area, just as they had for the last few years. But that wasn't what made this location ideal for his plans. The intelligence that gave Khalid the upper hand was not related to what the enemy would do, but what they couldn't do. He was in an area where fast air assets would not be allocated, indirect fire support would be limited to non-lethal ammunition and, when needed most, helicopters would be on task elsewhere. He had free rein to prepare and execute his attack without having to worry about a host of force multipliers being brought to bear against him. His handler had guaranteed as much, having made it clear to US military that this particular movement box was ground troops only.

The wait had given Khalid ample opportunity to consider what he was trying to achieve. The deaths of the enemy were important to him personally as marks of revenge – it was why he had decided to join the insurgent cause in the first place – but each successful attack was means to a bigger end. The havoc he helped create built his reputation and raised his chances of access to the upper reaches of the Taliban hierarchy. After each attack he made a report: either to the shadow Taliban governor for the district or the local Taliban military commander. These reports would wend their way up the insurgent structure until they reached the eyes and ears of the man in the Quetta Shura who had overall military responsibility for operations in Afghanistan.

Khalid felt no guilt about the support he was receiving from US intelligence. For now their purpose served his purpose. And at that moment the purpose involved the destruction of more American lives.

A couple of days before, Khalid had instructed his men to plant a crude IED on the track the soldiers were likely to use. The design of the device meant it would be activated when it was stood on, the weight pressing two electrical contacts together and completing a circuit to allow a current to flow to the detonator. Then boom. As colleagues moved in to help the casualty Khalid would set off a second IED, this one radio controlled, which they'd also concealed. He'd use a mobile telephone to dial the number of another phone attached to the device. The ringing would fire the detonator. Boom again. In the chaos Khalid's men would open up at close range with small arms.

Except the tactic wouldn't work.

The bitter experience of the attack he'd been involved with in which the old warlord had martyred himself – and for what? – demonstrated that. The mine on the track would be located by the metal detectors the enemy carried before it was ever trod on. The radio controlled device would be blocked by the enemy's electronic counter measures. And the weight of fire from the US soldiers would be heavier and far more accurate than anything he could muster from his own poorly equipped and barely trained men. Khalid knew all these things because he knew the enemy, and yet he remained confident that even as events unfolded and went against him he would still emerge with a significant amount of enemy blood on his hands. Because he understood how everything would go wrong he also knew how to put it right.

———◆———

The motorbike weaved up the dirt track, skidding in the dust, its wheels channelled by the ruts. The man grasping the handlebars fought to keep the machine upright and, more importantly, to the right of the track and away from the IEDs. As he drew level with the spot where Khalid was concealed he braked sharply and a young boy riding pillion had just enough time to scramble off before the rider opened the throttle and roared away.

The boy tumbled down the embankment and through the water.

"The Americans are coming," the youngster said reaching Khalid, squeezing in beside him.

"How many did you see?"

"Many of them, maybe 30 or 40 on the track, another 20 or 30 in the fields further back."

"Ok my friend, stay next to me and make no sound," Khalid ordered, lifting the hand held press-to-talk radio to his mouth.

His words reached the dozen men huddled in small groups to his right. Spread over 200 metres they covered the killing ground.

"You are all to stay low and are not to fire until the first explosion. Then do not move until I tell you. Remember your routes out of the area. You must stay on them. Do not deviate, do not run, make sure you move to the buildings I have allotted for you."

Khalid spoke slowly, emphasising each instruction. Under other circumstances Khalid would have been worried his voice communications would be overheard by the enemy. He well knew the infidels monitored Taliban frequencies. Khalid himself had been taught that very skill. However Khalid was confident the orders would go undetected. The frequency he was on was similar to that used with baby alarms. The enemy would play the percentage game, tending to monitor the more widely used VHF rather than the low frequencies Khalid had chosen.

"What about the civilians working in the fields?" a voice came back over the radio. "Women and children?"

"Do not worry about them, they will move fast enough when the shooting starts."

———◆———

Khalid and the others barely allowed themselves a breath as the American troops emerged into view, the height and angle of the sun revealing it was now sometime after midday. The sweat ran freely from beneath Khalid's turban, but he dared not move for fear of revealing himself.

The enemy movement was cautious, the lead man in the patrol conscious of the ever-present IED threat. The remainder of the patrol walked in the lead soldier's footsteps, on ground he'd checked with the metal detector he waved rhythmically from side to side.

"Stop!" he shouted.

The patrol froze but not in panic. This was a well-rehearsed routine; it was what you did when confronted with a bomb. Khalid blinked furiously to expel the moisture from his eyes but he only succeeded in blurring his vision further. Never mind he thought. His problems were nothing compared to those the Americans would have any moment now. The enemy soldier with the wand was yelling again.

"I've found an IED!"

"IED. Everyone down, standby!" came the order from a man just back from the one who had discovered the bomb. "Conduct your 5 and 20s."

The soldiers began checking the area immediately around where they stood. Another shout went up. A new voice.

"Sir, I have another one. This one isn't buried, looks like a Claymore."

With the Americans preoccupied, ever so gently Khalid connected a second wire to a small tin nestling in the grass at his elbow. Now, gingerly, he raised himself from his hiding place, pointing for the boy to do the same. He traced a diagonal route away from the track heading south. He had selected his path carefully. It was about the only way he could move and remain concealed from the enemy. Obediently the boy followed behind, clutching his superior's rifle in both hands. After a hundred metres the pair reached a deserted compound; its occupants were out in the fields tending their crop. Khalid knelt, fumbled for a small battery in his pocket and touched it to the end of the twin flex command wire.

The charge inside the tin he'd left where they'd been waiting was small but as it hadn't been buried the noise it made when it exploded was ear splitting. The insurgents took their cue. From their hiding places they poured fire onto the track. The enemy were still busy dealing with the two IEDs they'd discovered. Now they had other things to contend with. Frantically the soldiers tried to return fire.

Khalid urged his comrades on.

"Keep firing. Don't stop."

The insurgents' AK47s continued hammering out wild volleys of 7.62mm short, while the longer bursts of the PKM split the sky above the heads of the US soldiers. Periodically an RPG would weave out from the undergrowth, the signature noise and smoke of it being launched a prelude to the lethargic warhead looping over the track and exploding in a brown flash of shrapnel.

The noise was deafening and disorientating. At close quarters, and hemmed in by the vegetation, it was hard for the enemy to determine exactly who and what they were dealing with. Warily, a couple of soldiers started crawling towards the side of the ditch but the fear of more IEDs slowed them down.

Khalid sat away from the maelstrom, but he knew what would be happening because he understood the enemy's procedures. The soldiers on the track had become the firebase and were urgently trying to fix the insurgents in the tree line. The commander would order the second group of troops at the rear to ford the irrigation channel and outflank the insurgents' position. If Khalid's assessment was right then they should be passing in front of him in the next few minutes. Khalid looked along the watercourse. Within sixty seconds the first handful of enemy troops were moving through the undergrowth, ready to straddle the obstacle.

"Move now! All of you. Move."

On Khalid's instruction the insurgents abruptly ceased firing and began retreating from their positions using the pre-set routes Khalid had given them. Khalid heard the leader of the flanking group of Americans react to what he was seeing.

"Push forward now, the enemy are trying to escape!"

Egged on by their boss's words, the men picked up the pace. To their eyes the insurgent attack had failed; the IED had not initiated and the insurgents had opened fire in desperation, shooting wildly and blindly over their heads. If the flanking soldiers could move quickly and in depth they would be able to cut their enemy off. It was all about the kill, the body count; nothing else mattered to those on a high of blood lust.

The first cell of Khalid's unit had darted along the maze of small paths and disappeared through the doors of the ramshackle compounds that made up the small Kalay close to where he sat. The soldiers pursued them enthusiastically, confident that if they kept up the pressure through the claustrophobic vegetation they'd catch them.

The next explosion was also small, but infinitely more vicious: shipyard confetti – ball bearings, nails, bolts – erupted in all directions. The claymore had been wedged in the fork of a tree branch, about five feet off the ground, and was triggered by the American leading the charge tripping a motion sensor. It was he too who took the main force of the blast, together with his enthusiastic buddy who was just a pace behind.

The metal tore through the top of the men's shoulders, shredding their necks. Irregular hunks of ironmongery embedded in their skulls and the upper reaches of their torsos. A hand of one man was torn off – the muscle scythed away and the bone shattered. Still gripping a rifle, it fell to the floor. Both soldiers collapsed, the receding echoes of the explosion replaced by the high-pitched screams of those critically injured.

"Man down, man down!" a young soldier shouted. With misplaced bravery he advanced towards his stricken comrades but never reached them. With his third step he stepped squarely on an inconsequential stump of wood that he couldn't see because it was buried a fractionally below the surface of the path. The marine had always considered himself in good shape, more lithe and athletic than many of those he served with who carried their bulging muscles with obvious pride. But trim though he was, his 140 pounds were more than enough to compact the crush detonator the wooden limb concealed. The trigger was wired to a booster charge and plastic container holding 10kg of HME: plenty enough explosive power to blow him apart.

The blast mushroomed skywards, taking with it the soldier – what was left of him – in a macabre pirouette. The unbridled force separated him from his legs and tore at his helmet. The overpressure burst his eardrums and the blood vessels in his eyes. His jaw was shattered and metal shards ripped his nose from his face. Whiplash broke his neck. Unsurprisingly, mercifully, the unfortunate soldier was dead before hitting the ground.

There was pandemonium amongst the troops conducting the follow up. The commander tried desperately to regain control of his men and of the situation.

"Go firm all of you, stop where you are now! Do your 5 and 20s and don't go any further forward."

"We have casualties up there, Sir," came a frantic reply.

"I don't give a fuck – go firm or else you'll be next. Do you hear me?"

The men stopped, looking about them for solid ground where you would least expect to find an IED, trying to second guess what Khalid and his men had prepared. Most chose to stay on the track they had watched the insurgents run down. If the enemy had used it then there was every chance it must be reasonably secure. The men with the wands tried to find any trace of metal that might signify an IED, but there was nothing. Rooted to the spot, all the others could do was listen to the pitiful cries of their two wounded comrades and the shouts for the young soldier who was now missing. Repeatedly the commander called over his radio for air support only to be told that there was no CAS and the attack helicopters were on another task.

"Are you shitting me?" The commander swore into his radio. "I have injured soldiers here." The reply was unequivocal. Follow standard practice: get the wounded out of the area and to a secure landing site, away from the seat of the explosions.

Khalid waited patiently as the mayhem unfolded in front of him. He had achieved what he'd wanted: inflict casualties and halt the patrol's progress. He gently lifted the second white twin-flex wire. Without any apparent urgency he attached one of the two ends to the square battery that sat at his feet. He let the other end of the wire hover over the opposite terminal, waiting for exactly the right moment.

There was movement amongst the soldiers. One man stood up. He was followed by two others, and then a third, all of them ignoring orders. Together they edged towards their wounded colleagues, the man with the metal detector out in front.

They stopped; Khalid could see the front man kneeling down to conduct confirmation drills on a reading he taken from the bank beside the track. Turning around, a grimace on his face, he gave the thumbs down and his three companions inched away in the opposite direction, looking for safety. Khalid touched the terminal with the other end of the wire. A shot of energy raced 250 metres along the buried flex that had taken several days of painstaking work to dig into the landscape. It reached the spot where a carefully concealed yellow package stuffed full of ammonium nitrate fuel oil had been lying dormant. A number of ageing Russian munitions, each shell factory-scored for ease of separation on detonation, had been wrapped around the package. For good measure there was also a gallon-sized container of kerosene and when the device was given hideous life by the tiny pulse of electricity it was this liquid that created the brilliant flash of flame, followed instantaneously by blast and shrapnel. Caught at the centre of the conflagration were the three men who had retreated to what they thought was a place of refuge.

The commander died as the force of the detonation caught him square in the chest tearing off his body armour and slicing through his face, neck and head. The other two men where blown back, their limbs shredded and torsos blacked and scorched, the weapons they were carrying falling to the ground twisted and broken. The trio died on the spot.

Calmly, Khalid removed the phone from his pocket and pressed the number nine. The speed-dial number went directly to a second cloned phone. It too was connected to a twin flex wire. Khalid had predicted the ECM would provide a safety bubble out to about 100 metres: within that radius it would block a mobile signal. But Khalid's phone had been remote, out beyond the ECM bubble. On receipt of the call the second phone sent a current down another, also carefully hidden, command wire to energise the device the lead man had initially found. It too detonated. The blast blew the fourth man off the ground, his foot severed from his right leg and two of his fingers from his right hand.

As the reverb from the bombs died down, so more screaming and shouting took over: from the casualty, from the traumatised troops who had just witnessed their commander and two others ripped to bits.

The young boy looked at Khalid.

"You are a master fighter," he said admiringly.

"Maybe, but be sure you tell all you meet what you have seen here today. Spread the word of the good work we have done. Let them know we can beat the infidels."

Khalid moved to the rear of the compound, his disciple at his heels, and they calmly strode away from the chaos they were the architects of. The helicopters would eventually arrive to pick up the dead and wounded and he needed to clear the area.

"I want you all to move to our emergency rendezvous," Khalid said into the radio before turning to the boy. "Go and get the motorbike, and meet me in the next Kalay."

The boy scampered out of sight as he was bidden and Khalid pulled another phone from his pocket and replaced the SIM card it contained with one that had been pressed between the pages of his notebook.

"This is Tabasco," he said when he heard the connection.

A voice on the other end answered. In English.

"Yes, what have you got?"

"I have just conducted an attack to the southeast of Kabul, there are American casualties."

"OK."

"I need you to ensure the follow-up looks in any direction but northeast. Do you understand?"

"I understand, but you have to know we need to see some product and soon," the handler's voice was impatient.

"I will give you what you want but you must take care of your side of the bargain. You just look after my father."

"He is safe. Call when you have something."

"I will. But remember, no follow up northeast."

Khalid ended the call and reinserted the original SIM. Slowly he walked on, towards the next village and his next task.

Chapter 11
TABASCO – KABUL

It took Khalid less than twelve hours to reach the suburbs of Kabul from the scene of the ambush. He had changed his mind about remaining in the countryside, favouring instead the anonymity provided by the crowded capital's tightly packed, chaotic streets. The ring of high mountains that lay around the city's fringes created a natural barrier to Kabul's expansion and emphasised the claustrophobia of the city and the millions of inhabitants hemmed inside it.

Initially he had been accompanied on his journey by several of his colleagues, but as they progressed, the others peeled off one by one to seek the comfort and protection of their own friends and families. In this sanctuary and obscurity they would stay until mustered once more for another attack on the infidels.

Khalid's own refuge was one he'd used before: a dingy two-roomed house, shoehorned into a meagre space between two newer, multi-storey buildings. He wondered how this small piece of land had remained undeveloped. Khalid was only an irregular visitor, but there was a permanent occupant: a middle-aged man with a permanent stoop who made a living from renting out a room to anyone who wanted or needed it. It was he who had passed a message to Khalid from the local Taliban commander upon his arrival. Khalid was to go to another safe house located in southern Kabul district of Qala-e-Shada. And there he should wait until contacted again. Khalid's landlord had not asked the courier who brought the instructions for any further explanation because he was well aware none would have been forthcoming. Similarly Khalid did not question the orders he had been given, but simply followed them.

He had now been in Qala-e-Shada for over 24 hours and done very little except pray, eat, complete his ablutions and pay attention to his matted hair and beard. The cramped space that contained him was down in the basement: a mattress was jammed in one corner, a single blanket bundled on top. Sitting on the mattress he looked across at the only other furniture in the room, a wooden table sitting in another corner. There was no chair, but resting against the wall beside the table was a well-used AK47 without a wooden stock. The cellar had no window, no view and only one way in or out.

Khalid stared at the battered weapon and then at the thin leather bound notebook that sat on the table. He thought about how he had ended up here, how he had become what he had become. He thought about his sense of loyalty, honesty and honour. But mostly he thought about his father who was all he had left in his life and for whom he would die to protect.

Khalid felt a vibration in his pocket. He didn't rush to retrieve the phone, already well aware of who was trying to get hold of him and why. When eventually he had fished it from his trousers it had stopped ringing. He stared at the cracked screen. The missed call was from a Roshan number. No voicemail had been left. The call had been message enough. It told he needed to check in with his handler.

If the phone were ever found by someone of inquisitive nature who then attempted to return the call, it would lead to a feverously busy repair garage in the Kandahar bazaar. The man who would answer it, a local named Habibullah, had no links to either ISAF or Khalid and would sound harassed and say the call must have been the case of a wrong number. And that was what the handler intended. He had cloned the SIM of Habibullah; someone who received numerous calls daily and made even more himself. In essence two phones with the same number. All Khalid needed to know was that no one other than his handler was able to call him on that device.

Late the previous evening, after, as instructed, he had arrived at the second safe house, he had been informed he would be going to a meeting high in the Hindu Kush with a senior Taliban official. The man he would be meeting was the Taliban's finance minister.

Khalid retrieved the notebook from his backpack and placed the SIM card contained amongst its leaves into the Nokia. There was only one number stored on the SIM. Khalid called it.

"Please identify," a female voice said.

"Tabasco. Serial 843119."

"Hold the line."

He could hear the operator connecting the call and then there was a ring tone, that of an internal extension.

"Hello Khalid, how are you?" the handler came on the other end. It was the same voice Khalid had been listening to for the last two months. It was neither an American nor Pakistani accent but something neutral, indistinct, in between.

"Did you get my message?"

"Yes. Our MX reporting confirms a meeting of high level Taliban leaders to the north of the country. Very high. This fits with your information."

"What do you want me to do?"

"Our sources suggest the Quetta Shura are well aware of your work and are keen to use you as an IED facilitator and specialist within the wider network. We think they want you to go to Pakistan to conduct training for other bomb makers in preparation for a major offensive next year. It will be discussed at this meeting."

"Ok. So I will ask you again what do you want me to do?"

"We need you to mark the meeting for us."

"Why?"

"We will strike the target once you leave the area."

"How?"

"There will be a package left for you in the Shada cemetery. There is a single tree beside the western wall. The package will be at its base. Inside you will find instructions and some tracking equipment. I want you to collect it tonight, read the instructions and follow them exactly."

"I can't go back into circulation after this, not again, not this time."

"We know that. This is the last task. You will have done what we asked of you."

"And afterwards? What about me? When will I get a chance to go and see my father?" Khalid pleaded.

"It will be in the instructions you get tonight. It will deal with you leaving the area, dropping off the radar and getting out of Afghanistan," the handler soothed. "You have helped us and we will keep our end of the bargain and set you and your father up with a new life in Egypt."

"I will need money for travel once the job is done, papers, passports," Khalid persisted.

"It would be foolish of us to give you them right now. You will be searched, we can't allow your mission to be compromised."

Khalid did not respond, encouraging the other man to fill the vacuum.

"In the package, along with what you need to mark the target, will be a map. It will show the location of the next dead letter box to be used once your task is complete, all you need to escape will be inside."

"Understood, but I need guarantees," Khalid whispered.

"You will just have to trust us Khalid. As we have trusted you. Make sure you get the package tonight but not before 8pm. Understand?"

"Yes, ok."

"We're all close to getting what we want. Just a little longer."

The line went dead.

Khalid sat stock still, his brain whirring, working through the permutations. What were his options? There weren't any. He had to conduct the operation and facilitate the strike but he did not believe, had never really believed, he would be allowed to live. Not with all the information he now held in his head. He was dangerous to them and he was convinced they meant to bury his knowledge by burying him. That's what he would do in their circumstances.

Lifting his notebook from the table he flipped through to the last entry and reread it. He turned to the next blank page and jotted down the details of the conversation he'd just had. Then he lay down and closed his eyes.

The owner of the house arrived just after 6pm. He brought with him Khalid's supper: rice and fresh beans with some flat bread and a beaker of slightly curdled milk, mint leaves flaked on top.

"You will be leaving tomorrow, my friend," the house owner said setting the meal down on the table.

"I'm not sure," Khalid replied, mistaking the statement for a question. "Maybe tomorrow, maybe the next day."

"No, you will leave tomorrow. A courier left a message earlier today but you were at the mosque. He told me you would be leaving in the morning, after prayers, and you would not be returning. I was to inform you."

"Go on."

"They will collect you. Where you will go afterwards I do not know."

"Did they pay you?" Khalid inquired. "Do I owe you any money, do you need anything?"

"I am a poor man but they told me this was Allah's work and I should not ask or expect payment."

"Your name, Haji Rakim isn't it? I would like you to do me a favour Haji Rakim."

Khalid reached inside his pocket, retrieved some notes and counted out 6,000 Afghanis. The man shook his head.

"Thank you my friend but I cannot take it."

"Yes you can, for your trouble," Khalid insisted, pressing the money into the old man's palm.

"You are very kind."

"There is another 6,000 if you help me."

"Whatever you ask," the old man said bowing his head and touching his right hand to his heart.

"If I need to stay here again, without anyone knowing, the Taliban or the authorities can I count on you?" Khalid asked.

"Of course my friend, it is the Pashtu way. Hospitality to those in need of it."

By 7pm it was dark. With all the food consumed, Khalid wrapped himself in his long brown cloak and stepped out onto the streets. It would only have take about 20 minutes to walk directly to the cemetery but Khalid stopped at the mosque on the way where for nearly three-quarters of an hour he shared his thoughts with his God. Only when he left did he give all his attention to what he would have to do at the graveyard. Khalid had been taught the mechanics of live and dead letterboxes by his trainer while in US custody. They had been used as a system for exchanging information and equipment for decades. The terminology, it had been explained to him, was originally coined by the British in Northern Ireland in the 1970s. A live letterbox would be manned; with the information and equipment handed over in person. By contrast a dead letterbox was unmanned.

It wasn't until shortly after 8.30pm that Khalid stood at the base of the tree looking up at its bare leaves and jagged branches. He knew it acted as the primary marker, but there would be something else close by. In the gloom he searched at its base. Amongst the rocks strewn about it, a large oval stone stood out. Astride it was a Y shaped stick. Khalid had found the secondary marker.

Heaving the stone aside, Khalid discovered a cavity that stretched away under the tree's roots. He groped around in the hole, pushing his arm further and further in, until his fingers touched something plastic.

With an extra stretch he grasped the parcel and eased it out. Without inspecting it further, he stuffed it under his cloak and manoeuvred the stone back into place. Lastly he placed the stick back on top of the stone but this time reversed, a signal to his handler he had been. Throughout the brief visit Khalid had felt immensely vulnerable. It would have been simple for him to have been killed and disposed of. That he wasn't dead at least proved he still had some use.

He returned to his accommodation promptly and after lighting a candle – not unusually, the electricity had failed – locked the door to his dungeon. Perched on the edge of the mattress he lay out what he had collected. The flicker of the flame illuminated not one but two packages, joined tightly together with red electrical tape. He cut at it with a lock knife. Easing the two items apart he chose one to examine first. It was irregular in shape but, even wrapped in polythene, could not be mistaken for anything other than a pistol. Removing the covering he recognised the contents as the Russian-made Makarov he had had with him when he was first seized by the Americans. Pulling it free, he turned it over, checking for damage. Satisfied that it was intact and had a full magazine, he placed it to one side before picking up the other package. Underneath the plastic there was a box of ammunition and a large brown envelope. He studied the envelope for markings but there were none. He tipped out the items it contained: an official looking document with some writing in Dari scribbled at the bottom; a hand drawn map, also with a Dari inscription; and a manual for a Nokia mobile – once again with a note in Dari – together with a lithium ion phone battery.

As best as he could in the gloom, he examined the map. Holding it towards the spark of light Khalid could see Mazar-e-Sharif had been marked as the location of a vehicle and then a route traced back via Kabul to a dead letterbox about 10 kilometres short of the Khyber Pass. Against the drop an arrow had been drawn. The words accompanying it said what would be found there: passports, paper, money.

Next Khalid examined the intelligence report; a mission packet for Objective Vegas, the man he was going to see.

Once you have been taken to the meeting and Hakimulla Mahsud appears you are to activate the signal tracking equipment that is in the package along with the instructions. You are to switch on the beacon. We will give you 20 minutes to clear the area before it becomes a hot site. After the strike you must confirm the death of Hakimulla Mahsud and inform us using your normal Roshan number. The codeword for mission success is CAVIAR. Once we receive this code we will deposit your papers, money and passports for you and your father in the location shown on the map. You can make it to this location by using the vehicle also indicated on the map. The keys are under the right wheel arch.

Failure to attend the shura, light the beacon to paint the target and send the codeword will result in the death of your father. Afghan and PAK security services will issue a warrant for your arrest and all ties to this department will be severed. We will release documents to the media and on the internet detailing your involvement with ISAF and Afghan forces.

No further communication will be made and you are not to contact your handler until after the strike. Asset tracking will let us know if the meeting takes place.

Khalid lifted the Nokia manual, the small battery and the last piece of paper. The instructions for the battery were plainly laid out. He had to retain his secure SIM card but replace the current power pack with the one provided. The phone was to remain switched off. In the battery was a miniature tracking device, designed to activate a radio beacon the moment the phone was turned on. This was only to be done once he had confirmation of the arrival of Mahsud and was within 100 metres of him.

Carefully Khalid swapped the batteries of his phone. He crumpled up the remaining pieces of paper and burned them using the candle. Then he wrapped his notebook in the brown paper and Polythene from the parcel, securing it with the tattered remnants of red electrical tape before stuffing it under his cloak. He was ready.

Chapter 12
JOC – KHOST

Adam struggled to hide his frustration. Two days the team had been in Khost and the waiting was getting tedious. The only excitement had come from meeting Cyrus again. Not that the American had recognised him. He'd shaken Adam's hand and looked deep into his eyes, as he'd already just done with the others. But there was no glimmer of recognition. The name hadn't appeared to mean anything to him and he wasn't about to see in front of him the young man he'd confronted in the Upper Sangin Valley: the darkened skin, long hair and contact lenses ensured that.

Nevertheless Adam didn't trust Cyrus; regarded his words as hollow, manipulative and disingenuous.

"Peter can we talk?" Adam asked, walking up to the team leader.

"What is it?"

"I think we're getting the merry run around, we've been here 48 hours and nothing."

"I know," Peter whispered. "But we need to sit this one out."

"You know what Cyrus is like, you read the debrief notes from my last encounter with him, you know how ruthless he is."

"What do you think is going on Adam, seriously?"

"I don't know, maybe they're trying to get to Khalid before us. It's feasible."

"Maybe, but why?"

Adam thought about it.

"I don't know. Why do we want him alive? For information. Perhaps they've got the same motivation as us."

"So let's say they're holding back on us, what can we do? We're at the mercy of US intelligence and unless the UK can intervene then there's few options open to us."

"Will you brief UK, explain our concerns?"

"Of course, but do you really believe they can do anything to move this along? Like it or not the Americans hold all the cards."

"But why don't we just use Lal-Jan. Let's just go with his info and see what happens"

"Sorry Adam; that's not going to happen."

"Why not?"

"To put it mildly it hasn't helped that Lal-Jan was arrested. You know he's shown up on a biometric reading as an arrest and hold. Secondly I am not going charging around a CIA patch without clearance or support. And thirdly he's just not a reliable source."

"But I could talk to him, find out what he knows. Let's angle for the chance to debrief him."

Peter was dismissive.

"I'm sorry Adam, you are going to have to be a team player on this one."

Adam stood for a while thinking. He knew Lal-Jan was traced, they all did and they knew he was in this for the money and that made him unreliable. Peter turned to walk away. Then stopped and turned as if he had forgotten something.

"By the way, Cyrus wants to have a word with you."

"Me, why?" Adam asked.

"Really, do you have to ask?" Peter said. "It was inevitable; he was always likely to have researched you, picked up on your service with Khalid and clearly brought that forward to your time in Afghan."

"Great," Adam said sarcastically. "I thought I had got away with it."

"I know, but listen it doesn't matter, just stick with the brief, what happened in the past is in the past. We need to stick with what we're doing now."

Peter didn't invite further conversation. He was already heading over towards Simon, Al and Rocky who were lounging around on plastic chairs, soaking up the sun.

———————

Cyrus sat in his office. For the past couple of hours he'd been discussing with his planning team Khalid's forthcoming meeting. There were plenty of decisions to make and one by one they'd been going through their options.

"So we're agreed, Vegas is a top prize and we're happy to call an end to Operation Tabasco. Yes?" Cyrus said.

Each of the other three men in the room nodded but only one spoke.

"Yes Sir. But as discussed, we must ensure Bashir is completely out of the game. We can't have him popping up later with stories to tell."

"Agreed," Cyrus responded. There was more nodding.

"So it's settled. We take out Vegas and Tabasco together but we ensure we have a secondary option if that fails."

"Are you sure about the secondary option, Sir? It's risky and I'm not certain they will go for it."

"We need the Brits meshed in this. We need them hot on the trail of Bashir so if we miss they'll be able to fix him for us to strike."

The way Cyrus spoke indicated he wasn't expecting any more scrutiny of his intentions.

"I think in Captain Caine we have a hot head who is likely to move whether he has permission or not, let's see"

"Ok Sir, as per your instructions we've set the conditions in the JOC. All I need is for you to delay seeing Captain Caine long enough for us to ensure he has taken in all the information. He will either jump by himself or we can feed the team the info later."

"Good, I have sent for him, he should be here shortly. Let's get this thing wrapped up. You ensure Tabasco does what he needs to do."

A young man butted in with a hybrid US/Pakistan accent.

"That's done, Sir. He's ready to go."

"Ok," Cyrus replied, annoyed the handler had interrupted him. "Make sure asset tracking has him and ensure he is live when he switches the phone on. I want an immediate strike so have our UAVs are in the air at all times. Clear?"

"Sir, we already have positive feed on asset tracking. Reaper One is in the air now with Reapers Two and Three ready as follow-on, so we'll have 24-hour coverage for a couple of days. Can I just confirm the car has been fitted with the tracker so if it is activated we know Tabasco is still alive?"

The last of the three men spoke.

"The car is marked and as soon as it is started the tracker will go hot. I've also marked the hide so we have the opportunity to strike if he gets that far. Beyond that we'd have a problem if he disappeared into the wider population or crossed into Pakistan."

"Just leave that to me," Cyrus said. "Now get on with your tasks."

Cyrus watched the others go. Then he sat back to wait for Adam.

"Captain Caine my name is Paul, do you want to come this way?" asked the man who greeted him at the threshold of the JOC.

The guide showed his guest to a row of soft seats at the back of the room. Adam looked around him. A large whiteboard caught his eye. Listed on it were a series of names, addresses and what looked like asset codes. He squinted to make out what was there. Reaching the penultimate entry he read the word Tabasco. Just below it, Vegas. Concentrating hard on the list he jumped slightly when a hand was clapped on his shoulder. Adam turned to see who it was. Cyrus Vincent loomed large over him though he wasn't looking at Adam but at the same list he'd just been studying.

"You know, it's all to do with reducing the insurgents' ability to operate. It's not merely about cutting off the head to limit the command and control. Like the hydra there will always be another, no matter how many we sever. But even so, it is a victory for us and a worry for them if we can hit at the very top of their establishment."

Adam felt a surge of anger.

"You're right, at times we need to talk and at times we need to strike, its all about knowing what is the best thing to do at the time. Don't you agree?"

Cyrus didn't bite. Adam kept talking.

"Anyone interesting on the board? Objective Vegas?"

"Yes as it happens, a big shake in from the Quetta Shura, very rarely comes this side of the Pakistan border. We think he'll be scooping up the local talent for next year's campaign."

"Well that's what a good source can tell you, I'm sure you have many," Adam said, standing.

"Absolutely Captain Caine," Cyrus said, at last looking at Adam. "And you will know more than most how important good sources are."

The two men moved from the main arena of the JOC to the confines of Cyrus's office. Cyrus ushered his guest to sit in the same seat that Peter had taken when he'd popped in for his little chat.

"So how have you been Captain Caine?" Cyrus asked.

"Actually it's not Captain anymore, I left the military not that long after I left Afghanistan, but then you know that already."

"Yes I had heard, shame, but these things happen."

"Of course and I learnt a lot back then. I am less trusting than I was previously. More cynical about the world. And the people in it."

"It's a difficult game we play Adam, you don't mind if I call you Adam do you?" Cyrus asked. "At times it works for the best and at times it doesn't."

"I'd say I've discovered that to my cost, Cyrus," Adam responded, before adding. "You don't mind me calling you Cyrus do you?"

"Not at all. Did you ever hear what happened to your target Silab?"

"No I didn't," Adam answered genuinely interested.

"He died during the rendition process. A great pity. He would have been a useful asset."

"So it was all for nothing."

"Those can be the breaks, but when one door closes another opens. It's just percentages."

Adam wondered why Cyrus had gone into the whole Silab shit as he knew exactly what had happened to Adam after his meeting with him on the HLS. He wondered whether it was simply to get perverse pleasure from watching watch Adam squirm. Whatever, there was most definitely a motive.

"So I hear you know this Khalid Bashir?" Cyrus said.

"We met. At the Royal Military Academy as officer cadets. Not really friends but we were aware of each other."

"Indeed, what with you winning the sword of honour and he the overseas officer cadet prize. What do you think? That seeing you he will remember back to his time in jolly old England, become sentimental and hand himself over?" For the first time there was a hint of sarcasm in Cyrus's voice.

"Maybe, maybe not. We won't know until we track him down and we won't track him down until we get the clearance from you to move."

"Well I think we will have that in the next couple of days. Do you realise that intelligence suggests Bashir is fast becoming one of the top IED facilitators in this part of the world?"

"Yeah, I heard."

The conversation dried up. Adam left the office, walked through the JOC, out of the secure entrance and back into the main courtyard of the CIA compound within the Khost security base. Somehow he needed to speak to Lal-Jan. Adam was becoming increasingly concerned the

Brits were being sidelined. At best they were being played. He wanted
to take the initiative. He was in no doubt if he didn't move now, if the
team didn't move, Cyrus would manipulate events and there would be
no chance to take Khalid alive.

———◆———

Adam walked over to where the team was lounging about.

"So, what did he want?" Peter asked, putting down a well-thumbed
paperback.

"What you thought, nothing major, just a chat."

"No news on our move out of here?" chipped in Al.

Adam shook his head and took a seat on a small plastic chair facing
the sun. Lifting his chin he let the warmth brush over his face.

"Any word on Lal-Jan?" he asked of no one in particular.

"I saw him in the LEC compound earlier today," Simon replied. "He
looked pretty chirpy. No worse for ware after his stay at the detention
centre. In fact he looked pretty happy."

———◆———

Because of the time difference, Peter didn't make his daily sitrep call to
London until later in the afternoon.

"Any changes, Peter?" the man running the operation spoke.

"I think the US have taken the bait. I believe they are worried about
Adam's knowledge of Bashir and I think they will be making a move
soon."

"What are their courses of action?" the man pressed.

"I think they're feeding Adam snippets of information which may
lead him to Bashir. I believe they think he will either tell us and we will
move without their clearance or Adam will make a run for it himself in
an attempt to reach Bashir first."

"You think they are trying to suck us into their deception?"

"Without a doubt, I think we're getting close to the time we need to make it known to them we have information Bashir is their asset," Peter argued. "Once they are held to account they will be a little less obstructive in our attempts to influence trade in their patch."

"But we're not there yet," came the reply. "They can still strike and put this well out of our reach. I think we need to press further, what do you think?"

"Well that's why Adam Caine is here, he will either jump ship and get to Bashir first or he will get close enough so the US will have to come to us with the facts. Either way US intelligence will be forced to act."

"Will he go?" the man in London asked.

"I reckon so."

"Tonight?"

"Probably."

"Would you put money on that?"

Peter snorted.

"If you paid me enough, I might."

Chapter 13
THE GAMBLE – NORTHERN AFGHANISTAN

Adam lay stretched out on his bunk. Across the room, against the other wall, Al and Rocky were in their cots, sleeping soundly but for the odd snore and snort. The majority of their kit was stowed neatly on the floor at the end of their beds; weapons placed on top. Their remaining few pieces of gear – the personal stuff – was dumped on chairs besides their heads. Hanging from the chair closest to him, Adam could see a long red ribbon with a security tag at the end. He made up his mind and lifted himself up on to his elbows. Happy that there was no reaction from the others he levered himself up on to his feet. Still no sign of disturbance. He eased towards the prostrate Rocky, removed the camp ID from where it hung and tucked it into his pocket. Then crept back to his pit.

He stooped to retrieve his grab bag, slung it over his shoulder and grasped the HK M223 rifle. He had a last look around the room and headed towards the exit. The door opened out into a courtyard. Purposefully he strode diagonally across the open space. Passing first through a gap in the buildings, he made for the far corner of the CIA compound where he knew the vehicles would be parked up. He crept past the communal tent where the off-duty guys were relaxing. He heard their banter. And the sound of gunfire. Through the open flap he could see they were watching a movie. What Adam didn't see was the man watching him. Tucked away in the extra-dark shadows thrown by the large expanse of canvas, Peter observed his colleague climb into the driving seat of the nearest 4x4. There was the whine of the starter motor and the engine kicked into life. The vehicle inched forward, out of the Agency's enclosure and into the main, sprawling base. As Adam disappeared from view Peter raised the sat phone to his ear.

"Hello?" the voice at the other end said.

"He's gone."

"Right. I will inform higher and ensure they brief the Chief and PM."

"What do you want me to do?" Peter asked.

"Nothing, let's just see how the Americans react. Keep me informed."

The phone went dead and Peter pushed the antennae down, snapping it securely back into place. He felt a pang of guilt at the thought of using Adam. But he quickly reasoned with himself that it was Adam who was taking the initiative and anyway, this was why they had recruited him. From the day Peter met Adam at the Court Marshall centre in Catterick it was always going to end this way. He was an asset, no different from any other he'd used over many years. There was a bigger picture to all this. There always was.

Oblivious to Peter and his moral dilemma Adam drove to the part of the camp that housed the locally employed contractors, halted and went inside the living quarters. He waved the ID under the nose of the marine guard who sat, bored, at the entrance, and marched quickly off to look for the section where the interpreters were bedded down. He didn't get that far. Half way down the corridor Adam met the young Afghan who had been translating for him. The youth was on his way to the washroom, clutching a towel to his chest.

"There's no time for that. I need you now. Take your stuff back to your quarters and then we'll go and find Lal-Jan."

The interpreter scampered back the way he had just come. Within a minute he had returned, pulling a jacket on as he approached.

"So where is he?" Peter asked.

The man nodded down a side passage and they entered a room at the end of it. The sleeping quarters were dominated by a threadbare prayer mat in the centre of the floor. The metal bunk beds were arranged around it: clothes, towels and cooking utensils tucked in wherever there was a space. Adam spotted his man curled up under a blanket. He gripped his shoulder and shook him firmly, saying his name at the same time. Lal-Jan leapt up.

"Yes?" he said, confusion and sleep lending him an air of bewilderment.

"We need to talk," Adam said through the interpreter. "Do you have somewhere quiet we can go?"

"Down here," came the bleary reply.

Lal-Jan led the way to the brilliantly lit prefabricated mess area. He slumped down on one side of a table, with Adam stationed opposite, the interpreter at the end.

"Please?" Lal-Jan said.

"What did they want when they arrested you?" Adam asked.

"Nothing, they knew of my past, nothing more."

"Yet they let you go, why?"

"Because I am working for you, Peter vouched for me."

"Tell me about the Taliban finance minister."

Lal-Jan looked at Adam quizzically, as if he had just been asked the most stupid question in the world.

"I'm not sure what you mean."

"Yes you do. He comes to Afghanistan once a year to dole out money for the war. It's common knowledge. You know who he is."

"I was merely one of many fighters. I wasn't involved at that level. They would never let me know," Lal-Jan lied badly.

"Ok," Adam said, standing. He towered over Lal-Jan. "Let's get this straight. One word from me and they will sling you back into custody and you will never see your family again. Help me and I will ensure you get home to Kachkai. I will also make sure you have enough money in your pocket to keep you comfortable for a few years."

Lal-Jan didn't need long to make up his mind. He was used to trading information and loyalty – if you could call it that – for cash. These were no more than business transactions, trading arrangements, and in this case a matter of expediency. While the money would be nice so would staying out of jail. He sighed.

"His name is Hakimulla Mahsud a professor of theology in Pakistan."

"Where do they meet?"

"I'm not sure, high in the mountains, I can't…" Lal-Jan stopped short.

"You have come this far. You need to tell me now," Adam pressed.

"Jamadar kalay, northwest of Kabul."

"How far is that from here?" asked Adam, finally sitting down. "By road, how many hours?"

Lal-Jan shrugged.

"Maybe six hours until we get to the base of the mountain trails, then probably a day of walking from there to reach the village."

"Right, get your gear," Adam said standing up once more.

"What? What do you mean?" Lal-Jan asked, more than a hint of alarm in his voice.

"You'd rather stay here? I guarantee you will be in jail by the morning if you do. Now get your stuff." Adam turned to the interpreter. "You too. I'll meet you by the truck."

When the trio had congregated outside, Adam ushered the young Pakistani into the seat behind the steering wheel and Lal-Jan into the rear.

"Do you have your LEC badge?" Adam asked the driver.

"Yes Sir."

Adam swivelled round to look at the man sitting in the back.

"Lal-Jan I want you to put your hood up and say nothing. Just keep your eyes towards the floor."

Lal-Jan didn't reply but flicked his cloak over his head and stooped forwards. The 4x4 manoeuvred to the security post where

Adam jumped out with the driver's LEC ID and Rocky's pass in his hand. His own pass was around his neck. The marine sergeant eyed him sceptically as he approached. Dressed in his local clothing and sporting a long dark beard Adam knew the NCO would be wary until he identified himself. Holding up his ID he spoke quietly.

"Evening Sergeant."

"Yes Sir, how can I help?" the sergeant inquired.

"I just need to book out. Here are our temporary IDs which we were issued on arrival."

Adam took off his badge and passed it over for inspection together with the other two. The marine took the badges and studied them quickly before he looked down at his clipboard to which the patrol and movement forecast was attached.

"Sir, I have no information as regards you leaving the base."

"It's a short-notice op. I'm working with the Task Force setting up some local community contacts," Adam nodded towards the CIA HQ.

"I just have to crosscheck these IDs with our database."

"No problem, be quick will you. I'm already behind schedule."

The sergeant went over to a desk on which was plonked a large computer screen. Adam noted the layer of dust and grime covering it. He was a surprised it was working. Taking the ID cards one at a time the marine laboriously typed in the names of Adam Caine and Rocky Mallon.

"You arrived two days ago, is that right?" the sergeant asked, continuing to stare at the computer.

"That's right, we're a British NGO team on a fact-finding trip to Eastern Afghanistan," Adam explained.

"Ah right. Not what it says here, though."

"Well let's just call us NGO reps, eh?" Adam played along. "Seriously we're in a rush here; can you just book us out so we can get moving?"

Adam glanced back at the vehicle and the two men sitting inside.

He watched as another marine guard circled it, before stopping at the offside rear door and pushing his nose up against the glass.

"Is that us? Can we go?" Adam asked again of the marine sergeant, trying to sound irritated rather than nervous.

"I just need to call through to the JOC, make sure they have you logged down with your movement trace and flap sheet."

"Well can I get moving at least?"

The sergeant didn't answer. Instead he lifted the phone and pressed four digits.

"JOC security, hello?" came a voice over the receiver, loud enough that Adam could hear.

"Yes, this is S3 security at the main gate, we have a vehicle leaving with three pax. Can you give me confirmation please?"

"Sure – just a moment. Can you give me their details?"

The sergeant looked down so he could recount the information on the IDs. Adam decided it was time to move. With the sergeant distracted he bolted for the door and bounded down the two steps. If he could make it look like he had clearance from the S3, then the gate sentry would open the barrier and let him through. It was all a game of bluff. Jumping into his seat he yelled to the marine still loitering by the car.

"Right, all clear. Swing her open will you?"

"Yes Sir," came the marine's instinctive response to an order. He stepped back as a colleague unbolted the sheet metal exit. The vehicle engine kicked into life and the interpreter crept it towards the slowly widening gap in the perimeter fence. Adam could feel himself sweating. As soon as the sergeant had completed the call to the JOC he would realise there was no record of him being authorised to leave the compound. But if he could get clear while the call was still in progress then they'd be able to spin off into the night and quickly bury themselves in the back streets of Khost.

Not wanting to look around at the S3 post Adam kept his eyes fixed on the two marines who were now covering the open gate and lifting the barrier that was the last remaining obstacle between the occupants of the camp and the rest of Afghanistan. The pole was halfway up when Adam heard the call from behind him.

"Just hold it there," the sergeant barked. "Drop the barrier."

Immediately the marines dropped the barrier and took up positions watching the open ground ahead of the gaping gates. Adam held his breath; cursing. The marine sergeant tapped the window sharply with the end of his weapon. Adam slowly wound down the window.

"Sir, the JOC wants me to give you an out of bounds box which is effective as of 0800 hours tomorrow morning. It's on the west side of the town."

"Oh right, ok, thanks." Adam said with a sense of relief he was sure was all too obvious. He opened up his map and took the top off a permanent lumicolour stuffed in the door pocket. "What are the grid references and over-flight category?"

Adam dutifully noted down what he was told.

"Thanks Sergeant. I really need to be moving now. I appreciate your help."

"No problem Sir and good luck," the sergeant replied with a smile. "Lift the barrier."

"Drive slowly out of the gate and take the first turn left," Adam instructed the young Pakistani sat in the driver's seat. Leaving the camp Adam sighed, not quite sure how they had been allowed out.

"Ok lets get some distance between us and them," Adam said and turned to look at Lal-Jan who was till staring at the foot well. "You can breath again now."

Half a mile behind them the marine sergeant moved back inside the S3 post and sat behind his computer to make a record of the vehicle and occupants – two British soldiers and a Pakistani interpreter – who had just left. The phone rang and he answered it.

"S3, hello?"

"Have they gone?"

"Yes Sir, just a couple of minutes ago."

The line went dead. At the other end the JOC duty watch keeper turned to Cyrus Vincent, who was standing over him and nodded. Cyrus pivoted on his heels and headed for his office.

Chapter 14
KHALID BASHIR – THE HINDU KUSH

The 4x4 twisted and turned on the pitted track, forcing – yet again – the men in the rear to brace themselves against the metal sides and tailgate of the open-back truck. If the ancient Toyota Hilux had ever had reasonable suspension it had long since succumbed to the battering inflicted by some of the worst roads in the world.

Khalid swore as one of the other passengers lost his grip and slammed against him, the stench of his breath and body odour compounding the unpleasantness of the experience. He wriggled about, trying to find a more comfortable position but there was none, every inch of space taken up by a jumble of limbs, bodies and weapons: a whole arsenal of AK47s, PKMs and RPGs sticking out in all directions, a clutch of rockets protruded skywards from a sack as if a bag of baguettes.

Khalid didn't like being in the company of the arms or their owners. The fighters were amateurs and in their current configuration as part of a small convoy – a similarly laden truck was in front of Khalid's vehicle and another behind – they made an enticing target for any passing helicopter or government patrol.

———•———

The day had started early. Khalid was up, washed and packed by 0500 hours and by 0545 hours he was at the mosque for the call to prayer. After making his peace with God he returned to his room to find it already had an occupant.

"Are you Khalid Bashir?" the man had asked brusquely.

Khalid was irritated by both the visitor's manner and his intrusion.

"My name is Khalid Bashir, son of Farouk Bashir from Kachkai

Village in Northwest Pakistan. Who are you?"

"I have been waiting for you for thirty minutes," the man continued angrily ignoring the question. "My men have been waiting here for you. You are late."

"Maybe if you remember your faith and pray more to Allah he might give you some wisdom and some manners."

"Follow me," the man answered, moving forward to try and pass Khalid. But Khalid stood his ground in the doorway, determined to assert his authority.

"I will follow you when you tell me your name."

"Hafiz."

"Well Hafiz, grab hold of this."

Khalid picked his bundle from the table and threw it hard at the troublesome guest who had no choice but to catch it. Then he reached down and retrieved his own AK47. Now he was ready to go, on his terms. "Come on then."

Khalid allowed the man – a sour look on his face – just enough space to squeeze past. From the outset, the tiny group of trucks had steered clear of the major highways, sticking instead to the ancient drover routes forged over centuries by countless sets of hooves and more recently, by mechanically powered contraptions like their own. But progress was constantly impeded, not just by the state of the roads but the other traffic, often trains of animals herded without any sense of urgency by their minders. The job of propelling the beasts to market was clearly not one for the healthiest, most economically productive men folk. Instead it seemed to invariably fall either to the old and withered, or children with stick-thin legs that appeared barely strong enough to carry them over the harsh terrain.

Trying to ignore the stinking oaf at his left shoulder, Khalid shuffled on his arse and half-turned towards the slight youth who was jammed in beside him to the right. In his hand he grasped a folder. Khalid tried to raise a smile.

"Who are you?"

"Noor."

"What are you doing here, Noor?"

"I am an accountant," Noor replied, pulling the file closer to his chest.

"You are an accountant? For the Taliban? You work for the finance minister?"

"Not me," Noor answered innocently. "That would be Haji Mohammed Agha by whom I am employed. He looks after the accounts and ensures the money is collected. Each time the minister comes to Afghanistan he shows him the books detailing the payments."

"And from whom are the payments collected?"

"Village elders, wakiles, the local imams, warlords, those who run the opium into Northern Pakistan, rich Jihadi who want to support the fight against the infidels."

Noor seemed pleased someone was interested in his contribution to the struggle. Khalid imagined it was rare that anyone paid much attention to him.

"Where does the money go?" Khalid asked as the vehicle hit a rock and he was tossed forward.

"Across the border and on to Quetta. From there I have no idea."

"Do you do this all the time?" Khalid pressed, nodding towards the paperwork still clutched to the boy's breast.

Noor couldn't suppress a big grin.

"No, this is my first time. Normally Agha would bring it. But he is getting old and he is sick. He has asked me to do it for him. It is a great honour for me."

Khalid studied the boy. He was trying hard to grow a beard but all he had managed to acquire were a few isolated wisps and tufts of hair. There remained an innocence about him that was long gone from the furrowed faces of their travelling companions. As much as the boy yearned to be like them he wasn't. Khalid wondered whether he would ever lose the bookish look and nervous disposition. That he was a Hazara did little to inspire confidence that he would ever truly fit in with the Afghan Pashtuns around him.

"An honour indeed. And important work. Don't worry Noor," Khalid said soothingly. "Stick close to me. You'll be fine."

Noor offered Khalid a weak smile and they both settled into a silence as their vehicle, sandwiched by the others, rumbled on, a constant cloud of dust threatening to choke them. They had already passed, hurriedly, through Mazar-e-Sharif; seen and avoided a couple of government patrols; and stopped briefly for chai and something to eat in a compound inhabited by a family who had little sympathy for their cause but were too scared not to offer hospitality. For 30 minutes they had followed the track as it gained height before levelling off as it plateaued out onto a wide open plain.

It took them another half an hour to traverse to the northern edge of the ground where the terrain rose again, but much more sharply. What had been flat abruptly turned into seemingly near vertical, as if a giant had grabbed hold of one corner of the landscape and yanked it up. They halted at the base of the escarpment where a group of scrawny, miserable-looking donkeys awaited them. The vehicles began to disgorge their human cargo. Only Khalid and Noor remained seated, watching the others busy themselves, taking orders from an elderly man wearing a prayer cap who had emerged from the front of the lead truck.

"Everyone out. Drivers, as soon as we've unloaded you are to go back to Mazar-e-Sharif. You will return to this point by midday in two-days time."

Without hurry Khalid and Noor climbed out to join the others, taking with them what was most previous to each: Khalid his rifle and

Noor the sheaf of documents.

"Careful, please!" the accountant cried as he saw one of the guards carelessly fling down the bundles – cotton-wrapped packages – that had been strapped to the roof of their truck. Hafiz ignored the plea, aggressively pushing past the boy to retrieve one of the parcels that now lay in the dirt. Despite his surly behaviour Khalid guessed he was of little importance in the grand scheme of things. Like Hafiz, few of the other travellers hid their resentment – or was it actually jealousy? – of Noor, but Khalid sensed that the callow youth was the most important figure amongst them, not because of who he was but what he represented.

"I need to count the bundles as you pack them onto the donkeys," Noor insisted.

He scurried about trying to reconcile what he knew he had started the trip in Kabul with, with what he now found before him. Khalid had a fair idea what the parcels contained. Money. A lot of it. What else would an accountant be transporting? He saw Hafiz give him a scornful look then whisper to the elder.

"Why do you not help?" the old commander asked, approaching Khalid.

"I am not here to load your animals. I am a warrior. You make sure the donkeys are packed and you make sure we make it to the shura on time. This is not my task, it is yours."

"You are the foreign fighter trained by the British?"

"That is none of your business. Your men only need know I am a Jihadi who is fighting the infidel."

Khalid took a pace forward, threateningly. The old man didn't want to back down to Khalid. So he hesitated, sizing up his opponent, deciding whether to continue the confrontation and enter a trial of strength. Eventually he thought better of it and wheeled away, shouting more orders to the others, most of who had witnessed the standoff and made their own assessment of where the authority really lay. Khalid breathed a sigh of relief. Now everyone in the party understood he was not someone to be messed with. He'd created an aura of importance. His association with the most senior Taliban figures had been neither confirmed nor denied but it had been hinted at and that offered him protection. He doubted there would be a challenge to his position again. Except possibly from Hafiz who did little to hide his resentment towards either Khalid or Noor.

The ascent of the mountainside to the saddle between two ragged peaks took the best part of four strenuous hours, the donkeys doing the heavy lifting, carrying food, weapons and ammunition, and the bundles of money. As they approached the crest a vast landscape, hitherto hidden by the curtain of rock and scree they'd laboured up, was gradually revealed. As more of it became visible it was abundantly clear why the infidels had never managed to subdue the Taliban nor capture significant amounts of territory. Like the Russians most recently and the imperial armies before them, it was the terrain as much as its inhabitants that defeated the aggressors. Little wonder Bin Laden had not been caught in the Tora Bora; it was a natural, impregnable fortress, immune to siege and assault. Bin Laden's only mistake had been to leave such a sanctuary.

Positioned at the back of the train, a bundle and brown cloak slung over his right shoulder, rifle over the left, Khalid watched as the column of men and pack animals started to descend. The path twisted and turned with the contours and the travellers came in and went out of view as they followed its meandering route between rock formations and beneath escarpments. Immediately ahead of Khalid was the boy. Intermittently, Khalid could hear Noor talking with those he walked with, but what was being said remained indistinct. In the distance, and still far below, lay lush pastures; a vivid splash of green at odds with the desolate environment that dominated the view. Scattered across the pocket of lushness, like pebbles, were clusters of houses. Fingers of smoke rose above them. Khalid had never been here before; never visited these villages, but he knew exactly what they would be like. He could picture mothers and daughters cooking meals, men and their sons bringing in the sheep and goats and corralling them for the night. Soon it would be time for them to attend the mosques and afterwards eat. At last they would be able to sleep, enveloped by the protection the mountains offered. Khalid thought of what he had lost; his own family and the warmth they provided. He caught sight of a pair of children – still too young to be helping in the kitchen or tending the livestock – running along a path that dissected the fields, illuminated by the intensifying orange glow of the setting sun. Fluttering above their heads was a kite. Khalid did not know how to react. The innocent scene was as bitterly depressing as it was uplifting. It signalled everything that was right in the world yet also everything he had been deprived of. He could cling only to this fragment of hope: that his father was still alive. Through his own efforts lay the opportunity to be reunited with the old man and the slimmest chance of a sliver of contentment and calm. A shrill voice broke his daydreaming.

"We will be staying here tonight," Noor cried out, relaying the message that had been passed down the line.

Surprised, Khalid pressed past the others to find the commander.

"We are staying here? Why? Surely it is safer on the valley floor."

"I have been told not to go any further this evening. We are to wait here until tomorrow then go into the main village, there at the point where the river disappears from sight," the old man raised a bony finger to indicate the watercourse that cut through the scene laid before them.

"Is that where the shura will take place?"

"I think so. That is where it has been held every time I have been here."

"Does the place have a name?" Khalid asked looking down, tracing the river.

"It is known as Haji Jamadar kalay after the village elder and owner of the land," the old man explained. "He fought the Russians in the 1980s as part of the Mujahedeen under Massoud, the Lion of Panshir. He lost a leg and an eye but still he fought on and would be fighting today if he weren't too old. He is a great Jihadi."

"But if he fought with Massoud he would have been part of the Northern Alliance, an enemy of the Taliban?"

"My enemy's enemy is my friend," the old man said with a shrug. "And Haji Jamadar hates the West, hates the US and Britain. He has vowed to get rid of them, no matter what it takes and with whom he has to forge allegiances."

"Are you sure he can be trusted? Maybe his loyalties can be bought like so many of our Muslim brothers?"

"He lost one of his sons to the Russians, the other two to a US bombing raid in 2004 along with his daughter's husband. I trust him more than…"

The old man paused.

"Me?" Khalid finished the sentence. "You trust him more than you trust me?"

"Maybe…" his voice trailed off. "There's a small cave just up that slope. We will light a fire there, inside the entrance and out of view, and get some rest. The donkeys remain here with a guard."

Khalid hung back as the Talibs scrambled up the steep incline to his right and disappeared from view into a shadowy cleft in the rock. Only when he had checked that his pistol was secure beneath his clothing did he make to follow them. Noor was just ahead, skipping about, a child on an adventure.

The sun had dropped behind the mountain and darkness had smothered everything. But for the flicker of the fire, it would have been pitch black. Khalid had already considered what he would do once the moon rose and there was just enough natural light to see by. As best he could he would carry out a visual survey of the kalay, in particular the routes in and out. There wouldn't be time or opportunity to carry out a full close target recce as he'd been taught at Sandhurst, but at least he'd be able to identify a likely escape route that didn't retrace his steps.

Waiting, Khalid rested against the wall of the cavern, watching the fighters and their distorted shadows flitting about. Food was the focus of their attention; a heavy, blackened pot rested on the hollow pillar of rocks that surrounded the burning wood. In due course people started to dig into the communal vessel.

"Khalid, please come and eat," Noor shouted.

Khalid eased himself up and walked towards the group, stooping to avoid the low, jagged ceiling. Without saying a word he ripped off a hunk of the bread and cast around in the pot for his share of the rice, then retreated to his spot in the darkness to consume what he had just taken. He wouldn't have said so to any of his travelling companions, but the sustenance was welcome. Warm and filling, he realised it was what he had needed. Satisfied, he sat back against the granite. He resisted the temptation to go to sleep. Several of the others remained by the fire long after they had finished eating. Eventually there were just three left. Plus Noor. For a while they chatted in hushed tones. At last they all got up and made towards the exit. Despite the gloom, Khalid managed to catch the boy's eye and beckoned him over.

"Where are you going Noor?" Khalid whispered.

"They asked me to help with the donkeys. Make sure they're tethered and have something to eat. I thought I should help. I'm not tired," Noor replied. Before Khalid could respond he had turned and scurried after the others, out of the cave and away down the slope.

Khalid frowned, feeling uneasy. These men had all shown an open dislike for Noor so why encourage him to come out and help with the animals? Was it a trap? Noor was naïve and physically weak and if the others turned on him then there would be little he could do to protect himself. Noor's youth and innocence, his slight body and almost feminine features, the vulnerability that was a product of his youth and his personality: all this would make him attractive to the men. In a physical way. There was every chance the men did not want Noor to check the donkeys, nor that they wanted to simply beat him up, but that they intended to rape him. Khalid tried to convince himself this wasn't his problem; that the sexual abuse of young boys was a cultural habit; disagreeable, repulsive, grotesque but not unusual; that Noor was not his responsibility.

But his uneasiness lingered. Nothing about Afghanistan could be described as easy. Life conspired against you from the moment you were born. Poverty and all that stemmed from it – malnourishment, lack of education, illness and disease – were compounded by rough justice and repeated bouts of war. But for all routine hardship common to the region, Khalid's own upbringing had been as benign as any could be. His family had kept him safe and protected him. They had shown him love. Nowhere along the way was he subjected to the pain and embarrassment he feared Noor was about to endure.

Khalid remained motionless straining to hear what was happening outside but the only noises he could distinguish were the snores and occasional sleepy mutterings of the other Talibs sprawled about him.

Khalid got to his feet and padded to the cave entrance. He tried to peer down to where the asses were tethered but could not get a clear view. Against his better judgment but true to his own definition of the honour code he slipped down the hillside looking for the others who had left five minutes before. It was after slithering halfway down the slope that he heard the whimpering of a child: fear, pain and humiliation mixed together in a deep sobbing. Khalid followed the miserable cries. He swung around a craggy boulder and stopped in his tracks.

Noor was sat on the ground, his long shirt pulled down over his knees. He was without his trousers. They had been removed and tossed on the floor in a heap. One of the three men stood behind Noor, his own trousers around his ankles, a hand beneath his flowing, loose fitting shirt, working away at his groin, a look of excitement and lust spread across his sweaty face. His colleagues laughed expectantly, goading him on.

Khalid saw the tears streaming down Noor's cheeks, the marks and cuts on the side of his head testament to the pounding he must have suffered before being forced onto the dirt to submissively take his final punishment. Khalid locked eyes with the man whose trousers were at half-mast.

"What do you want you Western pig?" the man spat out from between blackened, rotten teeth.

"This is my friend," Khalid said, wanting to avoid a fight but struggling and failing to hide his anger. "I will not see him abused. You know the Koran. You have read it. It says you should not lie with another man. So what you are doing here goes against God's teaching."

"You should not dare to quote the words of Allah to me and my men. Who are you to preach to us? You have given yourself over to Western ways. You might call yourself a Muslim but you aren't one."

The venom in the man's voice, the same man who had collected Khalid from Kabul, made it clear diplomacy wasn't going to work. Already aroused, he and his henchmen were intent on taking their turns with Noor and they were not prepared to let Khalid interrupt.

Without warning Khalid stepped forward at speed, producing the clasp knife from beneath his cloak. Hampered by his state of undress the rapist was at a disadvantage. He made a clumsy lunge but Khalid sidestepped the lurching figure and got behind him, grabbing his head and snapping it back to fully expose the weathered neck. Grasping the knife with an overhand grip he ran the blade savagely across the skin. The metal sliced easily through the flesh and as Khalid drew it clear a spray of arterial blood gushed into the air. The smirks on the faces of the other two men had already evaporated, to be replaced with masks of shock as their dying colleague tried and failed to shout out. The carotid artery continued to spew blood, the fountain only easing as the victim's heart failed, leaving the rich, thick liquid to gently flow down the chest of what was now a corpse.

Khalid let the body slump to the ground and took up a defensive position facing the others. For a second they remained rooted to the spot, aghast at the sight of their mutilated colleague, a wide ragged gash beneath his chin. Then simultaneously they found their feet, scrambling back towards the cave. Noor remained on his knees, his head buried in his hands.

"Noor," Khalid said. "Noor, are you ok?"

The boy started to speak but he didn't look up, cowed by shame and guilt. He wept abjectly.

"I thought they were my friends. Why would they do those brutal things?"

"I am your friend. Let me help you," Khalid offered. With sensitivity he placed a hand on Noor's shoulders, an act completely at odds with the mortal violence he had just been responsible for. He leaned down and took the boy's arm, gently easing him up as he clung on to his trousers. Noor fumbled at his waist to secure the garment and Khalid turned slightly away to allow him some privacy, only to be met with a hammer blow. There was a blinding flash across his eyes and a shooting pain through his temple as the butt of the AK47 smashed into the side of his head. He dropped to his knees and then onto all fours, disorientated but just about clinging on to consciousness. He tried to twist to look at the assailant standing astride him but all he saw was the blur of the rifle stock arcing towards him again. There was no chance to get out of its path and this time it smacked him just above the left eye.

———•———

By the time he awoke he had been trussed up – ankles and wrists tied, head dangling between his outstretched arms – and slung over the back of a donkey. A deep, nausea-inducing ache wracked his skull, made a million times worse every time the animal took another step and jolted its human cargo. He felt dampness on his face. He managed to press his forehead against his sleeve and was unsurprised to see the crimson stain left behind when he pulled it away. Gingerly he swivelled his head. From his position the world was upside down. Just in front of him he could see Noor. His clothes were dirtied too; a bloody mark on the seat of his trousers a stark and very public indication of the buggering he'd received.

"Noor," Khalid tried to call but his mouth was dry. "Noor, hey Noor," he croaked.

It was enough. The boy looked behind him. There was immense sadness in his eyes, the pummelling he had taken sickeningly obvious. His expression, his wounds, the stain on his rear; no one would be in any doubt of what he had been subjected to. His humiliation was complete.

Khalid felt a profound sorrow, the strength of which he had not experienced since he learned of the loss of his family. His mercy was that the before he could linger on the injustice he had slipped back into darkness.

Chapter 15
HAKIMULLA MAHSUD – JAMADAR KALAY

The sunlight poured through the doorway, making Khalid blink. Backlit by the ball of fire a guard stood silhouetted in the aperture, his features impossible to discern. Stepping from behind this cut-out-of-a-man a second shadowy figure revealed himself and came towards the prisoner. Leaning forward to speak to Khalid his anonymity was preserved by the brilliance at his back, though when he spoke it could not conceal the stink of his breath.

"You will come with us," the guard instructed, simultaneously pulling a dagger from his belt and slitting the cloth that constrained Khalid's legs.

"Where are we going?" Khalid managed to ask.

"To see Haji Jamadar the village elder."

Khalid judged it to have been late in the morning, the sun almost at its zenith, when they had entered the village. By his estimate it was now several hours later and the day was well on its way to being over. In a couple of hours it would be dark again, a shroud once more drawn over the valley and its occupants. With his hands still clamped tightly together Khalid was led out of the compound he had been held in and along an uneven track that followed the meanderings of a river. After half a mile they turned abruptly right and strode over a rickety wooden bridge that was without railings and barely wide enough to take a cart. A few hundred metres ahead lay a cluster of buildings, a sizeable, stout compound at its heart. Approaching it they passed several labourers tilling a field with hand tools that had probably not changed in design for hundreds if not thousands of years. The workers made a point of ignoring Khalid's party, either uninterested in something the like of which they saw on a regular basis or smart enough not to show too much concern in business that did not concern them. The group came to a pair of gates, buckled by use and the weather, which marked the entrance to the larger premises. With the agreement of a sentry who controlled access they strode into the courtyard. Its layout was unexceptional, little different from every other such place Khalid had found himself in: at its heart was a raised dais for cooking on. As if to confirm its purpose it was populated by women fussing around the hearth. They too barely acknowledge what was going on under their noses, as if a bound man being led through their home at gunpoint was a regular occurrence. The prisoner party continued to the far corner of the compound and a door, painted garish red, which sat half open. Standing beside it was the man who had led the convoy through the mountains. He gazed at Khalid blankly then stepped back to fully reveal what was through the opening. The room beyond was illuminated by light streaming in through a row of small windows set high along one wall. A large, brightly coloured carpet dominated the room. It was covered with cushions on which, arranged in a circle sat eight, mostly elderly, men. Their age and their appearance – clothes that were similar in style to those worn by everyone else in Afghanistan but of better cloth, cleaner and without tears; long, grey beards that would have taken a lifetime to cultivate – marked them out as individuals of some significance within their communities. Each man had a glass of chai before him. The sturdy metal kettle used to make the brew sat steaming in their midst perched on a slab of stone. Khalid was manoeuvred to the perimeter of the circle.

"Salaam Alaikum," Khalid said in greeting, dipping his head slightly in respect.

"My name is Haji Mohammed Jamadar," replied the ancient-looking man directly opposite him.

Khalid would have recognised him without the introduction for

Haji Jamadar made no attempt to hide the vacant socket where his left eye had once been. Neither was the roughly carved wooden prosthetic that served as a left leg concealed from view.

"Greetings to you Haji Mohammed Jamadar and may Allah look down on you with favour."

"Greeting to you Khalid Bashir, son of Farouk Bashir from Kachkai village. Welcome to my village and may Allah protect you while you are here."

"Your words are kind and your wisdom legendary," Khalid replied, continuing the ritual of respect, well aware that whatever Jamadar said now guaranteed nothing in terms of his safety in the minutes and hours ahead.

"As is your skill and bravery against the infidels who would destroy our country," Jamadar said with a smile that soon faded. "But there has been a serious complaint made against you by the commander of these fighters. He says you killed one of his men. Why would he say that if it was not the case?"

"I humbly tell you that things are as he claims," Khalid nodded, again with a slight bow of deference. "By the grace of Allah, these are charges I happily plead guilty to."

"I have known Sardre Mohammed many years. He preaches the word of the prophet and he is a loyal and brave fighter. He is angered by the death of one of his followers."

"Is it a brave fighter, a student of the prophet Mohammed, who would let his men shame a young man against his will? To beat him, to abuse him, merely because he was young and vulnerable and they themselves were weak in body and soul?" Khalid replied softly. "Would you tolerate such a violation happening to a youth of this village such as that I witnessed against this boy who has come here to be at your service? If that is the case then I fight for the wrong reasons and Mohammed will surely abandon us all."

Khalid knew he was taking a gamble, but he calculated that the old warrior would not approve of such behaviour against someone so young.

Jamadar turned his attention on Sardre who stood in the shadows.

"Is this true?"

"My men had their pleasure with the boy but it was with his consent, he…"

Khalid cut him short.

"They beat him you lying son of a donkey. They hit and kicked him and they humiliated him and you allowed it," Khalid shouted stepping towards Sardre who had also taken a pace forward. Only the intervention of the guards stopped them from coming to blows.

"Wait!" ordered Jamadar, trying to re-stamp his authority on the proceedings. "Bring me the boy."

Noor must have been just outside for he appeared almost immediately, led in and paraded before the group, cowed and overwhelmed by the attention he was receiving and the reason for it.

"Why did you come here, young man?" Jamadar asked.

"To deliver money from Sher Agha," Noor said meekly, looking intently at his feet.

"Did these men shame you on your journey here?" Jamadar asked. Noor could not bring himself to verbally acknowledge the abuse but he did give an almost imperceptible nod.

"Were you willing or did they force themselves on you?"

Noor hesitated, caught on the horns of a dilemma, conscious that as a result of what he said someone, possibly he, was likely to lose their life. He decided in favour of the man who had stood up for him.

"They tried to force themselves on me and Khalid stopped them. Later, when I was on my own four of them shamed me again as a punishment for what had happened. I did not ask for it and I do not understand it."

Noor started to cry.

Murmuring bubbled up amongst the members of the shura; then the argument over what should happen became more heated. Voices were raised and fingers were pointed, though amongst the anger and the outrage Jamadar remained calm, speaking softly but with assertion. He was almost spiritual in his manner. Eventually he raised a hand. It was enough to hush the others.

"It is clear to me that Sardre's men abused this boy and Khalid Bashir tried to prevent it." He paused. "Yet this led to a death. I cannot allow the killing of one of Sardre's men by Khalid to go unpunished, however this did not happen in my village and therefore under Pashtu law it is not for me to take action against the perpetrator or ask for recompense for the dead man's family. We must wait until the arrival of Hakimulla Mahsud who will decide what action will be taken."

Jamadar had delivered his judgment.

———◆———

Khalid was pulled outside and directed just a few yards to a corner of Jamadar's compound where the final flickers of the evening sun still radiated. His position allowed him to witness the continuing stream of people coming and going, groups and individuals, all men, who would wait their turn outside the red door for an audience with Jamadar and the shura, for his wasn't the only business being sorted that day; these people too would have opportunity to present whatever grievance they demanded justice for or defend themselves against the allegations of others. Only one of the passers-by spared any particular attention to the man crouched against the dusty, crumbling wall. He had the deep blue eyes of a Hazari. Briefly he stopped and used them to stare at Khalid. A glimmer of recognition shot across his face, but his brow also furrowed as if he was puzzling where their paths might have previously crossed. Khalid was equally baffled. He also sensed they had met before but he was confused at his presence at the shura. The Hazaras' opposition to the Pashtun-led insurgency should have made him an uncomfortable visitor but he did not display any unease. A few seconds passed yet it brought no enlightenment as to their acquaintance and the man edged away.

Khalid studied all those who passed by but he remained none the wiser as to which one Hakimulla Mashud might be. No one stood out by either the entourage they travelled with or the preference they were shown.

The work of the shura continued unabated. Intermittently Khalid could hear raised voices from within the meeting room but never quite loud enough for him to be able to distinguish what was being said or who was saying it. The only other sound was the howling of dogs whose job it was to signal the presence of strangers. Their persistent yelping underlined the level of activity taking place.

The night had fully closed in; the only exception to the total darkness, a blade of light that stabbed through the gap created by the meeting room door standing ajar.

It must have been at least an hour after the last of the daylight had been banished that Khalid saw Sardre again. He swept past and disappeared into the meeting chamber accompanied by two of his men. Several paces behind trotted Noor, looking utterly crushed; his face still to the ground, shoulders hunched. Then it was Khalid's turn. An aide approached where he was being kept at gunpoint and indicated that he too should present himself to the shura. Stiff from the growing cold he stood and awkwardly did as he was bid, making for the beacon of brightness. Crossing the threshold he saw Haji Jamadar remained in his position as head of the gathering, a cup of chai still in front of him, the kettle still steaming. Khalid also recognised some of the other faces from earlier, but there were some new additions: the Hazara with the piercing eyes, and next to Jamadar a man with a huge turban which sat at an angle on his head. Khalid couldn't quite conclude why, but he thought this new comer was a man of education, a teacher maybe, perhaps of religion. His face and hands were clean and, Khalid noticed that his fingernails were neat; not dirty, torn and broken like those of everyone else occupying the space. It was this man who was first to speak to Khalid. He didn't stand on ceremony.

"You are the bomb maker?"

"Yes I am."

"I have heard many stories about you," the man went on. "My name is Mahsud."

Khalid's eyes widened, but he didn't miss a beat, betrayed no surprise.

"Then it is you I have come to serve."

"Haji Jamadar has told me what happened, that you killed one of Mohammed Sardre's men and you freely admit to it."

"I did, Sir," Khalid replied. "I did it to protect the boy who also serves you by bringing money from Sher Agha to enable us to continue the fight against the infidels."

"You were trained by the infidels were you not?" Mahsud asked, reaching out to pick at the latest offering of flat bread that had been laid before the council.

"I was trained by the British to serve in Pakistan." Khalid began to tell his story. Even the abridged version took him several minutes to recount. "But the very people I tried to serve murdered my mother and sister and I vowed to fight them until my last breath."

"And you have been very successful haven't you, Khalid?"

"It is Allah's will."

"You are here to help these men make mines to kill more of the infidel invaders yet how can I trust you if you kill one of my men? You have taken justice into your own hands, when you know there are processes for these matters. I need people I can rely on. People with

REAPER

discipline. You do not have the power or the authority to act as you have," Mahsud said.

"I did not kill to undermine your position or because I gained pleasure from it. I killed to protect your interests and to be true to the Koran as any faithful servant of God would be. My actions were those of a true Muslim and if you decide that I must forfeit my life then I will do so in the name of the prophet."

"All of that might be the truth, but you have given me a problem. You dented my trust in you before we even met. Why did you not wait and bring your problems to me? Put your faith in me? Do you disrespect me so?" Mahsud queried.

"On the contrary. I have nothing but respect for you and the struggle you lead and for your achievements. Everything I have done is in support of your goals. My admiration for you is boundless and so is my loyalty. If that were not the case then yes, I would have stepped back and let the violation of the boy take place. I would have let your accountant's lieutenant – your lieutenant's lieutenant – be mistreated and abused. If I came across the same thing again then I would act in exactly the same way. And I would be doing it for you."

Mahsud did not respond. The silence was broken by the man with the piercing eyes.

"I have seen this man fight the enemy," he began. "I was in his presence when he executed a British soldier without mercy. It was I who filmed the death of the non-believer and who put the video on to the internet for the faithful to see and the infidels to fear. I trust this man; he is brutal to his enemies and compassionate to his companions. If he can help us make better mines that can defeat the Americans and the British then I will support him and protect him and accept responsibility for him."

Blue eyes stopped talking.

A number of the others nodded their heads in acceptance but

neither Mahsud nor Jamadar reacted.

"Khalid Bashir," Mahsud began. "I believe your actions in the protection of this boy were noble and just and I believe you were protecting the word of the Koran and the interests of the fight against the infidel. But I judge that you must compensate the family of your victim and Mohammed Sardre for the loss of one of his men. You shall pay 20,000 Afghanis to the relatives and two donkeys to Sardre. Sardre, are you in agreement?"

There was a mumble from the claimant.

"Sardre, I cannot hear you," Mahsud said sharply.

"Yes, I agree," Sardre said sullenly but more loudly.

"Khalid Bashir do you agree to this sum?"

Khalid dodged the question.

"What about the boy?"

"Payment for his shaming has already been made by the dead man. Mohammed Sardre will apologise for the actions of his other men and will undertake to protect the boy on his journey back to Kabul."

"Then I must agree to this decision," Khalid answered, before asking. "May I have back the things which were taken from me?"

Sardre himself came forward and using Khalid's own lock knife sliced the bindings that tied him before handing it back to him. Sardre walked to the door and shouted out to someone. A guard arrived with a soft bundle and Khalid's rifle and pistol. Khalid checked through his belongings. Something was missing.

"May I have my mobile phone?"

"I will give it to you after you have paid me," Sardre said coldly. He looked towards those who were seated, seeking approval. There was a general nod of heads.

"I am not in a position to give you what I owe, not here. You know I have no donkeys. So let me suggest an alternative. Here, why not take my pistol?" Khalid suggested, offering the Makarov to his creditor. The man's eyes gleamed in anticipation. What he saw before him was very much prized. He could get donkeys from anywhere – commandeer them if he liked – but the pistol was of much more value and much harder to acquire. Sardre gleefully accepted the weapon. He turned it over in his hands, inspecting his bounty, weighing it up. Satisfied with the deal he fished in his pocket and gave the Nokia back to Khalid.

"Sit, Khalid," Mahsud ushered. "We shall talk and you shall eat. I am sure you are hungry. Take some of this bread."

Khalid sat where he had been standing and crossed his legs. His possessions beside him, the phone – silent, switched off – included. He urgently needed to turn it back on but that would have to wait. Activating the mobile would be the last part of the equation. Hakimulla Mahsud, the target, was just a few feet away from him, other senior figures surrounded him. Yet to initiate the kinetic strike the phone had to be sending a signal.

The discussion about the infidels continued and brought forth a rising amount of bravado and boasting as each of those in the assembled group battled to outdo the others with their own particular tale of fighting and slaying the enemy.

Mahsud massaged the egos of his disciples, listening to their tall tales, thanking them for their troubles, praising them for their sacrifices, reassuring them that men and equipment and money would continue to flow from the high command over the Pakistan border in Quetta. But he was not afraid to remind them of the realities of what they did. There would be no quick victory, he said, and the sacrifice to come could eclipse that already made. However there were things that made their winning inevitable. Allah was their guardian and their inspiration. And patience was their virtue. Time was on their side. The infidels were far from home and sick to get back. But for the Taliban, Afghanistan, Pakistan, these places were their home, either literally or spiritually. They wouldn't be going anywhere. He explained how well the poppy harvest had gone and what revenues were being received from the taxes he levied on the drugs runners, the village elders and tribal leaders, and local businesses. He spoke of the government-run district community councils and how it was possible to ensure those who served on them were sympathetic to the cause, happy to direct funds to Taliban-promoted projects to increase income. The money was important, an essential part of the recipe that would ensure their victory.

Mahsud finished talking by indicating that it was time for Blue Eyes, to make his representation. The Taliban information officer insisted his area of activity was as critical as any other: buoying the fighters, marshalling the people, scaring the enemy.

"The global media is key to our campaign. It carries our message to every corner of the world and does our job for us, putting fear in the hearts of the Americans and British and their allies, and courage in the hearts of our brothers. By uniting Islam we will not just defeat the infidel in this country but drive them out of all Muslim lands."

Blue Eyes went on to tell the shura about the exploits of Khalid, how he had fought with great strength and bravery, how he had killed without fear, how his actions had galvanised the non-believers, how Khalid's strength emboldened them all, his strength was their strength. As he spoke he locked his eyes on Khalid and sending out a signal to those present that he vouched for the fighter and that he was an asset not a liability: man of honour and trust to be revered and protected.

"Khalid," Mahsud said. "You will leave with me tomorrow. We shall go back to your country of birth and you will help with the training of more martyrs."

"If that is your will," Khalid answered and went to stand.

"Wait, you must eat first," Jamadar interrupted.

Khalid thought quickly. After they ate Mahsud might depart, go and sleep in another village. He didn't know. It was now or never. He needed to activate the signal and then take his chances. He was in no doubt he was already being watched by satellite tracking and if he activated the phone and dumped it they would be able to trace him as he left the area. The moment he lit the target they would fire, he would never be given time to get away. He needed someone to activate the phone for him.

"May I be excused to wash my hands before I eat?" Khalid asked the forum. "I still have blood on my hands and head, I should clean up. With your permission."

"Of course," Jamadar said. "We shall pray before we eat. You should go to the river to wash."

"I shall come with you," Blue eyes said.

"If you wish," Khalid replied as he stood and walked out of the room, feeling the presence of the other man uncomfortably close behind him.

Exiting the room and walking out of the compound Khalid found Noor leant on the perimeter wall. He stopped beside him.

"What troubles you my young friend?" Khalid asked.

"I am scared of Sardre and his men. What if they blame me for the death of Hafiz? What if they shame me again?"

"They will not touch you Noor, you heard the promise Sardre made to Mahsud and Jamadar. He has taken an oath to protect you. You will be safe. It is now more than his life is worth to try anything."

Khalid reached out to hold Noor by the shoulder. He could feel the boy trembling.

"I feel so alone. I have never been away from my family before, I want to go home to be with my father and mother. When I was asked to make this trip it felt like a great honour. I wanted to help. But I never dreamed things would turn out as they have."

Khalid sighed. Noor's wishes for a peaceful life – one without guilt or fear – were not unreasonable. They mirrored his. Yet he was as far from his dream as Noor was from his. The faces of the men he had killed haunted his every waking moment and accused him as he slept: the young soldiers hoping to return home to their own families thousands of miles away; the civilians caught in the crossfire, dead without ever knowing why they died or their families ever understanding what was achieved by their slaying; the young warriors he led into battle and onwards to victory or martyrdom and who blindly believed in him. They were all there in his mind's eye; lining up to reproach him for the lies he had told, the treachery he had orchestrated, the promises he had made but failed to deliver. But he had a greater goal. To avenge his own family and make good at least on the promise he had made to his father. He would not be deflected. Could not allow it.

"Noor," Khalid said with regret. "I have a phone, why don't you call home?"

"But we are not allowed to use mobile phones here," Noor replied.

Khalid turned to Blue Eyes but said nothing; in return Blue Eyes didn't speak.

"I think it will be ok," Khalid said to the boy and handed over the Nokia. "I want you to go over there. The signal is stronger. Make the call quickly and then stay there until I come back from washing and we can go to eat. Do you understand?"

"Thank you, Khalid."

"You know how it works?"

"Yes, I have one at home. I am glad I met you Khalid, may Allah protect you."

Noor walked away from the two men towards the centre of the compound holding the phone by his side. He stopped as Khalid shouted after him.

"Just wait a few minutes before you call, so you have some privacy."

The boy smiled at him.

Khalid continued briskly towards the river, his companion in his wake. Reaching the river the other man moved beside Khalid and they both squatted at the water's edge. It was no more than ninety metres back to the compound they had just left but the building was out of sight, curtained from them by the slope of the land and the fields of maze and poppy and the dark of the night.

"You are a kind and compassionate man Khalid Bashir," Blue Eyes said.

"Thank you my friend. I'm afraid I don't know your name but I am appreciative of the words you spoke in my defence."

"Maybe it is better that you do not know my name, but I spoke because I believed in what I said. But you do leave me with some questions. I wonder why you are here and I wonder what you have been doing?" Blue Eyes said continuing to scrub his hands.

"I'm not sure what you mean," Khalid said calmly.

"You were gone for a long time. You say you were injured, a bad wound. You claim a family in Sangin cared for you," Blue Eyes continued. "But I have not seen your wounds, you do not limp, you have no scars. What could have kept you away for such a long period? Were you really hurt?"

"Do you wish to see the holes from the Western bullets," Khalid asked. "Do you want me to tell you how it felt, how it burned, how I wept with the pain?"

Khalid's mind was spinning, memories were flooding back; he was losing control. Blue Eyes had provoked a response in him that he had not expected but maybe that was exactly what his companion wanted.

"Do you know what it is like to be used by the British, taught that your culture is wrong. Worse, to hear it ridiculed? Do you know what it is like to find your family has been destroyed? Do you understand what it feels like when you are drowning, when metal handcuffs are biting into your skin and an electric current is coursing through your body? Do you know…"

Khalid stopped abruptly. He had said too much.

Blue Eyes had finished washing and was watching Khalid, listening intensely as Khalid spoke, weighing up what he was hearing, trying to make sense of what he was being told. Then the realisation hit home. The two men glared at each other, frozen by the knowledge they now both shared. For a second neither seemed sure what to do.

It was the Talib who moved first. He pushed himself to his feet but slipped on the soft mud of the embankment. With the spell broken, Khalid lunged for him, finding slightly better purchase from a patch of firmer ground. As the Talib's mouth opened to cry out Khalid clamped a hand over it stifling the sound. He twisted the man and wrenched his head back, reaching around his neck with his other arm. The Talib tried to double over and for a moment Khalid found himself astride the Talib as if catching a ride, but Khalid's weight and momentum were too much for him to bear and the pair of them collapsed onto the boggy floor.

Blue Eyes struggled to slither away, but Khalid was kneeling on top of him, not allowing him to stand. With a clenched fist he threw a hard punch into his opponent's kidneys, taking some of the wind out of him. He followed up furiously with jabs to the head while trying to wrestle the man around so he could beat his face. Again and again Khalid punched, finally landing a blow squarely on the man's nose. He felt the bone give way. There was a rush of blood, the hot sticky fluid pouring out and covering Khalid's fingers as he followed up.

With a strength and determination that flowed from the understanding that he was fighting for his life the Talib kicked desperately with his legs. Then Khalid felt a knee jerk up hard into his groin. He moaned as the sickening blow to his balls spread through his body. It was all he could do not to recoil backwards. He needed to finish his opponent.

He kept lashing out at the man's face with his fists, parrying the Talib's attempts to gouge the open wound above his left eye. With a mighty heave the Talib erupted beneath Khalid and half threw him off. The pair of them barrel-rolled in the mud. The positions were reversed; now Khalid was pinned down. He felt his opponent's rough hands grasp him by the throat, attempting to squeeze the life out of him. Instantly he started gasping for breath. He knew he would weaken quickly. There was only one chance to break the stranglehold. With a monumental effort he thrust upwards with his arms, straightening them as his hands impacted with the man's chest, using them as ramrods to push him back. He felt the fingers at his neck slip away, the nails clawing his skin.

Unsteadily, Blue Eyes scrambled to his feet, his back to the fast flowing river. Khalid remembered what he had learned on the rugby field at Sandhurst. He stooped and rushed at his enemy, dropping his shoulder as he made contact below the man's ribcage. The blow lifted Blue Eyes into the air and he collapsed into the freezing water, Khalid tumbling after him.

The shock of the icy cold made both men gasp. The Talib fought for a breath of air but Khalid forced his head under the surface, ensuring it was the glacial liquid that he sucked into his lungs. The man struggled violently. He was on the edge of life and the fear of death gave him the strength for one last effort. He flailed like a madman but, muscles tensed, Khalid kept his grip on his cloak, not allowing him to emerge. The Talib twisted in an attempt to dive away. Khalid followed him down towards the bottom of the torrent, knowing he had at least thirty seconds more air in his body than the man he was fighting. He had to make it count. Even as the resistance from the Talib eased and then ceased and Khalid's lungs began to burn he stayed under to guarantee death. Only at the last second did he erupt from the water to refill with air. The body of the Talib bobbed up beside him and gently started to float away, face down, robes billowing in the flow.

Khalid staggered back to the riverbank and hauled himself out on his hands and knees, shattered by the wet and the chill and the exertion. His groin ached terribly and free of the fight he succumbed to the nausea, vomiting several times before he felt able to move.

He was aware time was short. He couldn't be sure how long he had been fighting but it must have been several minutes since Noor had switched on the phone and initiated the attack sequence. The strike could take place any moment. He could not stay where he was.

Khalid stumbled away, following the river upstream and towards the mountains. His legs barely worked and his joints were numb from the biting cold. But if he was going to survive then he had to force himself on. No choice. He hadn't evaded death at the hands of the Talib only to succumb to the drone attack. Wouldn't that be the bitterest irony?

———

A couple of hundred metres away Noor had stood patiently. At last sure he was alone, he powered on the phone and dialled his parents' number. A male voice answered. Relief washed over Noor. He spoke briefly to his father and, conscious of what Khalid had said, just as briefly with his mother. It didn't matter that the conversation was short. It was enough to hear them speak. He reassured them he was fine and that his job was nearly over and he would be back within the week. As he hung up the phone there was a smile on his face.

It was a peaceful night. There was almost no noise. The dogs had stopped barking and the only thing to trouble his ears was the distant murmur of the river as it tumbled through the valley. Noor felt content and, for the first time in a while, safe. He stood and waited for his friend to return.

It was into this sea of calm that the missile descended unseen. There was no time for Noor to appreciate what he was experiencing before his life ended in a brilliant flash of light and a giant detonation. The compound evaporated. The heat reached him first, blistering and peeling away his skin. His eyes bulged and exploded as the overpressure washed over him. Blinded, he fell to the ground, the force of the blast sucking the air from his lungs and tearing at the flesh that remained. He never knew what hit him, never had time to feel fear or pain. His only reaction as his body disintegrated was to try and utter a primal call for help. It was instinctive, not considered, but the scream was not for those who had borne and nurtured him but for the man he had only just met; the man who had so recently saved him.

"Khalid!" he mouthed as death overwhelmed him.

———◆———

When Noor died Khalid was half a kilometre away. A couple of hundred metres earlier he had forded the river to put another barrier between him and anyone who might come in pursuit. The current had almost been too much for him but he had discarded his cloak to stop it acting as a drag and just managed to make the far bank. Breathing heavily and soaked to the skin he had allowed himself a brief pause, sitting against a large angular rock which marked the point where a goat track diverted away from the course of the water to wend its way steeply up into the mountains. When the missile struck Khalid was struggling to make out the location of the village. The intensity of the light had taken him by surprise, but it prepared him for the blasts that followed as the second and third missiles drove into the compound.

Khalid did not know how high the death toll might go, but it was certain Noor, Mahsud and Jamadar would be part of it.

Khalid forced himself up. He knew that if he allowed himself to sit there longer he'd be hit by feelings of sorrow, of guilt and shame over how he had used Noor and how his actions had killed him. He set off up the track telling himself that whatever had taken place was another stepping stone on the road to being reunited with his father and a future he had to believe they might have.

Chapter 16
BDA – KHOST

As Khalid had been battling in the river, Cyrus was stood at the back of the JOC staring intently at the big screen on the opposite wall, tapping his foot impatiently. Normally the image projected onto it would be a map, but this time it was a live aerial video-link, a black and white bird's-eye view of Jamadar Kalay sent back by the Reaper circling high above. For a few minutes there had been a flickering red light at the centre of the view, throbbing hypnotically. Cyrus could feel the frustration growing inside him and still the red dot pulsed, taunting him. Cyrus said nothing, knew better than that. Those who were speaking did so in urgent whispers, passing messages into their headsets. Others sat hunched at their computers, moving their mice, tapping at keyboards, sending and receiving and analysing information. The atmosphere in the room grew increasingly tense. Cyrus could see the furrows deepening on more than one brow. He put his hand to his own forehead to rub away the tension.

And then the crimson blip disappeared from view, subsumed by a brilliant flash of light that swallowed up the village. When the whiteout dissipated the pulse of red had vanished and so too had much of the surrounding settlement. At fucking last Cyrus thought to himself as the two subsequent missiles struck the same spot.

Within sixty seconds a handful of blobs were converging on the epicentre of the blast: first responders arriving in trucks. The vehicles clustered together and smaller blobs started to appear alongside them, occupants spilling out to try to help or to stare at the bleak vision before them. A series of smaller explosions erupted amongst the new arrivals and all movement stopped.

Nobody in the JOC cheered or showed obvious signs of satisfaction beyond a grunt or two of muttered approval; they simply remained glued to the unfolding carnage. Cyrus Vincent had seen enough though. He stepped back inside his office and closed the door with more force than was necessary. He sank into the chair behind his desk and reached for the computer. He had some electronic paperwork to do, filing his report on the strikes he had just witnessed against objectives Vegas and Tabasco. Thirty minutes after the strike and he was still busily typing when there was a tap at the door and the duty watch keeper came in.

"So, are you going to tell me what happened?" Cyrus said not bothering to look at the new arrival.

"Sir, we can confirm bingo on Objective Vegas. Satellite tracking has shown no movement from the compound and monitoring of signals from the area show that the deaths of both the village elder and the high ranking visitor are being reported."

Cyrus stopped what he was doing and confronted his visitor. There was a look of anger spread across his expansive face.

"I'm not asking who the fuck is dead, but why it took us so fucking long to kill them? Why the four-minute delay between the signal being activated and the first strike?"

"I don't know exactly, Sir," the watch keeper replied. "I think there was a communications issue between here and Creek. They're still looking into it."

Cyrus stood up and banged the table, making the young man take a step back and automatically straighten up.

"I don't want any fucking excuses from you or anyone else. Do you know how much can happen in that space of time? How far a man can travel? Ever heard of the four-minute mile? That delay means Bashir could have made his escape. It means we could have missed one of our targets. It means that all this planning could have been for fucking nothing. Do you get that?"

There wasn't much the watch keeper could say.

"I get that, Sir," he tried.

"No, not fucking 'I get that, Sir'. That's the wrong answer. I want immediate coverage of the surrounding area for any movement out of the mountains and I want eyes on the vehicle in Mazar-e-Sharif. Understand?"

"Yes of course, Sir." Hesitantly, he added, "May I finish my report?"

"What else have you got?"

The man read from a script on his clipboard detailing the strike and the expected casualty count. He explained how it was confirmed that the man who switched the phone on was still holding it when the first missile hit. The monitoring of the airwaves indicated a high-ranking Taliban figure had been killed. HUMINT sources were already starting to say the same thing. Radio and phone traffic amongst militia leaders and warlords was confirming the village elder Haji Jamadar was dead.

"Early stages but at this point the casualty count is looking like fourteen insurgents KIA, eight non combatants dead and about twenty wounded," the watch keeper concluded, relieved that he had not been interrupted again.

"What information control measures have we got in place?" Cyrus asked, more calmly now.

"We've got the District Community Counsel in our pocket. The District Governor has been bought off and we have inserted a bit of cash into the local hospital, police station and local community services, such as they are, to ensure the story is clean. Fourteen insurgent dead will be the headline that's put about."

"What about news release on Vegas?" Cyrus asked.

"Sir, we think it would be good to say that Mahsud has been killed along with Jamadar."

"OK approved. Now I want feedback on Tabasco. As soon as you can get it. The earlier we call bingo on Bashir the easier I will sleep.

And the easier I sleep then the quieter your life will be. Let me know the moment you have anything." Without further comment Cyrus dropped his head and returned to his own report.

He had been at the spy game for too many years to take anything for granted. He didn't want hunch or rumour or 'chances are'. What he wanted were heads served up on silver platters, or as near as damn it. For sure he was very pleased that Mahsud was dead. After all that was what all this had been about. As for the other twenty or so who had died, he cared nothing for them. All he needed to know was that Khalid was among their number. For if he wasn't then the house of cards could still come tumbling down. The whole Bashir affair had been high risk but, he reasoned, it had to be seen in the context of what this was part of. A global ideological struggle. Still he was well aware not everyone was as committed to total war as he was. There were too many people with too many sensitivities. The politicians were the worst. Especially those coming to the end of their electoral terms. Most were fine at the beginning; carried along on a heady tide of popular support and nationalistic ideas about making America great again. But the enthusiasm waned as the years passed and fear of the ballot box, and the history books, overtook fear of the enemy. Better men than he had been cast adrift by nervous presidents, senators and congressmen, keen to retain their seats and unwilling to be revealed up to their necks in the blood and gore of a vicious battle.

And if details of what had been happening with Bashir reached the media then his country's leaders would be engulfed by the scandal. There was no way the UK government would turn a blind eye to a US asset murdering a young British soldier in front of the cameras, not to mention the attacks he had orchestrated on coalition forces out in the field. Equally, the administration in Washington would turn as pale as the White House at the thought of the US public knowing what they were prepared to do, and the young men they were prepared to sacrifice, to prosecute a campaign many already thought they shouldn't be involved in. Yes, Cyrus told himself again, it was in everybody's interests that Bashir was dead and one way or another he would be. The beauty of it all was that the British were providing the insurance policy. Adam Caine had left the base at Khost with a known insurgent and was on his way to try to meet up with Bashir. The Brits were well and truly caught up in the Bashir deception. Up to their mother-fucking necks. Cyrus couldn't suppress the smile trying to break out on his face. This had got so big that in truth he was fucking enjoying it.

———◆———

Peter Ryder clamped the phone tightly to his ear, struggling over the bad line to hear what he was being told.

"We are getting reports of a major kinetic strike by the Americans north of Mazar-e-Sharif. There is a good chance it was triggered by our man Bashir. He could be one of the fatalities."

"And the main target?" Peter asked.

"The Taliban finance minister, plus a couple of local warlords."

"That fits in with my intelligence. Question is: did they get Bashir along with Mahsud?" Peter muttered, talking more to himself than the man on the other end of the line.

"Is there any chance Caine is there by now?"

"No chance. I have eyes on and regular updates. He is still at least six hours from the site, maybe more."

"Are you sure?" the voice pushed.

"Absolutely, and if necessary I have the ability to slow the whole thing down a bit."

"Do you have the ability to end it? Now?"

Peter Ryder thought for a moment. He knew exactly what was being asked. This was about damage limitation. Controlling the situation if things went wrong or government thought it best to eliminate the problem.

"I can end it whenever you want. You understand why I wanted the sixth man," Peter explained reassuringly.

"Will he act if we need it?" the voice asked again.

"He'll act when I give him the call."

"Well let's hope we don't get to that stage."

Peter stood for a while after the connection was broken. Things had got complicated. What he was doing was just part of much bigger manoeuvrings between two countries who were supposedly allies. It was all good old-fashioned colonialism. The US wanted a regional base to allow them rapid access to Eastern Iran. The UK sought to continue exporting military hardware and knowledge and influence to Pakistan. And the two aims weren't necessarily compatible. So every ounce of leverage was useful. Every bargaining chip worth having. And at the moment none were more useful than Khalid Bashir, and by extension Adam Caine.

Chapter 17
CAPTURED – HINDU KUSH

Khalid scrambled up another steep scree slope, struggling to get up and over the peak and out of the valley. He hated stopping, but the exertion and the altitude left him breathless. He needed a second or two to recharge his lungs. Trying to steady himself on the shifting cascade of stones, gulping in oxygen, he glanced back the way he had come. A thread of rising smoke marked out where the village was – or had been. He fought against a desire to think of Noor. It took all his will power to banish him from his mind. Resolutely he turned back to the task at hand and eyed the slope ahead. There was still another hundred metres or so of vertical distance to cover before he crested the ridge above. The depressing succession of false peaks already conquered had made him wary of believing his goal was in reach. Recent experience had shown there was as much likelihood of encountering yet another ascent beyond this one as there was with being confronted by a clear route down to the plains beyond.

His pace was measured. He knew he had to preserve a rhythm he could keep up with no more than a few intermittent breaks. Speed was of the essence but so too was endurance.

Sometime earlier he had passed close to the cave where he had spent the night before last, fighting with and killing Hafiz, but he ignored its meagre comforts and kept clear of the well-worn path. Instead, as best he could, he remained several hundred metres abeam of the defined route, picking his way through the broken terrain, wincing as he turned an ankle or felt the knife-sharp stone edges dig into his soles.

Khalid paused once more and this time he allowed himself a sigh of relief. From the top of the ridge he was finally afforded a view of the easier ground below. It wasn't all downhill – there were still points where he would need to give up height only to regain it again – but overall the land dropped away. So far his exit had been by foot but he knew he would need mechanised power. His best hope were the vehicles that had dropped them off as they began their journey to Jamadar Kalay. Sardre had told the group to be back at the drop off point two days later and Khalid's estimation was this meant midmorning. Time was against him. He needed to keep going. He forced himself to move, stretching his aching limbs and feeling his damp, clinging clothes trying to smother his movement. At least he was warm, though. That was another reason to keep going; to stop the chill setting in and stiffening him to a board.

The goat path he now followed was indistinct. Every few paces he thought he had lost it but intuitively he would follow the course of least resistance and within a handful of steps find himself back on the path almost imperceptibly marked out by the animals.

After fifteen minutes of knee-jarring descent he dropped into some dead ground which flattened out then rose sharply again to a parapet of rock and stone. Reaching the top of this he studied the scene before him. And cursed. Two trucks were snaking rapidly away from the base of the mountain towards Mazar. He hadn't seen the vehicles when they were stationary but their rapid retreat made them glaringly obvious. Either the allotted time for their departure had arrived or else they had been tipped off about what had happened in Jamadar. It didn't matter which, the upshot was the same – his transport was receding into the distance.

Khalid sank to the floor, fatigue and disappointment gaining an advantage. He put a hand to his forehead and fingered the crusty residue left by the drying sweat. He didn't feel hungry, but was in desperate need of a drink. He looked about for a stream. Over to his left a small silvery trail of icy liquid meandered amongst the rocks. Eagerly he ducked his face into it and felt his skin tingle as it was chilled. As he quenched his thirst he tried to figure what to do.

The absence of the pick-ups didn't change the basic plan – Khalid still needed to get to Mazar – it just made things a whole lot harder, and longer, and more dangerous. With every passing minute there was a greater likelihood that his handler would determine he had not been one of the victims of the missile strike and come after him with all the resources the CIA could muster. He would be chased down and killed. Chastened by the thought and refreshed by the water Khalid hauled himself to his feet and plodded on.

Since leaving Khost Adam's progress had been steady. When he had been sure they were clear of the base he had ordered the driver to pull over so they could get their bearings. He checked the route on his map then input the coordinates for Mazar-e-Sharif into the satnav and waited for the technology to set a course via a number of waypoints. As the markers were shown on the small screen, he checked them off against what he was expecting. Hitting save, he had given the young Pakistani driver a small nudge and pointed down the road into the darkness.

"Keep your full beams on and drive no faster than sixty miles per hour," Adam said. "Understand?"

"Yes Sir."

"You ok in the back Lal-Jan?" Adam asked via interpreter.

By way of reply, Lal-Jan posed his own question, "Where are we going?"

"We will make our way towards Mazar-e-Sharif, skirt the town and then head north into the mountains. From there I want you to direct me towards the village."

"If I can remember the way," Lal-Jan responded, non-committal.

"You know the way Lal-Jan and I know you know the way."

As the 4x4 flew along the road Adam clung to the handle above the passenger door, considering his actions. He understood he was taking a serious gamble separating himself from the Det and setting a collision course with US intelligence. However he calculated it was the right thing to do. Throughout the briefings received ahead of the mission it had been stressed that Khalid needed to be taken alive and something within him thought that in many ways Khalid was owed that. He thought back to Sandhurst, conjuring up recollections of how hard it was for the foreign cadets who had to constantly swim upstream. Khalid had stayed the course and was presented his reward by Royalty. It must have engendered in Khalid some sense of pride and, if not exactly devotion to the British way of doing things, then at least a respect. Yet what he had subsequently endured was enough to pitch any man against such a system.

Adam believed the British Government and the military retained a duty of care towards Khalid. He also couldn't help but believe there was more to the whole affair than the US was admitting to. Why else would they go out of their way to obstruct UK Intelligence finding him? Why would they deem him such a threat that they would actively cross a friendly government's plan in order to eliminate him?

Adam needed to reach Khalid ahead of his US counterparts. Instinctively he looked down at his watch and tilted it towards the glow of the dashboard lights, but still couldn't make out what it read. It didn't really matter. In these circumstances time was not absolute, but relative; relative to the progress the Americans were making. Adam leaned back and closed his eyes.

———•———

Khalid examined his shin. It was scraped and bloodied and hurt like hell but if anything was actually broken then the pain would have been worse still. He took comfort from the fact it was still in a straight line rather than at an acute angle that would confirm serious damage. The slab of stone he had trusted and put his weight on had given way and, without warning, sent it and him, sliding down the slope. That was until his sledge had wedged between two rather more steadfast pieces of the landscape and he was hurled forward.

Rubbing the injured spot furiously he lifted his head only to be left bewildered by what he now saw in the morning light. Far below him, tucked into the lee of the hillside, still a mile or more away, was a silver square, two parallel shafts of brilliant white light protruding from it into the shadows. From this angle it was impossible to say what kind of vehicle he was looking at but its very presence raised Khalid's spirits. Was it one of the trucks he had seen departing earlier come back for another look? At first Khalid thought the odds favoured this explanation; who else would be making the journey to such a remote part of the country? But then he began to doubt that conclusion for on this day Jamadar Kalay would be a magnet, people would flock there: comrades and followers of Haji Jamadar coming to help, and if they couldn't do that, at least witness for themselves the aftermath of the attack; and Mahsud's enemies, those who wanted to confirm his death – and that of the man who had been instrumental in achieving it. Khalid tried to make out more detail on the vehicle, but his point of view didn't allow it. So what? he thought. He needed the vehicle and he would dispose of the people inside it as required – whoever they were.

———•———

Adam was in a quandary. He had to decide how best to now proceed to Jamadar Kalay and that choice was going to have to be made on the basis of what he was being told by a paid informer. Should they hike in on foot from here or was there a way of taking the vehicle all the way to their destination, skirting around the massif that confronted them?

"Well?" Adam asked Lal-Jan. "What's the best option?"

"There is a track from here which leads into the mountain, it'll take you to a pass that eventually leads to the village."

"How long from here?" Adam asked. "On foot. How long?"

"Maybe five or six hours. If we move quickly and bring no equipment."

Adam said nothing, staring ahead. The sun was rising and Adam watched as a thin mist rose from the valley floor as the earth heated. It had been a long night's drive from Khost. They had not been completely alone on the roads. Sporadically they would be passed by trucks heading in the opposite direction, mainly farmers heading to market, their precious loads of animals and produce bumping about in the back of the pick-ups, the goats and sheep bleating nervously. There were also taxis, doing who knew what in the early hours of the morning. Then, just minutes earlier, there had been the men with guns in two jeeps that swept by going the other way, the weapons of the men pointing skywards, the dull metal giving off just a hint of a reflection in the glare of the main beam. For several minutes afterwards Adam looked over his shoulder to see if they would stop, do a u-turn and come back after them, inquisitive as to their identities and intentions. But he saw nothing and eventually swivelled back to face the way they were travelling. It was only a few minutes later that they'd arrived at the point where any further progress would have to be on foot.

Khalid moved briskly but worked hard to keep obstacles – rocks, bushes, occasional small trees – between him and the truck below. He would have preferred to have made his move during the night, but time was against him. Waiting risked seeing the 4x4 depart. Already there were exhaust fumes billowing from the tailpipe, but Khalid hoped the engine was running to keep the occupants warm rather than a prelude to hitting the road. That being the case, at least it offered an opportunity. If they were warm then there was every chance they were also drowsy, relaxed, unsuspecting.

Getting closer now Khalid slipped off the goat path and dropped into a boulder field. Moving from one giant block to another, it took him more than a quarter of an hour to finally make it to the bottom of the slope, though he was still a hundred metres from the prize.

Inching forward he could make out two men sat in the front of the car but the darkened rear windows made it impossible to see who was in the back. He hoped there was no one there but he couldn't rely on wishful thinking. He began to creep closer conscious he was unarmed except for the lock knife. How he wished he still had the Makarov he had handed over to Mohammed Sardre.

He moved in slow motion, checking before planting a foot, careful not to disturb anything and give away his position. He understood the art of movement, how to break up the ground up into small bounds, constantly scanning for escape routes and cover if he was seen. He came to the spot he had decided would be his launch position. He was no more than 20 metres from the driver's side of the vehicle. Khalid prepared himself. He believed he had speed on his side; if he could cover the distance quickly he would catch the occupants unaware. It was his only hope. This was the point of no return. Once committed, he would have to follow through. There would be no easy retreat. He knelt and prayed.

"I must be bold. Allah will protect me, my fight is just and I have served him."

———◆———

Adam folded away the map on his lap and checked his satnav one last time. The windscreen had steamed up, the film of moisture still thickening. He rubbed his forearm against the glass but it only afforded him a limited view of what was outside. He felt vulnerable.

"Just wait here," Adam ordered. "Let me just have a look around and then we'll move on."

He unlocked his door, grabbed his rifle and jumped out into the growing heat only to be dazzled by the sun. Shading his eyes he looked across the roof of the vehicle but still it was too bright to adequately make out the lay of the land. Bending down he reached back into the foot well and felt for his sunglasses, looping the cord over his neck. Then he stood his full height, let his eyes adjust to the light and strode off towards the higher ground.

———◆———

Khalid was up and running, a sprinter out of the blocks, the sun at his back masking his movements for a few moments more. He closed rapidly on the vehicle. There would be no time to check if the door was open or not so he needed another way in. Two or three metres out, and without breaking stride, he raised his right arm and launched at the side window the lump of rock he carried. The glass shattered easily, collapsing inwards. Khalid was right there. Reaching through the opening and transferring the open clasp knife from one hand to the other he stabbed at the neck of the driver who sat stock still paralysed by surprise. The blade buried itself deep into the flesh, jinking slightly as it struck bone.

There was no noise from the man and no blood, just a look of open-mouthed horror on his face.

Lying across the dying man's lap was his AK47, the barrel pointing into the centre of the truck. There had been no chance for him to raise it, let alone twist it round, aim and fire. The occupant of the passenger seat also had an AK. For a second he was equally dumbfounded and disorientated by the exploding glass and the attack it heralded. But he recovered quickly and moved to lift his own weapon. Khalid beat him to it. Leaving his knife embedded in the driver he lunged for the trigger of his rifle and pulled it. The gun bucked, the uncontained recoil sending the bullets on wild trajectories. But most found their target, ripping through the passenger, shredding organs and tissue, one striking his chin and tearing it off. He screamed in fear and pain and died almost immediately.

Clutching the tatty AK Khalid levered himself back out of the broken window, releasing the door catch as he withdrew. He looked at the driver and the knife still protruding from his neck. The man moved his hands to grasp the handle and with a tremendous effort he wrenched it out. With the seal broken, blood began to spurt from the open wound. Instantly the man knew he had done the wrong thing. With a look of despair he dropped the knife and tried to clamp his hands to his neck, but with each heartbeat more blood escaped and drained him of both strength and life.

Staring into the driver's eyes Khalid changed the weapon from automatic to single shot, levelled it at him and once more squeezed the trigger. The 7.62mm short round smashed into the man's temple, bored through the frontal lobe of his brain then, as it exited, splintered the skull, fracturing it all the way from the back, over the top of the ear, to the left eye, splattering the corpse in the passenger seat with a sticky human mess.

Khalid glanced into the back of the vehicle. Content there was no one there he rummaged through the glove compartment and map pockets to see what he could scavenge, in particular desperate to find ammo. With relief he discovered three more AK47 magazines, all full. A few loose rounds rolled about in the foot well. Plus there were the remaining bullets from the other weapon's mag. He gathered together the haul and stuffed everything into his pockets before stepping back to survey the damage he had caused. His train of thought was rudely interrupted. A flurry of bullets churned up the dusty earth just a few feet from where he was standing. Khalid dived to the floor as a second fusillade shattered the front right headlight cluster. Judging by how the rounds were landing Khalid reckoned he was being fired on from above. Someone was up on the mountain.

———◆———

Half a mile away Adam had cocked his head at the various sounds of gunfire: the initial burst then a single shot, and now repeated volleys from more than one rifle. It had to be related to Khalid.

Turning, he ran back to his vehicle and leaped into his seat.

"Follow the track north, that way there," Adam said, pointing his finger up the valley.

"Sir, I am listening to the news from Kabul on the car radio," the interpreter said. "They are reporting that the US has carried out a missile strike in the mountains and killed a number of Taliban and Al-Qaeda fighters."

"Did it say where?" Adam asked.

"No, Sir. Just that it was northeast of Kabul, up in the hills."

Adam pictured the map in the CIA JOC at Khost; remembering the markings on it for objectives Vegas and Tabasco.

"Just keep it steady," Adam said. He swivelled in his seat and handed something to Lal-Jan. "Here, take your pistol. You know how to use this right?"

Lal-Jan slipped the magazine out and inspected it. Snapping it back he said:

"Don't worry, I can use it."

———◆———

Khalid tried to kneel up. He felt and heard the rounds zip over his head, the distinctive crack making him duck again. Gingerly he crawled towards the rear of the truck and peered around it. With his

214

eyes he followed the contours up the mountain until he saw a trio of men with a donkey. Khalid brought his rifle to bear and fired a shot at the group. As the bullet landed close by the men scattered leaving the animal rooted to the spot, held fast by a tether. Khalid shifted position slightly and fired again before his opponents could settle. This time a pair of rounds flew up the hill. They brought a furious response and the flurry of return fire drove Khalid back into cover behind the rear wheel. As the maelstrom died Khalid pulled the rifle hard into his shoulder, braced himself against the wheel arch and peered round the bodywork, scanning his opponents' positions. He saw one of the fighters step out onto the track. Khalid aimed, steadied his breathing and took a shot. The round flew true, striking the man in the groin. He fell to his knees shrieking. Khalid followed up with two more shots. One hit the man square in the chest. He toppled backwards.

Khalid pushed himself to his feet as a retaliatory burst tore into the dust around him. More bullets thumped into the body of the car. Not allowing himself chance to think and hence hesitate Khalid dashed four or five paces, crouching low, hoping the vehicle would block sight of his movement from his adversaries. He dived into a hollow and started crawling. He knew those he faced couldn't shoot, but the truck was a big-ass target and it was drawing plenty of fire. He wanted to get away. Reaching the cover of a group of boulders he huddled behind them, occasionally daring to take a look to check whether the remaining two gunmen were on the move. Khalid had two problems: first he needed the car, but it had already taken a pasting, and second he wasn't completely sure who his opponents were and so whether they were after him or the transport.

There was a thunderous explosion and a fireball erupted from the back of the truck followed by billowing smoke. Then came shouting. Despite the distance Khalid could clearly hear what was being said. And who was saying it.

"You are no martyr Bashir. You are the infidels' pig and Allah has rewarded you for your treachery," yelled Sardre. More rounds poured onto the blazing truck.

Khalid needed to move again. With his enemy's attention focused on vehicle he squirmed through a gap in the rocks and made for the slope to try and outflank them. He scrambled higher. It took him only a couple of minutes to get above and behind the pair. Dropping into a crook in the boulders he took aim at the white skullcap perched on the head of one of the men but even as he fired his target lurched to the right, the round flying past his ear. Confused by the noise the man turned to locate its source. He found himself looking directly at Khalid, no more than twenty metres away. Khalid fired again, the bullet hitting the man on the bridge of his nose, destroying the bone and obliterating his right eye. Screaming, he fell to the ground, his ripped and deflated eyeball hanging by tendons from an empty socket, blood pouring down his face and dripping from his chin.

Khalid strode past the fatally wounded man and made for the donkey. The animal was braying and shivering in fear. As Khalid got closer it started to buck, trying to free itself from the rope that restrained it, frantic to shed the load still strapped to its back.

Khalid hesitated, wary of the beast's thrashing. He never heard the round being fired, only the searing heat as it lanced into him just below his ribcage on his right side. The blow dropped him to all fours.

Panting, disorientated and confused by the body blow, he struggled to raise his head. In his peripheral vision he saw the donkey still skittering about. Its wild movement revealed Sadre attempting to creep up behind it unobserved. He had a rifle in his hands. Khalid tried to shift his position, but his physical being did not respond to the mental command. He tried again, urging himself to move away from harm. He managed just a few feet before slumping to one side and ending up half lying, half sitting in the stones.

Sardre was still coming towards him, more confident now, mechanically changing the magazine in his weapon. Khalid resigned himself to what was going to come. Khalid muttered fatalistically, reciting a favourite saying from his Sandhurst days.

"Those who lived by the sword die by the sword."

Sardre halted ten metres short of his target, content that he didn't need to pick his way any further across the boulder-strewn slope to achieve a kill. He raised the AK47 to his shoulder, went to pull the trigger, and disintegrated. Khalid watched as Sardre was literally blown apart. His head separated from his body. So did his right arm. Then his left leg shot out from underneath him at a macabre angle, the kneecap exploding. What was left of him collapsed into a heap. There had been no chance for him to utter a sound.

Khalid understood where the violence had come from. He didn't need to look to the sky to confirm it. Instead, as the Cobra continued to pummel the area with its 30mm cannon, he ignored the pain from his wound and huddled up into a ball, trying to roll into the shadow of a rock. He knew the beaten area would extend many metres beyond the original target and he had as much chance of being hit as Sardre. The shooting continued and the earth vibrated as the shells struck. An eternity later the firing stopped. Khalid waited several seconds then finally glanced up, swivelling his eyes rather than daring to turn his head. The aircraft was banking to port, circling overhead, the menacing clatter of its rotor blades audible. Khalid worked out the sequence of events. It was likely it had been sent into the area to conduct some kind of battle damage assessment following the missile strike in Jamadar kalay and then to track down the party spotted leaving the village with the donkey.

The helicopter had not fired in Khalid's defence; more likely it had arrived during the gun battle, alerted by the vehicle exploding. Once the crew had spotted the combatants they would have requested clearance to engage. This had helped Khalid stay alive for a few minutes longer but if he was seen still breathing then he'd go the same way as Sardre.

The Cobra was scribing a wide arc through the sky, perhaps scanning for other survivors of the drone attack, but eventually it would be coming back to inspect the havoc it had just wrought. Even if the gunner did not visually identify any sign of life the thermal imaging would pick Khalid up as a heat source. There was nowhere to hide and in his condition he was certainly not able to run.

Khalid hauled himself to his feet, gritting his teeth against the surge of pain. He stumbled down the track, back towards the blazing 4x4. If he could get close to the burning vehicle he could let the blaze conceal his own heat signature. Passing Sardre he stooped down, felt below his blood stained clothing and retrieved the Makarov pistol.

"He who lives by the sword… well you get the idea, you fucker," he said out loud.

He also sidestepped the man he had shot in the face, somewhat surprised that he was still alive, squirming in agony, a low moan coming from his mouth. Khalid ignored his plight and concentrated on getting back to the wrecked vehicle. The pain was searing but the thought of being disassembled by the Cobra drove him on. Reaching the truck he collapsed, exhausted from the effort, as close to it as the heat would allow. He clamped his hands on the wound. He was hopeful none of his vital organs had been hit but the injury bled profusely. Hearing the sound of the helicopter again Khalid let his head sink into the dirt. Almost immediately he drifted into a deep and welcome unconsciousness.

———•———

As soon as Adam had seen the helicopter he'd ordered his driver to stop.

The car Adam was travelling in pulled over, as close to the side of the mountain as it could. He had heard the heavy, unmistakable sound of 30mm cannon fire and had looked up through the windscreen to see the attack helicopter circling. It wasn't the time to be driving into a US operation. In the main, attack helicopters operating alone fired first and asked questions later.

He kept his focus on the helicopter as it repeatedly circled the area. After twenty minutes it veered away, flying off south, having either completed its task or run low on fuel. For ten minutes more Adam remained where he was then gave the order to head for the epicentre of the engagement.

"Just keep us close to the side of the mountain," Adam warned the driver. "And keep the speed down to around thirty."

Tucked in close to the cliff face, they drove parallel to the track that ran down the centre of the valley. The ground was rough and littered with fallen boulders but there was room to navigate around them. Adam dragged his rifle up from the floor and checked the magazine again, ensuring there was a round chambered. Content, he placed it back down at his feet. Behind him Lal-Jan had the pistol on his lap. Adam ushered him to hide it under his cloak and Lal-Jan slipped it beneath the folds of his brown kameez.

"Sir, look, over there," the driver shouted, gesturing out of his window. Adam peered over the driver's shoulder. Also moving north, out in the centre of the plain were two trucks running just ahead of a dust cloud. As they all moved further up the narrowing defile it was clear the two parties would converge.

"Lal-Jan. The vehicles over there. Who do you think it is? Locals?"

"Locals, Taliban, the local warlord. Whoever it is they will be armed. We should not go near them," Lal-Jan said, a degree of panic in his voice.

"Agreed. We will drop back and let them pass."

But as the driver eased off the throttle the other trucks mirrored the action and slowed down too before heeling left to head directly into the path of Adam's vehicle.

"Shit," Adam swore under his breath as he kept his eye on the unknowns. As they closed in it became obvious that the trucks were packed with fighters bristling with weapons. Adam opened his window and threw the map out. The satnav and the rifle followed. There was no way he was going to be able to fight his way out of this encounter so better off without the trademarks of Western soldiers. Instead he'd have to bluff it.

"Listen to me, when we get stopped you are to say I am a Swiss journalist. Do you understand?"

The driver said nothing. Adam could see him sweating, he eyes wide and full of dread.

"Did you hear me?" Adam shouted, grasping the young driver's forearm. "I am a Swiss reporter. Do you get that?"

"Yes, Sir," the driver mumbled.

"Lal-Jan is our guide, tell him."

The interpreter spoke rapidly to Lal-Jan then addressed Adam.

"They will kill us, they will take our property and our car. They are thieves."

"Just be calm, let them do the talking, you just give simple answers and translate for me. Lal-Jan I need you to say you are our guide and that we are heading into the mountains to interview a Taliban commander, that you've organized it, give a name, Jamadar, anyone from this area."

The insurgent vehicles had closed in rapidly and now bracketed Adam's own transport, one in front, one behind. For a couple of hundred metres they continued, the strangers studying their prize. Then, harshly, the lead truck skidded to a halt. It was all Adam's driver could do to avoid ramming the rear of it and all the occupants were thrown forward. Before he could do anything Adam's door was flung open and he was heaved out. He cursed as he banged a kneecap hard on a rock. The driver and Lal-Jan were also being ejected. He heard them yell as they were punched and kicked and flung to the floor at gunpoint.

"Stay calm" Adam whispered. "Look down, don't look into their faces, don't antagonise them."

Adam tried desperately to remember his SERE training: survive, evade, resist, escape. His own head bowed, he was vaguely aware that their vehicle was being searched. The strangers might find the Blue Force Tracker but he was betting they wouldn't know what it was, mistaking it for part of the truck's electrical system. They were throwing everything out now: water bottles, the wheel brace and jack, a couple of rucksacks, but there was nothing there to indicate the team's true identity. Overseeing the activity was a tall, thin man with a patch over his left eye. One of those doing the searching went over to him shaking his head and saying a few words in Dari. The senior man snarled and spat. He pushed past his subordinate and strode up to Lal-Jan and the driver. The boy started to panic.

"Sir, Sir," he blurted, "I am just an interpreter working for this journalist."

The leader motioned to the men guarding the pair. They grasped the driver by his shoulders and yanked him to his feet, roughly going through his pockets and feeling under his clothing, but all they recovered were some tattered papers and a crumpled old photo. Satisfied there was nothing else to find they shoved him towards the leader who slapped him about, shouting questions at him. It was clear the answers offered in return were not satisfactory because after each one the boy would receive another blow. The interrogation went on for several minutes before the one-eyed man lost interest. Instead he motioned towards Lal-Jan. He too was hauled to a standing position and frisked. Lal-Jan remained silent, looking directly into the eyes of the leader. Groping under Lal-Jan's tunic, one of the guards shouted excitedly and triumphantly withdrew the pistol.

"Fuck," Adam said silently.

The pristine weapon was given to the commander. He examined it carefully. For all his experience of, and familiarity with guns this was the first time in his 38 years that he had handled a 9mm Glock; its name and calibre stamped onto the metal in English. Adam listened as the man spoke to Lal-Jan but he couldn't understand a word. He lifted his head fractionally to see Lal-Jan leaning in towards the leader, his hand on his heart as if pleading innocence, swearing on the life of his mother. The discussion was heated and as it continued the men went on frisking Lal-Jan.

A shout made Adam raise his head once again. A mobile phone had been pulled out of Lal-Jan's pocket. Adam didn't recognize it. As with the pistol, this latest find was passed dutifully to the leader. He rolled it over in his hand then stabbed at the power button. Opening the menu he looked at the call list, there was only one number. He looked hard at Lal-Jan and hit redial.

Almost immediately there was an answer. The leader didn't understand what was being said but he knew the language it was being said in. English. He didn't bother replying.

For the first time Lal-Jan looked truly scared. He started to tremble. He dropped his head, his chin coming to rest on his chest, as if he knew what was coming next. Without warning or ceremony the leader paced over to him, put the Glock to the crown of his head and, holding the phone alongside the gun barrel, calmly pulled the trigger. Lal-Jan crumpled.

———•———

At the sound of the shot Adam flinched. He tried to get to his feet only to receive a fierce blow to his knee from the butt of an AK. His leg gave way and he twisted and half-fell. A second blow caught him on the back of his neck and he went face down into the Afghan dirt. Then they started to kick him. As the pummelling went on the leader dropped the phone to the ground and stamped on it repeatedly, the brittle plastic case and the circuitry inside splintering easily.

The punishment lasted half a minute until the leader yelled out an order to stop. The guards attempted to get Adam to stand but his knee wouldn't support his weight. He buckled and sank back down. The leader leaned over him and took hold of a fistful of hair.

"Infidel!" he spat. "Infidel!"

He struck Adam across the nose with the handgrip of the pistol. Then he did it again. The skin split and blood quickly flowed from the deep gashes.

"Take him," the leader shouted.

The same men who had tried to raise Adam to his feet now dragged him towards the second truck where he was dumped in the open back next to his driver. One of the guards clambered in beside them and removed his scruffy turban, using it to bind Adam's arms. They were already under way, the truck making a tight turn and barrelling back south. Adam ached all over from the kicking. But more than the pain was the worry as to what might still be to come.

Chapter 18
CIA HQ – KHOST

Peter jerked the handset away from the side of his head at the deafening sound of the gunshot, shocked by its intensity and by what it implied. After a few seconds he dared to put the phone back to his ear. He still couldn't hear any talking but what sounded like a scuffle going on: grunts and groans, thuds and thumps. Finally the line went dead.

He had been surprised to hear the phone ring, automatically looking at the screen to see who was calling. It was needless effort because only one person had the number. What was confusing was why Lal-Jan should be ringing rather than texting.

"Yes Lal-Jan what is it?" he had said, his irritation obvious. Now there was no chance of the Afghan providing an answer.

Peter scrolled through the messages Lal-Jan had sent over the last six hours. It was hardly a high-tech method of keeping in touch, but it kept Peter informed. The handful of communications had succinctly documented the journey out of Khost, northwest past the capital, and given updates on their positions as they made their way through Mazar and into the mountains. Peter's phone had last vibrated thirty minutes previously, the SMS pinpointing them to a valley en route towards the village of Jamadar. Then nothing more until the phone had rung. Now Peter had to assume that his sixth man – the man he had plucked from the Camp Torchlight holding facility at Bastion and recruited as a HUMINT source – was dead and there would be nothing from him ever again.

Peter sat down heavily on the trestle bench outside the accommodation block, resting his head against the cool concrete. He needed a chance to think. He was a man who saw a lot of sense in sticking to the rules, following protocols and guidelines. Without doctrines and standard operating procedures where would you be? War was chaotic enough; it didn't help if participants acted on whims rather than discipline. Everyone would be second-guessing everyone else. Decision-making would become a lottery, a matter not of best practice but the toss of a coin; hunches, emotions, would rule. Peter hadn't always thought this way. Not in the old days in Belfast, first as a child growing up in the province, witnessing daily the bitter struggle across the sectarian divide; and later as a young man, a member of 14 Intelligence Company, helping take the fight to the IRA. He had been more willing to take his chances back then; some had come off and some had not. On more than one occasion he lad lost an asset to a Provo hit squad and been told their loss was of secondary importance to the mission; the question being not whether a human had died but whether the operation survived? Peter had found it hard to reconcile the loss of life, often for minimal gain, and had raised it with his superior. He had been told to shut his mouth and stick to the rules or leave the team. Over time he had come to accept the ordered way of doing things, became a convert, and took his newfound zealousness for protocol with him when he developed the Det after 14 Int had morphed into the SRR.

Peter knew what would happen if he went straight to London with news of his loss: watch and wait, let things run, see what US intelligence did next – but inaction seriously jeopardised Adam's life. Peter was clear about that. What he had just heard over the mobile underlined it. And he wasn't sure if he was ready for another death in the team.

He could go to Cyrus and hope to get a bit more out of him, but ultimately any rescue mission would require UK Special Forces and the tasking for that would have to be cleared by UKSF in Kandahar.

The sound of stones crunching under boots caused him to look up.

A young marine was striding across the gravel. He halted smartly.

"Mr Ryder, Sir."

"Yes?"

"Sir I have been asked to escort you to the JOC. Mr Vincent would like to have a word, Sir."

Peter allowed himself a wan smile, bemused by the marines' habit of bookending every sentence with the word Sir.

Peter followed the marine. He almost bumped into Cyrus as the door to the JOC was opened.

"Ah Peter, I was coming to look for you. I thought we might take a walk. As it happens the JOC is a bit busy at the moment."

"Sure, no problem, lead on," Peter said, backing out of the way as Cyrus strode past him.

"I love this time of the morning over here," Cyrus said. "The sun is up but the heat is still bearable. It's a great time to get your head straight, set your targets for the day ahead."

Peter shrugged noncommittally.

"I suppose so, never really thought about it to be honest."

Cyrus stopped abruptly and turned to look at Peter, taking half a step forward, barging into his personal space.

"One of your soldiers left the base last night with a local national, Lal-Jan," Cyrus said.

"Yes, I'm afraid Adam Caine exited without clearance either from me or from London," Peter explained. "I believe he is heading northwest towards Mazar-e-Sharif."

"Why?" Cyrus asked.

"I guess he believes he has a lead on Khalid Bashir and he thought he would act on it."

"Think. Believe. Guess. Don't you know?" Cyrus said mildly, maintaining his calm. "I suppose you're aware that Caine has a history of going off the reservation? I have had dealings with him before."

Peter ignored the slight.

"I've only just found out about Adam, I was coming to find you to see if we could trace his movements."

"What about the man you've got with him? Hasn't he told you anything?"

Peter paused. Then said falteringly, "How did you know?"

"Know what? That you had a sixth man in your team, a local facilitator, a man who could give you information as and when it was needed?" Cyrus stared at Peter. "We knew the moment we lifted him when he arrived on the base. Faced with a long time in Bagram's holding facility it didn't take long to get his tongue moving. As soon as we threatened to transfer him he told us he was working directly for you on the mission, outside of what the rest of your team knew."

"That's why you released him so quickly," Peter said.

"Of course. Well, we held him for a while but when the time was right we let him out."

"So you suspected Adam was going to make a run for Bashir?" Peter pushed. "But if you knew that why did you let Lal-Jan go?"

"Now I'm not sure I want to let you in on that yet," Cyrus answered. "Suffice to say a UK intelligence operator – under your command – has left the base with a known insurgent in an attempt to meet up with another known insurgent who was trained by the British. It doesn't sound great if you say it like that, does it?"

"No it doesn't," Peter admitted. "And we might have another problem."

"Really, what?"

"I think Adam has been taken captive."

"How do you come to that conclusion?" Cyrus asked already in possession of the answer.

"I got a call from the sixth man – just before he was shot, executed I think."

Cyrus thought for a while, formulating his response.

"We know where Adam Caine is," Cyrus said.

"How? Where?"

"What did you think, that we wouldn't keep an eye on him once he left the base? We control everything that goes on in our patch, and to be honest everyone else's patch too. We've had satellite surveillance on their vehicle since it left Khost."

Peter was confused.

"Yet you did nothing to stop him?"

"Why would we? There was a chance he would find Bashir and there was a chance he would also lead us to some important Taliban and Al Qaeda leaders."

"So what now?"

"Good question. What do you want to do?"

"I want to mount a mission to get Adam out of there and to do that I will need your intelligence and support."

Cyrus made a point of mulling over the request, of taking it seriously.

"Ok you have it, but the US will not be committing any men on the ground, this will need to be a British affair."

Now it was Peter's turn to pause. He was playing with smoke and mirrors but to get London to agree to a SF mission to get Adam out alive he would have to tell them the CIA had intelligence as to where Adam was and were willing to provide the details if required. He also had to convince London that Adam was worth saving; that he had information key to getting their hands on Bashir. But that presupposed that Bashir was still out there to be taken.

"Can I ask you a direct question, Cyrus?"

"Sure. Go on."

"Is Bashir alive?"

Cyrus didn't hesitate.

"No. We conducted an operation last night to kill a high-ranking insurgent commander. You have probably already picked up it up on the news this morning, if not then you will. We are certain Bashir was with the commander at the time and died in the strike."

"How certain?" Peter pressed.

"You know as well as I do we can never be one hundred percent but my reports are pretty accurate and they're telling me he's dead."

"So our mission is over?"

"Looks like it."

"But you will help us with Caine?"

"Yes, but you need to make the call. I will leave you to it. I will brief my chain of command as to the situation."

Cyrus brushed past Peter and headed towards the JOC. Peter called after him.

"What will you tell them?"

"I'll tell them a British operator has been taken captive while helping us with the Vegas strike. What else would I tell them? More to the point, what will you say to London?"

"I'll tell them Adam Caine was captured while working on his mission and in support of US intelligence," Peter lied. Cyrus didn't respond, just kept walking.

Peter watched him disappear into the air-conditioned prefab, then made for the accommodation block. Simon saw him come in.

"What's up Peter?"

"We got a bit of an issue here," Peter explained. "Adam has done a runner with one of the vehicles. Can you grab the other guys and see what kit we have lost?"

"What on earth is going on mate?"

"I'll explain later but right now I need to speak to London."

Peter took the sat-phone from his grab bag. He extended the telescopic antenna to its full length and hit speed dial. In London another phone started to ring. Still Simon hadn't moved.

"Mate, can you get the others and do that check?"

"Of course," Simon replied reluctantly.

The call was answered by Peter's handler. He listened patiently as Peter ran through events: what had happened, the fact that he had lost his sixth man, probably dead. He explained how he believed Adam had been taken prisoner and was now being held in a village outside Mazar-e-Sharif. He also detailed the US strike on the village and how the official American position was that Khalid was likely to have been one of the casualties. Finally Peter said he wanted to mount a mission to get Adam back and that US intelligence was happy to provide satellite coverage.

"But what's the point? If Bashir is dead then there is little else we can gain. Why not just leave him to his fate. Nobody will know," the handler laid out a scenario over the line.

"I can see your angle, but there is something else."

"What?"

"They pretend not to be, but they're nervous here. I'm not sure Bashir is dead. I think there's a chance he might have made it out and if he did then we could still get to him first," Peter argued.

"That's your impression or you're sure?"

"It's a hunch. They released the information of his death to me so quickly, almost as if they're trying to get word on the street to see if anyone refutes it. If he is still alive then the need for Adam remains."

The handler went quiet, considering the options. The easy decision would be to simply call an end to the mission and report the death of Khalid Bashir to COBRA. If he subsequently turned up alive then the UK government would just have to go cap in hand to the US. The other option was to keep the operation going in the anticipation that Bashir had not been killed. To do this the handler would have to get permission from COBRA to approach Director Special Forces for help. He made up his mind.

"Ok Peter, I am going to give you five more days. If after that there's no Bashir or no lead to Bashir I'm pulling you all out."

"Thanks. What about the rescue?"

"I'll go and get clearance now. I want you ready to act on anything we pass onto you."

Peter hung up. The rescue mission would be out of his hands. DSF would speak to his US counterparts in Afghanistan. At government level the Foreign Secretary would brief the PM searching for authority for the mission. In turn the PM would speak to the US President requesting official support for the rescue.

Chapter 19
MALALAYA – MAZAR-E-SHARIF

The room was cool, the shaft of sunlight shining through a narrow opening just above Khalid's head offering a little light but no real warmth. As he regained consciousness his blurred vision slowly cleared, but it was not what he could see that immediately concerned him but what he felt; the lancing pain in his side. Reaching down he ran his fingers over a bandage wrapped around his abdomen. The tight binding bit into his skin as he clumsily shifted position, making him wince.

He lay on a low wooden bed with a straw-filled mattress. A bright yellow blanket was crumpled beneath him, dappled with the dark stains caused by blood seeping from the hole in his body. Stained too were the ragged clothes he still wore. On the floor beside the bed was a metal bowl stuffed full of sodden rags that someone had used to clean his wound.

He tried to muster enough strength to raise himself onto one elbow, but the pain defeated him. Groaning, he tried again. Teeth gritted he managed to get into a half-sitting position just as the door opened and a small man with a stoop entered. The new arrival shuffled to the end of the bed and studied his patient, squinting into the light that now bathed his deeply lined face.

"You should remain still," the man said. "The bullet passed through you without too much damage but you have lost a lot of blood and you should rest. You're very weak."

Khalid fought to catch his breath.

"I am indebted to you my friend. What is your name?"

"I am Gul Mohammed. You are on my farm and you are the guest of myself and my daughters."

"I must thank you Gul Mohammed for taking care of me," Khalid said with deference, lowering his head.

"It is my duty. I did nothing more than any good Pashtu would do; take care of those who are in need. Miraculously the wound was clean and the stitches easy to put in. Really, there is little to thank me for."

"What happened?" Khalid asked, easing himself back, flat, onto the bed.

"I watched the helicopter from a distance. When eventually it left the area I made for the smoke rising into the sky and found your vehicle burning. You lay beside it badly hurt. I had a quick look around but all the others I found were beyond help. So I hauled you into my truck and left. I think I was just in time because as I reached the bottom of the valley I saw another vehicle arrive. I was worried they would see me and come in pursuit, so I moved off quickly. They didn't follow."

"You were brave to do what you did."

"I did what I could."

"How long have I been here?"

"Not long, maybe ten hours, the sun will set soon."

Behind Gul the cloth covering the entrance to the room twitched and was then pulled sharply aside. A young woman strode in. Khalid watched as she crossed the floor and went to retrieve the bloodied rags. She did nothing to acknowledge Khalid.

"Let me introduce my daughter, Malalaya," Gul said.

The woman halted as her name was mentioned. For the first time she looked directly at Khalid revealing to him her deep brown eyes, smooth olive skin and bright full lips. What she didn't display was any sign of emotion, certainly not a smile.

"You are welcome... whoever you are."

Khalid noted she spoke with an assuredness rare amongst Pakistani and Afghan women, especially those as young as Malalaya appeared to be. How old was she exactly? Khalid wondered. Nineteen? Twenty?

"Forgive me lady with little patience," Khalid replied with as much lightness as he could muster. "I am Khalid Bashir, son of Farouk Bashir from Kachkai village in Northwest Pakistan and I am your servant."

Khalid went to stand but the pain bit deep and he groaned. In a flash Malalaya moved towards him.

"Please, you must not try to get up," she said firmly. But there was also the first hint of tenderness. "I have not spent all day looking after you just so you can do yourself harm again. It would be a waste of my time and yours."

Khalid looked at Gul as Malalaya eased him back down. Now the old man was smiling too. He shrugged his shoulders.

"My daughters have free wills. Their lives and minds are their own and they are not afraid to show it."

Khalid accepted the assistance and his chastisement.

"Do the Taliban leave you alone?" Khalid asked Gul Mohammed, only for Malalaya to jump in and answer first.

"We do not talk about the Taliban here, they are barbaric, they kill people and they kill ideas, they do not represent the true Afghanistan or true Afghans."

"You must be careful what you say," Khalid answered politely.

"I do not care if they come here to take me away. I will go telling them what I think of them," Malalaya shot back, unrepentant.

Khalid did not protest as she tugged at the rough blanket and tried to tuck it around him. He noticed her broken and blackened nails. They were at odds with the delicate, clean hands and white palms. She wore a large shawl, wrapped over her head, across her chest and over her shoulder, but as she leaned forward he caught a glimpse of her slender, tanned neck. Her face was strong yet gentle, fine but with pronounced features. Her jaw was firm and lent her an air of authority. Khalid couldn't remember when he had last been in the presence of a woman, not like this. He was drawn to her. She had a beauty that life had failed to blunt. He was mesmerised by her self-assurance. It wasn't arrogance, but a sense of being, of self-worth. Clearly she regarded herself as anyone's equal, refusing to be cowed because of her sex or her heritage. Malalaya caught Khalid studying her. She looked back at him, her face deadpan, betraying neither pity nor curiosity nor embarrassment.

"Khalid Bashir son of Farouk Bashir from Kachkai village in Northwest Pakistan, you will remain here," she said, now mocking his own introduction. "I will bring you food in a while. And when you are stronger there is something my father would like to talk to you about."

"If that is ok, Khalid?" Gul added.

Khalid didn't take his eyes of Malalaya.

"Of course. I am in your debt."

With his eyes he followed her as she left the room, her father trailing behind. Certain that she was gone he collapsed rapidly back into sleep. It was deep and black and without dreams. He had not slept this way for years, not since before he discovered the bitter news of his family. He was dreadfully tired but there was more to his calm than that. For the first time in an age he felt secure. Strange though it was to think it, he also, almost, felt loved.

He awoke not knowing how long he had slept. The only light in the room was cast by a candle sitting in the corner that he had not been aware of being lit. Staring into the flickering flame he was momentarily lost in thought. With the greatest effort he forced the images of those he loved most dearly from his mind only to find their faces replaced by that of Noor. Khalid sensed he was not alone; that someone had entered the room. Comfortable in his surroundings he turned over slowly, relieved that the careful shifting of his body was rewarded with only a mild sensation of pain. Malalaya was standing there.

"I have brought you something to eat."

She sat beside him and watched as he devoured what he had been given. Rice, some flat bread, lumps of chicken. Despite the company he made no attempt to disguise his craving, barely finishing one mouthful before stuffing in the next. All the time Malalaya studied him.

"You're hungry. Perhaps I should get you some more."

Khalid stopped eating, suddenly conscious of his gluttony, his cheeks bulging with food as he tried to speak.

"Very hungry," he spluttered, spitting out rice. He tried to apologise before deciding it best not to attempt to say anything further until he had finally finished what he had been served.

"Forgive me, Malalaya," Khalid said at last, embarrassed. "You must think me an animal."

"You do not need my forgiveness. I think you are smart. Probably educated. But maybe a little lost. Why are you here Khalid?"

"Did your father tell you what happened, how he found me?" Khalid asked.

"Of course. But this makes no sense even to my father. That is why he wants to talk with you. It is not my business. But I would like to know, will you bring grief to my family?"

"I am not a bad man, Malalaya," Khalid said, trying to skirt the issue. "I would do nothing to hurt those that do nothing to hurt me. You are right to say I am educated, you are right to say I am lost but with Allah's help I will find my way and I shall find peace."

"Can you read words?"

"Yes I can read words," Khalid responded, smiling.

"Will you teach me?"

Before Khalid could answer they were interrupted. Gul entered the room. Silently his daughter gathered the plate and left.

"Malalaya is my eldest. She is special to me. Her mother is dead and she is now the woman of this house. She cares for me and also for her sister. My only son is also dead, but she is as strong as any boy I have known, both physically and mentally. When we talk she runs rings around me. Her mind is agile and inquisitive. Always questions."

"Why would she not be married yet?" Khalid asked Gul. "Surely she has the charm and beauty to have suitors?"

"In truth, I will not give her to any man. Not for a dowry, nor for tribal allegiances. Her marriage will be her choice and not mine. She has not chosen a partner yet and until she does she will remain unmarried and I will stand against any man who would try to change this against her will. Maybe she will never marry. If that is her choice then so be it. All I care is that the decision is hers."

"Your wife and son are dead you say?"

"Yes," Gul replied. "My wife died peacefully a few years ago, may Allah protect her. My son was young and foolish and lured to fight with the Taliban by money and for false cause. And for his trouble he was killed in an accident high in the mountains."

"I am sorry," Khalid offered.

"Inshallah. He believed what he was told. He hated the infidels because he was told to. For the mere fact they were foreign. He gave his life cheaply. But foolhardiness is a trait of the young. I should have done better in preventing him from going. The fault is mine as much as his and I pray for forgiveness for not teaching him better."

Gul became reflective. He was motionless, not even blinking, just staring into space. Then with unexpected suddenness he turned back to Khalid, startling him. He had the most earnest look on his face.

"Mohammed has delivered you into my hands, it is Pashtun-wali and I take my responsibilities to you seriously, just as if you were my own son."

Khalid listened respectfully, not daring interrupt this man with the long white beard. Then his host asked the same question his daughter had.

"Tell me Khalid, do you fight with the Taliban? Will you bring more tragedy to my family?"

Khalid thought for a moment.

"Gul Mohammed I speak the truth to you and I ask for your understanding. I am a servant of the Prophet and I serve those who are his disciples. I fight those who fight against us and I have killed while doing this. My fight is one of vengeance and in honour of my family in Pakistan, destroyed by the infidel. My mother and sister were killed, my father lives, but only just." Khalid felt his throat tighten when he thought of Farouk. "I am not evil. I do not want power or money. Ultimately all I crave is peace and the opportunity to live simply on my own farm. But to get there has required violence. My hope is that my fight is now over but, to answer your question, my being here might put your family in danger. I shall leave now."

Another voice broke in.

"No Father, please," Malalaya urged. "He is too weak to leave, I feel a goodness in this man. We should help him."

"You should not have been listening daughter," Gul said angrily, turning to look at the figure in the doorway. Then more soothingly. "But I agree, Khalid will remain here until he is well. And then he can go. If he wants to."

"Gul, your hospitality humbles me," Khalid said. "But I must ask. What of the others who died at the bottom of the mountain?"

"When I went back I saw their bodies being taken away. By tribesmen or some of the local warlord's fighters. I can't be sure. But they have gone and only the vehicle remains, your secret is safe for now."

Gul pushed himself to his feet. He walked to the candle and blew it out, ushering his daughter to follow him. As they left the curtain fell. And so did the darkness. Within a few minutes Khalid slipped back into another deep sleep.

It was early the next morning when Khalid left his room for the first time since he'd arrived. He stepped through an anti-chamber and out into a brilliantly bright day. Pausing to absorb the warmth of the sun he saw his quarters were little more than a small annex of a much larger complex surrounded by a high perimeter. To his right, dominating the compound, was a two-storey building, constructed not of the more common mud bricks but hewn stone. Clean and bright it clearly belonged to a man of influence and wealth. Busying themselves in the yard were half a dozen men and women; tending animals or baking or cleaning and mending.

Khalid paused by a set of gates in the compound perimeter. Beyond them he could see more workers, these ones tending the surrounding grounds and fields. Beside the gates, sat a man of vast stature. He was more in attendance than on guard for there was no sign that he carried a weapon or would have even been able to leap into action if intruders approached.

"Good morning Khalid Bashir." The gentle voice of Malalaya took him by surprise, "Did you sleep well?"

"I did," Khalid answered, noticing her flushed face and the burgeoning basket of vegetables she carried, he added, "May I help you?"

"Yes you can, I am not here to tend you," she said teasingly.

Khalid reached across and took the basket from her. The effort made him wince in pain, a stabbing sensation in his side. He caught his breath but did not release his load.

"You should not have him working," Gul shouted from somewhere across the courtyard.

"He is strong Father and I think a little light work is good for him."

Khalid followed Malalaya towards a raised working space where she motioned him to set the basket down.

"I have something to show you," she said.

Malalaya led the way into a long room with a table and a stove in the corner puffing smoke. Next to it was an alcove packed with food vessels: jars, urns, drums, bottles, sacks.

"Look, can you read this?" Malalaya said, handing over a thin book with a battered and tatty, but colourful cover. There was real excitement in her face. He took what was offered and turned it over in his hands, opening it gently so as not to break the spine.

"This is not Pashtu or Dari Malalaya, it is in English," Khalid said.

"I know. I like the pictures, they are romantic. They are what I wish my life to be like."

"It is a fairy tale, not a true story. Make believe."

"Will you read it to me? Please," she asked again.

For the next hour Khalid did as he was bidden, reading the story to Malalaya, over and over. On the first occasion he had to keep stopping as she constantly interrupted with questions. But by the time he was reading the book for the fourth time she was enthralled, listening almost in a trance as the fantasy played out. Looking up from the text once or twice he caught her watching him. It gave him a rush. He had loved his family, but the warmth he felt towards this woman was not the same as he felt for those to whom he was related by blood. Never before had he sensed this kind of affection. And he liked it.

"How do you know English, Khalid?" Malalaya asked eventually as he came to the end of the book yet again.

"I learned it when I lived in my village, my grandfather taught me a little," he thought for a moment. "It was partly because of this that I was chosen to go to England to attend a military college. And there I mastered the language."

He could tell she had a flood of questions for him and that each answer he gave would only trigger more. He didn't see how he could deflect them and it left him torn. He was desperate to share his experiences with someone he was growing fond of and who was interested in him. But he was equally wary of putting her in a position where she knew too much. Not for the first time his saviour was Gul.

"I have brought you some food and clothes for your journey Khalid, as you requested."

"Thank you Gul. You are a very kind and honest man."

"You are leaving?"

"Yes Malalaya, I must. It is too dangerous if I stay here. For me and for you."

Malalaya turned to her father.

"You knew he was leaving and didn't tell me?" she said accusingly.

"It is the right thing to do; he cannot stay here. He might bring trouble to our household and he is correct to think this. But you are always welcome to return to us Khalid when you business is finished."

"May I ask you one more favour, Gul? Do you ever go to Kabul?"

"Yes, quite often. Probably once a month."

"Can I ask if you would do me a great favour? Would you go to the suburb of Qala-e-Shada and find a man there called Haji Rakim? He will direct you to a cemetery, to a hidden place where you might find a book that I left there. It would do me a great service if you retrieved it and looked after it. Can I ask that of you?" When Gul nodded agreement, Khalid explained where the house was and how Gul could reach it. Finally Khalid turned to Malalaya and looked into her imploring eyes.

"I will come back to see you Malalaya if your father allows me to."

"And what about me? Do I not have a say in the matter?" she replied. Khalid smiled. "And what is your say?"

"That when the time is right you should return to visit us."

Khalid shook Gul's hand, then shook Malalaya's. To do anything more would have been inappropriate. He picked up his bundle and turned to walk out of the room and out of the gates.

"Do not forget about us Khalid Bashir son of Farouk Bashir from

Kachkai village," she shouted after him. "Don't you dare."

Khalid smiled to himself but did not turn round. He had a journey to focus on. First he would go to Mazar-e-Sheriff and collect the car that had been left there for him. He was reluctant to, he knew how dangerous it would be, but there seemed little option. Then he would go to Pakistan and get his father; there was nothing else to be done. As soon as they knew he wasn't dead then they would kill his father. He was sure of it. He had to go and quickly.

———•———

Eight hours later, at the JOC HQ, the electronic warfare operator was about to end his shift. It had been another quiet day. He didn't like them like this. It was hard to maintain concentration and time dragged. He had spent much of the time thinking what he would do when he finished his tour – just three weeks away now – and got home. Much of his planning had centred on his rather plump but entirely enthusiastic wife. A flashing warning message jerked him back to the present.

"Sir, I have a mark here," he shouted.

"Go on," responded the duty watch keeper taking a bite from a sandwich.

"We have a red signal from a monitored source in the north of the country. It's coming up as Tango 411," the EW operator said studying his computer screen.

That was enough to make the watch keeper set down his sandwich and hurry over and view the signal for himself over the operator's shoulder. Having confirmed the signal he grabbed the phone and dialled the number he had been given for exactly this eventuality.

"What is it?" Cyrus said.

"Sir I have Tango 441 lit up heading from coordinates 41R PL 2425677 southeast towards sector 5 in the same grid indicator," the watch keeper reported, reading from the screen.

"Speak fucking English will you man."

"Yes Sir. Sorry Sir. It's a car heading from Mazar-e-Sheriff towards the PAK border. Objective Tabasco, Sir, his vehicle is on the move."

"Assemble the primary team now," Cyrus instructed.

"What shall I tell them, Sir?"

"Tell them they best move their fucking arses."

Chapter 20
RESCUE – NORTHERN AFGHANISTAN

Ever so gently Adam tried to ease the numbness in his backside, shifting his weight from one cheek to the other. Sitting cross-legged on the cold stone floor he had barely dared move since being dragged in and dumped in the corner. His hands were tied behind him, a thin rope chaffing at his wrists. Around his neck a padlocked metal collar forced his chin in the air. From it ran a chain. It wasn't taut, resting on his chest, but where it ended he could not see; the blindfold bound tight over his eyes prevented that. The fridge-like chill of the cell made him shiver.

Adam fought the temptation to move. He couldn't be sure he was alone. He had to assume he was being watched over by guards and he didn't want to attract any attention by revealing his discomfort. He was in deep shit but needed to remain calm, not cocky. Show fear when it was expected of him, but remain focused on the jobs at hand: staying alive, finding a way out. He considered how he might forge some link with his captors: whoever they were and however many there might be.

He estimated the journey from where he had been lifted had lasted no more than thirty minutes. Given the terrain that meant they'd probably covered no more than fifteen kilometres. On arrival he had heard people shouting and animals bleating nearby as he was hauled from the truck. It didn't mean much. There were kalays at every turn in Afghanistan. He had passed dozens on his way to the mountains from Mazar-e-Sharif.

As he was half shoved, half carried to the dungeon, there was another sound: the Pakistani driver protesting wildly. The cries had quickly trailed off as his fellow captive was, presumably, led away in a different direction.

Adam didn't waste his breath screaming. What was the point? Crying out in English would only have made those holding him more excitable than they already were at having caught a Westerner.

He wondered about Lal-Jan. Why had he had the mobile phone? Whose number had been programmed into it? From the gunman's reaction when it was answered it clearly hadn't been an Afghan on the end of the line. Adam's conclusion was that it was one of Cyrus's team; maybe Cyrus himself. Adam wanted to believe this was the case. If so it allowed him to hope someone knew he had been captured and, even as he trembled in the darkness, there was a rescue mission under way to get him out. Then he remembered. He wasn't a British soldier anymore. He no longer had the might of the British Army behind him. He was a mere contractor, a private security operator without backup. There would be no grand plan in place to get him out. Still, he had to cling onto something and the slim chance that someone was concerned enough about his fate to intervene was what he grasped hold of. The other scenarios weren't worth dwelling on. Torture, summary execution and then his body dumped in some miserable corner of Afghan. Only marginally better was the prospect that a ransom would be sought for his release; except there was no one to pay it, which took him back to the prospect that sooner or later he would be shot.

The more he considered the permutations the more likely it seemed he would have to shape his own fate. If any opportunity arose then he would try and escape.

He heard a bolt scraped back until it struck the hasp, and a door being opened, creaking. He felt a slight breeze wash lazily over his face. There were a few muffled footsteps before the sounds were repeated but in reverse. First the door and then the bolt slotted back into the secure position.

There was more movement, shuffling. He reckoned there were two people. He smelt sweat and tobacco, heard a cough. A sniff followed. The stench got closer. He braced himself as best he could. His only protection was his physical strength and the hope that any strike would be a fist or stick.

When the attack came it was more violent than Adam had anticipated. He gasped as he was flogged with a leather thong or belt, its edge ripping through his clothes and digging deep in to his flesh. Kicks started to land too, not the stamping of bare feet or those covered with nothing other than soft sandals, but concussing blows from heavy boots. One caught him just above the temple and he toppled over.

He struggled to curl into a foetal position, his hands still bound uselessly behind him. As he scrunched up, trying to protect his vital organs and his face, he was stunned by a ferocious punt that caught him on the nose in exactly the spot where he had been pistol-whipped. The old wound opened up. He felt warm sticky blood begin to flow, mixed with snot. The beating continued. Adam felt as if not a square inch of him had been left untouched. His mind began to cloud over. For all the world he wanted to give in to the temptation to fall into unconsciousness. But he understood it would be the death of him. He wouldn't wake again. He used every ounce of his strength, physical and mental, to tense against the onslaught, forcing his muscles to resist the attacks.

Then, as quickly as the assault had began, so it stopped. Through it all there had been no utterance from his tormentors other than deep intakes of breath, indications of the effort they were putting into their task.

Still panting, the attackers took hold of Adam, one of them fumbling to release his collar. They manhandled him towards the door. Someone grasped a fistful of his hair and jerked his head upwards. Adam wasn't in a position to care. Once again there were squeals of protest from the bolt as it was jerked free and then they were through the door and into the open. His blindfold had been torn off during the punishment and he took in as much as he could as he was propelled along by his captors. He noted there was an audience, mainly women and children, standing silently watching the spectacle. An image flashed up in his mind; from the old Hollywood blockbusters set in ancient Rome and the inevitable scene where the slave or the barbarian or the Christian or the traitor was paraded before the crowd in the Coliseum to be given the thumbs down by the emperor.

Adam felt another sharp blow to the back of his leg and he folded forwards onto his knees, the wickedly sharp corner of a stone digging deep into his patella. Something was jabbed into the rear of his skull. He braced against the gun barrel determined in his final moments not to appear cowed. He fought to keep his dignity, straining to keep his head up despite the downward pressure of the weapon. He knew it would be quick. There'd be no pain but his life would end here.

As he knelt in the position of prayer, one of his enemy started on a sermon, shouting out to the assembled gathering of onlookers. The words were spat out venomously. It was a harsh lecture, almost an act of incitement: the orchestration of a mob. Adam received another blow, this one to the back of his head. It sent him reeling forward, sprawling onto the deck. Now there were many pairs of hands clawing at him. Without any great skill but with earnest endeavour the baying crowd ripped at his clothes, raking his skin with their nails. Within seconds the hyenas had stripped him almost bare. He felt the scorching sun blazing onto his back. The sensation was almost therapeutic, the heat penetrating and soothing his wounds and bruises. Still a few sets of hands pawed at him, doggedly working to ensure he was completely naked.

A shattering volley of automatic fire halted the sacrificial ritual. Adam sunk further into the dust and lay there bleeding. Again he felt the pull of unconsciousness. Teetering on the edge of awareness he felt himself moving, being dragged through the dirt. He presumed it would be back to his cell where he would be revived, ready for the next ordeal.

———•———

It was a small convoy. Just two vehicles making their way along the wadi. Land Rovers, but not the sort you'd buy off the shelf or from the dealer. These were bespoke, skeletonised battlewagons, akin to the panthers used in Ulster twenty years previously. They were light on armour but heavy on weapons and their compact size and lack of weight gave them an agility that beat the Jackal and made them perfect for the job.

Each Land Rover carried three men. In the lead vehicle one of the crew scanned the ground ahead with his .50 calibre Browning. Behind him in the second Landy another soldier, grenade machine gun at the ready, watched to the rear for anyone who might decide they were worth a closer look.

None of the troops had a helmet; instead they wore baseball caps, wraparound sunglasses tucked in beneath the peak to protect against the wind and the dust. Over their mouths and noses they had tightly wrapped shamages.

There had been no conversation between the men since a pair of Chinooks had dropped them off three hours previously. They maintained their course through the series of waypoints plotted on their satnavs. Of the things that concerned them, IEDs were low on the list. An EW burn had been carried out only an hour before they were set down. It would have removed most of the seeded IEDs in the area, not that there were likely to have been many. The route they had chosen was pretty much random. The chances of striking an IED was about as remote as being hit by lightening.

———•———

Backed into the corner, Adam waited for the beating to begin again. The sound of footsteps got closer and he felt himself trembling at the thought of the pain and the shock. But when hands were laid on him they weren't inflicting harm, instead they roughly grasped at his arms and brought him up into a seating position. Someone tore off the blindfold that had been repositioned after the mock execution. Adam sat nervously, staring at the floor, waiting for the next stage of the procedure. There was a stinging blow, a slap, to his cheek, the sort you'd expect if someone was urgently trying to raise you from the deepest of sleeps.

Adam looked up. There were three people gathered in a semi-circle around him. Two men were standing whilst a third was down on his knees. It was the Pakistani interpreter.

"They want to know who you are," the lad said quietly with fear in his voice.

"Do you think they speak any English?"

"I don't think so. They haven't given any sign of it. That's why they came for me."

"What have you told them?" Adam said, his parched throat making him croak.

"I have only told them that you work for the television, that you are here to do a story in Afghanistan. About the war."

"Good, " Adam mumbled. "Stick with that story if you can."

On the edge of composure, the boy mumbled his affirmation.

"I know you're scared, but they are interested in me. If we can make them believe our story they may ransom me and let you go. Do you understand?" Adam said trying to reassure the lad.

The interpreter nodded.

"Have they hurt you, have they beat you" Adam asked.

"A little but…"

A slap to the back of the interpreter's head shut him up. The man who had struck him shouted out. The gaolers were clearly bored of listening to the boy talking to the prisoner and wanted their questions answered.

"They have asked me your name," the interpreter said after a moment.

"Tell them my name is Adam Caine."

The boy did as he was told. The older of the two guards asked another question as his colleague looked on, his rifle pointed at Adam's chest.

"They want to know exactly why you are here."

"I have come to speak to some of those fighting in the war against the Americans," Adam bluffed. "I heard there was an old warrior in the hills who might have fought with the Americans in the eighties but now fights against them. I wanted to talk to him. It sounded like a good story."

"Now they want to know which film company you work for? Who pays you? Are you American?"

"No, not American. I am Irish," Adam said opting for as neutral a country as possible. "I work independently but I am producing a film for the American company CNN. Have you heard of them?"

The interrogator spat on the floor contemptuously.

"He says they are lying scum. That they tell the American story, not theirs," the boy explained.

Adam had agonised over his fictional employer. His choice had eventually come down to one thing. Money. He had yet to meet an Afghan who didn't believe Americans to be stinking rich and if they thought he worked for a US firm then it might set the dollar signs ringing. CNN seemed to tick the right boxes. To his captors it was famous enough for them to have probably heard of it and American enough to have limitless funds to secure the release of one of their workers. Hopefully they would see Adam as an opportunity for wealth and a reason to delay killing him a little longer.

"They want to tell your story, the Afghan story. Attitudes are changing and they want to hear from you," Adam continued.

The man started shouting and slapped Adam across the face, hard.

"I am telling you the truth. I don't speak your language, I have no weapons. Why as a spy would I be here with no protection?" Adam pleaded.

"Maybe not you," the man said through the boy. "But the Pakistani with you had a gun and a phone, he had contact with the infidels."

"I knew nothing about this, maybe the Americans wanted to keep an eye on me and sent this man, I don't know, he was my guide, he was recommended to me," Adam begged.

There was a moment's silence as the two Afghans whispered to each other, their voices hushed but loud enough for Adam to pick up their confused and uncertain tones. To Adam it suggested they weren't the ones pulling the strings. They were two-bit players who had stumbled across something they didn't know how to handle. They'd never planned for something like this. The likelihood was that they were just local hooligans who would eventually approach a warlord and try to sell him on. The older man turned back to Adam.

"We are going to kill you if you do not tell us the truth."

"I am telling the truth," Adam said. "Call CNN. Ask them if they know who I am, they will vouch for me, they will pay money for me."

"Do you have the number?" the man asked.

"You can find it on the Internet. Just look it up," Adam said with slightly more confidence, putting the ball back in his captors' court.

The men started to talk. This time their conversation was louder and they were more animated.

"What are they saying," Adam risked whispering to the interpreter.

"They are talking about handing you over to the local Taliban leaders," he said.

"Are these men not Taliban then?"

"No, they work for a militia, they are not important. There are about twenty, maybe thirty, of them in the village."

Before Adam could warn him the butt of a rifle struck the interpreter between the shoulder blades, sending him flying.

"No, please don't hurt me," the interpreter yelled only for the younger guard to turn his AK47 round and jab it into the boy's mouth. Adam heard the crack of enamel, teeth breaking against the unforgiving metal of the gun.

The mood had changed in an instant, the men now extremely agitated and annoyed; maybe because of their own indecision or maybe as a result of the suspected scheming going on between their detainees. The older man kicked out with is boot and struck Adam in the balls. He let out a groan, a wave of nausea passing up his body. A rifle was pushed against his ear. Adam cursed. Perhaps they did have a plan after all. Kill their prisoners and rid themselves of the aggravation.

———•———

The arrival of UH-60 helicopter had not gone unnoticed by the locals. They were first aware of it when it was high above them. It was not an unusual sight, frequently, if not routinely, enemy aircraft came into view. One or two of the inhabitants had watched as the helicopter crossed the skies far above their territory and disappeared out of sight. What they couldn't then see and wouldn't have guessed was that five clicks beyond them the American pilot had applied the stealth noise suppressor and descended rapidly, turning through 180 degrees before flying low and fast on the reverse heading to the one the locals had just witnessed. Just short of the kalay it had dropped the last few metres to the deck, taking the impact on its sprung skids, relaxing onto its haunches as it hit the earth. Within ten seconds, its human cargo had disembarked and gone, the Black Hawk's pilot lifting the aircraft – now 1000 kilos lighter – vertically and swing away. With the chopper already a small smudge in the sky the unit of ten it had left behind divided: six turning south, the remaining four continuing westwards towards the settlement.

The smaller team fanned out, checking mud huts and compounds as they progressed. At first glance each appeared to be dressed like the local population, their heads covered with a turban, the end of which was hooked around the front of their faces. They wore long tan coloured cloaks that concealed their equipment and all but the bottom of their combat trousers. The only things that immediately set them out as different were the silenced M4 rifles with optic sights that they carried in their Oakley-gloved hands.

The quartet moved on, relying on momentum and confusion to keep them out of trouble. On the outskirts of the village men and women worked steadily in the fields, concentrating so hard on their labours that they didn't see the soldiers closing in on the heart of their community. Others had seen them trot past, but did not react, unsure of who the strangers were or what they were doing. Next to a well, shaded by a thicket of trees, a group of elders sat about, talking with several younger men. Without fanfare one of the new arrivals stopped and took up a watching position over them. His stance was neither aggressive nor defensive. He was simply there, his M4 held at his side. Forty metres further on another member of the team covered a short alleyway that opened out on to the fields and the main track in and out of the village. The remaining pair jogged on towards their target.

Eighty metres south of the village the half-dozen men in the second group had settled down to watch and wait, forming an extended line on raised ground. Lying on their bellies they readied their weapons: an assortment of rifles and light machine guns, and a single, heavier, general purpose machine gun. None of them were encumbered by native dress; instead they wore UK forces' MTP, plates carriers and belt order. Each had a baseball cap and ballistic glasses; none said a word.

Patiently they awaited their cue.

The lead duo of the assault team stacked beside the slightly open door of the cell. The senior man looked back at his colleague and gave him a small nod. Raising his rifle the second man looked over the top of the sight and scanned the entrance waiting for the signal to go.

———◆———

Adam winced as the rifle muzzle was jabbed hard against his ear. His head was turned on its side, the pressure from the rifle pinning it against the floor. He swivelled his eyes to catch a glimpse of the light streaming through the door. He blinked uncertainly. Something had appeared at the bottom of the jamb. It looked like a tin of beans. The toe of a boot appeared to give the can a gentle kick and it rolled slowly in to the room. Adam closed his eyes, ready for what would come next.

The grenade was commonly known as a 'flash-bang' but its nickname seriously undersold the violence of the weapon. The detonation was ear splitting and the creation of the universe couldn't have started with a more brilliant flare of fire and light. Adam's head started to resonate in tune with the reverberations of the explosion bouncing off the walls of the small chamber. He knew exactly where he was but felt utterly disorientated. He thought he could make out the low muffled sounds of a silenced rifle being fired on automatic, but his confused state meant he couldn't be sure. Half-heartedly raising his head, he watched as a gunman paced into the room, pulling his rifle into his shoulder and scanning for targets. The first he found was the Afghan who had been standing over Adam ready to dispatch him out of this life.

The would-be executioner shuddered as the bullets struck him. This was no double tap, no single shot to the head, just the sustained ferocity of rounds pouring from a weapon on full auto.

Bullets struck the victim in the torso, legs, chin and shoulder, boring into flesh and shattering bone. The low impact dumb-dumb projectiles had enough energy to do the damage but lacked the penetrative power to pass right through the body and hit anyone behind. The effects were lethal.

Stricken by the numerous 5.56mm rounds that had hit him the first man collapsed. Already the gunman had turned his attention to the younger Afghan. Lumps of expanding lead tore holes in his throat. He went down face first, falling across the shocked interpreter. The boy tried to shrug off the corpse, appalled by the splintered body resting on top of him. He tried to stand.

"No! Stay still!" Adam yelled.

The boy didn't hear him, or else ignored the warning. Clumsily he got to his feet, raising his arms for balance. He was left facing the duo of men who had entered the room. Without hesitation they turned their weapons on him and pulled the triggers. Way too late Adam shouted for them to stop but already the youth's body was ragged and wrecked.

Adam closed his eyes and let his face rest on the floor. Behind his back he felt a knife cut through the bindings on his wrists and yet again he was conscious of someone hauling him off the floor. Kneeling unsteadily he stared into a pair of deep blue eyes just inches from his own.

"Adam Caine, can you hear me?" the voice said.

"Yes I can hear you," Adam replied.

"This is UK SF. We are here to get you out. Can you walk?"

"Yes I think so" Adam nodded.

"Ok let's try."

The Special Forces soldier helped Adam to his feet and then stood holding him for a moment while Adam steadied himself. The second trooper hovered at the exit, on the lookout. There was more gunfire. Not silenced this time.

"How does that feel?"

"Yea good."

"Right stick this on," Adam's rescuer instructed, removing his cloak to reveal his UK military uniform beneath. Adam took the woollen robe and draped it over his naked shoulders.

"Here." The SAS trooper handed Adam a Glock 9mm pistol. "It's made ready. Are you happy how to use it?"

"Yes of course," he replied.

"Well just be careful where you fire. We have other men out there. Now let's get the fuck out of here."

The three men grouped by the door and peered out. There was now a lot of activity. Some of which they could see, most of which they could only hear: the whiz and heavy impact of rounds coming from the high ground; the bullets ripping up the ground, tearing into compounds, whistling along alleys, creating a wide beaten zone inside which nothing that moved was going to survive.

The flash-bang going off had initiated most of the mayhem. The moment it exploded the two troopers in the village raised their weapons and engaged anyone who looked like they might pose a threat. Simultaneously the two heavily armed Land Rovers that had been dropped off by Chinook hours previously and made their way across the desert emerged from the wadi they had followed all the way to the kalay. The combination of the .50 cal and the GMG helped fuel the panic. The famers in the fields scattered and insurgents dived for cover. But the firing wasn't random. It created a clear corridor down which Adam could be ushered away.

"Lets go!" shouted one of the troopers and the three men darted into the open, Adam taking one backwards glance at the broken body of the young interpreter.

The trio moved quickly. Fire seemed to have erupted from everywhere. Instinctively Adam ducked every time the heavy weapons of the support team went off. As they passed across the open ground the other two team members collapsed behind them to cover their withdrawal. Adam and his escort reached the edge of the village then stopped for a moment so the leader could gather them all in and make sure everyone was accounted for.

"Just wait here," he ordered.

Adam leaned against the wall of a compound, left exhausted and dizzy by the short dash. The pistol he held in his hand felt like a tonne weight and his arm hung limply by his side. His vulnerability attracted predators. From behind a mud wall a wild-eyed man with a rifle walked out. Adam harnessed his last reserves of energy and hauled the Glock to the horizontal, struggling to control his quivering arm. Without taking proper aim he fired twice. The pistol kicked hard and he almost dropped it. The rounds flew off wildly. Adam slumped to his knees as the attacker raised his rifle, somewhat surprised that he was getting the chance to do so. Adam tried to level his pistol once more but he was out of strength. Now it was his turn to be surprised as a volley of shots brought the Afghan down. Adam turned to see one of the troopers towering over him, his own weapon pointed in the direction of the motionless figure. The trooper shot again, putting another fistful of bullets into the body. Then they were on the move again, towards the spot where the Black Hawk had put down ten minutes earlier, the last part of their retreat covered by the so far unused and unnoticed half-dozen troopers concealed in the tree line. Their moment came. A group of insurgents had regrouped and were charging out of the village. As they broke clear of the buildings their progress was brought to a shuddering halt. In the first seconds of the ambush most of the insurgents were in the low trajectory volley and went down. A couple managed to turn away but were simply shot in the back. One or two more dragged themselves into a ditch at the bottom of which they cowered.

The UH-60 appeared, skimming the ground, aiming for the billowing green smoke now marking the HLS. As it brushed the ground, Adam was shoved forward. He was the first to board, followed rapidly by the assault quartet and then the ambush team. Within half a minute the Blackhawk was airborne again, spinning on its axis and departing to the south. Adam lay on the floor of the chopper drained of will to move, his rescuers crammed in around him. His nose to the floor Adam closed his eyes. The last thing he saw was a black boot. It was the most comforting thing in the world.

At the kalay the Land Rovers had dropped back in to the wadi to begin their own journey home, travelling north to the pre-arranged pick-up point some three hours drive away. The mission success would only be real to them once they were safely onboard the Chinook routing back to Kandahar.

Chapter 21
THE JOURNEY EAST

The old man kicked the tyre of the car and rubbed his beard in contemplation. Khalid watched impatiently.

"Look, I want to sell my car," he said again to the garage owner. "Do you want to buy it or not?"

The proprietor of the back-street workshop was in no rush.

"How much for? Is it stolen?"

"Maybe it is stolen but not by me," Khalid said. "All I want is another vehicle to replace this one."

The man eyed up what he was being offered then set off for another walk around it. He had to admit that for an Afghan vehicle it was in pretty good condition: the rubber had plenty of tread, the engine sounded smooth, even the interior was reasonably clean.

"Are you in trouble?" he probed again.

"I do not have time to tell you my life story. If you do not want to do business then I will go somewhere else and let them benefit. It's up to you."

At last the old man nodded slowly.

"Yes, I think we can do a deal."

He ushered Khalid to the back of the premises, past a variety of pistons and cylinder heads and brakes and drive shafts and radiators, and then out into a yard, in the middle of which sat a vintage Datsun missing its rear bumper and window. Khalid studied it sceptically. It didn't look as if would start let alone get him to Pakistan but he didn't have many options. The car he had arrived in had been parked just where he was told he'd find it, the keys tucked into a rusty crevice in the wheel arch. Driving towards Kunduz he wondered when the drone strike would come; the one that would obliterate him and solve a problem for the Americans. For reasons he was unsure of he survived the journey but he wasn't going to stay in the vehicle any longer than he had to.

"Does it run?" Khalid asked.

"Of course it runs. It is my car. I have had it for many years and it has never failed me."

Khalid exchanged the keys to his car for those belonging to the one before him. Slipping inside he put the key in the ignition and turned it. The engine cranked into life. There was a roar from the holed exhaust, but the engine sounded strong.

"I think you have problems my friend. Do you want something to eat before you continue on your journey?" The offer of hospitality appeared genuine but Khalid shook his head.

"I need to be on my way."

The deal complete, Khalid nosed out of the garage. He set off as if tracing the route back to Mazar-e-Sharif. But after a short distance he turned left. The road headed south towards Baghlan and Kabul beyond. From there he would make for Jalalabad and the Khyber Pass. At that stage, almost in sight of the frontier, there would be another critical decision to be made. The arrangement was that he'd find there a dead letterbox containing money and passports for him and his father. Yet to collect what awaited there might be complete folly. It was ludicrous to think the drop wouldn't be watched. And if they were he was likely to be caught.

———◆———

Adam woke with a start. Raising his head slightly he looked towards the bottom of the bed. Peter stood there looking down at him.

"How long have I been here?" he asked groggily.

"Not long, you got in yesterday evening, slept through the night." Peter replied, "How are you feeling?"

"I'm fine," Adam lied wincing as he tried to sit up and swing his legs on to the floor, uncertain of his surroundings.

"Looks like it."

"Where are we?"

"Kabul. At the ISAF medical facility in the main airport."

To demonstrate the point there was a roar overhead as a plane took off.

"Well I guess the shit has hit the fan. What's being said?" Adam asked.

"Nothing."

"Nothing? Why not?"

Peter didn't answer straight away. Instead he looked around the room to confirm no one was within earshot.

"I knew you were going to go for Khalid," Peter started. "It was obvious and in a way I thought it was a good idea. We had been held back by the Americans and I guessed, as you had, the reason was they were trying to get to him first."

"But if that's the case why didn't you offer me some support instead of making me go it alone?"

"There are two answers to that. First is, I did support you, with our sixth man."

"You mean Lal-Jan? What the fuck was that all about?" Adam asked angrily.

"He was my man on the inside. Like it or not, if I hadn't sent him with you the likelihood is we'd never have known what had happened to you," Peter replied.

"But he paid with his life?"

"Yes he did. And as you know well enough that's the game we're in. As for the reason we stayed back, well if Cyrus knew we had made a break for it he would have closed us down. This way I could use the 'rogue man' approach to try and hold him off for a bit."

Adam weighed up the explanation.

"And now?"

"Now I have a bit more of a handle on what is going on and why they want him dead."

Adam stood up gingerly and moved towards Peter. He felt the pain of his beatings keenly but he also understood that the more he moved the quicker his muscles would loosen up. He stopped in front of Peter.

"What exactly have you learnt?" he asked.

Peter thought for a moment; things were moving fast; lots of talking and bluffing going on between US and UK intelligence, as well as between the governments. But as far as he was concerned nothing had changed, his mission to capture Khalid was still very much on. Khalid Bashir in UK custody with details on his work for US intelligence and how this led to the deaths of UK and other ISAF forces would be explosive. A huge bargaining chip for the UK government to negotiate whatever they wanted: a trade deal probably – weapons or oil or gas; something big and important and costly, that was for sure. There was little that was moral about politics. It was about the practical. The art of the possible. Important men playing their games through their pawns. It had ever been thus, particularly in this part of the world. For God's sake thought Peter they even called it the Great Game.

"They knew about Khalid all along," Peter said. "They had a chance to grab him but let him continue in the hope he would lead them to some kind of big fish."

"They knew?"

"Yes and two days ago he delivered them the prize, the Taliban finance minister. The Americans took him out not far from where you were taken."

"So was Khalid killed too?" Adam asked the obvious question.

"That is the presumption. What I do know is Cyrus wants to speak to me, in fact us, as soon as you are able to walk."

"In Khost? We have to head back there?"

"Ah no, Cyrus has thoughtfully made the trip to Kabul. The team has also made its way here. I suppose he will tell us Khalid is dead, our mission is over and we can head home."

"We failed then. I failed."

Peter did nothing to correct Adam's view of what might have happened to Khalid.

"Don't be too hard on yourself. The mission was always a long shot given the CIA's spoiling tactics."

Peter stuck to the half-truths, unwilling to divulge the full picture of what had been going on.

Adam bent over, deflated. If the mission was terminated they would return to the UK, each man going his separate way: some to be recalled for future ops, others like Adam, to be conveniently forgotten and never used again. The last few days had taken a lot out of him and he was unsure what was going to happen next. He wasn't convinced Khalid was dead, something told him that those men that had taken him captive were picking up survivors. One of those survivors could have been Khalid.

"You ok?"

"Never better," Adam replied. "Let's go see Cyrus and get this over with."

———◆———

It had taken Khalid five hours to reach Kabul, but he didn't pause in the capital. Instead he drove hard along the main artery between Afghanistan and Pakistan heading for the border. He wanted to believe the change of vehicle had thrown the CIA off his scent but he still hadn't determined what he'd do next. He knew by heart the location of the drop east of Jalalabad, just off the highway up a small feeder road to the north.

Yet the odds of it being under surveillance were high. Either it would be marked electronically or else there might be human eyes on it. Maybe both. He could take a chance, do a drive by and see the lay of the land; alternatively he could head straight on to the porous frontier, hoping to slip through without credentials. He was still mulling over what to do as he approached the turn and swung left.

———•———

Amid the ruins of the crumbling building the two men sat quietly, drinking tea and eating the rice they were scooping out of the pan positioned between them. They were local to the area, a region that had suffered badly over the previous 20 years. A long time previously, as a boy, one of the pair had helped guide tourists. There had been none of those for an age. And their absence meant the opportunity of making a half-decent living was all but nonexistent. Most of the population followed a way a life that, before the visitors, had not changed for centuries: one of toil and subsistence. It meant scavenging for work, the sort of work that would have been familiar to the countless generations that preceded them: labouring, farming, harvesting the poppy. Neither the man nor his companion was particularly fond of the Taliban. Their ambivalence extended to the government forces, but they would happily do jobs for either if there was money on offer; so when, the previous day, they had been asked to watch the ancient graveyard that serviced the ruined village they were quick to accept. Their orders were simple enough. Shoot anyone who approached the cemetery. They weren't to ask any questions or verify anyone's identity. There wasn't any point in worrying about innocent casualties. The village had been abandoned long ago and it was unlikely anyone had come to mourn the dead for years. The two men weren't worried about the prospect of killing. They had murdered before, in the course of the robberies they'd been forced to commit to try and survive. The difference here was that they knew upfront what their reward would be.

Khalid pulled up about five hundred metres down the track he had just taken. He turned off the engine and stayed still for a minute, letting the silence envelope him, looking out for anyone who might have seen him drive up. The only people he could see were now someway behind him, stallholders who had laid out their wares on flea-bitten rugs back at the junction. The drop was about one kilometre further on. He thought it better to continue on foot. If anything looked untoward he could at least sneak a retreat back to the car without compromising it. He moved north, handrailing the track, staying a good hundred metres away from it. His destination was a burial site and in that site was a small grave adorned with a yellow and red banner. There would be a pile of stones at the head of the grave with a small, roughly fashioned wooden plaque carrying no name. If he lifted the plaque it'd reveal a hollow in the stones where the documents and cash were hidden. So he had been told.

Striding along the slightly rising scrubland he came to a spot that afforded him good sight of the landscape beyond. He dropped to his stomach and slid up to the lip of the viewing platform. The village with the graveyard was clear to see but there was no sign of life. Khalid waited patiently but nothing stirred. Content with what he had seen, he eased himself backwards and off the skyline. Then he froze. He had caught the movement out of the corner of his eye. Khalid remained stock still. At the edge of the track a man was carefully adjusting his position in the lee of a shallow drainage ditch that had become overgrown. He was peering down the track in the direction where Khalid had parked, but because of the lay of the land he wouldn't have seen him drive up.

Khalid started to creep towards the sentry, trying to stay in his blind spot. He got to within fifty metres and then sprawled out on his stomach again. He studied his prey. The Afghan held his weapon with both hands. He seemed alert but all his attention was towards the track.

Back on his feet, Khalid slipped into the drainage ditch and closed in on his quarry, using the foliage smothering the channel to mask his progress. Held in his right fist was the clasp knife that had already served him so well. Ghost walking, he checked where he placed his foot before committing to each step. One dislodged rock or broken twig and the man would turn around. It would be game over. Khalid was right behind the lookout. He could see the rise and fall of his body as he breathed. Khalid held the knife tighter in an overhand grip. His knuckles went white. Raising himself to his full height he covered the final steps as rapidly as he could. The man was almost within arm's reach. At the last moment the man jerked up, sensing danger. But Khalid was already on him, wrapping his left arm around the man's head, his forearm covering his mouth. His right hand shot forward, burying the knife deep between the man's shoulder blades alongside the spine. Khalid ripped and tore with the knife, feeling the metal slice flesh and then catch on bone. He was hopeful he had hacked through the spinal cord. The confidence was well founded. His opponent sagged to the ground, alive but immobilised. Khalid yanked out the blade and put the bloody tip under the man's chin. The sentry looked at Khalid with a mix of helpless terror and incomprehension. Khalid kept his hand over the man's mouth as the tip of the knife pressed against the skin, breaking it.

"Are you alone?" Khalid demanded.

The man didn't answer; he just stared. Shock had taken control of him. Khalid pressed the knife a little further trying to break the spell.

"Are you alone?" he hissed, more menacingly. "It will take no effort for me to drive this knife into your throat. Tell me, are you alone?"

"No there are two others. Please help me, I can't feel my legs, my arms."

Khalid looked down at the lifeless limbs, noticing the stain spreading on trousers, a sign that he had lost control of his bodily functions either from fear or the damage done by the blade.

"Where are they?" Khalid asked trying to focus on his task.

"In the building close to the burial site. They are watching it."

"Are they armed?"

"Yes. Please help me," the man pleaded.

Khalid raised his head slightly and looked across the ground towards the village. There was a ruined compound just back from the burial site. His guess was that's where they'd be.

"Please you can't leave me like this," the man whimpered.

"Sorry," was all Khalid said before he put his weight behind the knife, feeling it slide easily into the man's throat, tearing his windpipe. There was a strange gurgling noise and blood began to dribble from the man's mouth and through Khalid's fingers as he kept them pressed over the man's face. For a few seconds the eyes looking at him widened in horror, then they simply froze over, lifeless. Khalid cautiously pulled his hand away to reveal a gaping mouth set in a look of utter bewilderment. He tried to clean some of the blood off on a tuft of grass then snatched the rifle still held possessively by the corpse.

He checked the magazine of the battered AK47 and pulled back the cocking handle to confirm a round was chambered. He clicked the change lever from automatic to repetition then shuffled to the edge of the drainage ditch and viewed his surroundings once more. He made a mental note of the route he would take; it would give him cover from view although not fire if he were seen. He heaved himself out of the channel and jogged off gently in a slight stoop.

Besides the cemetery, the larger of the two guards rose to his feet and lifted the simple press-to-talk radio to his mouth.

"Gulum?" he said. "Gulum, can you hear me?"

The radio that lay in the scrub besides Gulum crackled but there was no one who could answer it.

"Gulum, Gulum, are you sleeping?"

The man stood up and tried for a third time to raise his colleague. Worried now, he stepped towards the crumbling entrance to the building to look in the direction of the main highway.

"I am going to check on Gulum, lazy bastard."

"Ok," came the disinterested response from his friend who continued to pick away at his food.

The first guard went to leave but a shadow darkened the threshold. It was followed by a figure holding a rifle. The guard moved to raise his hands but Khalid ignored the gesture and pulled the trigger of his rifle twice in quick succession. Two rounds impacted the man's chest and he fell to the ground. The second man, still eating and with his back to the door, had no time to register what he had just heard. Even as he sat there, ready to scoff another handful of rice, Khalid had turned his weapon on him and fired again. The 7.62mm short round smashed through the rear of the Afghan's skull, tore through the cranial cavity and exited through his cheek, taking with it a bloody spray of bone, brain and food. The man slumped forward, what was left of his head landing on the cooking pot.

Khalid spotted the radio. He hadn't noticed the sentry back up the track with any communications kit but he assumed he was the only person this pair would have had electronic contact with. Khalid stepped past the bodies, out of the rear of the hut and across the road to the burial plot. There were only two graves decorated with banners and only one of these had a cairn on top. Khalid squatted down in front of it and moved aside the plaque. He leant further forward and took out the small package inside.

———•———

"Call Cyrus," the duty watch keeper in the CIA HQ said to the operator.

"Yes, Sir," he replied. "What would you like me to say?"

"Just tell him the hide has been activated, I am looking for authority to engage satellite tracking and deploy a Reaper to the area."

The operator dialled the number for Cyrus and when it was answered passed on the message.

"Put the watch keeper on for me please," Cyrus said as calmly as he could.

"Duty watch keeper speaking."

"Ok, tell me how long since the hide was activated and explain to me why we didn't have eyes on it?"

"Sir," the watch keeper replied. "It was activated less than three minutes ago. I believe we did have eyes on it via a local HUMINT source, he is now trying to raise communications with his men on site. As yet he has heard nothing, suggesting they've either bunked off or been bumped off."

"OK, lets get the satellite over there, no point deploying the Reaper now, too late, but lets see if we can identify the vehicle he is in."

"Yes Sir."

"Did we locate the control vehicle he took from Mazar-e-Sharif?" Cyrus asked.

"Yes Sir, it was found in a garage in Kunduz. Unfortunately the NDS has lifted the garage owner and we haven't yet had the opportunity to talk to him."

"Fucking Afghans," Cyrus said and hung up.

Chapter 22
OPERATIONAL BRIEFING – KABUL

Adam and Peter strode out of the medical facility heading for the nearest vehicle parked in front of the building. Clambering inside Peter nodded acknowledgement to the driver, uniformed in canvass trousers and a tan shirt, the regulation pair of sunglasses concealing his eyes. Nobody spoke. Doors shut, the driver pressed the accelerator and they sped off towards the airfield, barely slowing for a barrier that was rapidly raised as they approached. Airside, they stuck to the road tracking the perimeter. Hitting a straight section of tarmac the driver put his foot down further.

They were headed for a non-descript set of prefabs close to the end of the runway, surrounded by a high link fence atop of which were perched rolls of razor wire. At each of the enclosure's four corners sat a sentry tower. This time there was no automatic entry and they stopped before a horizontal bar that was flanked by two heavily armed US soldiers, wearing almost identical grim expressions. Without a word the driver showed his ID card and was ushered inside the gatehouse. A minute later he was back and driving his passengers the last few metres to their destination; the smallest of the half dozen or so buildings on the plot.

Adam could see the Det boys standing outside the door, their equipment and weapons with them. Peter was quick to dismount.

"Hi fellas, sorry to keep you waiting."

"What's going on boss?" Simon said moving towards his team leader.

"Not sure, about to find out I hope," Peter answered.

Adam followed Peter from the vehicle. He stood for a moment

facing the other Brits. At first he thought the guys were going to blank him: it must have crossed their minds that this Rupert was a bit of a dick for heading off on his own initiative. Al approached with a none-too-friendly look on his face. Adam was relieved when it mellowed into a grin.

"Good to see you made it out, mate," Al said thrusting an M4 carbine in Adam's direction.

Adam took the rifle; instinctively checking the safety was on.

"Ah yeah, none too clever I think," Adam replied sheepishly.

"Well, we have all done that shit before, only you seem to have done it more than most. We've the rest of your kit here."

They walked over to where Rocky, Simon and now Peter stood.

"Pleased to see you safe sunshine," said Rocky, patting Adam on the shoulders. Adam winced as he did so; the whipping and beatings he had received would take a while to heal.

"Never thought I would say this to such an ugly pair of heads but it is great to see you."

"They seem to have given you a thorough going over," Rocky observed.

"I know a woman in Thailand who could leave you like that," Simon added. "But she would charge you about two hundred dollars for the pleasure."

"Know from experience, eh?" Al chipped in. "Trust you to have to pay to get some. You'd get it for free if you weren't such a big ugly cunt."

Adam felt overwhelmed; the men had cracked on as if he had never been away. He was tempted to say something to thank them but thought better of it.

Al filled the silence

"Do you think you got anywhere near Bashir?"

Adam pondered.

"Not sure. I think I was on his tail, but the CIA beat me to it."

"So do you think he's dead?" Simon asked.

Adam shrugged.

"I reckon we're going to find out soon enough."

The five-man team chatted for a while, Peter slightly aloof from the rest listening more than talking. He knew they had not come all this way just to get some sun, but now he had to go through the motions with Cyrus and see what the plan was going to be, and whether a tan really would be the main highlight of the trip.

"I hate to interrupt the tearful reunion guys but I'm going to need you lot to wait here for a while longer while I go in to get a brief from the CIA chief. Meanwhile double-check that kit of ours. If you're lucky you might still get to use it and have a bit of fun."

Peter gauged the guys' reaction. They seemed pleased there was still the chance for some action. Apart from the insertion and the move from Kachkai to Khost the men had done very little. They were impatient: keen to either leave the country and the mission, or get on with it and take it to a conclusion.

"Adam I need you to come with me," Peter said turning for the building.

"Sure no problem," said Adam and jogged gently after his boss.

———•———

Khalid crossed the Afghan side of the frontier with ease, his progress aided by the handful of US dollars he had found on the three men he killed. He had used ten of the greenbacks to bribe the border guard. It helped he had left his passage until it was late. The headlights and continuous, chaotic stream of traffic had made the policeman flustered: he was fed up because his colleagues had disappeared on their meal break leaving him to fend off agitated and impatient travelers. He waved vehicles through with only a cursory glance, his mind concentrated on getting his share of the food. Khalid raised his hand in thanks as he was ushered on. Now he sat in no-man's land having left Afghanistan but not yet passed into Pakistan. There was another checkpoint ahead and the sentries on duty there seemed ten times more vigilant, or at least ten times slower.

Stuck in the queue he looked over to the passenger seat to check how much American currency he had left; just five crumpled single-dollar bills. He didn't think it would be enough.

His heart began to beat faster. The Pakistani officials were asking drivers for their travel documents and all the lorries were being searched, as was every second car or so. Khalid edged forward at a snail's pace following an overloaded bus full of what he supposed were migrant workers heading home. He knew the risk he was taking. While the steady stream of vehicles and people helped mask his movements and made it all but impossible for US intelligence to lift him here – there were too many variables and the operatives would be at the mercy of the mob if anything went wrong – it was increasingly difficult to see how he was going to get across without a passport or a meaningful amount of money.

His decision to go to the graveyard had always been a gamble, but even so the realisation that he had wasted his time while putting himself in extreme danger for a nil return was a bitter disappointment. When he'd thrust his hand into the crevice and retrieved the parcel he'd momentarily thought he'd struck gold. The flush of success evaporated when he examined the bag's contents. He'd flung the wad of blank paper to the ground in a fit of rage. But his anger wasn't going to solve the problem he now had.

Khalid counted the guards. There were two of them checking credentials, working as a pair, one covering the other. A third man occupied a sandbagged bunker in the middle of the road, trying to watch the streams of traffic that approached him from both directions.

Khalid hung slightly back from the bus. If he leaned towards the side window, he was afforded just enough space to get a glimpse of the string of cars and lorries coming along the other side of the highway. The dull orange glow of the sodium lights at the checkpoint was barely enough energy to illuminate the immediate vicinity of the crossing point, leaving the rest of the area in the inky darkness of a moonless night, pierced only by headlight beams. But Khalid didn't worry about these. In fact they were a blessing, helping – with the sodiums – to destroy any night vision the sentries might have hoped to have.

The bus had reached the front of the queue. Khalid waited as the guard went first to the driver's window and then walked around the front of the vehicle and went inside, up the steps. His colleague followed behind, covering the movements with his weapon. It was systematic, ordered and professional. Routine.

Khalid revved his engine as high as he dared and dropped the clutch. The tyres spun briefly before finding purchase in the dust and the car shot forward crunching violently into the bus's rear end. There was the rending of metal as both vehicles buckled under the impact. Khalid was thrown against the steering wheel gashing his forehead. Inside the bus occupants were sent flying. Immediately the air was full of cursing and shouting. Horns started to blare as other travellers waiting their turn further back realized they'd now be stuck for even longer.

Stepping unsteadily out of the car Khalid held his arms out, open palmed, in protestation. The second guard edged towards him, nervous now. They were both immediately engulfed by the passengers pouring off the bus to see for themselves what was going on. Amongst them was the furious driver, clutching a handkerchief to a head wound weeping blood. Indignantly he inspected the damage. Some of those in surrounding vehicles whose evenings had been ruined joined the melee, complaining and gesturing. Khalid kept up his act. Trying to remain calm, arguing he was the innocent party. More soldiers appeared from the guardroom, but none took control merely adding to the chaotic throng. In the confusion Khalid had lost sight of the man with the gun and he shadowed one of the passengers as he walked back towards the door of the bus. But where the man went inside Khalid simply kept going straight on, shielded from sight by the bulk of the vehicle. He ducked under the barrier and increased his pace. He dared a look round but no one was coming after him, no one shouting out that he should stop. Another few metres and he became lost amongst a mass of stationary trucks, tired travelers and roadside hawkers.

Khalid didn't rest until he was more than a kilometre down the road. Then he put his hands on his knees and tried to catch his breath. He allowed himself a weak smile. He was home, back in Pakistan. But he wasn't going to get all the way to Peshawar by foot. He needed another form of transport. He felt in his pocket and grasped the lock knife. He didn't want to kill again, but if that is what it took then he needed to be ready for it.

———◆———

Cyrus Vincent was deep in discussion with a man in uniform when Peter and Adam walked in and approached him. Cyrus terminated his conversation but gave no words of welcome. He perched himself on a rickety-looking chair beside a large projection screen. He pointed to two more chairs facing the screen. The British pair took the hint and sat down. The fourth man – the odd one out in dress terms – remained standing and started to talk.

"My name is Bret Andrews. I am the operations officer for all CIA kinetic strikes in the north of Afghanistan, as well as liaison officer for all activities with Regional Command Southwest. What I am going to tell you is for our-eyes only. We ask that no notes are taken. And please don't interrupt."

"Seven days ago our sources in Kandahar picked up information that a senior Taliban figure was going to be visiting Afghanistan from the Quetta Shura. Further MX reporting from Quetta confirmed this senior figure was Mahsud, the Taliban finance minister, designated Objective Vegas. As you can imagine the White House suddenly became very interested indeed in what was happening. Initially our biggest issue was that we had no leads as to where the meeting would take place or when. That changed when we picked up radio traffic from your man Khalid Bashir. It became clear that Bashir would be attending the meeting so it was a case of triangulating the signal and tracking Bashir down, which we did to a house in the western suburbs of Kabul."

Bret halted as an aerial photograph of a densely packed urban area appeared on the screen. After a few seconds it was replaced. Peter and Adam watched as a series of images flashed up; the same subject but from different angles and varying times of day. Then they were into pictures of individuals milling around in a rural compound.

"Along with MX reporting and satellite surveillance we were able to follow Bashir as he left the house in Kabul and moved to a village in the mountainous region northwest of Kabul and north of the town of Mazar-e-Sharif. Local informants identified the settlement as Jamadar Kalay, home to a high-profile supporter of the insurgency. This gave us confidence we had the correct location, but we could not be one hundred percent sure because poor atmospheric conditions meant we lost track of Bashir. However we then took this shot of Jamadar."

A single image appeared on the screen. At its centre were a couple of trucks.

"And eight hours later, this one."

There were now several vehicles and a much larger number of people.

"Thank you for not interrupting. Now do you have any questions?" Bret asked.

"You believed the increase in vehicles signified the arrival of

Mahsud?" Peter asked the obvious.

"Yes we did and permission was requested to conduct a kinetic strike against the village and the intended target Objective Vegas.

"And Bashir?" Adam asked.

"He didn't factor in our decision making," Bret answered.

"Did you know I was en route to the same area?" Adam queried.

"Yes we did but that didn't factor in our decision making either."

There were no more questions. Cyrus stood up and moved to a position just behind Peter and Adam. He stayed silent as Bret went on.

"Permission to strike Vegas was given and a target set was worked up in pretty quick order. What you are about to see is the imagery of the attack."

Technically it wasn't cockpit video but a recording made by the surveillance camera mounted on the Reaper UAV. The film was typically grainy but the images were clear enough to show the settlement nestled high amongst the mountains. In the bottom right hand corner of the frame various digits rattled by showing time, altitude and coordinates. The video jumped and suddenly Peter and Adam were watching a point of view shot taken from the nose cone of a Hellfire missile as it closed in on the target marked by the cross hairs. The ride was mesmerizingly addictive. Like watching car crash TV. The building at the centre of the frame loomed larger and larger until, in the last instant, it filled the screen. As the missile tore into its target the video jump cut again to play an aerial view of the demolition job. There wasn't just one blast, but a series of three; the screen whiting out each time a weapon hit the spot.

The haze cleared and the village came back into view. At the epicenter of the strikes the target building had simply disappeared. Around the spot where it had stood other compounds were badly damaged, rubble strewn about. The flat-bed trucks and 4x4s that had been parked together were now scattered, upturned and twisted. Some were on fire. One had toppled into a crater created by a warhead. Amongst all the debris there were also bodies, at least a dozen could plainly be seen. From the varying sizes it was clear not all were grown men. A couple of the blobs moved.

Other people started to appear, running around, at a loss as to what to do.

The video jumped once more and the viewers were riding with a fourth Hellfire. It fell amongst the largest congregation of survivors. In a blazing flash they were gone. The film ran for a minute or two longer as the Reaper continued to circle. But there was little else to record. Now there was barely any movement. No need to fire a fifth missile. The screen went blank.

"We believe our objective was eliminated along with a number of other insurgents. Bingo was called on Vegas and MX reporting has confirmed a successful strike."

Bret stopped talking and Cyrus started.

"All in all we deem it to have been a very successful and important result. Both the US and UK governments are happy with the outcome as are ISAF HQ and the Afghan president," Cyrus summarised. "The collateral damage was as minimal as could be expected."

"Collateral damage was minimal?" Adam questioned.

"Not important, Adam," Peter said standing up to face Cyrus.

"So what about Bashir? Is he dead?" Peter asked.

"We were hoping he was killed in the strike," Cyrus answered. "But to level with you we think he managed to make good his escape. It was a surprise shall we say."

"So what now?" Adam butted in.

Cyrus looked at Adam then turned back to Peter.

"Let's put our cards on the table here," he started. "You want Bashir alive, and we want him out of circulation."

Peter interpreted.

"Dead you mean?"

"Dead would be really good, but if we had to, we'd settle for him being taken alive as long as we never saw him again."

"So what are you proposing?" Adam asked.

"Well Captain Caine, if you think you can control your impetuous nature we suggest a joint snatch operation to…"

Adam cut him short.

"I remember your last snatch operation Cyrus. It was done to benefit you and fuck us up. Perhaps it's a case of you controlling your impetuosity and arrogance rather than me," Adam said angrily.

"Captain Caine," Cyrus tried and failed to be conciliatory. "Don't get self-righteous with me. I understand you have a vested interest in this man. I know of your friendship and your attempts to inform him – the enemy – of our plans. But we are happy to forget all that if you finally decide to become part of the solution rather than the problem. We need you if we are to get close to him. If you help achieve a mutually acceptable outcome then we can let bygones be bygones. If not I will go to the absolute top to make sure you are prosecuted for aiding the enemy."

"Aiding the fucking enemy?" yelled Adam.

"Whoa you two," Peter stepped in. "Let's not get excited here."

Adam stopped talking and looked at the CIA man, smarting at what he had just heard. He was not ready to roll over and take shit from Cyrus again. He had been played in Sangin and he had been played when he was allowed to go after Bashir alone.

"Have you any idea where he is going?" Peter asked.

"Of course we do," Cyrus answered.

"Well are you going to tell us?" Adam chipped in testily.

"He's heading to the main hospital in Peshawar. He is going to get his father. Where else?"

Khalid pulled off at the next junction and drove away from the main road for a couple of clicks. He was in striking distance of Peshawar but was exhausted and desperate to rest. He'd made good time, aided by the careless driver who'd left the keys in the ignition as he stopped to have a piss before reaching the border. Khalid was relieved he hadn't had to use his knife.

Still sitting behind the wheel, Khalid pulled his cloak tight across his chest. He turned off the car's lights; left the engine running, taking comfort from the warm air blowing from the vents. He felt the heat lulling him towards sleep. On the edge of dropping off he turned the key and silenced the engine. He locked the doors and was asleep in seconds. But not at peace, the image of Noor flashing before him.

Chapter 23
INSERTION – PESHAWAR

The sun had set hours earlier, the night sky long since having gone through the gentle transition from red to deep blue to matt black. Sixty minutes before midnight there was another shift. The rising moon threw a grey light over the landscape, just enough to see by but without the intensity and definition of daytime.

The quartet of men stood patiently at the edge of the helicopter-landing site. It wouldn't have been cold except for a slight chill whipped up by a freshening breeze. On the far side of the HLS was another group, much larger in number. Adam counted at least sixteen of them. Like the Det the OD-A – Operational Detachment Alpha – were heavily armed and wore the same irregular dress – a mix of civvies and military gear – plate carriers covering their vital organs. Most packed M14 carbines, a couple M1014 combat shotguns, all silenced.

There was a third gathering of troops, just a brace, their weapons marking them out for what they were: a sniper team with US Marine M40 rifles, a suppressor attached to the end of each barrel. Their attire was more obviously forces, US Marine fatigues and desert hats.

A fourth team had left earlier; an eight-strong command and control unit which would orchestrate the forthcoming operation, monitoring radio communications and calling in backup and air support if that was what it came to. From their mobile operating vehicles they'd have direct comms with those on the ground. Going the other way there'd be connection – via Khost – to CIA HQ in Langley Virginia.

The snatch team was all Det. It would be their job to watch the target area, identify the objective and send the codeword prior to moving in and lifting him before he reached his destination. The codeword was

Tabasco, the destination was Peshawar hospital and the objective was Khalid Bashir.

The OD-A and the snipers were there to provide a loose cordon, quick reaction and a bit of point muscle if and when required. They also had the medical skills to pick up the pieces if things went tits up.

The first helicopter emerged out of nowhere. Lost in his own thoughts, the arrival of the distinctive tilt rotor Marine Osprey made Adam jump. On landing the rear ramp of the airframe went down and a loadmaster appeared, giving the thumbs up. The knot of OD-A men walked as a tight group towards the entrance. One by one the aircraft swallowed them up. Hard on their heels came the sniper duo. As they too disappeared from sight, the ramp closed, masking the blue internal lamp. The twin engines roared as the pilot put on the power and the helicopter was on its way, lifting, hovering, dipping and lurching eastwards. After a couple of minutes, by now well out of view of the Det, the twin set of prop-rotors dropped into the horizontal position and the Osprey picked up speed for the flight to the Pakistani border and Peshawar beyond.

"What's the ETA of our lift?" Al asked absently, filling the silence that had returned to the HLS.

"You know already, Al" Rocky answered. "After the first chalk we have a fifteen minute wait, so I guess that's 0215 hours matey."

"Is that quarter past two in the morning?" Al mocked.

"Ha, I forgot you were signals," Rocky shot back. He turned to Simon.

"How many charges have you made up?"

"I'm holding two and Al and Adam have one each," Simon explained. "I have enough kit to make another couple of devices but there is no point until we see the lay of the land."

"Method of initiation?"

"Just one with electronic initiation unfortunately, the rest are command detonated."

"Let's hope we won't need any of them," Rocky said, absently kicking a stone around with his boot.

"Adam, when you identify Bashir it's important you move quickly to intercept. The only way we are going to stop this getting noisy and a bit messy is if you can close the gap and get into his space."

"I'm clear about what has to happen. As long as Al keeps his distance and the rest of you keep out of sight we'll be fine."

"Make no mistake mate, if he isn't playing ball you have to go for the head, put him down and make sure he's down."

Adam kept quiet. Al answered for him.

"Rocky, he knows what to do. Let's just make sure we get into our OP and have good sound and vision or this whole thing isn't going to happen."

"Fair point mate," Rocky said. Then, looking up: "Our lift has arrived."

The flashing orange light closed in on them. In the greyness it was difficult to gauge distance and it was a bit of a surprise when the Blackhawk suddenly loomed overhead and set down, enveloping them in its wash. Shaking into a stick in typical British military style the four men knelt with their faces away from the down draft, pleased to be wearing ballistic goggles. They had all removed their baseball caps conscious that the storm of air from the helicopter would do the job for them if they weren't quick enough.

As the tornado eased and the noise of the engine moderated the side door of the chopper slid open. A single green light gave them the all clear to board. Rocky led them to the aircraft then stood aside, counting them in.

"Just confirm unit and destination, Sir," the loadmaster shouted as Rocky boarded too. Rocky didn't attempt to make himself heard above the whine of the engine. Instead he held up an orange flash card, the dim light of the cabin just strong enough to reveal the information written on it.

OP Name: TALISKER
C/S: Delta 30
Freq: Preset 2 CF(E)
Load: FOUR PAX
DOP Grd: PQ 8825 5181
Codeword: PILGRIM
Safe colour: GREEN

The loadmaster seemed content. He gave the thumbs up then navigated his way to the cockpit. Leaning in between the pilot and co-pilot he confirmed on a map where they were headed. Al looked at his seat. On it was an amplivox-style headset. He picked it up and stuck it on his head, allowing him to listen in on the aircrew's conversation. A small switch for his right hand meant he could butt in on what was being said. Pushing it forward he spoke to the loadmaster.

"How long till we are on the ground mate?"

"We are working on about a forty minute transit and maybe ten minutes on task before we set you down," the loadmaster replied.

"Ok, can you let me know when the Osprey lands?"

"Sure, no problem, I'll give you guys a call ten minutes out."

Adam looked out the window of the Blackhawk as the ground unfurled below him. The contours were clear, the landscape flecked with trees, tracks and houses. The view, rushing past at 140 miles per hour, had a mesmerising effect and Adam kept on staring. After twenty minutes in the air the helicopter crossed into Pakistan, not that it was obvious to Adam, the landscape not marked by any change that betrayed the fact they were moving from one jurisdiction to another.

Chapter 24
PLAN B – QUETTA

The phone in Abdul Sadeek's pocket vibrated into life. There were no numbers displayed, only the words *Blocked Call*. Sadeek wasn't deterred from answering it for he knew who it would be: the same man who had rung him early the previous day to ask if he was up for another job. Nothing too difficult, the voice had assured him, similar to the work he had previously done. Deliver a car from Quetta to Peshawar had been the request. A 350-mile drive. That was all.

"Can you do it?" the man enquired.

"Yes of course," Sadeek had replied without hesitation. He was not one to look a gift horse in the mouth. The money had always been good and better still it came in the shape of dollars, delivered promptly by a courier on a motorcycle.

"It will take you most of today and all of tomorrow. Are you sure?"

"Yes. I can do it, no problem."

If Sadeek was being truthful he needed the cash. He'd got used to these little windfalls and was spending as if they were steady income. "Please, let me do the job."

"OK, I will arrange delivery to you of the keys to the car and $500. You'll also get instructions as to where the car is and where you are to take it to." The voice on the other end of the line had been calm and deliberate. "I will call later tonight to check you have reached your initial destination."

Before Sadeek could confirm what he'd been told the line had gone dead. It was less than half an hour after the call that the motorbike turned up and its rider handed him a small package. As on previous occasions the messenger wore a full-face helmet, his identity remaining a mystery to Sadeek. Taking the delivery inside the house Sadeek shooed his wife and children, under protest, out of the main room. Protectively he turned his back to the door and ripped the parcel open to find the worn key to a Toyota Corolla. The money was there too. The handwritten note accompanying the other items explained that the car must be driven to the village of Shahbaz Khel on the N55, south of Peshawar. Once there, Sadeek would have to sit and wait until the phone rang again and he was told about the second stage of the job. Sadeek had left the house immediately, barely pausing to kiss his wife and hug his son and three daughters.

"I will be back in a couple of days," was all he'd told them as he set off on the short walk into the heart of Quetta. The car was where it was supposed to be, tucked away down a side street that proved a devil of a job to negotiate out of.

The journey north was long and slow. Mercifully the N55 was not particularly busy but the car had very little power and was heavy to drive and so still he felt tired. He had noticed, but wasn't particularly worried about, the vehicle sitting very low on its rear axle; the front of the car rearing into the air as if a horse startled by a gunshot. In this part of the world murdered car suspension and broken springs and shattered shocks were par for the course. There was hardly a vehicle on the road that didn't totter or tilt this was or that. Anyway even if there was extra weight at the back, he had been told not to open the boot and he knew better than to deviate from his instructions. The promise of another $500 on completion of the trip meant much more to him than satisfying his curiosity. Not that it was just the money. The voice that had given him his orders had been local but Sadeek did not doubt that behind this level of organisation and finance was a foreign power and in all likelihood that meant America. He was not going to offend his paymasters. The consequences didn't bear thinking about. At best he would simply be killed for his trouble. At worst he and his family would be denounced as traitors and then all of them slaughtered for collaborating.

As a younger man he had not taken part in the series of regional conflicts that raged around the country. Instead he kept his head down steadfastly rejected joining his kinsmen who crossed the border into Afghanistan to help in the fight against the Russians. As the decade-long war wore on his city became increasingly impoverished and he along with it. In the end he had no choice but to take up the opportunity of work smuggling the poppy crop along the old silk routes on behalf of the Balush tribe, and by extension the Mujahedeen. When the Taliban took control of Afghanistan the drugs trade was one of the first things they suppressed and once again Sadeek was left facing poverty. His refusal to join the battle against the Soviets meant he was shunned by many of the returned veterans. Employment was sparse especially for one who had not demonstrated loyalty to the cause. Which was why, when a little bit of ad hoc work came his way, he jumped at the chance.

In circuitous fashion that initial task – simply reporting what time a convoy of cars passed close to his house – had led him to where he was now: Shahbaz Khel. He pulled over at a spot close to a small chai shop and watched the steady stream of customers going to and from it, almost all of them travellers. He had been dozing off when the phone rang.

"Hello?" he said sleepily, trying to remember where he was.

"Have you rested?" the voice asked Sadeek.

"Yes, I have slept a little. I am alright to drive again."

"Good. I want you to leave for Peshawar now, but you must not arrive there before two in the morning. Do you understand that?"

"Yes" Sadeek answered.

"Once you do arrive, park in front of the main hospital. Do you know it?"

"The Lady Reading hospital."

"That's right. Just stop there, switch off your engine and wait," the voice instructed.

"What will I be waiting for?" Sadeek asked.

"For further instructions from me via this phone, you are not to leave the vehicle and you are not to talk to anyone."

"How long will I be there for, how long will I have to wait?"

"Do you want to be paid the rest of the money?" the voice asked brusquely. Without waiting for an answer it continued. "If so then you will do as you are instructed and wait as long as it takes."

The call was terminated. Looking at the screen he could see it was 10pm. Four hours to reach his destination. Throwing the phone onto the passenger seat he turned the ignition, switched on the headlights and moved off. In the mirror he could see a big group of drivers relaxing outside the cafe.

Khalid woke desperate for a piss. He was cold and knew he would get colder still by leaving the car but he needed to go. He got out reluctantly and relieved himself, shivering but also savouring the release of pressure on his bladder. The moon was high. He reckoned it was well after midnight but he was only 90 minutes or so from Peshawar. He didn't intend to follow the Kabul road straight into the heart of the city. Rather he'd keep going until he hit Hayatabad, then track south around the ring road, until he meet the eastern route in. There he would lose the car and weave through the back streets on foot, cutting through the bazaar to the hospital.

His mood was much more subdued than the previous evening, completely at odds with the adrenaline charged rush of excitement he had felt at being back in his country. A wave of pessimism swept over him and he became convinced he would not find his father. Certainly not alive. But deep down he understood that was not the point. Whether the old man was dead or not was almost of secondary importance besides his need to fulfil his promise and do his duty to the person who had done everything for him and given him boundless love. Khalid felt tears well up in his eyes. He wept for his losses, but also for what he had become and what he had done. The lives he had taken and the lies he had told. He tried to persuade himself that every step he'd made and every immoral act he'd committed was justifiable as he strived to keep his word and by extension his honour. But hadn't he long since become dishonourable? What would his father say if he was aware of what his son had undertaken in his name? Would he regard as acceptable the choices he had made? Khalid half hoped Farouk Bashir was dead. For then there would be no explaining to be done. Khalid remembered all too vividly the lessons he'd been taught on his father's knee. Self-respect had been at the heart of what he'd learned. *There is no good way of doing the wrong thing,* he'd been told. Khalid tossed the arguments over and over in his head. Had he done the wrong thing? Was it wrong to revere your parents? Was it wrong to do everything in your power to protect them? Perhaps sometimes there was no good way to do the *right* thing.

He thought back on the pride he had felt at being selected to go to Sandhurst and the immense satisfaction he'd felt at standing in front of the whole Academy to be recognised as the best overseas cadet by the Prince of Wales. If he had then simply returned to the Pakistani Border Force he would have been venerated and marked out for advancement. Promotion would have followed and he would have become part of the establishment. It was not his fault that life had taken another, much more darker, direction.

He thought about getting married, of having a wife and a family of his own, and land and a home. He thought of Malalaya. Would she dare come to Pakistan to live with him? He didn't believe it was possible. Khalid envisioned a life of loneliness, devoid of the family who loved him and a wife whom he could love. The future seemed one of emptiness.

His sadness fuelled the anger. He looked for someone to blame for his misfortune and he focussed on the Americans. But they were not the only ones he raged at: there were also the British and the Taliban. For years now his life had been manipulated by others. No longer. Whatever happened he would not wear a harness again. Life or death. It didn't matter what awaited him. He would not be in the hands of others. Khalid got back into the car and headed off.

———•———

Sadeek took the N55 Indus Highway into the heart of Peshawar, slowing as it narrowed and he had to negotiate more and more junctions. It took him right to the hospital. He pulled over to the side of the road and turned his lights off, studying the layout of the building. As far as he could tell there were three entrances: the main one used by the walking wounded and visitors; a staff entrance; and one for accidents and emergencies. He decided to head for the A&E entry. He calculated that its regular users would be too preoccupied with medical matters to worry about him. If anyone asked he'd say he had dropped off a friend who'd come in to see someone recently rushed in. He turned the headlights back on and drove steadily past the front of the building before turning left and entering the car park. There were plenty of spaces. The entrance was bathed in light but he was just far enough back so it didn't spread over him.

He sat quietly and quickly the drowsiness returned. But he didn't drift straight off to sleep. When he had retrieved the vehicle in Quetta he'd leant over and tried the glove compartment. It hadn't budged. Now he tried again. He pulled harder. On the fourth tug the brittle plastic catch gave way and the compartment flew open. A pile of leaflets spilled into the foot well. He picked one up. The words on it were in

Pashtu. The message was a declaration from the Islamic Emirate of Afghanistan. It spoke of Jihad and of how the Pakistan government was as much a puppet of the US as its Kabul counterpart. It explained how the Taliban was taking the fight against the Westerners into the heart of Pakistan and urged the people to join the cause.

Sadeek paid little attention to the propaganda. For a few minutes he pondered whether this meant his paymasters were actually the Taliban or whether this was material planted by the Americans for a reason he could not fathom. Then he told himself off. *Stop thinking, follow orders, remember what this is all about, the money.*

Chapter 25
RL COPPER – PESHAWAR

"Zero this is Oscar Delta One Five how copy?" Michael Quinn said over the handset.

With the rest of the mobile command centre he had flown in direct from Kabul by Globemaster, arriving at Qasimabad airport west of Peshawar, the previous day. Alongside the human cargo the cavernous aircraft had disgorged a couple of heavily armoured vehicles decked out to look like diplomatic cars. The side and rear windows of the second vehicle had been blacked out to allow the communications and tactical specialists who sat inside to travel unobserved. In the lead vehicle, along with the driver and commander, was a pair of CIA operatives. In the rear of the other vehicle Peter sat with Michael, head of the OD-A. Now they were on the road, accompanied by an escort; a pair of Pakistani police jeeps manned by Intelligence Bureau operators. They had been bought and paid for by the ISI commander in Peshawar who in turn had been bought by, and got paid by, the CIA.

"Zero this is Oscar Delta One Five how copy?" Quinn repeated as the truck struck a pothole.

"Zero, good copy, confirm touch down and movement to report line gold," the voice on the other side of the net came back.

"Will be at report line gold in approximately ten mikes."

"Confirmed Oscar Delta One Five. Hello Oscar Delta One Five Bravo. How copy?" the Khost controller spoke to the second rebro vehicle. "Can you confirm satellite up link?"

"Roger, we have link to satellite and will be beginning test feed in about three mikes."

"Confirmed three mikes stand-by," the Khost controller said. He punched instructions into a computer to help route comms from the vehicle to Khost via satellite and spoke again. This time he didn't need any technology to make himself heard.

"We have confirmed link with the forward control team, Sir."

Cyrus nodded and turned to the person sat at the neighbouring desk. "Do we have a link to Langley, London and Washington?"

"We will be able to transmit live pictures as soon as the team hits the ground."

"Splendid. Wouldn't want anyone to miss the show."

———•———

The pseudo-diplomatic convoy moved through the dark Peshawar streets at a steady speed, the vehicles' headlights on full beam to dazzle anyone trying to look in. They hardly blended in with the surroundings but at that time of the night there were few people about and the presence of the Pakistani police cars also dissuaded unwanted attention.

They pushed on up the Khyber Road towards the point where it met Hussain Road. The buildings were set tight against the highway edges. As the vehicles hit the junction and turned right, the ground opened slightly with the compounds and markets stalls falling back from the sides of the road. Reaching Bara Gate and the large expanse of open space that surrounded it, the two core vehicles pulled up side by side facing opposite directions. The police trucks moved to the perimeter and spilled their contents of men who fanned out to create a cordon.

"Do you have comms with the lead helicopter, Peter?" Quinn asked.

"Yeah I've good comms, the first chalk should be in at around three, the second chalk about thirty minutes later."

"Chalk?" Quinn looked confused.

"Chalk stick, you know, the first lift," Peter translated.

"Ah right, the first packet in."

"Yeah we call it that too," Peter said.

He relaxed back into his seat and studied the map of the city roughly taped against the window. The chart also appeared on the finger-marked screens of the secure laptops he and Quinn had open on their thighs. Their own position was already flashing on the screens: a single blue dot with a scripted call sign and designation number beside it. All the members of the inbound teams had their own personal locater beacon. When they arrived they would register with the tasked surveillance satellite so they too would be represented on the computer maps as dabs of different coloured light.

"Do we have eyes on the HLS yet?" Peter asked Quinn.

"Yes, Reaper sitting on task, they can give us cover as needed, or just keep eyes on. Apart from that we're clean."

"Fuck this is going to be tight."

"As long as your guys know what they are doing we shouldn't have any issues."

"It's not the ability of my men I'm concerned about. It's the getting out that's the problem – with or without our target."

———◆———

The Osprey flew on until it hit the Kabul River canal that ran into the heart of the city. The pilot contacted forward control.

"We have you on tracker," Peter reassured them.

"We are looking for permission to land. Can you confirm HLS is clear?"

"Roger Osprey approach from the north and clear to the west, over."

"Moving to drop off point now."

Crammed in behind the flight deck, the OD-A listened in to the conversation through their headsets. Now they prepared themselves. Those who had bothered fastening their seat belts unclipped them. Each man hefted his rifle into the alert position for offload. The team leaders checked again the maps tucked into their small Perspex forearm grips.

The loadmaster picked his way to the rear of the aircraft struggling to avoid the jumble of legs, feet and equipment. He looked at his human cargo and gave them a triple fingered sign: three minutes to landing. The troops shuffled to the edges of their canvas seats, M14s made ready, a round seated in the chamber. Closest to the exit was the shotgun pair. Their job: to leave the helicopter first and blast any close quarter targets if that is what it came to.

Only the two marines sat completely still, clutching their sniper rifles tight between their legs, knees locked, the sights nestled in their groins.

The pilot of the Osprey saw a sharp bend in the waterway approaching. As the watercourse veered off ninety degrees to the east he held his course. Almost immediately he came upon the old British cemetery. He flared sharply and dropped firmly onto the deck. He counted in his head the time it took for the aircraft to empty. On 21 he was lifting back into the sky and away.

Peter tracked the Osprey as it went.

"Hang on, what the fuck is this all about?"

Quinn leaned over to look at Peter's screen.

"The Osprey. It's just landed again. On the polo ground west of the Pakistani Army base."

"Show me."

Peter pointed to the aircraft with a fat finger.

"The aircraft that dropped off the cordon team has landed again."

As he spoke the dot in front of him began moving, clearing the city to the west. This time it didn't stop.

"What's going on? That wasn't in the plan?"

The two snipers moved steadily, covering the ground in the shadows, confident of which route they should take, which alley to dodge down, which compound would be empty and which had guard dogs, where there would be movement at this time of the morning. They had already run the route many times: virtually, on the computer. They reached the central mosque and stepped inside. A set of ladders led to the base of the minaret. From there another set let them to the next floor. Then there was a third set. They clambered up until they could go no further. Squeezing through an arch they found themselves behind a low parapet where they sat down and allowed themselves a few moments of recovery, letting the sweat flow down their faces. They slipped their small rucksacks off their shoulders and pulled out the laser range finders they contained. Making themselves comfortable they positioned their equipment on the wall and looked out over the bazaar and the hospital. Then they started ranging various points. Somewhere behind them the Blackhawk was approaching the HLS.

The loadmaster sat just behind the pilots and studied the ground through a window. The door gunner manned the M-240H scanning the compounds as the helicopter flew by, the scene on the deck brought to life for the air- and flight-crew by their passive night vision goggles.

"Simon," Rocky yelled. "Once we set down I want you to head straight to the junction beside the cemetery and meet up with the escort from the cordon troops."

"OK mate."

"Fellas," Rocky addressed everyone this time. "We will move along our prepared route as discussed and once in the OP we will get changed."

Three thumbs up came back in acknowledgement. Adam slipped his Glock from its holster and twisted the suppressor into place over the end of the barrel, giving it a tug to make sure it was secure, then dropped the weapon back into its holder, conscious that the weapon was now longer.

The Blackhawk had been following the same flight path as the Osprey and touched down almost exactly where the other aircraft had first landed. Simon led the way, running towards the north wall of the graveyard, reaching into his pocket as he moved to activate the Infrared firefly that marked him out as the man to talk to. Two figures rose to their feet, the monocle PNVGs that had picked up Simon's strobe worn over their left eyes.

"Hi fellas, sorry I'm late, needed to get a hair cut."

"What?" one of the OD-A operators said.

Simon's humour was lost on the US soldier.

"Never mind mate. We'd like to get moving as quickly as we can."

"No problem, we have teams out covering your route."

"Can you just make sure they know that when we reach the OP we'll be changing into local dress?" Simon said.

"You got it."

The other three members of the Det shuffled up behind Simon.

"Well? What we waiting for?" Al said.

"Yeah what we waiting for, Simon?" Rocky echoed sarcastically.

"Right, so I'm leading the way then, am I?" Simon replied.

"Oscar Delta One Five, this is Simon we're on the move over. We'll give you a shout when we reach the compound."

"Roger Simon," Quinn replied as he inspected the trace on the laptop.

Like mother duck Simon made sure he had his brood strung out behind him, one of the OD-A guys included, then he traversed the wall and stepped out onto the Jamrud Road, moving to the far side of it, followed by Rocky. Adam kept left, Al in his wake. They moved as a formation, keeping up momentum until they wheeled into Hospital Road.

Simon paused briefly and knelt as Adam and Al jogged across the street then pushed on. Now they were on Fakir-e-Alam Road, passing the Lady Reading hospital, the letters IRNUM stencilled in gold above the stained glass entrance. This was the principle target area and they took a moment to absorb as much of it and its surroundings as they could.

Simon glanced at his watch. Just before 3.30am.

In front of the hospital a number of people were busying themselves. A handful clustered at the back of a vehicle, probably fussing over a patient. Two more walked past as if they had seen it all before; cleaners, wondered Simon? Or kitchen staff? Or porters? Arriving for the early shift?

Briskly the soldiers moved on.

The team came to the point where the road ran sharply left. This was their marker and final RV point. In the shadows of the bazaar Simon stopped and scanned down the road as Rocky came towards him.

"Fucking hell mate I'm breathing though my arse. You couldn't have moved any quicker could you?"

"Ah come on mate, just a bit of youthful enthusiasm."

"This the FRV?"

"Yeah, we should be at our target in about fifty metres or so."

"Do you have time to put your RC device here? A major junction? Just think it might help when it comes to getting out of here," Rocky argued.

In response Simon flicked his day sack off his shoulder. He searched around for a suitable place to set his charge and found a small sewer grate. He lifted the grate and wedged the bundle safely beneath it, careful to ensure the trail antennae protruded slightly. Feeling around he flicked the switch to activate the bomb. An LED glowed green for a couple of seconds to confirm the power was on then faded out. Simon kicked some dirt, old straw and general crap from the road over the device. Happy with what he had done he retrieved his day sack and nodded to Rocky, mouthing the words 'that's me'.

Adam spotted the old man first. He'd come out of nowhere but was now standing in the middle of the street staring at Simon. He must have watched him place the charge. Flicking his M4 around his body, the sling guiding it to fall by his hip Adam drew his pistol and took aim at the old man. He kept dead still for a moment and watched as the old man walked towards where Simon stood. Still Simon hadn't noticed him. Adam coughed and Simon froze. He swivelled his head to locate the danger and ended up staring into the face of the curious passerby.

The man was innocent enough. That morning he was simply repeating the routine that accompanied every market day. He liked to get to his pitch early to make sure everything was set up correctly. His stall was close to the road and he was one of the busier traders. He had to make sure he was ready to serve his customers when they started to flock in. On any other day this would have been the right thing to do. But not on this one. He now found himself in the wrong place at the wrong time and had seen something he shouldn't have. His body crumpled to the ground as the first 9mm bullet struck him in the base of the neck and a second buried itself between his shoulder blades. The muffled sound of the pistol being fired was barely susceptible, hardly louder than the tinny noise made by one of the ejected cartridges as it bounced off a rock.

Adam moved toward the lifeless man. He reached down and grabbed the corpse by the shoulders. It weighed almost nothing. Relieved, Adam dragged it past a few stalls and dropped it into an irrigation channel that was more full of rubbish than it was water.

He raised his hand to Simon and the rest of the team to indicate the job was done. Simon moved on. Rocky gave a wave to the OD-A operator at the rear of the brick and then held a flat palm across his chest: the clear signal. The OD-A op replied with a diver's O sign and let the others proceed without him.

The pace of the team was slower now. They were at the hub of the city: the sprawling bazaar that was flanked by the railway station at one end and the hospital at the other. Adam felt very much as if he was on enemy territory yet they were following in the footsteps of thousands of British soldiers before them, the places they passed testament to the Empirical history of both Peshawar and the region: the hospital itself, the military graveyard, the polo fields and the train tracks.

The team moved on until they hit a narrow alleyway just before the major crossroads with Barbar Islama Road. They ducked down the passage in single file. Simon still leading, then Rocky, Adam and Al. Twenty metres along it they came to a wooden door, green paint peeling off of it. It was what they'd been expecting.

"This is it, Rocky" Simon said.

"Roger mate, give it a check will ya?"

"Hey, Al," Adam said turning to the man behind him. "I hear you like it in the rear."

"Fuckin' funny mate." Al changed the subject. "I'm sweating like a fuckin' prod at a Sinn Fein conference, when are we getting inside?"

Simon turned the handle and the door gave a little, scraping on the uneven brick floor. He put more of his weight into it and it opened just enough for them all to squeeze through and into the courtyard beyond. Last in, Al shoved the door shut. He took a heavy chain that hung on an eyelet in the jamb and looped it over a hook on the back of the entrance. It wouldn't stop a determined pursuer but it would slow them down. Moving on they found the stairs to the upper floor. Being careful to check each room as they went, they shuffled along until they reached a window overlooking the bazaar and the front of the hospital.

"One Five this is Simon we are now at OP location."

"Roger, Simon," Quinn answered. "All call signs this is One Five. OP set. Moving to Report Line Copper."

The forward control vehicles pulled away gently allowing time for the Pakistani vehicles to load up and follow on. Together they travelled to Notia Gate at the southern end of the city but only half a kilometre from the heart of Peshawar. The gate was manned by a mixed team of border guards and police. Peter tapped his fingers impatiently against his laptop as their Pakistani escorts negotiated with their colleagues to allow them to pass through. After what seemed like an age the command vehicles were ushered forward and parked up. If things turned sour they had a clear exit south towards the emergency HLS or the main highway out of the area.

"All stations this is One Five. We are now at Report Line Copper. Out."

Chapter 26
GULBAHAR DISTRICT

The project team stood around an oblong table in the conference room pouring over documents and maps. The team leader was at its head, looking slightly nervous. The operation was crucial to his boss and hence crucial to him. Failure would not go down well.

"Everyone is now in position, Sir," he started.

"And the British?"

"They have inserted, Sir, and made it to their observation post without difficulty. They've got good eyes on the bazaar and the main entrance to the hospital. They have communications with the OD-A and mobile control."

"What do we know of Bashir?"

A new voice entered the discussion.

"We have had no positive sighting or knowledge of his movements since he took out the three men at the hide location. We are confident he must have crossed the border some time last night so we now think he is in Pakistan," said the man, tracing a finger over the map along the N5 through the Khyber Pass and into the Northwest Frontier Province.

"Confident? What makes you so sure he has crossed?"

"Well to be honest, Sir it is our best guess, supported by our sources on the ground. Last night there was an incident at the border where a car collided with a bus. The driver left the scene quickly and the vehicle was traced back to a garage in Kunduz. Although the target vehicle wasn't found in Kunduz it all seems too much of a coincidence to be anything else."

"I agree. What about our plan for Bashir?" This was directed back to the project leader.

"We have a set of Task Force 82 snipers in an over watch position covering the hospital, the bazaar and the Det."

"Task Force 82? Are they from SEAL Team 6? I told you I didn't want major SF involvement."

"No Sir, they're not. Your orders were clear. These guys are contracted privately. They are used for force protection but we have a direct call on them."

They stood for a while studying the map calculating distances and routes from the pass to Peshawar, and the bazaar to the hospital.

"What orders do the snipers have?"

There was a pause as the four men in the room looked at each other. None had previously been in a position like this and for all the training and talk of targets and assets and imperatives they weren't completely comfortable with what they had to do, even if it was in the name of national security.

The team leader finally filled the silence.

"The snipers have orders to watch the Det and identify the target once they approach him. They have been told to eliminate the target and to eliminate the man making contact with him."

"And what if they fail? What if they don't get him before he reaches the hospital?"

The last of the four men around the table finally spoke.

"Sir, we have a HUMINT asset sitting at the hospital in a car loaded with two thousand pounds of homemade explosive. This is packed around a further fifty pounds of commercial explosive. Combined, it's more than enough to drop the front of the building, it will be detonated if the target reaches the hospital."

Cyrus nodded appreciatively.

"Good. And where will the trace take us?"

"The homemade explosive was from a find we had in Helmand a few months back, the driver is from Quetta and trackable back to known insurgents. We have various Taliban propaganda leaflets in the car. As far as anyone is concerned this will look like a Taliban attack on the Pakistan infrastructure."

Cyrus stood for a while thinking.

"Where is Peter Ryder?"

"In the mobile command centre."

"Who is with him?"

"Quinn, Sir."

"OK – has he been briefed?"

"Yes he has. On command he will take the action you requested."

Without saying more Cyrus marched out of the room leaving the three men to continue their discussions. He went to his office and sat wearily behind his desk. He wondered if it was all worth it and tried to reassure himself that it was. What he must do was speak to his boss at Langley and ensure he was primed to speak to his counterpart in UK intelligence. He was in no doubt that by the end of the day both Khalid Bashir and Adam Caine would be dead. Not completely ideal but if that was what it took to keep things out of the public domain then so be it.

—◆—

Khalid dodged through the Gulbahar district of Peshawar. There was a familiarity about it born of the time, long ago now, when he had paid visits here with his father, and more recently as a recruit in the fight against the infidels.

He kept one hand in the pocket of his shalwar kameez, gripping the Iraqi made Tariq pistol.

It was a strange gun to find in Pakistan but the movement of weapons was big business and where there was demand there'd be supply. Such were the economics of rifles and pistols that, strange though it seemed to him, he could have picked up an AK47 for half the money he paid for the 9mm. In his other pocket he felt the weight of the ten-round spare mag as it bounced against his thigh. As he threaded his way between the stalls of the market the call to prayer started to wail from the minarets. Emerging from the bazaar he halted and looked around. A steady trickle of people – men – was appearing, heeding the summons. He was pleased to see the streets getting progressively busier. They would help cover his movements to the hospital and then away from it again, with or without his father. He strode on towards his fate.

Chapter 27
GREEN ON GREEN – PESHAWAR

The window was narrow but offered a sweeping view of the road leading to the bazaar and hospital. It was a view Rocky and Simon – sat on rickety chairs, close to the aperture – studied meticulously. Behind them Adam and Al crouched against the rear wall, either side of the door that had let them in.

In his mind Simon retraced the steps he and the others had taken to reach the OP, recovering the mental notes he'd made along the way of reference points and rendezvous locations. What he was searching his brain for were defendable locations where they could stand their ground as they waited for the OD-A to come to the rescue.

"Can you see the large stalls to the left of the road?" Rocky asked.

"Yep got them, that's where I left the RC device," Simon said, leaning forward and peering round the rough edge of the window.

"What range have you got on that mate and what's the blast radius?"

"Range is pretty good, from here with line of sight we have no problems. We'd hit it first go. As for blast radius, lethal out to about five, maybe ten, metres. After that its likely to cause casualties for another ten."

Rocky wasn't completely impressed.

"That's pretty localised?"

"Its all you need in a confined space or if you want a distraction."

Rocky looked east. The sun was getting higher in the sky, cars were moving along the road, weaving around a growing mass of wheelbarrows and handcarts laden with the wares the traders were bringing to market.

Rocky turned to Adam, struggling to see him as his eyes adjusted from the brightness outside to the gloom around him.

"It's starting to get busy. Do you want to come up here and take a gander?"

Adam shuffled forward with his binoculars and took the space Simon had vacated. He didn't get too close to the opening, wary of being pinpointed in the light. He knew it was going to be difficult spotting Khalid from this position but he was confident he would be able to do it. There would be things that would distinguish him: size, weight, gait; the traits that, put together, made him an individual. Like all soldiers Adam had been taught the basic A-H method of identifying a target, a skill that had been honed and refined as part of his HUMINT training during the Achilles program. He heard Rocky make a call on the radio.

"One Five this is Rocky?"

"One Five, this is Peter, send, over."

Now there was an informality to the radio communications, the call signs having been ditched to make things simpler and quicker.

"Can you confirm the cordon troops?" Rocky asked.

"You have four teams covering the main access points, I will move them to you if required. I have you on Blue Force so just concentrate on the target."

"Confirm the single point sniper coverage?"

A look of surprise crossed Peter's face. He looked accusingly at Quinn sitting beside him in the back of the vehicle by the Notia gate.

"What?" Quinn said indignantly.

"Sniper? I don't have anyone on the Blue Force?"

Quinn shrugged.

"No idea buddy. Maybe they just got them confused with the OD-A."

There was nowhere for Peter to go with this. He felt deeply uncomfortable about what his guys were suggesting but this wasn't the moment to translate that to the troops on the ground.

"Rocky, they are likely to be with the cordon troops. Any tasks through me."

"Ok, will let you know what the atmospherics are like, if nothing to report we will remain quiet."

"Roger, out," Peter said, setting the handset down to study the digital map on the laptop in front of him.

LONDON

The Prime Minister sighed.

"I have just got off the phone to the President. He is sorry for the whole terrible affair with Bashir and Private Akers and he has promised that he will take action against the CIA heads for taking their brief too far. He wants this whole issue to be resolved and will help in any way he can to facilitate a mutually acceptable conclusion."

To a man the PM's audience nodded. General Adamson, the Chief of the Defence Staff, was there, together with the heads of MI5 and MI6. So too, the Secretary of State for Defence. They looked exhausted, frayed by events in Afghanistan and Pakistan over which they felt, until now perhaps, they had very little control. Adamson cleared his throat.

"Prime Minster if I may. The Det is now in a position to intercept Khalid Bashir and to take him alive if required."

"The US government doesn't really want that," the MI6 chief interjected.

"If you'll let me finish," General Adamson spoke to the head of the security service without bothering to look at him. "We have the ability to eliminate the target, but we must have your explicit authority to do so. He is a foreign national and if we were to get caught doing this then there might be more than a bit of fallout at the UN if Pakistan complains."

"Secretary of State?" the PM looked for help from his political ally.

"I have briefed the Foreign Office and they are pretty confident they can stop it going to council."

"OK General Adamson your team has clearance to eliminate Bashir," the PM articulated the order he had decided on before the meeting had started.

"Understood, Prime Minister," Adamson said, before continuing, "however we have another problem."

The PM sighed again. Why was it that people always seemed to come to him with their dilemmas?

"And what is that?"

The MI6 boss filled in the blanks.

"The CIA thinks that Adam Caine, one of the Det, is too close to the subject and may already know too much for comfort."

"Listen, all of you. Before you continue, I am not sanctioning the elimination of a UK national," the PM's voice rose. "Am I making myself clear?"

"Perfectly."

The five men stood without anyone speaking. In their minds they all knew how this was going to finish, but they were all reluctant to put their name to it. In the end General Adamson broke the impasse.

"We shall be manning COBRA until this operation is complete, that should be by the end of the day."

"I have meetings throughout, but you make sure I am informed the moment this is concluded," the PM answered.

The gathering broke up, Adamson and the Defence Secretary going off on their own. They marched down a warren of tunnels until they came to a heavy wooden door outside of which stood a uniformed soldier. Ignoring him they entered to be confronted by scene of purposeful activity involving at least a dozen people: security analysts, communications experts, military planners, civil servants from the Foreign Office. At their centre was a map of the operational area. The new arrivals made for a pair of chairs and sat down. Beside the one in which the Defence Secretary plonked himself, was a red phone. It had no keypad, but was wired directly to the switchboard and hence the world beyond.

A young woman brought in a tray of coffee and unbidden started pouring each of the senior men a cup. Briefly distracted, Adamson followed her with his eyes as she left, concentrating in disgust on her fat arse, feeling nothing but disdain for the poor physical state of the nation's youth.

KHOST

Cyrus wanted to be doubly sure of what he had just been told so he repeated it back into the phone.

"So there is no doubt, that it is a go for the elimination of Bashir regardless of the location of the British team?"

"Yes, I have just talked to the head of MI6 who has received permission from the Prime Minister to execute the order," the CIA chief answered.

Cyrus considered for a moment. He knew the next question was going to be a difficult one.

"And if the British get in the way? Do we have permission to remove them?"

"No you don't, not in so many words. But if in the heat of the operation they were to lose one of their men then we are pretty much covered. These things happen, but I don't need anything that will bring suspicion on us, so hold off on the use of your courier. He's the backstop. Got it?"

"Understood."

"I am sending you the MI6 chief's number. You have direct liaison authority. Let me know what the outcome is so I can brief the President. Let it be good news."

Cyrus hung up. He had his clear list of priorities. One, eliminate Bashir. Two, eliminate anyone who gets in the way. Three, eliminate anyone he could have talked to and passed on details of what he had been mixed up with. Cyrus moved to the main operations room. He found the team leader leaning over the comms table next to the digital wall map. Cyrus touched him on the shoulder and ushered him into the side room. Cyrus closed the door behind them.

"We have the go for taking out Bashir."

"Thank goodness," replied the team leader, relieved that all the work that had gone into setting up the op was going to come to something. "We don't have clearance to take out Caine though?"

"Not officially."

"So what do you want me to do?"

"I want him dead. Is your team up to it?" Cyrus responded.

"The sniper team has its orders, they just need the word from me. They'll engage the target and then they'll engage Caine."

"What about Peter Ryder?" Cyrus queried. "If he suspects there is something going on he will be all over it."

The team leader shrugged.

"It's your call Sir. I have a man there who can take care of Ryder if required."

"Who?"

"His name is Quinn. Works for the NSA, normally assists with the indigenous population training programme. At the moment he is attached to the OD-A."

Cyrus did some calculations. He was moving well outside his brief but if it all worked then no one would bat an eyelid. Bashir would be gone, Downing Street would have won a trade agreement and the whole story of how the British trained a Taliban IED facilitator would be literally dead and buried. This could work.

"You seem to have covered every base," Cyrus said smiling.

"I think so, but there's a backup plan or two, just in case," the team leader said confidently.

"Right well let's get on with it."

PESHAWAR

"Stand-by," Rocky said. "Tango moving along the stalls on the right of the street."

Adam's binoculars gashed to the man Rocky identified. He halted and started to chat to one of the vendors. His pause gave Adam a clear side view.

"Nope, not him, mate."

"Are you sure?"

Adam didn't bother answering. If he wasn't sure he wouldn't have said so. Behind him he could sense Al fidgeting, getting restless. The minutes dragged on. Directly below the team, the road was now chaotic with carts and pedestrians and livestock and buses and scooters and cars, all jostling for their bit of space. Adam's job was becoming increasingly difficult. A couple of times he thought he had his man and readied himself to move only to reassess and dismiss the thought.

"Could you have missed him Adam?" Rocky pressed.

"No, I haven't missed him. He is waiting for the crowd to mask his movements."

By 8.30 the street was rammed. Adam barely dared blink as he strained to make out Bashir. His eyes ached, but he resisted the temptation of rubbing them. When the Adhan sounded out across the city, the voice of the Mu'adhin boyish and sweet, calling people to midday prayers, Adam breathed a sigh of relief. It would give him, and his eyesight some respite. People started flowing towards the mosques. Many more lay out prayer mats where they were.

"One Five, this is Rocky," there was a hint of weariness in his voice.

"Rocky, Peter. How's it looking?"

"Yeah ok, bit of a lull thanks to prayers and still no sign of the target."

"Be careful when the mosques begin to empty."

"We've got it covered, out."

"I bet he said be careful when the mosques empty?" Adam said with a rye smile.

"That's exactly what he said, as if we hadn't thought of it."

A mile away Peter sat in the back of the vehicle, the tracker in front of him. The blue symbols of the Det hadn't budged since they moved into the compound and OP position, while the OD-A was broken into four groups, the members of each in such close proximity to each other that their signatures were blending together. Two groups were to the south and southeast of the hospital, near the railway station, close enough to the Det to support it, but also within range of the control vehicles if they had bother. The other two teams had taken positions to the north of the hospital: one securing the route to the HLS and airport: the other directly north of the Det, no more than three hundred metres away.

"What are the OD-A reporting?" Peter asked Quinn.

"Normal activity, positions secure, nothing else," Quinn replied.

"What is Khost saying?"

"Nada. Our radio transmissions are rebroadcast to them, if they have anything for us they will break in."

"And the downlink from Reaper?" Peter persisted.

"No link yet. Again I think Khost have the link, if they have anything they will send it our way."

Peter went silent. He felt as if he was being told everything, but nothing. His intuition was that he was outside the loop. The mission wasn't his, and probably never had been. He considered stepping outside and calling his handler to see what he could find out. He decided against it. He would wait. An excited voice broke his train of thought.

"Standby, standby."

It was Rocky.

He waited too. And he watched, concentrating on the figure Adam had pointed out, meandering along the line of stalls towards the junction. If it were for Rocky to judge then he would say there was something that marked the subject out. He held himself more erect than many of those around him. There was something deliberate about the way he moved, even as he tried to look casual. He lingered at the stalls, picking things up but showing little intention of actually buying anything. He appeared more preoccupied with his surroundings.

"Well?"

"Not sure," Adam replied.

Behind Rocky and Adam the others were as still as stone, Al poised on one knee, ready to make a dash for it, Simon sat with his RC transmitter in his hand.

"Is it him?" Rocky hissed.

"Not sure," Adam said again.

"You said you'd …" Rocky began to protest, but was cut short.

"Wait, quiet."

He studied the man as he stooped to pick up something from a table. It was a laboured movement as if he were carrying an injury. The man inspected the item with a cursory glance then turned back to that which he regarded as more important, the way towards the hospital. For a second he looked up at the window Adam was peering out from. Adam dared not move. He said his own prayer. The man's gaze moved on.

"It's him," Adam cried. In a heartbeat he was on his feet and darting for the door.

Al beat him to it and was out of the exit and bounding down the stairs. At the bottom he was forced to stop momentarily to drag the chain off the gate. He released it and swung it open, peering out, scanning the alleyway in both directions. The hesitation allowed Adam to catch up. Al held up an arm to hold him back.

"One second, mate," Al shouted.

"I don't have one second, we need to go."

Adam pushed Al's arm aside and barged past into the alley, sprinting towards the street. Al took off after him, his rifle bumping at his thigh.

"One Five, this is Rocky. We have target confirmed. I say again target confirmed. Two foxhounds now moving to intercept."

"Make sure they understand that if he is not willing to come peacefully they are to use lethal force," Peter ordered. "This has to happen."

Bit bloody late to be issuing orders like that thought Rocky given that the chase was on. Simon was now crouched beside him at the vantage point. Below them, but not yet quite in sight, Adam had reached the alley entrance and stepped left into the road. He was hit by the confusion of Peshawar daily life: the throng of people and things; the noise; the smells and the harsh light of the sun. At street level his view was severely restricted. He had to make contact with Khalid immediately or else he would be lost in the swarm. He barged into the crowd, shoving bodies aside, driving through the crowd. He thought he heard Al shout behind him, telling him to slow down, but he ignored the instruction.

"Fuck sake, mate," Al swore to himself. "You're like a fucking whippet."

"Roger out."

The sniper pair sat patiently at the top of the mosque, observing the city laid out beneath them. Propped up in front of them was a range card. It pinpointed landmarks, detailed distances, showed the positions of the Det OP and the OD-A cordon. Their rules of engagement had been gone over a million times. First they would engage whoever identified Bashir. Only then would they take out Bashir himself. Someone had been thinking ahead to the operation post mortem that was bound to follow. This way it would look as if the whole shooting match had started as a deliberate attack on a Western military asset by a Pakistani national rather than an unsanctioned foreign hit on a militant. All they needed was a go for lethal action.

———◆———

Quinn spoke into his handset.

"Tiger team this is One Five, you have permission to engage within mission parameters, over."

"Tiger, roger, out," came the acknowledgement from minaret.

Peter stared at Quinn in exasperation.

"You're losing me, mate. Who the fuck is Tiger team?"

"You know we can't allow Bashir to get away. Tiger team are our insurance to make sure he doesn't."

"Don't give me riddles? Who the fuck are they and what are their mission parameters?"

"Snipers. They have been given the task to engage Bashir if your men fail," Quinn lied.

"But they will be given the chance to take him first, right?"

"Of course," Quinn lied again.

Peter turned to his map and picked up his handset. Now he knew he wasn't being kept in the loop. He reached for his handset.

"Don't!" Quinn said grabbing his hand firmly. "It will only confuse the situation."

"Let me fucking tell you something Quinn, if any of my men are hurt because of what you are doing I will take your fucking head off," Peter snarled, jerking free of the American's grasp.

———◆———

Adam surged through the crowd oblivious to the protests he was generating. Anyone hindering his progress got an elbow in the ribs or a kick in the shins to move them on. Breathing heavily and with his hand grasping the Glock in his pocket, he reached the stall where he had last seen Khalid. But he wasn't there. He scanned frantically, turning rapidly, taking a step in one direction then another. He reached up onto his tiptoes to try and see over the human roadblock. Was that him? Thirty metres away? Walking calmly towards the junction and the spot where Simon had concealed the RC device. Adam fell in behind him, the pursuer covering the ground more rapidly than the pursued. Adam wondered how he would make contact with Khalid. There really was only one way. Now he was just a few metres behind.

"Khalid," he shouted. "Khalid Bashir."

Khalid faltered, then stopped in the middle of the street, responding instinctively to the shock of his name being called; In English; by someone with an English accent. He was back in Sandhurst. His hand tightened on the Tariq pistol. He turned, slowly, to see a man standing five metres from him. He was sweating. The pair faced each other like Wild West gunslingers. Neither moved, taking everything in.

Adam spoke again.

"My name is Adam Caine, I'm…"

"I know who you are," Khalid interrupted. "Do you think I wouldn't remember standing with you in front of your future King?"

"We must talk Khalid, you know why I am here."

"You are here because I am your enemy. You are here to kill me. You know I cannot let that happen."

"No wait," Adam pleaded. "That is not why."

"Really? Why then?"

"What happened Khalid? After that day at Sandhurst. What happened to you?" Adam fought to keep his voice calm. "What would make you go against us, murder those who trained you and who looked after you?"

Khalid sighed.

"You have no idea. You have absolutely no idea what your precious allies did to me and my family."

"Then tell me Khalid, I want to know, I want to help you."

Khalid laughed bitterly.

"No, you are working for the CIA. You are here to silence me and kill what I know."

There was sadness more than fear in his voice. Adam shook his head. He tried to explain.

"Khalid, I'm here to take you alive, to take you back to the UK. I promise you I am here to help."

"Don't be naïve Adam. If you want me alive then you must be the only one. The irony is that I was proud to be a cadet at your officer school: to learn to fight against terrorism and for my country. To secure its future and my family's future. I was prepared to embrace what I was taught and what I was told. I really came to believe that the West wanted to achieve something good… for all of us. I wasn't scheming or plotting or playing a game against you. I simply wanted to live my life with honour. And that day in front of the Prince, that was what I thought I was doing. There was me, a simple man from a village high in the Pakistan mountains, immersed in your traditions and your customs. I looked forward to sharing them with my men and with those that I loved. But you prevented that. You took me in. You deceived me. And it is you who has led me here."

Adam tried again.

"Please Khalid, come with me."

Twenty paces away Al broke through the crowd. Slowly he closed in, gently withdrawing his pistol and holding it low by his side, two-handed, trying to lose its shape in the folds of his cloak. He ignored the shifting throng of people, reserving his concentration for Adam and Bashir. He saw their lips moving but couldn't hear what they were saying. In front of him the Pakistani begin to back away.

"No Adam. If I leave with you now my father will be lost to me forever. I have already been robbed of my mother and sister. I will do what I have to do to try and keep my father."

"We will help you. It's not possible for you to look after your father alone. Too much is loaded against you."

Khalid sneered.

"That is what they said Adam, the Americans. But they used me. They made me promises that were nothing but lies."

Adam stepped towards Khalid, matching his movement, trying to keep the distance between them constant.

"Adam, back off or I will kill you," Khalid yelled, drawing his weapon from its place of concealment, but not yet raising it. Adam knew he was about to run. So did Al. From their observation point, Rocky and Simon sensed it too.

"Out of the way Adam!" Al warned, bringing his own pistol up into the aim.

Adam pirouetted to come face-to-face with Al, his back now to Khalid. He took half a step to the right, to put himself more squarely between the other two. He shook his head.

"Not yet Al. You must let me talk to him."

"Get the fuck out of the way," Al growled, shifting position to try to get a cleaner shot at Khalid. Adam moved too, narrowing the angle. Adam watched his colleague's finger start to squeeze the trigger.

The muted crack of the heavy round being fired from the minaret would not have been heard by anyone in the street. Certainly Al was not aware of anything before the bullet felled him. His arms flopped down, his mouth fell open, the shock on his face evident to all. How had this happened? He was the one pulling the trigger but somehow he was also the one who'd been shot. The legs that had carried him so far in his life, through so many difficult situations, gave way and he buckled. He found himself kneeling. He urged his body to follow orders and get up out of the dirt but nothing happened. He was stuck, blood streaming from a neck wound inflicted by a 7.62mm round from a sniper's rifle. Al could count himself unlucky. The bullet had been intended for Adam, but it was Al's deep misfortune that even as the US Tiger Team sent the bullet on its 446 metre journey, a farmer who was in the habit of making the usually uneventful trip to Peshawar each month from his home south of the city, had stepped forward, drawn by a shouting match going on in a language he didn't understand. The bullet had glanced off his skull, barely losing velocity. Its diverted path led it towards Al where it smashed into one of his vertebrae. The impact directed it downwards, following the spinal column. With its energy almost expended the bullet was just able to exit Al's body from his right hip. He slumped forward, making no visible attempt to avoid his face being buried into the dirt. His body twitched momentarily as it went through the last throes of life. Then it was still. Adam sprang towards the corpse.

Confusion turned to pandemonium as those in the street started shouting and screaming. Adam heard another gunshot and a local fell to the ground just a yard in front of him. People were fighting to get away, panic impeding their progress. The air by Adam's ear rippled as a third round flew past just inches away. He wasn't sure who was shooting but it was clear he was the target. Out of the corner of his eye he saw Bashir backing further away. Then he was gone.

Adam took a last look at Al and plunged back into the melee. He had to keep contact with Khalid or else everything was in vain. He pulled out his Glock. There was no attempt to hide it now. As Adam ran he took aim at the retreating shape and fired. The bullet missed but was close enough to make Khalid duck out of the way. Losing his stride and his balance he careered into an old woman and they tumbled to the floor, Khalid clinging desperately to the Tariq pistol. He forced his way back to his feet, ignoring the woman's fury as he trod on her stomach. Adam was drawing closer, his arms pumping like a sprinter, but instead of a baton he carried the Glock.

All Simon and Rocky could do was watch. They were able to see but not influence.

"Man down, man down!" Rocky screamed over the net.

"Man down, roger" Peter repeated, turning to Quinn. "Get the cordon moved in now, I need support for my men and the road to the hospital closed off."

Quinn showed no reaction. Ignoring Peter he kept staring intently at the tracker. Then he made his own radio call.

"Tiger this is control. Confirm you still have target in sight."

"Target heading west. Engaging. Over."

"Target? What the fuck is going on, Quinn?"

Peter reached over and grabbed the man sitting beside him.

"What's happening? It's simple. We have been given authority to take out the target, something your team might also want to consider. If you want to do anything worthwhile I suggest you get with it and encourage your team to drop him before he escapes." Quinn responded, yanking himself free of Peter's grip on his fatigues.

A million thoughts churned in Peter's head. It was all moving so quickly, the meeting with Khalid, the engagement, a man down.

"Rocky, this is Peter."

"Al is down. I say again Al is down. I need support now," implored Rocky.

"Rocky, support is inbound," Peter said in as calm a voice as he could muster. "Listen to me. I want you to take out the target."

"What?" Rocky replied. "Adam is giving chase already."

"Just listen. Drop Khalid now, regardless of whether Adam is in the way or not. Do you understand? This has to be brought to an end."

Rocky didn't answer but looked across at Simon who'd heard the exchange. His colleague shrugged.

Outside in the street Khalid had turned and got off a shot. It was a hurried and un-aimed but Khalid's intention was to hamper Adam's progress. But there was a down side to his action. Around him people scrambled for cover, ducking under stalls and crawling behind cars and carts, falling over themselves to get out of the way. It left Khalid feeling more vulnerable. As his human shield dissolved he was left in plainer view. But at least he was now close to the corner of the road that created the T-junction.

Adam was running as fast as he could and felt as vulnerable as Khalid for evidently he was as much a target as the man he was chasing.

"Fire the RC device," Rocky ordered.

"What?"

"You heard me, fire the fucking device."

"Adam's in the danger area," Simon said as he turned to look down the road.

Khalid had reached the junction and taken a right turn, north towards the hospital entrance. Adam tracking him, weapon raised and finger on the curve of the trigger, his eyes constantly refocusing between the foresight and the target. Rocky leaned towards Simon.

"Fire it, or I fucking well will."

Reluctantly Simon lifted the firing device and flicked the switch. An LED on top of it lit up as the radio-controlled signal was sent. The bomb detonated a millisecond later, the blast moving upwards then outwards, ripping apart the cylindrical metal tube, tearing through the shoddy concrete paving that surrounded the drain and ripping up the grate cover below which it had been concealed. The mass of debris was sucked up and spat out, flying lethally in all directions. The blanket of shrapnel engulfed those in close proximity to its epicentre, Khalid amongst them. The shock wave sent him skidding across the street, his side peppered with shards of metal, concrete and stone. A jagged piece of iron embedded itself in his hip, scything muscle before hitting the bone. Colliding with the ground he splayed his arms to try and cushion the impact. The pistol went spinning from his grip. The explosion kicked Adam to the floor as the storm of debris, noise and heat swept over him. His chin burned where a large fragment of shrapnel buried itself deep. He cried out in pain.

———◆———

Peter grabbed his secure sat phone and heaved himself out of the seat, barging past Quinn. He reached for the handle and flung the rear doors of the vehicle open. Pacing away from it, he dialled the number of his handler in London and put the phone to his ear. Impatiently he waited for the connection, but it wasn't made. He checked he had a good signal and tried again. Still nothing. Just the flat, miserable tone that indicated the line had been discontinued. Peter swore. In all his years working outside the formal boundaries of the UK secret service and military intelligence he'd known that theoretically he could be dropped, cast adrift. But he'd never have bet on it happening. Not after all the service he'd given them. Not at a time like this. He refused to believe he had been dumped, literally cut off. He'd give them all a bollocking when it was time for the debrief. Everyone: the handler, the Det commander, everyone involved in this whole sorry business. What did they all know about life out in the field? Who the fuck did they think they were? There was noise behind him. He twisted round to see Quinn jumping out of the truck.

"Monitor the net, will you? I'm coming now, we need to get moving," Peter said angrily.

Quinn didn't move. He stared straight at Peter with cold, hard eyes. Peter thought about giving the man a piece of his mind but then he understood what was really going on. He dropped the phone and heard it shatter on the ground. His right hand slipped to the drop holster that held the Sig Saur and he dragged the weapon clear. He brought it up as quickly as he could, twisting into a side stance to try and present as small a target as possible.

He had trained for moments like this all his life: in Ulster; through operations in Iraq, Afghanistan, South America; with the security services fighting home-made British terrorists. He knew the drill, get a round off as fast as possible to distract the other guy, to make him go defensive. It was the second round that would count. Then he would keep firing until his opponent was no longer a threat. That was the theory and he was about to put it into practice.

But it was a race Peter was never going to win. Quinn already had his M4 in the aim and he had acres of time to make sure his shots found their mark. The first bullet struck Peter on the right side of his chest; the second, more squarely in the centre of his body, nicking his heart. He fell backwards, striking his head on a rock. Dazed and dying the last thing he saw was Quinn standing over him. Peter had always been prepared for a violent death. What he couldn't countenance was that it had come at the hands of those who were supposed to be his allies. It was a betrayal he hadn't expected. Sinking into the blackness he was almost glad to be out of it all.

Chapter 28
LADY READING HOSPITAL – PESHAWAR

A grey dust cloud hovered over the scene of the explosion, in no hurry to disperse. It was sixty seconds since the bomb had gone off. There was movement and noise in all directions.

Many people were still trying to get away. Bloodied and confused, one man crawled on his hands and knees, his right ankle shattered, his foot sticking out at ninety degrees. But others were converging on the carnage: some disorientated and wailing; others to help; still more to try and comprehend what the hell was going on. Simon was getting close now. He passed a body. Al's. He barely gave it a second glance. His priority was on the living, not the dead. His aim to prevent

Adam suffering the same fate.

"Rocky," Simon called on his radio as he sprinted.

"I'm about fifty metres back from you," replied Rocky, trailing behind.

"Can you confirm we have support and what direction they are coming from?"

"No comms at the moment but if they're coming they should arrive from the north," Rocky said, sucking in air.

Simon reached Adam. He was still down, blood trickling from his left ear, his eyes bloodshot and filled with grit. He was blinking furiously. There was a jagged wound just below his mouth. Simon crouched down and put a hand on his shoulder.

"Adam, it's Simon."

Adam struggled to talk.

"He's just ahead."

"Are you ok?" Simon asked looking about for Bashir.

"I'm fine, I'm fine, you go."

Simon stood up. A few yards away Khalid was shaking his head, trying to clear his jumbled brain. He caught sight of someone moving towards him. The figure was dressed in the local getup and had a long beard. But there was no disguising the Mendle desert boots he was wearing; even less so the M4 he carried. A few feet away from Bashir lay the pistol. He crawled across the ground and grabbed it, the gun being infinitely more valuable to him than the money. Bashir lifted the Tariq and took a shot. Simon ducked behind a stall, knocking off half of its contents: fruit, vegetables, a cage full of cheeping birds. Peering round the trestle table he fired back, the round scuffing the ground in front of Khalid who was unsteadily getting to his feet. He staggered off, making for an alleyway, firing again as he retreated. Simon replied in kind but was wide of the target, then he too was up and moving. Khalid bounced down the claustrophobic passage, adrenaline suppressing the pain in his hip, but unable to make up for the loss of tissue. Simon was close behind, repeatedly forced to press himself into the recesses as Khalid fired back at him. They weren't alone. Simon almost fell over the mother and her two tiny children as they emerged from the doorway of a house to find themselves in the middle of a gun battle. Simon hesitated, turning his attention away from his quarry to shove the family out of danger. His actions saved their lives but jeopardised his own. Simon felt a blow to his shoulder. It was as if he had been smashed with a sledgehammer. The gun fell from his hand. The two bullets that followed fast behind both found his upper body. He willed himself to stay standing but the strength had gone from his legs and he collapsed against the earth wall and slid to the floor.

Even above the cacophony of other sounds, swelled and dominated by the sirens of the first ambulance to leave the hospital for the scene of the explosion and the frantic, persistent blast of a horn of a police car, Rocky and Adam heard the shots. Hampered by his injuries and blurred vision Adam battled to keep up with Rocky as he made for the passage, helped when the lead man paused at the entrance and peered warily down the narrow funnel. Forty metres along it lay a body; someone stooped over it. Adam realised that whoever it was they were going through Simon's pockets. Angrily he pointed his pistol into the air and fired. The report echoed down the passage. Seeing Adam, he ran off. Rocky reached Simon first and put his fingers to his neck, checking for a pulse. There wasn't one.

"Bashir must be heading to the hospital. Try and cut him off."

"You get onto One Five and tell them to tighten the cordon."

Glenn Sinclair cursed again. Then he made the call. He was furious at their failure to nail their target. He couldn't remember the last time he and Scott had started a job and not finished it. They were the best, proud to call themselves snipers. They could be relied upon to deliver. That's why they got the tough assignments. Only this time they'd screwed up. He tried to keep the disappointment out of his voice but wasn't convinced he managed that either.

"One Five this is Tiger. We have lost the targets."

"Roger Tiger, I want you to withdraw back to the HLS over," ordered Quinn, concealing his fury. "All call signs this is One Five you are to withdraw now to the HLS."

Rocky listened in, confused. Why the hell was everyone heading to the HLS when he had two of his men down?

"One Five, this is Rocky, how copy?"

There was nothing but dead air. He was talking to himself.

"Peter this is Rocky over. Simon and Al are down. I need that support now."

Rocky stood up, Simon's lifeless body splayed out at his feet, bloodstains beside it, the colour literally drained out of him. He just caught a glimpse of Adam reach the end of the alley and disappear round the corner. He kept staring, caught up in a debilitating mix of sadness and bitterness. Two figures materialised where Adam had been standing a few moments earlier. They had raised rifles that were pointed towards him. Then they marched down the passage, shouting. Rocky saw they were dressed in Pakistani Army uniforms. Behind the advance guard several more troops followed. In resignation Rocky slowly raised his hands above his head, clearly showing the pistol. When his arms were fully extended he threw the gun to the floor.

"For fuck's sake," Rocky mumbled to himself. "Now what the fuck do I do?"

The nervous soldiers kept yelling, gesturing for Rocky to put his hands behind his back. He did as he was bidden. The youngest of the Pakistanis grabbed him by the throat and forced him down. The second moved behind him and bound his wrists. They both edged aside as a senior figure came between them. He seized Rocky's turban and tore it off his head, confused at what it revealed. What was a Westerner doing knelt at his feet?

"British soldier, British soldier," Rocky shouted but nobody took any notice of him. He just hoped this was the same story that would be coming from London when they heard of his capture.

LONDON

The Defence Secretary didn't want to make the call but the Chief of the Defence staff insisted.

"Listen Secretary of State. We have come too far. If any of those men get out alive we will have a lot of explaining to do," the General explained bluntly.

"Is there no other way? Something surgical maybe. Surely we cannot condone loss of life on this scale?" the Defence Secretary scrabbled around for more palatable alternatives.

General Adamson sucked in through his teeth. He was fed up with this weak politician who wanted the end result but wasn't capable of taking the hard decisions needed to get there. Had he ever been a military man then he would have understood and wouldn't be wasting time now.

"If there was another way we would be taking it, but we have to go down this route. The MI6 chief has already briefed you. MI5 have the aftermath and fallout in hand. We can manage the information campaign on this one and in the end it is a CIA asset we are talking about. Now, make the call," the General said brusquely, his patience exhausted.

The minister dialled the preloaded number and was patched through to the PM's aide. He explained that it didn't matter what the Prime Minister was doing – he could be shagging the Downing Street cat for all he cared – he had to be put on the phone, in private. The voice of his political master eventually came on the other end of the line.

"Yes?"

"It's Bashir. He has escaped the trap. We need to collapse this now and the US are looking for permission to withdraw their forces and target Bashir with, shall we say, a blunt instrument."

"What are you talking about?"

"Let's say that there will be civilian casualties."

"And the Det?"

"We don't have any firm information, but it is likely Adam Caine will be part of the collateral," the Defence Secretary admitted.

"But I said I didn't want to order the killing of a British national."

"Sir, I appreciate that but we are now in a precarious situation. If we don't act decisively there is a good chance Bashir will escape and if he does then we have to presume that the story of this whole sorry affair is going to get out. To kill Bashir we will have to sacrifice Caine, there is no choice. As it is we have already taken other casualties."

"Other casualties?" the PM's voice flagged.

"We have lost some of our men to enemy fire."

The phone was silent for a while as the PM thought. The Defence Secretary could feel his job slipping away.

"Prime Minister, I am going to have to press you before it's too late."

"Damn it, give the order."

The Secretary of State turned to the General and nodded.

PESHAWAR

Khalid skipped through the traffic on the main road, trying to ignore the growing pain in his side, pausing only once, briefly, to turn his back to the flow of vehicles as a string of military trucks swept past. Then he was in the hospital's car park. He tried to compose himself. He wiped his face clean with the sleeve of his cloak and slipped the pistol back into his pocket. He calculated that the first of the ambulances carrying casualties from the bomb attack would be arriving at any moment. Who would pay him any attention when everyone was concentrating on the carnage wrought by a bomb a few hundred metres away? This was his best chance. He glanced around then entered the building.

Forty metres away across the car park, Sadeek watched Khalid disappear from view. No more than two or three minutes later he saw a hurrying figure follow the same route. What marked him out as a curiosity was the gun he carried at his side. Sadeek had heard the gunfire and the explosion and seen the response from the medical teams. He'd tried to convince himself it was nothing to do with him or his task. He'd been told to wait and that was what he intended to do. He considered calling the number of his mobile but thought better of it in case his handler got annoyed. He was determined not to risk losing the money he would be due if only he remained patient for a little longer. He turned the car radio up and sat back to listen to more of the Bollywood music.

Inside the hospital Khalid walked straight up to the reception desk, a spotty youth stationed behind it studying a dusty old computer.

"Excuse me," Khalid said. "I am looking for someone."

"If you just wait over there," the man said, pointing to a group of about a dozen people huddled on benches in the corner of the foyer.

"No, you don't understand, I am looking for someone, urgently."

The man raised his hand again and gestured once more to where the others were waiting. Khalid wasn't going to argue. He leant over the counter and slapped the man hard across the top of his head. His victim yelped. When he looked up he saw the butt of Khalid's pistol jutting out from his cloak.

"Make no mistake, I will kill you if you do not do as I ask," Khalid hissed. "If you shout out I will kill you. If you talk too loud I will kill you. If you do not focus on what I am saying I will kill you. Do you understand?"

The man nodded dumbly.

"Say it," Khalid ordered, keeping the menace in his voice.

"Yes I hear you," the man said weakly.

"I want you to check your records and see if you have a Farouk Bashir here."

The young man tapped at the keyboard, first typing in first Farouk's name; then asking Khalid his father's date of birth and where he was from. He waited, trembling, as the search took place.

"Yes there was a Farouk Bashir here. Serious brain injuries caused by an explosion," the man read out.

"Was here? Where is he now?" Khalid asked leaning across to try and look at the computer for himself.

"It doesn't say. Just tells me he is no longer here, that's all."

"But it must say something, if he was transferred it would say so wouldn't it?"

"It would if he was transferred or discharged, but if he died it would be registered at the Governor's offices."

Khalid took a step back, his world spinning. Surely his father could not be dead? Khalid had never been confident that he'd find the old man at the hospital, it was always a possibility that the CIA would move him to another facility, in Islamabad maybe or the main Cairo hospital in Egypt. But he'd hoped there would be a trace of him. What now?

Khalid turned and strode off down the main corridor, tracing a path he'd taken what seemed an age ago now. The passageway stretched into the distance but after a few metres there was a branch off to the right. Khalid took it. Thirty metres on there was a nurses' station and behind it an office. Inside was a man in a white coat. Without hesitating Khalid walked in. He had not dared to believe he'd find the same doctor he'd spoken to all that time ago. But here he was. Khalid moved towards him. There was no hint of recognition from the doctor.

"Do you remember me?" Khalid asked.

"I'm sorry no I don't," the doctor replied blankly.

"We spoke. A long time ago now. About my father, Farouk Bashir. He was here with a serious head injury and you were treating him."

The young doctor looked flustered, he was busy and he had been stopped from going about his duties.

"I'm sorry, how long ago was this?" the doctor asked. He shook his head sadly when Khalid told him.

"I'm afraid that…"

The doctor broke off as the door to his office burst open. Khalid swung round as Adam exploded into the room, pistol raised. Khalid didn't bother withdrawing his weapon from his pocket. He simply raised it and fired through the material. Two shots. A frosted window disintegrated as Adam flung himself out of the way, colliding with the corner of a heavy metal filing cabinet and ending up behind a desk. As he fell, he let off a shot of his own. There was a scream of agony but not from his intended target. The doctor collapsed, clutching at his leg, his right knee shattered by the 9mm bullet.

Khalid jumped forward, slipping on shards of glass, letting off more unaimed rounds. Adam watched him disappear. Too slow he brought the Glock to bear but his target was out of sight. Adam forced himself to his feet, ignoring the cries of pain from behind him, and darted out of the office. Another shot sent him diving for cover behind the registry desk. There was a thud as a bullet buried itself in the woodwork.

Adam risked a peek down the corridor. He caught sight of Khalid dissolve into a wall at the point where there was a sign with the symbol of a set of steps on it. Adam lurched after him, pushing aside a shuffling patient who had a look of fright and confusion on his face. He reached the place where Khalid had gone from view and gingerly opened the door into the stairwell. He heard the rapid clang of boots on metal steps as someone ascended them. Adam raised his head and caught a glimpse of Khalid skid round a half landing four flights up. He pointed the Glock and pulled the trigger. The noise was deafening but there was no break in the sound of running feet. Adam bounded up the steps two at a time, checking himself at each turn to make sure his adversary wasn't waiting for him. As he closed in on level five he saw a door shutting gently, the elbow of the hydraulic closer narrowing as it moved. Adam took a couple of deep breaths and grabbed the handle. He turned it and eased himself into a foyer busy with people. He wrinkled his nose up at the smell: piss and vomit and the stench of ill people. Adam had a choice to make. Two corridors ran off in opposite directions. Which way was he to go? The presence of an orderly down on his hands and knees, cursing as he retrieved the contents of a tray of medical equipment that lay scattered on the floor, gave Adam the clue he needed. He sprinted past the flustered medic, running at full tilt. He negotiated another corner. Khalid was only just ahead of him, looking around as if he had lost something, checking his bearings. Then he seemed to make up his mind and yanked open a side door and went through it.

The room Khalid found himself in was just as he remembered it: the same stained bed and bedding; the window with the tattered mosquito mesh; the shaft of light that played on the grubby wall. Only one thing was missing: the patient. The room had an aura of foreboding as if it was a place where people came to die, not to get better. Khalid felt utterly bereft, overwhelmed by loss. Drained of the last vestiges of hope, he sagged with fatigue. He had no will to go on. There was no point. All he wanted to do was lie down where his father had been, get as close to the old man as he could. He circled the bedstead and stood on tiptoes to look through the aperture that gave a view of the street. He could see the car park and an ambulance flying through the gate, siren screeching. There were Pakistani troops too, carrying rifles, running towards the building. It was all over.

KHOST

"Sir?"

"Yes?"

"Bashir has entered the hospital. Caine is there too."

"Is everything in place?"

"Yes Sir, just waiting for your authority."

"You have it."

"Understood. We shall use the Reaper to send the remote signal."

"I'm not that interested how you do it just get on with it and give me a sitrep once you have."

"Yes Sir."

The team leader marched out of the office, leaving Cyrus sitting behind the desk, mulling things over. He had been awake the whole night as information from Peshawar had first trickled, then poured, in. This had gone as far as it needed to go and it was time to put an end it. He felt no emotion, no qualms when the order to eliminate the Det boys was received and none now that he had permission to take

334

the necessary action to shut the thing down regardless of how many casualties there would be. He sipped his cold coffee and lifted a cigar from the half-full box of Havanas in front of him.

It wasn't a celebratory smoke; just something to help him think.

Cyrus had long since given up being surprised about the outcome of his operations. Things happened. Sometimes they worked in your favour, sometimes they didn't. That was how it was working in shit places with dodgy people with strange ideas and big guns. You couldn't guarantee success, but you could mitigate failure, you could clear things up so there wasn't a mess left that'd later trip you up.

He wondered what his own future would now hold? About time he vacated the Near East Desk and got a posting to Washington. Christ, he'd worked hard enough to get it.

PESHAWAR

Adam crashed through the door and into the room. Momentarily disorientated by the gloom, he instinctively fired at the dark shape that he had to assume to be the fugitive. The bullet creased Khalid's neck and blood quickly flowed. The jolt shook Khalid out of his inertia and consumed him with fury. He staggered forward firing the Tariq wildly. Three, four shots he unleashed, the last of which found its target, grazing Adam's hip. The blow threw Adam off balance and he tumbled inelegantly into the side of the bed. Under his weight it rolled easily on its unsecured castors and pinned Khalid to the wall.

Adam tried to get to his feet but Khalid was quicker, shoving the bed away from him and crawling over it. He sent Adam toppling with a kick to the ribs then stamped repeatedly on his wrist, crushing the tendons until he released his grip on the Glock. Khalid punted it away and stood over his opponent. Groaning with discomfort, Adam stared at the muzzle of the Tariq pointed unwaveringly at his forehead, waiting for the shot that would end his life. It didn't come. Not yet at least. He remained frozen, waiting for what happened next but still Khalid did nothing and said nothing. Cautiously Adam tried to prop himself up, shuffling slightly away until he was able to lean up against the doorframe. Khalid's gun covered his movement but didn't prevent it.

"Why Khalid? Just tell me why," Adam said trying to stall him.

"They killed my family, they killed them all. My mother, my sister, and now my father. What other reasons do I need?"

"But the death of your family wasn't deliberate. You're a soldier. You know these things happen. However terrible they are, you aren't the first person to suffer. You know that."

"Maybe. But you see things differently when it is your own flesh and blood. The Americans don't care who they kill. The lives of Afghans, of Pakistanis, are worthless to them. We hold no value. They do whatever they want to protect their interests, with no thought of the trail of destruction and misery they leave. Why do you think so many countries, so many people, oppose the US? Hate the US? Now I know why and I loathe America too."

Adam shook his head.

"But you fought against the very people who would have helped you, those who trained you, who honoured you, who had set you on a path to opportunity. You threw it all back. You killed my countrymen. You murdered Danny Akers. You are no better than those you criticise."

"You don't know do you, Adam?"

"Know what?" Adam answered, confused.

Khalid lowered the pistol but kept eye contact with Adam.

"At Sandhurst we were taught to write everything down, to keep a diary, to look back at the lessons we were taught and the lessons we learned when we got things wrong. You remember that, right? I kept my diary; took it with me when I left. It was my prized possession from Sandhurst; the crest, the fine paper, the red line on each page. I kept it and I kept writing in it."

"I'm not with you. What has your diary got to do with anything?"

"I fought you and I fought the Americans, I used everything I could and everything I had available to fight you, but I fought in an honourable way. My IEDs are no better or worse than your mines. Where you used mighty companies to produce your high-tech arms I used improvisation and ingenuity. I harnessed the skills and dedication of the jihadists for whom the war against the West is a life or death struggle. And I expected to suffer the same fate as so many of my countrymen. Death at the hands of the enemy. But it didn't end like that. I was captured by the Americans and held in one of their prisons."

Khalid stopped for a moment.

"They tortured me, they beat me, to get me to submit. I resisted it all. But then they played the card for which they knew I could not trump. My father. His fate was in my hands, they said. They offered me the chance to see him again."

Adam still didn't understand.

"But how did you get away from them?"

"I didn't get away. Not in the sense that I escaped. They let me go."

"What do you mean? Why?" Adam answered confused.

"They said they would release me if I worked for them. They said they would take care of my father if I gave them information, if I would lead them to senior Taliban and Al Qaeda figures."

Adam said nothing, shocked at what he was hearing. Outside there was more shouting as another ambulance screamed into the hospital compound. Khalid was pulled to the noise and glanced towards the window. He looked back in time to spot Adam scanning the floor for his pistol.

"Don't try anything, Adam. I will kill you," Khalid warned. "It's not as if I'm not used to it."

"But why the young soldier, Khalid?"

"Once I said I would do what they wanted the Americans took me to the south of Afghanistan on the Baluchistan border and released me. I used the money they gave me to get myself to Kandahar and from there I joined another local Taliban unit and simply continued my fight against the West. But now the Americans were aware of everything I did. More than that, they assisted. They passed me information, gave me details of troop movements. They helped me with my attacks against coalition forces. They explained where I'd find patrols, where ISAF was its weakest; anything that would give me an advantage and elevate me in the eyes of the Taliban leaders. And then they sat back while I killed their colleagues, your colleagues. It worked like a dream. I rose through the ranks and was treated as a hero. And the higher I got the more I found out things that were of use to my handlers."

"Are you telling me the CIA used you to target British and US forces in order to give them intelligence? I don't believe it." Adam was incredulous.

"You should believe it. They led me to a target and then they led me safely away. They prevented kinetic strikes against my position and stopped aircraft from supporting their patrols so I could escape."

"And the young British soldier? Danny Akers?"

Khalid shrugged mournfully.

"We captured him by accident, we were intending to hold onto him and have the British pay a ransom or else sell him to one of the warlords. I didn't even consider killing him. But the Americans had other ideas. They insisted he be executed and that it be filmed. I killed that young man on the order of the CIA. They calculated this would prove my commitment to the insurgent cause and leave no one in any doubt as to what I was capable of. And they were absolutely right," Khalid finished.

"You're lying to me. You're trying to dodge the blame for your crimes.

"But it is true. And now I have outlived my usefulness you are here to kill me. Yet that's not quite all is it? For you must now realise what will happen to you. You'll die too. You're as expendable as I am. You and I: we are in the same position. We know too much," Khalid looked down at Adam with a hint of sympathy.

"But why would the Americans use me, use the British? Why not deal with you themselves?" Adam asked the question of Khalid, but it was as much addressed to himself.

"Because they were aware that we had a connection. Because they wanted to implicate someone else in their plot. If you think the Americans are your friends then I am afraid you are mistaken."

"Who was your controller?" Adam asked already suspecting he knew the answer.

"The man who offered me a deal I couldn't refuse? He was called Vincent."

"Cyrus Vincent?"

"Cyrus Vincent. You know him? Well his name is in my diary along with everything else. It contains the whole story of what has taken place. I might be killed but they can't destroy my record."

KHOST/LONDON

Cyrus sat in the CIA HQ in Khost listening intently to the rebroadcast feed from Adam's personal radio. He suddenly wondered whether that posting to Washington would materialise. 4,500 miles away, in London, the Defence Secretary and General Adamson, also heard what Khalid had said, but they didn't respond. What was there to say? They all understood the business they were in. Anyway, shock, revulsion, outrage, indignation; none of it would do any good now. It was too late. The path had been trodden. Deals had been struck and trade contracts were secure. Thousands of jobs and billions of pounds; that was what they had gained. So what if a few soldiers died along the way? They were expendable. So what if a few people in an overpopulated third-world country were killed? No one would miss them. Not really. It was a price well worth paying, in the national interest.

"Switch it off General," the Defence Secretary said wearily. The General looked at the politician. He seemed deflated.

"War is a dirty business," said the soldier.

"No," the Secretary of State corrected him. "Business is a dirty war."

PESHAWAR

Abdul Sadeek was concerned. He had been studying the comings and goings since the explosion in the market and he had seen the two men enter the hospital. Then he'd heard the gunfire. He'd sunk down into his seat at the arrival of a flurry of trucks out of the back of which had spilled armed police and soldiers who fanned out around the hospital. He thought about his wife and children in Quetta. What would they be doing at this time? He desperately wanted to be back with them. For some reason the money didn't seem as important as it had. Sadeek was worried that one day the money was going to come with too many strings attached and that he would be asked to do something that would not reward him handsomely but instead lead him to lose everything. He promised himself that this would be his last job.

He looked in the rear-view mirror and wondered again about the way the car sat low on its back axle. Out of the corner of his eye he spotted a leaflet he'd failed to return to the glove department when he'd prized it open.

He picked up the small mobile phone and held it in his hand unsure of what to do. Hesitantly he pushed the green button that brought the screen back to life. Then he made up his mind. He'd call the number he had and say he was leaving the car and returning home. Forget the money. If anyone wanted the vehicle they could simply pick it up from where it was.

There was a crackle of static from the radio. His favourite Bollywood track was distorted by interference. Annoyed by the strange, grating noise he started to lean forward to turn down the volume. He never got to do it.

The explosive in the boot exploded with a blinding flash, unleashing a huge destructive force. Sadeek and the car were vaporised. The blast took the route of least resistance, throwing police cars onto their side. The shock waves burst through the hospital foyer shattering the plate glass in the entrance doors. The sullen young man at the desk died immediately, shredded by flying shards of silicon. The old brick walls of the Lady Reading had not been built withstand the force of a bomb and they crumbled. The whole façade of the hospital buckled and disintegrated. There was no screaming from those caught up in the overwhelming attack because there was no time. The victims could not even gasp a breath of oxygen because all the air had been sucked up in a ball of fire and heat.

Towards the back of the building, Khalid was thrown violently off his feet and against a wall that was itself crumbling under pressure from the car bomb. Adam was bucked into the air, the floor fracturing and twisting beneath him. Slowly the front of the building slid forward, putting more and more pressure on the internal support columns that were now exposed to the outside world. These too twisted and broke. The entire hospital was collapsing, the upper floors crashing to the ground, crushing and trapping those unfortunate to be lower down. Adam and Khalid went with it.

EPILOGUE

The man clung to the mangled, lifeless hand as the smothering, choking dust started to clear the air. Taking a last look at the tattered human remains of what had been his sworn enemy he felt a wave of bitterness. Not towards his opponent, but against those who had manipulated and corrupted their actions and destinies. At that moment he made a vow: that this would not be the end of things; could not be the end while those responsible for the trail of death and deceit lived on.

He heard people scrabbling about on the rubble and the anguished cries of the wounded. He felt pain too, but did not cry out. Close by two ghostly shadows appeared, the colour of alabaster except for the streaks of blood that hinted at their injuries and their hurt.

The man let go of the body and rose up. Unsteady on his feet, wincing with each step, he stumbled over the giant chunks of concrete and through the mangled steel reinforcing rods. He bounced off a mattress, avoiding what looked like the remnants of a child's cot. Someone tried to approach him, putting out his arms to help, but he shrugged off the offers of assistance and ignored the fascinated stares from those arriving to gawp.

Market day had been forgotten. Hoards of the curious now pushed and strained to get closer to the extraordinary scene, their inquisitiveness getting the better of their fears that there might be more violence to come.

The man pushed through the tightening thicket of onlookers, heading for the maze of alleyways and passages that lay beyond. The wounds slowed him but he drove on, conscious that he had to escape before the net closed in once more.

For 24 hours he ran, picking up lifts, catching on the radios of cars and trucks snippets of news about the attack on the Lady Reading Hospital. Thirty-seven dead the reports said. 214 wounded. They hadn't got that quite right. There was at least one more injured person. It was just he hadn't stayed around to be counted. There were details too of the murder of a pair of Western aid workers, gunned down in Peshawar shortly before the hospital was demolished by the car bomb. The work of an Al Qaeda cell or perhaps a local Taliban unit; so ran the speculation. Again, the man knew better than the journalists.

It was by taxi that he travelled the last few miles up the Khyber Pass, over the border and on to the Afghan capital. He made the driver drop him well short of his next destination. The final leg of the journey he undertook on foot: to the cemetery and the hole at the base of the tree where the prized possession remained where it had been left. He smiled to himself as he unwrapped the diary and fingered the embossed Sandhurst emblem adorning the front cover. Flicking through the pages he quickly came to what he was after: the hand drawn map, an address, a single name.

————◆————

The man's landlord had attempted to suppress a look of surprise when he'd opened the door to find him standing outside but wasn't quite quick enough. He ushered him in, showed him to the bedroom and brought some food. The man showed his gratitude but made it clear he was to be left alone.

Behind the closed door he studied the diary more carefully, reading thoroughly each entry as they detailed the events of recent months. Satisfied as to the existing contents the man added information on the last few days. There was a lot to write and he was exhausted but he completed the task, leaving nothing out. At last he felt able to lie down and wrap himself in the blanket that had been enticing him since his arrival. The sleep was deep and dream free. It was also miserably short.

After what seemed like only moments later he felt the hand shaking him roughly. When he managed to focus his eyes it was to see Haji Rakim standing over him. He was pointing at his watch.

"You asked me to wake you before dawn," Rakim reminded him.

The man mumbled some thanks before rolling out of the bed. It took him a few moments to get his balance. Grimly he gathered his few belongings and left the chamber.

In the street he found the small-engined motorbike Rakim had acquired on his account. The streets were already getting busy and it took him a while to negotiate the twists and turns of the city before he was out in the open and on the main highway towards Mazar-e-Sharif. He had stiffened up in his sleep and each pothole sent a heavy jolt of discomfort through his body. He felt it especially in his damaged right knee and broken ribs. Several of the puncture wounds started to seep blood, forced open again by the shaking. He rode for the best part of six hours before the machine started to splutter. A look in the fuel tank confirmed that petrol starvation was the source of the problem. Leaving the bike at the side of the road the man looked around for somewhere to lie up and rest. A couple of hundred metres away stood a battered compound, its walls breached either by time and weather, or something more sinister: shells or air-delivered ordnance.

He crossed the scrub ground and ducked through one of the more recently created entrances only then to realise he was not alone. Tethered to a wooden post that supported the winding gear of a well were a couple of scrawny goats. The man viewed them for a while before skirting round them and collapsing onto a pile of hay that was clearly there to feed the animals. He vowed to himself to keep his stay short but he was defeated by fatigue. Before he had chance to fight it, sleep had overcome him once again.

He woke, startled, to the sound of the goats moving, the bells around their necks tinkling feverishly. What had disturbed them, and hence him, was a young boy, the goatherd. He was urgently fiddling with the knots of the animals' leashes to free them and lead them away. The boy tried to back away as the man rose to his feet but he tripped and fell. The man tried to smile. He raised his fingers to his mouth as if feeding himself.

"Food. Have you any food?"

The youngster said nothing.

"Have you got anything to eat?" he repeated. This time the boy pointed towards a small cloth sack by the wall. The man shuffled stiffly over to the bag and examined what was inside. He retrieved from it a small piece of cheese and a large flatbread that had been folded. Beside the bag was a plastic pitcher with a cloth top held in place by a scrap of cord. He peeled back the lid and sniffed the contents.

He ate the food and drank the goat milk without talking and without taking his eyes off the boy who sat on the floor against the well. He thought about what he should do.

His choices were clear: he could do nothing and leave, knowing the boy was likely to go straight to his family after which word would quickly spread that there was a stranger in the area; he could kill him; or he could tie him up and at least buy a bit of time before it was noticed the boy was missing and people came to find him.

There had been so much violence and death that he could not now, not in these circumstances, countenance any more. His battle was not with the innocent but the guilty. He set down the pitcher and rummaged through his pockets, pulling out the keys to the motorbike. He lobbed them at the boy and lifted his chin, nodding, as if to say Go. The boy took the gesture for what it was. Without further prompting he scooped up the keys and stuffed the pitcher back into his bag. Then he hurried away, leaving the goats behind.

The man counted to ten and followed him out. He trudged back to the main road and turned right. He knew Mazar lay not too far away: and before that, the village where he would make his next stop. No one seemed to pay him any attention as he approached it and made for the largest compound.

He walked as straight as he could but his knee throbbed and caused him to limp. He headed for the imposing set of red double doors that marked the main way into the property. A guard stood before them.

"Yes, what do you want?"

"Please, Gul Mohammed."

"And who would you be?

"Khalid Bashir."

The sentry turned away, stepped through the entrance and walked away across the wide courtyard, leaving the doors ajar so the man could watch his progress. He saw the sentry stop and talk to a tall young woman.

When Malalaya heard who had arrived she did not wait for her father. She could barely believe what she had been told. She sprinted to the opening and barged through it, then stopped abruptly.

Adam Caine stepped forward. He well aware of who he was looking at, despite no introductions having been made. The description of the woman that Khalid had made in his journal had been completely accurate. Now that woman started to cry.

"Please don't," Adam said, handing the diary to Malalaya.

She took what was being proffered.

"So he is dead?" she said.

"Yes."

A thought seemed to occur to her.

"Was it you who killed him?"

Adam considered this.

"No, not really."

"Will you tell me how he died?" Malalaya said and the tears began to stream down her face.

"Yes, I will do that," Adam answered. "But I will also tell you how he lived."